Blood in the Desert

~ A Novel ~

You Left In Me the Faith - Book 1

Mary, Hope you enjoy the novel!

By C. Douglas Gordon

10/1/17

Blood in the Desert - You Left In Me The Faith - Book 1

mbsmith@parkcitiespublishing.com
Mary Beth Smith
Park Cities Publishing

DEDICATION

To my late brother, Michael Gordon:
You left in me the faith.

This painting of my deceased brother was done by his son, my nephew Steven Gordon. Steven's inscription, "You left in me the Faith" was the inspiration for the title of my book series.

CONTENTS

CAST OF CHARACTERS

HISTORICAL PERIOD 284 AD – 340 AD

Main Fictional Characters

Quintus – A brutal Roman officer responsible for persecuting Christians in Syria.

Miriam – Quintus' slave girl.

Philip – Miriam's blind son and Quintus' bastard child.

Barnabas – Philip's close friend and lifelong confidant.

Puella – An orphan girl who is adopted by Miriam.

Simon of Petra – A traveling merchant and patron of Miriam and Puella.

Thomas – A young hermit who befriends Philip and Barnabas.

Lupa – A mysterious female wolf who nurtures and protects Miriam.

Main Historical Characters

Diocletian – The only Roman Emperor to retire. His bureaucratic skills saved the Empire. He conducted the last and most vicious Christian persecution.

Galerius – Quintus' superior - Diocletian's liege charged with governing the Empire's southeast region.

Constantius – Father of the first Christian Emperor who governed Gaul and Britannia under Diocletian.

Constantine the Great – General and controversial first Christian Emperor who consolidated the Empire under the banner of Christ.

Eusebius of Caesarea – Bishop, early church historian and Constantine's biographer.

St Helena – Constantine's mother, a devout Christian and patron of Christian Churches. She discovered the true cross of Christ as well as his tomb. She built three Churches on sacred Christian sites in the Holy Land.

St. Lucian of Antioch – Martyr, Presbyter of the School of Antioch and early Christian scholar.

Arius – Student of Lucian. Arius' teaching sparked the "Arian Controversy" which was resolved at the Council of Nicaea in 325 AD.

St. Peter the Hermit – Solitary hermit living in the eastern desert of Egypt.

St. Procopius – Christian hermit who built numerous monasteries in Egypt establishing the first system of organized ascetic communal living.

Stories of Martyred Saints

St. Mark the Evangelist

Sts. Sergius and Bacchus

The Theban Legion – mass martyrs

St. Procopius

St. Barbara

December 302 AD Nicomedia Martyrs – mass martyrs

St. Peter of Alexandria

November 311 AD Nicomedia Martyrs – mass martyrs

ACKNOWLEDGMENTS

I would like to acknowledge and thank my editor, Jean-Marie Dauplaise, publishing consultant, Mary Beth Smith, and graphic artist Kathrine Tripp for their contributions to turning my concept and words into a book. Additionally, I extend my humble thanks to my ad hoc review committee of friends and family who have read, re-read, proofed and offered critique throughout this process.

BLOOD IN THE DESERT

~ A NOVEL ~

You Left In Me the Faith - Book 1

DISCOVERY

Nag Hammadi, Egypt 1945

Three hundred and ninety miles south of Cairo, Egypt, sits Nag Hammadi, a small village that has existed since ancient times. Primarily an agricultural and fishing community, it has survived for millennia, its inhabitants harvesting the rich gifts deposited there since the beginning of time by the Mother Nile, upon whose fertile shores the village rests. From the ages of the Pharaohs, it had proven itself of little historical significance until this particular day.

On this particular morning in 1945, two peasant brothers were digging for fertilizer near the base of the Jabal al-Tarif cliff, northeast of the village, a task they'd long since grown accustomed to carrying out routinely. One can imagine that the brothers knew the area well, not only for its rich soil, but also as a favorite site for youthful fun and adventure, well away from the usually watchful eyes of their parents and elders. Left to themselves, they never tired of exploring the caves, whether in search of mythical beasts or relics from the great imaginary battles that clashed in their minds as they combatted one another with sticks, rocks, or the handles of broken tools. As peasants, they were steeped in the lore of their own ancestors and the folk wisdom of their al-Samman clan, but were both illiterate and uninformed about the history of their native region and unaware that any of their findings, either real or imagined, might prove to be of historical significance.

This day, however, would be different. They trekked to the site, their mules equipped with empty satchels intended to be laden with rich fertile soil. As the peasant farmers dug, they unearthed a large clay vessel with four handles near the opening and fashioned from Coptic red slip. The opening was sealed with a dark wax-like substance. Old myths and mysteries rose from their memories as they examined the artifact. The brothers, Muhammad and Khalifah, were suddenly struck with the fear that the vessel might contain a djin, or jinni whose freedom would unleash horrific terrors.

Alas, children no more, their fear gave way to visions of bountiful riches. Their excitement swelled as Muhammad took his mattock and struck open the jar. The flying debris contained neither the mist of a jinni, nor riches of gold, but rather fragments of ancient parchment, which ultimately proved to include thirteen, leather bound manuscripts. Unwittingly, they realized that today's mysterious finding might indeed contain riches, but they were unable to surmise their significance.

They immediately shared their discovery with close acquaintances who were camel drivers. Seven lots were drawn in preparation for dividing the treasure. Fearing they might be tricked by the brothers and prompted by suspicions that the manuscripts contained sorcery, the camel drivers declined their shares and the brothers were left with the entire lot. Wrapping the manuscripts in his tunic, Muhammad returned to his home and hid the cache in a straw pile next to their household oven.

As with many such discoveries of antiquities, these artifacts were subject to mishandling, partial destruction, and separation. Thinking them worthless, a portion of one book was inadvertently used as kindling by the brothers' mother to light a fire in their home oven.

The treasures were subsequently bartered between illiterate peasants until eventually, several manuscripts found their way to a Cypriot antiquities dealer in Cairo. Realizing their potential value, the dealer traveled to Nag Hammadi to purchase the remaining books. He did so, and then sold the lot to a Belgian antiquities dealer who unsuccessfully offered them for sale via newspapers in both New York City and Ann Arbor, Michigan.

On the 10th of May 1952, the Belgian dealer's widow sold the collection to the Jung Institute in Zurich and the documents came to be known as the Jung Codex. As the collection was deciphered, it was returned bit by bit to Cairo. Full publication was delayed amidst a maze of scholarly obstructionism, well into the 1970's.

Today, the collection is known as the Nag Hammadi Codices and consists of 12 codices and 8 pages of a 13th. In all, these codices incorporate 52 texts. All were written on 4th Century papyrus. All were declared heretical Christian writings and had been ordered to be destroyed soon after the Council of Nicaea in the year 325 AD. The titles of the 52 texts are:

Codex Titles
I.
1. The Prayer of the Apostle Paul
2. The Apocryphon of James
3. The Gospel of Truth (1st copy)
4. The Treatise on the Resurrection
5. The Tripartite Tractate

II.
6. The Apocryphon of John (1st copy — long version)
7. The Gospel of Thomas
8. The Gospel of Philip
9. The Hypostasis of the Archons
10. On the Origin of the World (1st copy)
11. The Exegesis on the Soul
12. The Book of Thomas the Contender

III.   13. The Apocryphon of John (2nd copy — translation 1 of short version)

14. The Gospel of the Egyptians (1st copy — translation 1)

15. Eugnostos the Blessed (1st copy)

16. The Sophia of Jesus Christ (1st copy)

17. The Dialogue of the Saviour

IV.   18. The Apocryphon of John (3rd copy — long version. Copy of same Coptic translation as II.6)

19. The Gospel of the Egyptians (2nd copy — translation 2)

V.   20. Eugnostos the Blessed (2nd copy)

21. The Apocalypse of Paul

22. The (First) Apocalypse of James

23. The (Second) Apocalypse of James

24. The Apocalypse of Adam

VI.   25. The Acts of Peter and the Twelve Apostles

26. The Thunder: Perfect Mind

27. Authoritative Teaching

28. The Concept of Our Great Power

29. Plato, Republic 588a-589b

30. The Discourse on the Eight and Ninth

31. The Prayer of Thanksgiving

a. Scribal Note

32. Asclepius 21-29

VII.   33. The Paraphrase of Shem

34. The Second Treatise of the Great Seth

35. Apocalypse of Peter

36. The Teachings of Silvanus

37. The Three Steles of Seth

VIII.   38. Zostrianos

39. The Letter of Peter to Philip

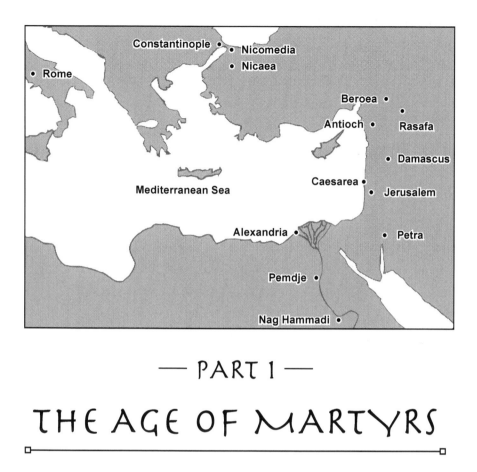

— PART 1 —

THE AGE OF MARTYRS

In an effort to eradicate early Christianity, the Romans conducted no less than ten intensive persecutions to eradicate the new religion during the three hundred years that followed the crucifixion of Yesua. The last and most vicious of these began in 284 AD, under the reign of the Emperor Diocletian. The Coptic Church refers to this reign of terror as "The Age of Martyrs." Born to slave parents, Diocletian rose through the ranks of the military to become a cavalry commander. He was proclaimed Emperor by the Army in 283 AD, after the death of the Emperor Carus and Carus' son, Numerian, who were on a military campaign against Persia. Carus' lone surviving son, Carinus, claimed the Imperial throne, but was defeated in July of 285 AD by Diocletian at the Battle of Margus in what is now known as modern Serbia. Legend purports that Carinus was killed in the battle by one of his own officers.

The pattern of commandeering the title of Emperor by popular Roman generals was commonplace in the third century AD. This age of Roman military anarchy began with the murder of the Emperor Alexander Severus in 235 AD by his own troops. Following his death, for the next fifty years, as many as twenty-five claimants assumed power over all or part of the Empire.

For fifty years prior to Diocletian's accession, the Roman Empire was plagued by civil wars, invasions, plagues and economic depression. A state of near-collapse had supplanted the realm previously known for the stability of "Pax Romana." The Empire had many enemies, both within and without.

Like his predecessors before him, Diocletian had many faults. He was, however, an excellent bureaucrat whose reforms brought stability to the Empire, thus ensuring its existence for another century. He devised an ingenious governance structure that provided stronger regional control and a stabilized succession plan. First, he divided the Empire's Imperial leadership by naming fellow officer Maximian as co-Emperor in the West. Each co-Emperor was supported by Junior Emperors, or Caesars, providing a succession plan for the co-Emperors. Constantinius, father of the future Emperor Constantine, was appointed Caesar in the West and Galerius, Caesar in the East. Together, each governed a quarter of the Empire. New administrative centers were established closer to the frontiers in Nicomedia, Mediolanum, Antioch, and Trier. Diocletian's skills ushered in a period of bureaucratic and military growth fueled by constant military campaigning. By standardizing imperial taxation, construction projects multiplied throughout the Empire and trade routes were secured once more.

During a sacrificial ritual attempted to predict Diocletian's future, Roman priests were unable to read the entrails of the animals that had been slain for the divination. The failure to divine a prophecy was then blamed on the presence of Christians, who were surmised to be dwelling covertly within the Imperial household. Through this twist of fate and the concomitant scapegoating of Christians, Christianity itself, on a larger scale, was thus presumed to be a bona fide internal enemy of the state. Diocletian surrounded himself in public with avowed opponents of Christianity. He condemned the Christian sect of Manicheans to death and tenaciously purged the army of Christians, particularly within the officer ranks. Over time, through a series of edicts imposed by each of the four Imperial leaders, Christians were stripped of their rights and eventually subjected to persecution. The persecutions were less severe in Gaul and Britannia and were most severe in the Eastern Empire under the reign of Diocletian and Galerius.

— CHAPTER 1 —

BANISHMENT

I

Rasafa, Syria 293 AD

In full battle regalia, the Roman officer Quintus Flavius Scipio, a Supernumerarius in the Roman Legion of the Caesar Galerius Maximianus, reveled in parading through crucifixion sites on a large Persian stallion that was given to him as a reward for his brutal efficiency. The Supernumerarii were elite officers who served the cavalry, military intelligence and other special assignments as determined by Regional Governors. He distinguished himself in the Legion's Cavalry in campaigns against the Persian invasions of Roman Mesopotamia.

Apart from his razor sharp Roman sword, the horse was his prize possession. Quintus had named his mount Narseh, after the Persian General who fought Galerius to a standstill after eight years of ruthless conflict. His black-eyed equine trophy was stark white, except for its black chin, lips and proud nostrils. His long flowing mane and tail glistened silver-white in the bright sun. The stallion served as a perfect extension of the rider's equally imposing figure, clad in a brightly polished breast plate and a helmet with a long, flowing crimson mane. With nostrils flaring, both horse and rider trotted past the tortured victims. Eye to eye with the crucified, the officer taunted and berated his prey. Onlookers cowered beneath his imposing gaze. Others fled at their first sight of his arrival. This brazen ceremonial ritual was a reminder to the entire local population of the Emperor's resolve to punish the empire's declared enemies, those who persisted stubbornly in the futile worship of an inferior Man-God deemed by those who were then in power to be of little to no consequence, Yesua.

On this day, Quintus came upon a woman who was on her knees praying beneath the wretched figure of a crucified man. The Supernumerarius approached her at a quick trot. Upon reaching her, he halted and raised his steed's imposing head, holding it outstretched above the head of the cloaked woman whose eyes remained closed, hands clasped, steadfast in prayer. Both Quintus and Narseh drew themselves up self-importantly, as if the woman's public and devout display were far beneath the dignity of either. Angered by her seeming indifference and presumed effrontery, Quintus dismounted, drawing his sword.

"Impudent woman! Is this man known to you? Answer me!"

"He is my son," she said softly. Her eyes fixed on the tortured figure of her only son, who slumped, dying before her.

Mocking her, he asked, "And what is it you are praying for? Is it for his miraculous salvation, or perhaps for his resurrection after certain death?"

"Neither. I am praying that he forgives you," she replied.

This blatant act of disrespect further enraged him. Quintus spun about to face the dying man, then thrust his sword deep into the man's chest and pierced clean through his aorta, releasing a copious fountain of vivid crimson blood upon both his horse and the lowly peasant woman.

Still she prayed, unfazed by the carnage and brutal sacrifice of her son.

"Woman! Do you not know that your son can forgive no one? In your so-called god's own words, 'Give thee unto Caesar what is Caesar's.' Your son is dead only because he refuses to give Caesar his due, the allegiance Caesar's worth demands!"

Undaunted, the woman spoke, quoting the Gospel of Thomas, "Yesua says give to Caesar what is Caesar's, give to God what is God's and give to me what is mine. Those are His words."

"Why precisely ought I to consider yours, ignorant woman? Your son is dead. All that you have left to give is that which I just exacted from him, your own paltry life. I suppose that you expect that I should spare that, as well?"

"No. Mine is the power to forgive, and I forgive you for what you have done, as well as for what you are now about to do," she said, her voice soft, yet unwavering in its conviction.

"Enough of this insolence!" he cried as his sword fell upon her, violently severing her head from its frail, slender neck. Spurting blood splashed across Quintus' now immobile form, soaking his legs, cloak, sandals and feet. Relishing the tactile sensation of spilt blood, the unmistakable scent of its coppery tang, Quintus drew himself up, his strong jaw jutting forward, as if to better please his absent Roman audience. Only the gleam of his ice-blue eyes betrayed the otherwise seeming indifference of his chiseled visage. The woman's now pallid body fell forward, nearly exsanguinated and altogether lifeless. Quintus stood triumphantly, posing as a victor, indifferent to the motionless corpse of the woman, now joined in death with the suspended form of her tortured son, completing the gruesome tableau of twisted loathing and decimation he had fashioned.

Quintus relished the cacophony of battle and of death. Success depended on an instinctive command of his senses. Spiritual renewal, he felt, is born of survival. While the chaos of battle accelerated time, the rituals of beheading, torture and crucifixion slowed its pace, heightening the experience. Beheadings, in particular, he savored as enjoyable sensory affairs. The sound of his Roman sword sliding from it sheath, its weight and the almost buttery ease with which it sliced through the neck, all were intensified, underscored by the sound of the head as it hit the ground. As it rolled to a stop, there befell a brief silence followed by the dull, but certain thump of the decapitated body as it struck the ground.

Diocletian's junior emperor, Galerius, handpicked Quintus not for his valor in battle, but for the cold dispatch with which he executed his assignments. Even his spiritual being was defined by a brutally callous and god-like dominance. Quintus Flavius Scipio was the perfect instrument for conducting the ruthless persecution of stubbornly devoted, pious Christian believers. From his Imperial seat in Antioch, Galerius appointed Quintus as the chief persecutor of Christians in Syria.

Quintus' memories of his "special assignment" were replete with corporeal predilections. Mass crucifixions were laden with the stench of decaying bodies and the sounds of death. The screams and moans of dying men, a chorus orchestrated by demons, were punctuated by the occasional squabbles of feeding vultures and the wailings of roadside women. The sight of foaming mouths paled in comparison to the guttural gasps of victims drowning as fluids accumulated in their lungs. Habitually, he would close his eyes, not in an effort to shield himself from the sights of slaughter, but to better attune and enhance his other senses, particularly to the symphony of death and torture and death again, which he conducted with the supreme effectiveness of a maestro.

Quintus' loyalty was generously rewarded. In addition to his glorious steed, his accumulation of wealth included vast tracts of land and a lavish villa, complete with slaves. Among these was a particularly treasured possession, the daughter of an Egyptian Christian leader whose family was sold into slavery after her father's brutal, attenuated torture and eventual beheading. Quintus had acquired the girl three years previously, when she had just turned thirteen. She was a gift from the Roman governor of Syria, a reward for Quintus' efficient persecution of Christians. Her father had been martyred when she was only ten; she was taken east by a Roman official who was reassigned to Syria and had subsequently fallen from the governor's grace.

As her nascent beauty unfolded, her petite, feminine frame softened, her smooth, olive skin seemed to glow and her delicate hands were slender and soft. Her golden-brown skin was accentuated by long, straight, ebony hair, which fell, glinting blue in the sun. Her physical comeliness radiated an aura of purity apt for a service which Quintus reserved for her alone. After returning from his "special assignments," the girl was required to perform a thorough purification ritual. First, she bathed him. Afterward, she massaged his body with oils and groomed both his hair and his beard. He preferred to remain standing throughout, although her small stature required him to be seated so that she could best serve him. Her perceived innocence made her, he thought, the perfect choice for this ceremony.

Although he suspected that she had been sexually violated by her previous owner, Quintus regarded her as untouchable, and he intended to keep her that way, not out of any sense of honor, but instead, as a tempting luxury he reserved only for himself. He compelled her to strip bare before she was allowed to perform the cleansing ritual. Lusting for her succulent body intensified his purification ritual, as did the touch of her skin and the smell of her hair. For three years, now, he had watched her body mature, her breasts gradually budding, her womanly shape evolving. The longer he refrained from enjoying her as any master would have long ago, the more he stoked his prurient delight.

Never once did he think to ask her name, an oversight that satisfied her, for it was all she had left of her father who had chosen her name, Miriam. When she administered to him, he would stroke her thighs and the backs of her arms, tracing his fingers over her shoulders and across her breasts. He would gather her hair in his hands, smelling her sweet fragrance. His taunting strokes made the girl tense with fear, which she strove to stem through silent, yet fervent prayers.

Somehow, this day, this ritual, would be different. As Quintus journeyed toward home, his yearning for the slave's touch, his yearning to touch her, would vanish, for the peaceful tone of the beheaded woman's voice haunted him as he traveled toward his lands, his villa, his household. Upon his arrival, Quintus dismissed his livery servants. Uncharacteristically, he personally cleaned his body armor and groomed his horse. The blood was exceptionally difficult to remove; it tinged the legs of his white horse with stains that, against all reason, he feared might prove permanent. His gore-encrusted garments disgusted him. He burned them. The blood's unusual tenaciousness delayed his arrival for the cleansing ritual.

For her, the wait generated even more anxiety than usual. The silent, cool surroundings chilled her naked body, and goose flesh raised the soft hairs on her arms and legs. Her body was tensed more so than ever before; she dreaded his beastly toying even more. When he entered the room, she could sense an uneasiness in him that was quite unfamiliar. His ordinarily palpable air of dominance seemed to have diminished, a loss of puissant authority that he sensed as well. She sensed his reticence, yet discerned that he wanted something from her, that he longed for a gesture, perhaps … something more, surely, than the ritual performance. But why? What could this mean? Tangled uncertainty gripped them both.

Normally, she would begin by bathing his head, then his shoulders, working her way down his torso toward his feet, which she reserved for last, just as he'd insisted time and time again. Noticing that both his legs and feet were stained with blood, she silently retrieved a bucket of clean warm water, dropped to her knees and began to wash his legs. Her strokes were gentle and soothing. The blood dissolved with her touch.

His uneasiness waned. He touched her hair. Its softness eased him further. He stepped back from her and gently pulled her to him. Face to face with her, she averted her gaze as he lingered over her features, which seemed, he thought, to have been sculpted by the gods, replete with a perfectly proportioned aquiline nose, thin lips and a gently pointed chin. Thin, charcoal black eyebrows and high cheekbones framed her most striking feature, deep-set hazel eyes that glinted celadon green. Curious, he thought, until this day, it seemed he'd long assumed they were merely brown, ubiquitous brown and universal. Mysterious, reflective and unsettlingly haunting, her eyes simultaneously spoke volumes, yet revealed nothing at all. Cupping her face in his hands, he pulled her closer as they breathed the air in unison. He stared into her eyes, his dominance giving way to submission, which discomfited him deeply. She stared into his soul, seeking his spirit, sensing his desolation.

Sensing a need to speak, she said, "God's love will save you. Yesua says, 'Ask for forgiveness and you shall receive.'" Her words startled him; Quintus suddenly recalled the image of the woman whom he had desecrated earlier that day. Miriam's words commingled with those of the slain mother, her face with that of the beheaded woman's; voices and visages converged, fusing into one. Overwhelmed and alarmed by his mind's deceptions, he exploded with rage, grabbed her, shoved her violently to the wet floor, caught up a fistful of black hair, and plunged her head into the bucket of blood-stained water. He wanted to drown her, drown the mother, drown them both, so as to silence forever their impudent and uncannily similar words. No need to rush, he thought, he could do better than that. The experience had, in fact, he realized, brought him to a state of full arousal.

He yanked at her, assuring himself he had not lost the upper hand at all. Raising her hips with his hands, he plunged into her from behind. Blinded with pain, she instinctively struggled, grasping to right herself, but the bucket overturned, spilling its contents. His dominance reasserted, he grabbed her hair and, as if clinging to the mane of a fine Persian charger, reined her back forcefully. Once satisfied, he released her hair, and then brutally forced her to the blood soaked floor, where he pinned and held her with his foot. His moment of domineering pleasure had been, for her, an eternity of pain and blindness. And silence. She had not cried out. She would not. She lay sprawled across the floor, motionless; she gasped as he drew his foot back, only to ram it back down onto her face, his last corporeal insult to her as he strode off to his quarters, summoning another slave to attend him. Although Quintus never touched Miriam again, nor she him, he continued to govern her in a manner even more peculiar than he had done previously.

Quintus replaced Miriam's role in the cleansing ritual with a young adolescent boy just entering puberty. The boy's looks were striking, thought Quintus, as handsome as she was beautiful, yet still pure and unblemished. From that moment on, she was forced to stand and watch the ritual. Miriam's cheek now bore a permanent crescent-shaped scar that she incurred when, in the force of his rage, Quintus had slammed her face to the coarse stone floor and then held it there against the chilled floor beneath the ruthless weight of his foot, where it had remained until she bled upon its stones. In her new role as observer, he ordered that she be fully clothed in a dark tunic and veil that exposed only her eyes, which made her virtually indistinguishable from the devout mother as he had first seen her before decapitating her on that same, fateful day that he had raped Miriam. As she watched, Quintus played out with the young boy the same sort of sensual performance that she had endured. She could see the fear in the boy eyes, as well as the sadistic gleam in her much loathed master's.

Quintus' moment of weakness and his subsequent violent assault against Miriam resulted in the inception of a child. From the moment of conception on, she was forced to endure the cruel purification ritual as if she were but a living statue, her immobility a perpetual reminder of the dead, beheaded woman Quintus had slain while patrolling.

Throughout her pregnancy, Miriam feared that the child she carried would one day be forced to perform the same ritual with its demon father that she had borne and which the boy, Marduk, now suffered to endure. As she watched, she prayed that her child would never experience the horror of Quintus' touch or the evil of his domineering gaze. Ten moons after his conception, Miriam gave birth to a blind son. Her motherly instincts could not ascertain whether the blindness was due to the trauma endured at his conception, or as a response to her constant prayers for his protection from Quintus.

After his son's birth, Quintus compelled the boy to accompany the mother to the cleansing ritual. She was allowed to speak to her son in his father's presence only if it were in praise of his father. Because of his blindness, or perhaps because of her prayers, the boy could never see or feel the fear what Quintus provoked in others. Miriam had named the boy Philip, an apostle of Yesua's who preached in Greece, Phrygia and Syria. The boy cultivated an odd attraction toward Quintus. Bright and inquisitive, the blind boy was adroit in using all of his other senses, which blessed him with keen insight and perception, an aptitude that he may well have obtained from his sire. Despite this, none of Philip's other five senses ever discerned the miasma of evil surrounding his biological father, an aura Miriam never failed to detect. In fact, however, Quintus never allowed the child to come near or to touch him. In fact, as with the child's mother, he never asked, nor cared to know the boy's name.

Often the boy questioned Quintus about his military armor and weapons. As time passed, Quintus altered his ritual and disrobed in the room, allowing the boy to clean his blood-stained sword and armor. For the boy, it was a treat filled with tactile delights. He gently touched the cold metal and razor sharp edges of the sword. His fingers traced the decorations on Quintus' breast plate armor. He savored the feel and the scent of its wet leather straps.

Although Miriam lived in dread of the ritual, Philip waited in anticipation for his father's return. Although he had grown vaguely fond of the boy, Quintus' deliberately avoided contact with Philip at any time, save for the ritual cleansing ceremony. Ultimately, the child served as a reminder of that day when his mother's touch had momentarily pierced through his spiritual armor. Quintus never allowed either himself, or Miriam, to forget that moment of frailty.

II

From the moment she discovered his blindness, the mother was riddled with questions. "How do I explain what a rainbow is to my blind son? What about the blue sky, puffy white clouds or stars sparkling in the inky black night? How will he know the difference between a sunset and a sunrise?" She was determined that the boy would live an active life in spite of his blindness. Instantly, she recognized the challenge of communication between them without the benefit of eye contact. She studied his body language, noting corollaries to feelings like exploration, excitement, and anticipation. She discovered that the boy expressed a wide range of moods, interests, and emotions that were nowhere evident on his face. His hands and arms flailed wildly with excitement when he was pleased. When happiest, his feet and legs joined in, a response that the scent of his mother, or the sound of her voice never failed to elicit. Curiosity produced a slow wandering of his hands. When exposed to the warm sun, he would gently touch his skin with his fingertips.

Throughout his infancy, she allowed her soft, long black hair to dangle against Philip's face while he was feeding. He often suckled with one hand grasping and kneading her silken hair, as the other stroked her face, and always, his fingers would gravitate toward the scar on her cheek, studying its terrain. The infant Philip radiated a palpable sense of contentment to Miriam. During his waking hours, she would frequently blindfold herself so that she could learn how Philip, sightless, would perceive and experience his surroundings. As his motor skills developed further, she introduced tactile objects to him, which they both learned to recognize in blindness. She burned fragrant candles to encourage and stimulate his sense of smell; he enjoyed both the touch and the perfume of the various aromatic flowers native to their region, and above all, she relished sharing with her son in the unique scents, touch and glorious tastes of the many fruits Miriam herself most favored.

Before sharing each object, she kissed and cuddled him as she hummed a sweet melody. He could feel her happiness. As he learned to mimic sounds, she said the object's name while placing his hands on her mouth as she spoke the word. They shared the same bed. On stormy nights, he would fall asleep in the safety of her arms. Holding him close, she could smell his sweet scent and hear the steady thumping of his tiny heart. She taught him about the world not as she saw it, but as they experienced it, together. He taught her how to love again, to love without the pain of loss.

As he learned to speak, expressing thoughts and ideas, she taught him about life and a love that transcended the love that they two alone shared. "There is a spirit that is in you, which is also in me," she would tell him. "It is the spirit of God, the creator who birthed us. The spirit is all around us. It has always been and will always be. We are one with the spirit."

Her faith was an oral tradition passed down through eight generations of her family. Her first Christian ancestor was baptized as an adult by Mark the Evangelist. Because of her banishment to a life of slavery, her knowledge of Christianity had not progressed beyond what she had learned as a child. Her youthful understanding thus consisted of the Yesua's sayings, the story of his life and the wonder of his miracles. Although somewhat convoluted by local traditions about creation and the nature of good and evil, her faith was simple and pure.

Three times daily, each day of his life, together they prayed to Yesua. Invariably, this daily routine generated questions from the gentle, but naturally inquisitive blind boy. She never attempted to answer his questions directly. Instead, she would recite the stories of Yesua, the words of Yesua, which she herself had learned as a child, choosing carefully, so as to tell Philip truths that would lead the boy to the answers he sought. The nature of good and evil was particularly troublesome to the child. Responding to his queries, she would thoughtfully and carefully retell the very creation stories told to her by her parents. She had little concern for the theological issues spawned by complex explanations of good and evil. When the discussion became too deep, she would redirect him to the words of Yesua. The boy loved the story of Yesua's life, death and resurrection. He revered how Yesua forgave his murderers at the hour of his death. When he was not yet quite eight years old, Philip told his mother, "only Yesua can love like that." "To love is to forgive," she replied. "To forgive is to love."

One day, they were sitting arm in arm at the villa's open gate, waiting for Quintus' return from an "assignment." It was a cool day with a fresh breeze. Philip huddled near Miriam, stroking her hair and anticipating the rumble of hooves raising clouds of dust that he could feel, smell – even taste, the dust a harbinger of the aroma of lathered horses, hooves pounding his way. He softly traced his fingers across his mother's face, touching her lips, nose and eyelids. She closed her eyes, embracing the cool breeze and his gentle touch. His fingers paused as he once more examined her scar.

He raised his head and asked the question she'd been dreading since his birth. "Mother, why is this cheek uneven, not as smooth as your other?"

She hesitated. "Ah, my son. When I was your age, both of my cheeks were equally soft and smooth."

What a curious answer, he thought. "How then did one change, but not the other, Mama?"

Again, she hesitated. Some day he must know the truth. "Your father was angry with me and he pushed me down. My cheek hit the floor, which split open my skin."

"Like when I fall and scrape my knees?" The boy asked.

"Yes, but much worse," she answered softly.

He could feel her anxiety. "Why did he push you so hard?"

Her speech shifted to a slower, more deliberate pace. "He grew angry because he did not want to hear the words that I spoke to him."

"What words could have been so awful, Mama?" The boy felt he must know, if only so as to avoid inadvertently speaking them himself.

"The Truth." Her gaze was blank as if she was reliving that moment.

He could not see her face, but he could hear her disgust, her agony. "The Truth?" he asked.

"I told him, God's love will save you. Yesua says, 'Ask for forgiveness and you will receive,'" she whispered to her son.

The thundering commotion of the returning cavalry ended their conversation abruptly. Both mother and son scurried off to the bathing chamber. Miriam assumed her statue-like position in the corner of the room, and Philip located the wash buckets needed to clean Quintus' armor. Silently, they waited, each preoccupied with words unspoken.

Quintus entered the chamber and disrobed before the boy, who began cleaning each piece of armor as it was discarded. The young slave, Marduk, entered the chamber for his part in the ritual. Both master and slave were nude. In the past, the blind boy had questioned Quintus about his armor hundreds of times. The officer's responses were curt, devoid of detail, and stopped abruptly the moment the cleansing rite commenced. Quintus felt the boy's questions corrupted the sacred realm of the purification process. The chamber's silence was interrupted only by the sound of water trickling down the far west wall and seeping slowly out, across the floor. So it was this day. Miriam watched from her corner as the terrified boy Marduk bathed their officious master and as in utter silence, Philip attended to his father's armor.

The silence was broken unexpectedly by the blind bastard son who had sliced his finger on the sword's razor-sharp blade.

Perturbed by the outburst, Quintus shouted, "Silence boy! Stop! You squeal like a frightened girl!"

His words stung the boy, whose emotions were still raw from what he had learned from his mother's admission earlier, before Quintus had returned to the villa. Angered, the boy snapped back, "Why must this sword be so sharp?"

"To better slice off the heads of obstinate Christians, Christians who squeal like little girls. Now be quiet and go about your business." Quintus was impatient to return to his meditative state.

For once, please listen to your father, Miriam prayed silently.

Moments passed. Quintus' trance resumed; the anguished mother waited for what she hoped would be a calm dismissal.

The boy's anger subsided as he thought about the tortured, bloodied Yesua on his cross, just moments from death. "Father, forgive them." Thoughts of Yesua soothed his angst.

The boy spoke. "Father?"

"Silence!" The second interruption exasperated Quintus.

The mother was thankful that the boy could not see his father's rage. She prayed that her son would not feel his fury.

"Father?" The boy's voice was calm as he repeated the words his mother had spoken earlier. "God's love will save you. Yesua says, 'Ask for forgiveness and you shall receive.'"

Instantly enraged, Quintus exploded with fury, pushing aside Marduk, whose dark eyes opened wide, his mouth forming a perfect O of astonishment and fear. Quintus was already crossing the room, knocking over both Marduk and buckets of water as he dove toward Philip. He grasped the boy's slender, tan arm, and dragged him toward his mother, who had stepped as far back into the corner as she was able. Quintus slung the boy toward her, roughly dashing the boy's head against the dripping wall. Philip's blood now mingled with the water and began, slowly at first, to join the rivulets' inevitable trek across the floor and toward the gurgle and glug of the drain.

"Get out! Slut! Sorceress! Go! Go and take your bastard son with you!" He spat the words at Miriam, and then pulled Philip up from the floor, the boy's feet dangling and flailing helplessly in mid-air, where the brutal Quintus held him fast; clutching the boy and consumed with disgust, he spit first upon one blind eye and then the other. After spewing his hot, angry saliva into the boy's eyes, Quintus pulled his helpless form still closer, roaring, "And you! You little freak bastard, another outburst like that and it shall be your neck that my sword next severs," he growled, first shaking the stunned boy, then dropping him abruptly onto the floor, where he landed pitifully and painfully, tears springing loose.

Addressing Marduk, who had wisely risen and whose face now bore a slave's mask of benign subjection, Quintus ordered, "We are finished here now. Bring me my riding clothes, and report here instantly when I return."

Quintus strode swiftly to the stable and ordered the liveryman to saddle his horse. "I must spend some time with the only living creature who understands me," Quintus declared, grasping the readied reins, then wordlessly mounted Narseh and vanished in clouds of dust and clattering hooves.

III

It was a fateful day in 303 AD that would change all of their lives forever. A servant summoned Quintus to the front gate of the villa, which faced south at the northern edge of the town forum. A small band of Roman soldiers had arrived at Rasafa. They were waiting for him in the square that fronted the villa's gate. It was clear that they had been traveling for many days. With them was a sorely battered prisoner who was shackled and chained. His feet were caked with dirt and blood. One could not distinguish one soldier from another. Looking more closely, Quintus felt that the man looked oddly familiar, that he resembled an older version of a courageous and distinguished Roman officer with whom he had once served in battle.

The commanding centurion inquired, "Sir, are you Quintus Flavius Scipio, Supernumerarius in the Legions of Caesar Galerius Maximianus?"

"I am," Quintus responded.

"Sir, I have been ordered to deliver this prisoner to you by Antiochus, the military commander of Caesar's legions in Barbalisso."

Quintus circled the man, examining him. His eyes, lips and nose were crusted with dried blood and severely swollen, as well. Quintus stared intently at the battered face, struggling to recognize the man beneath the telltale evidence of hardship and brutality. At long last, he spoke, addressing the prisoner with but one word, "Sergius?"

The man nodded. Quintus turned and addressed the centurion, "I know this man. He is a Roman citizen, as well as a high-ranking officer, valiant and loyal."

"This man is a traitor and a Christian, one who stubbornly refuses to sacrifice to the gods," the centurion replied. "Tales were reported to Galerius Maximianus, Caesar of the Eastern Empire that his legions, and more specifically, his officers, were secretly practicing Christian beliefs. Two officers, Sergius and Bacchus, in particular were suspected to be secret practitioners. Galerius set a trap for the two by assigning them to the ranks of his personal guards. He then arranged for an extravagant sacrifice at the Temple of Jupiter, honoring the great god. When the entourage entered the Temple, Sergius and Bacchus remained outside its edifice; they did not cross its threshold. Pressed by the other guards, the two both refused to enter the temple. It was thus their secret was laid bare. When confronted with threats of torture and death, they both, each of them, refused to renounce their Man-God, the Nazarene, Yesua."

Quintus moved closer to Sergius. An icy stare brought them eye to eye. Without losing his gaze, Quintus asked the centurion, "Why have you brought me just this one? Where is the other, the traitor Bacchus?"

The centurion continued, "The men were stripped of their military garments and dressed as women. They were then paraded throughout the town, but despite such indignities, it seems their popularity amongst the troops, who revere them as fearless and dedicated leaders, caused great unrest within the Legions. Therefore, Galerius sent them to Mesopotamia, to be tried by Antiochus, a close friend of Sergius and the military commander of Barbalisso. In spite of Antiochus' persuasions, both officers remained resolute in their loyalty to this Yesua. They were sentenced to be tortured – to death. Both were flogged and beaten. Bacchus could not endure the lash and the beatings. Sergius lived. Nails were driven into the soles of his sandals and just so, through his feet. Orders were given to march him here to Rasafa. If fate allowed him to survive such a march, we were ordered to deliver him here, to you. You are to finish his sentence. We have marched for three days, now, yet he refuses to die. There is sorcery at work here. I am glad to be rid of him. He is yours to do with as you wish."

Again, Quintus's gaze was met by Sergius', whom Quintus addressed, "look carefully into my eyes and know my resolve, man."

In a weak, but steady voice, Sergius replied, "Yesua says, whoever has ears should hear. There is a light within a person and it shines on the whole world. If it does not shine, it is dark."

Raising his voice, Quintus roared, "I say whoever has ears should hear! Look into my eyes, traitor, and learn now my resolve!"

"I have," said Sergius. "I see only darkness."

A substantial crowd was gathering. Quintus turned to his servant and ordered, "Bring the slave girl and her blind son, so that they may see and hear what must now come to pass."

When the mother and child arrived, he positioned them both facing toward the prisoner. Stepping back into the center of the crowd, Quintus addressed the gathering. "Let it be known to all here, and especially to those of you who worship the Nazarene called Yesua, that it is great folly to worship this false god!"

The boy tensed as he heard the familiar sound of his father's sword being slid out of its leather sheath. Using the flat side of his sword, Quintus struck Sergius across his back, driving him face down to the roadway's surface. The boy clung to his mother when he heard the metal strike the chains as the man fell helplessly to the stone pavement.

Addressing the pair, Quintus commanded, "You two! Stop standing idle! Lift him to his knees. Now!"

The mother then knelt, and gently lifted Sergius' bloody head and whispered, "Yesua is with you."

Sergius replied, "and also with you kind woman. Tell Quintus that I forgive him."

"Do as I command! Do it now!" Quintus railed.

Each grasped a shoulder burnt red by the sun, battered and slick with sweat. With great effort and great care, for fear of injuring him further, they hoisted Sergius to his knees, steadied him, and then stepped back. Quintus swung his sword again, this time blade to bone, decapitating the man. The head rolled to the boy's feet, blood jetted from the severed flesh, splattering Philip's face as the lifeless body fell forward to the ground for the last time. Miriam clutched her son and wiped the blood from his eyes.

Quintus stood above them and placed the tip of his sword under her chin, forcing her head upwards. "Look at me."

Then he shouted, "Look at me!! What did he say to you?"

Calmly, she answered, "He told me to tell you that he forgives you."

Slowly, he lowered his sword. Then, grasping its handle with both hands, he raised his outstretched arms above his head, determined to rid himself of the endless nuisance of this woman.

Suddenly, the boy ran to Quintus, shouting "Father! Father...... I can see!"

The crowd was deathly still. Quintus lowered his sword. He looked into his son's eyes. It was true. The boy ran back to his mother. Quintus paced quietly around the body of the fallen martyr. Slowly, he walked counterclockwise along the perimeter of the crowd, returning to stand before the woman and her boy.

What kind of sorcery is this? he wondered. Whatever it was, he was more determined than ever to put an end to it. He whispered instructions to his nearest body servant and sent him back to the villa. The servant returned with a scribe and a small, brown sack of denarii, which jingled just slightly when the slave came to a halt.

Quintus turned, addressing the crowd, "Is there a traveling merchant here?" A man stepped forward.

"What is your destination?"

"Egypt," the merchant replied.

Quintus had neither the will to murder the mother, nor did he wish to harm the boy, for deep within, his sinister mind reasoned that he would suffer retribution through whatever dark magic protected this witch and her child. At the same time, he seized upon the ideal solution to his problems, a fate worse than death for both of them. He would separate them, forever.

He dictated a note to the scribe, sealed the note and instructed the merchant to take the boy to the military commander of the Roman Garrison in Alexandria. "Here are 50 denarii for your trouble. This note bears instructions to give you another 100 denarii when you deliver this boy. The commander is a friend of mine. He knows my seal. He will honor my word."

"Does the boy have a name?" the merchant inquired.

Quintus neither knew nor cared to know. "Tell him your name boy. Now!" he barked.

The boy replied with bold aplomb, "It is Philip."

Then Quintus turned to the centurion, "Are you returning to Antiochus' garrison in Mesopotamia? "

"No. We have been redeployed to Aelia Capitolina in Syria Palestina."

"Fine," Quintus muttered, gruffly. "Take this creature with you and leave her there. Do not look at her. Do not talk to her. Do not listen to her. Do not touch her. Let her find her Nazarene god there if she can," he declared smugly.

He addressed Miriam, "You will never see your son again. My Roman brethren in Aelia Capitolina will be far less tolerant than I have been. "

"What is her name?" asked the centurion. Again, Quintus neither knew nor cared.

"My name is Miriam," the girl replied.

Addressing the crowd, Quintus shouted, "Depart this place....all of you....and leave the body of this traitor for the dogs and wild beasts."

Miraculously, the dogs and wild beasts did come, but they never disturbed the body. Instead, they guarded it until Sergius' fellow Christian brethren arrived, so as to remove his remains for proper burial.

Over the years, the legends of St. Sergius and St. Bacchus grew in popularity and veneration. In 425 AD, a shrine was constructed in Rasafa. Later, the city of Rasafa became a bishop's diocese and was renamed Sergiopolis. The shrine in Sergiopolis became the site of eastern Christian pilgrimages, until Islam spread through the region three centuries later. Sergius became an enormously admired saint in Syria and Christian Arabia and remains now the Patron Saint of desert nomads.

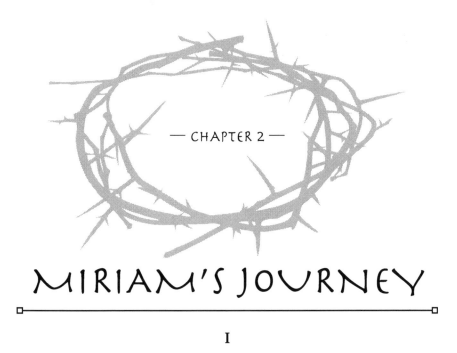

— CHAPTER 2 —

MIRIAM'S JOURNEY

I

It is generally held that Mark the Evangelist established the first Egyptian Christian church in Alexandria between 50 and 60 AD. By the end of the third century, nearly all of the population of Egypt was Christian. In fact, the end of the third century marks the beginning of the Coptic Church and is referred to as the Age of Martyrs. The Diocletianic persecutions were particularly brutal in Egypt.

In the year 286, the Roman Theban Legion was ordered from the Eastern Empire to Gaul in an effort to quell an uprising there. It was common to move legions from far away regions in order to prevent them from fighting in their homelands. Upon arriving in Gaul, the Legion was ordered to participate in a sacrifice and to avow an oath to advance the elimination of Christianity there. The Theban Legion was entirely Egyptian and entirely Christian. Upon hearing the orders, they refused to either participate in the sacrifice, or to take the oath.

The Emperor ordered a decimation of the Legion, meaning specifically that every 10th legionnaire be put to death. A legion consisted of 6,600 men. That day 660 men were put to the sword and the names of the men were written on the helmets of their officers. Still, the Legion collectively refused. Enraged, the Emperor ordered his loyal legions to annihilate the remaining Thebans. On September 26, 286 AD, the entire Theban Legion was martyred. Not one man raised his sword in defense. All accepted their fates willingly.

Undoubtedly, the insolence of The Theban Legion had a strong influence on the focus of the Diocletian Persecutions. Not only was there a concerted effort to purge Christianity from the ranks of Roman legions everywhere, but the Emperor also ordered the systematic dismantling of the Christian religion in Egypt, including the destruction of churches and the burning of Christian writings. Organized bands of Christians fled to the eastern and western Egyptian deserts to escape persecution and to live in prayer and contemplation. Christian Monasticism claims its roots in third century Coptic Egypt.

In 287 AD, Miriam's family fell victim to the Emperor's wrath. Miriam's father Abāmūn was an influential Coptic Christian in Pemdje, an ancient village one hundred miles south of modern day Cairo in Middle Egypt. In an effort to extract a denial of Abāmūn's Christian faith, Miriam's mother, Sarah, was subjected to excruciating torture in the presence of Miriam and her father. First, Sarah's body was raked with sharp iron combs, tearing her flesh. Then a boiling mixture of vinegar, lime and swine hair was rubbed into the wounds. Abāmūn did not recant. Next, the soldiers carved a hole in Sarah's face and gouged out her eyes. Abāmūn remained steadfast. Finally, after two soldiers skinned Sarah's flesh from her shoulders to her chin, a boiling mixture of oil, lead, gum and tar was drizzled on to her head, oozing into her open wounds.

Racked with pain, Sarah screamed, "Mary, Sweet Mother of the Light pray for them. Yesua, you are with me, forgive them." As her mother succumbed to violent convulsions, a centurion grabbed Miriam by her hair and dragged her to Abāmūn's feet. He stripped Miriam naked and addressed her father, shouting, "Recant you wretched fool!"

"I cannot deny Yesua for he is in me and I am in him," Abāmūn replied.

"And what of your wife and daughter?" spat the soldier.

"He is in them and they are in me. Our being is eternal. If we deny Yesua, then we deny eternity. They are safe with Him, no matter what you do!" Turning to his subordinates, the centurion said, "Take this little bitch to the slave market. See to it that she is sold to a demon that will make each remaining day of her life an eternal hell!" As Miriam was dragged away, the naked and vulnerable ten year old girl screamed, "Father! Mother! You left in me the Faith!"

II

For a few brief minutes, they stared at each other, mother and child. No longer blind, Philip traced his hands across Miriam's face, touching the scar he'd so often felt, but had never before seen. "Why, mother! You are so beautiful," he said. She stared into his once lifeless eyes for what seemed like an eternity. Before she could speak, soldiers responded to Quintus' orders and wrenched the child from her arms.

The moment was traumatically resonant with that day, sixteen years earlier in Pemdje, yet Miriam knew that separation was inevitable in the temporal realm. She hoped that she was leaving Philip in the Faith that would reunite them in the spiritual realm. Her faith was based on oral tradition that included sayings and parables of Yesua, as well as stories about saints and martyrs, including Miriam's mother and father. For his sake, she bound Philip by oath to never speak of these teachings in front of Quintus. Had she erred? What good were these teachings without an unfailing commitment? How much of his father's spirit did Philip inherit? Would a lack of open commitment equate to fear, a weakness Quintus loathed? Would Philip interpret her teachings this way? All of these things she wondered as she was led away by the soldiers.

As the crow flies, Resafa was three hundred sixty miles northeast of Aelia Capitolina. Miriam's destination was the site of an ancient city that was reconstructed by the Emperor Hadrian in 135 AD, following its destruction after the Jewish Revolt of 70AD and the Bar Kokhba revolt of 132–135AD. The ancient city was once called Jerusalem. Their arduous passage meandered through various trading routes in what could best be described as hostile environments. The first leg of the trip was south through the Syrian Desert on a caravan route that passed through the city of Palmyra. There, the troops turned west to Damascus, then south again to Aelia Capitolina. The journey encompassed nearly five hundred miles and took a full thirty days to complete.

Miriam was accorded little sympathy by the soldiers. Out of respect for Quintus, or perhaps for fear of him, the soldiers gave Miriam just enough water and food to keep her alive. She walked the entire route. Upon arrival in Jerusalem, the soldiers halted at the temple of Venus to offer a sacrifice in exchanged for their safe passage. As a final gesture, they left Miriam at the foot of the steps leading to the temple entrance.

Two Jewish revolts had resulted in the complete destruction of Jerusalem by the Romans, including Solomon's Temple. In 135 AD, the Emperor Hadrian rebuilt the city as a Roman garrison to house his legionnaires. The city was renamed Aelia Capitolina and Hadrian changed the country's name from Judea to Syria Palestina. Jews and Jewish Christians were prohibited from entering the city under penalty of death. Gentile Christians were permitted to stay, but worshiped cautiously. Venerated Christian and Jewish sites were reduced to rubble, covered completely and replaced with Roman temples.

Miriam was deserted by the soldier escorts at one such site, three quarters of the way up the slope of the western hill across the valley from the site where once the magnificent Temple of Solomon on the Temple Mount had stood. For two weeks, she roamed the precinct surrounding Venus' Temple, reduced to begging for food; her efforts were met with little success. Already weakened by her torturous journey, she survived only by virtue of her hoped for reunion with Philip and her undying belief that Yesua was with them both. On the north side of the temple, she slept in a small alcove she'd discovered amidst the ruined remains of a deserted building on the edge of the narrow stone street.

Late one morning, she awoke from sleepless delirium to a commotion in the street. As she stumbled from her hovel, she observed a procession of soldiers further up the hill, taunting a lone man carrying a cross. Their pace was slow, and in spite of Miriam's weariness, she was able to join the small band of bystanders who followed along. The man had been horribly tortured. His face and torso were swollen and bloodied. On his head was a grotesque crown of large thorns. One thorn angled through his right temple, exiting the corner of his eye socket. The man obviously was a Christian, most likely a leader of some sort who openly taught the Faith.

The procession moved up the narrow road past the temple precinct. Suddenly, a soldier on a white horse galloped up the road from below, his sword raised high. As he passed, he struck the man on the back of his head with the flat face of his sword and continued his gallop past the group. The blow drove more thorns deep into his weary neck, just below the skull. The man fell helplessly to the stone road and struck his head, driving still further thorns through his eyebrows, very narrowly missing his eyes. His face bled profusely, making it both difficult for him to see, as well as for onlookers to know his face, for all it was suffused with blood and sweat. Soldiers then ordered bystanders to help the man to his feet. Miriam struggled forward and fell to her knees before him. As he raised his head slowly, she tore her own garment and wiped the man's face clean.

He spoke gently to her saying, "The Light shines in your kindness. Your Faith has saved you."

As she stared into his eyes, an uncanny sensation first subsumed, and then overwhelmed her; it was if she were looking into a mirror, seeing a spirit deep within her own self. Before she could speak, the soldiers had their prisoner on his feet and moving again, despite his excruciating agony. They taunted him saying, "Easier for us to leave you here, you beast, but then we'd hate for you to miss all the entertainment to come. Yes! Death awaits you when we reach the heights. Better for you, though, to keep moving, than to be left here now to be eaten alive by wild dogs."

Addressing the crowd, the soldiers said, "Beware to you who know this man, for his fate shall also be your own." Slowly, the bystanders slipped away. The procession lumbered on. By the time the man reached the crest, Miriam alone remained. The soldiers went about their seemingly perfunctory task in methodical silence. A surreal apparition overcame Miriam; it seemed to her these were actors, repeating a script that had been rehearsed and enacted for hundreds of years. The man's blood-soaked garments were torn from him. Standing naked, his frail, bloody body presented itself, it seemed to her, like a newly born child's, just slipped from the womb; a body resonant with her own first glimpse of her son, Philip.

The soldiers lowered the man to the cross and carefully positioned his body so as to pinion him there. Holding his knees and feet together, they bent his legs toward his chest. Two soldiers aligned his feet and placed them on opposite sides of the mast. A third uniformed minion drove a metal stake through each foot at a point centered inside the Achilles tendon between the heel and ankle bones, just where the bundled nerves enter the feet. They positioned his arms on the cross beam with a slight bend at the elbow. Four soldiers completed the task of mounting their captive. Two held each arm in place, while two others drove metal stakes through precisely the points on each wrist where the bundle nerves enter the carpel tunnel.

Two of the soldiers then positioned themselves at either end of the beam and two others were stationed on each side of the intersections of the beam and the mast. In a synchronized movement, they hoisted the cross to its final placement into a hole, which was several feet deep, and centered in a scrabbled mound of rubble and debris. The entire assembly, man and cross, slammed into place. The position of the stakes, the bend of the knees and elbows were all calculated for effect. The stakes were at points that simultaneously ensured maximum pain as well as skeletal support; the bends in his limbs would allow movement. His fate was not only to hang on the cross but to ride it as well.

For three hours, he rode the cross. First, to relieve the pain in the arms, he would rise up, then, to relieve the pain in his legs, he was forced to slide himself down. These motions were followed by increasingly lengthy periods marked by utter stillness, as well as labored, even arduous breathing. Each movement up was accompanied by a painful groan; each movement down with guttural utterances; some were prayers, some were pleas. Miriam, who knelt at his feet, fixed his gaze with her own, feeling viscerally each of his prayers, every one of his pleas to a sacred Spirit within them both.

Oblivious to these excruciating minutiae, the soldiers busied themselves gambling. As he endured the cross, the skies darkened to a deep, foreboding purple. The dice match paused occasionally as the soldiers reacted to distant thunder and lightning. Finally, all movement ceased. His last plea was one for the forgiveness of his tormentors. It was greeted by a tumultuous lightning bolt and cloud burst.

The soldiers quickly ended their game and approached the cross. "Is it over?" one asked. Another responded, "Let's make sure, for it is too dangerous to stay here." Grabbing a lance, he approached the cross and thrust it into the man's heart. "Orders are to take him down so that he does not become a symbol for his followers. Leave him for the dogs." Quickly, they pried the spikes from the cross. The body crumpled to the ground. The soldiers gathered their wares and trudged off hurriedly down the road and out of sight.

Miriam was now alone with the fallen man. Moving beside him, she pulled him to her. As she rocked him in her arms, she began to cry. Her salt tears mixed with the blood soaked rain.

III

The remnants of the passing storm softened the morning's sunrise on the deserted hill. Miriam awoke slowly, finding herself in a disoriented state. She rolled onto her side, and then realized that she was surrounded by a pack of wolves, all resting peacefully beside her. Carefully, she rolled over to protect the man's body. The body was gone. A nursing she-wolf lay at Miriam's head, offering her swollen teats. There were no pups anywhere to be seen amidst the pack. Miriam's severe fatigue fell away as her unwavering instinct to survive rose to the fore. The she-wolf's futile search for her pups had given way to her life-giving instincts. Miriam became her bella and the she-wolf suckled her back to life.

The hill was silent that day. Miriam rested. The she-wolf continued, protecting her. The next morning, the pack itself was gone. Only Miriam and the she-wolf remained. The animal was on her feet, and nudging Miriam to rise. The she-wolf turned and trotted down the hill toward the temple. Miriam rose up, so as to follow. The bloody scene had been washed clean by the storm. She saw no evidence of the fallen man as she trailed behind the she-wolf, which had now wandered down to the street. When they reached the temple precinct, the animal raced ahead, and then up the stairs, which led to the entry portico. Sniffing the ground, she paced excitedly around the portico landing.

Miriam followed her up the steps to the entrance. There, on the portico floor, were bloody footsteps. A burst of energy charged through Miriam from head to toe, as she hurried her pace in search of the man. The footsteps continued to the center of the sanctuary and then, mysteriously, stopped. Miriam slowly turned, looking about for evidence of the man. Finally, she turned again and faced the entrance. Silhouetted there in the gentle balm of the morning sun, was the she-wolf. As they made eye contact, the she-wolf turned and disappeared down the steps. Miriam did not hesitate to follow.

The she-wolf trotted back up the road to the crest, and then turned left into a field that traversed the hillside opposite the city's west wall. When she reached the wall, the she-wolf followed the partition down the hill to a shallow ravine, where she stopped to wait for Miriam. The storm had washed away a weakened area of the barrier's foundation. The she-wolf slipped away then, just beneath the wall.

Miriam attempted to follow, but the opening was partially blocked by a rock of substantial size. While large enough for the she-wolf, it was too small for her. Miriam lay beside the wall, and began to dig furiously with her hands. The hard earth felt like solid stone; the soft skin of her hands and fingers scraped and tore; Miriam grimaced with pain. She then tried the rock, but found it far larger than she'd expected, for it seemed to weigh as much as did she herself. She went on digging for nearly an hour, further ripping the skin from her fingers and tearing at her bloodied fingernails, then suddenly, the stone slipped, trapping her right arm to her elbow. She dug now with her left hand for another twenty minutes. Bracing the rock with her left hand, she wiggled her right arm free. The rock shifted again, giving just slightly. Miriam prayed that the space might now be large enough as she contorted her body through the passage. She slid first her right arm and then her shoulder. Next, she craned her neck, her head breaching its way, followed by her aching left shoulder. As she struggled to move her hips through, though, it was only then that she realized that the space remained too small.

Exhausted and begrimed with dust and filth, as well as her blood, her sweat and her tears; she closed her eyes, convinced that all she had accomplished this day was to prepare for herself a rocky grave. She had struggled for nearly two hours, only to travel a bit more than five feet. Resigned to her fate, she made final preparations for her Spirit's eternal journey. She prayed. She prayed to Yesua. She prayed to her parents. She prayed to the Spirit within. As she prayed, she entered a trance, which was interrupted by the howling of a wolf. All this while, her protector had been waiting patiently. Hearing the animal's low howl, Miriam gave one last push forward, freeing her hips. Belly down, she wriggled through the hole, and then raised herself up on her elbows, gasping for air. The she-wolf greeted eagerly, licking her face and her neck. Miriam craned her neck toward the wolf, pressing her head against the warm fur, now brow to brow with her sole guardian.

"My sweet Lupa; please lead us to Egypt." With that, Lupa turned and trotted southward.

PHILIP'S JOURNEY

I

Philip's first sight was his mother's face. His second, his father, scowling brutally, standing above Miriam, his blood-drenched sword raised high. His third, the grotesque, haunting remains of the decapitated martyr, Sergius. Conceived in rage, born into darkness, Philip was now reborn – into violence. His mother had taken pains to teach him of Yesua. He loved the story of how Yesua died so that His Spirit would endure forever, living on in everyone. His father's callous murder of a man who would not, could not deny Yesua, struck him as purely incomprehensible.

Separated from his mother, Philip now traveled with a band of strangers into unknown lands. Carrying rare and pungent spices from the east, the caravan traveled westward in hopes of selling their wares. The merchants were from Cochin in India, a major port city on the west coast of India near the Arabian Sea; the Apostle Thomas had visited there two hundred and fifty years previously. The group's members were all related: two brothers, their two sons, a cousin and his own two sons. They had been making this journey for ten years. The oldest among them was forty-eight, the youngest, just nineteen.

The merchants' journeys re-traced the routes traveled by Yesua's disciples centuries before: Peter and Paul in Antioch, Barnabas in Mesopotamia and the disciple, Thomas, through Syria, Persia and India. Following established eastern trade routes, Thomas was the only discile to take Yesua's message well beyond the boundaries of the Roman Empire. During his mission to southeast India, near Mylapore, Thomas was speared to death. His relics were later returned to Edessa in Mesopotamia. For hundreds of years, the acts and teachings of Thomas were handed down through oral traditions. These traditions greatly influenced eastern Christians, not the least of these, this traveling band of merchants. Quite unknowingly, Quintus had ordered Philip to be shepherded by none other than believers of Yesua who had been taught in the Thomasine tradition.

The merchants were un-phased by Quintus. They had seen the heinous deeds of his ilk many times before. However, the great miracle of the martyr's blood and the blind child who could now see, affected them deeply. By this alone, they understood just how very precious their new cargo was, and they certainly had no intention of actually delivering Philip to the Romans in Alexandria. Furthermore, these men also understood how brutal Miriam's mother's journey would be, knew there was little hope of her survival.

The first day, they traveled in silence. Philip's mind was filled with a myriad of new sense-experiences. Strange humped beasts lumbered onward, bearing both men and materials. New scents, new sounds, escorted the visual wonders attending this new gift of sight. The heat on his face was now accompanied by a blinding light, yet flashbacks from the day before shattered the wonders before him. How quickly his life was changing. Late in the day, the caravan stopped. Camels were fed and bedded down. A large lean-to canopy tent was raised. As the sun set, the entire group gathered under the tent to pray. They dropped to their knees and sat erect upon their heels. One among the group spoke:

"Let us give thanks for this day. Let us pray as Yesua taught us."

All in unison, the group lowered their heads to the ground and prayed.

"O Birther! Father-Mother of the Cosmos
Focus your light within us - make it useful.
Create your reign of unity now-
through our fiery hearts and willing hands
Help us love beyond our ideals,
to sprout acts of compassion for all creatures.
Animate the earth within us: we then
feel the Wisdom underneath supporting all.
Untangle the knots within,
so that we can mend our hearts' simple ties to one another.
Don't let surface things delude us,
but free us from what holds us back from our true purpose.
Out of you, the astonishing fire,
returning light and sound to the cosmos."

The prayer reminded Philip of his mother. There was one phrase Miriam had repeated to him so often, particularly during stressful times. She whispered the day before as the soldiers separated them.

"Yesua, focus Your Light within us".

Twilight came upon them as they prepared the evening meal. The eldest addressed the others.

"Feed the child first and let him sleep. His soul is tired and confused. His soul needs a good night's rest."

Philip was fed and led away to a soft mat under the canopy where he was covered with several blankets to protect him from the cool night air. For the first time in his life, he feared the darkness. Since birth, his dreams had been solely auditory. Last night, his first visual dream had been a cruel rerunning mish-mash of the nightmare events that had comprised that dreadful, fateful day. Tonight, his traveling companions' kindness eased his fears. This night he would have his first peaceful visual dream; it was of his mother, surrounded and supported by a white gold cloud of Spirit, which then broadened in scope. He saw his father, Quintus, step forward.

In this dream, Quintus rescinded his order to separate mother and son. Instead, Miriam and Philip would be exiled together. Unlike the night before, tonight Philip's dream was soothing. Miriam and Philip rode together on a camel; he sat before her atop the great beast; she clutched him from behind, her slender brown arms fast about him. As they rode, she whispered in his ear, explaining each new sight and how the sounds and smells related to what he was seeing. Although otherwise somewhat vague, the sights, smells and sounds he recalled upon waking were vivid.

The most vivid visual sequence included the sight of his mother's face up close, her penetrating gaze and the crescent shaped scar upon her right cheek, both close enough to feel, to touch. This vision repeated each time he turned to ask each a question of her. "Why does this animal have such a funny shape? What do we call this beast? Why do they smell so odd? Why does this hot wind blow? From whence does this hot wind come?" Her sweet, gentle scent and her murmur-soft voice were always present as he dreamt. Her whispers clung to him like a blanket. Indeed, his soul was at peace, both happy and content in equal measure.

A new smell he'd never before encountered entered his dream. It was so odd that it woke him from his slumber. He lay awake, silently gathering his thought. This was but the second day on which he was to wake possessed of his sight. It was still dark, but he could see clearly. It took several moments to gather his thoughts as he looked about, taking stock of his surroundings. Realizing that he was alone, he rose in search of the men who had carried him so far to this place.

He followed the smell. It was then that he saw all of the men, their silhouettes danced as the campfire flickered. The smell that had roused him was of food, of his breakfast meal still cooking on the fire.

The eldest of the group addressed him, "Philip, peace be with you. Welcome to this wonderful day that has been made for us. Please sit and eat." He gestured for Philip to sit beside him.

Philip approached the group with caution, but then sat alongside the man who had so invited him.

"Did you sleep well?" the elder queried.

"I dreamt of my mother. I could see her in my dream."

"Let those who can hear know that the Yesua gave you sight so that you may see her always."

"I miss her," he blurted out, then began to cry.

The group of men glanced at one another. Finally, the elder spoke, "Come. Eat." He broke the bread, dipping it into the thick soupy mixture that bubbled atop the fire. He handed it to the child and said, "Take this bread to feed your body. Use the spirit of Yesua within you to feed your soul."

The group ate in silence, each pondering the circumstance of their curious guest and the strange miracle that had restored to him the sight he'd never before known.

Philip's inquisitive nature broke the silence. "Who is the 'Birther?'" he asked.

"Are you referring to our prayer last night?" the elder inquired.

"Yes," the boy replied.

"The 'Birther' is the creator of everything that is now and ever will be. The 'Birther' is both Father and Mother of the Cosmos. We learned the prayer in our travels through your land, now many, many years ago. It was taught to us in Aramaic, the native language of Yesua, who taught the prayer to his disciples when they had asked Him how they might pray."

"Where is the 'Birther?'"

"His kingdom is spread throughout and across the Cosmos; thus, it is in everything."

Philip paused for a moment, thinking. "The 'Birther' is in you?"

"Yes."

"In me?"

"Yes."

"My mother said that the Spirit of Yesua is in me."

"Your mother is correct," replied the elder.

"So is the 'Birther'....a....a Spirit?" Philip asked.

"The 'Birther' is Spirit. There is no 'other.'"

Confused, Philip paused again, and then inquired, "But you said that my mother was correct and that the Spirit of Yesua is in me. How can there be two spirits in me, when there is no other Spirit?"

"The Spirit of Yesua is one with the 'Birther,'" replied the elder.

This puzzled Philip greatly. He ate in silence as the bread was passed again. After much thought, he spoke once more.

"How did Yesua's spirit become one with the 'Birther'?"

The elder responded, "Yesua said, 'If you don't bring forth what is inside of you, then what is inside of you will destroy you.' Yesua understood the Spirit within and brought it forth with such perfection that he achieved total harmony with the 'Birther'. Not even death can destroy it. Yesua's way is the only way to achieve total harmony with The 'Birther.' The salvation he gives is salvation from the destruction from within."

The explanation brought a pause to the conversation. The others had gradually been drawn into the dialogue between the wise elder and the curious boy. Smiles crossed their faces as they watched Philip, once more deep in thought. The group exchanged glances. Philip's inquisitiveness tickled them. His response shocked them.

"My mother told me that my father did not have Yesua's Spirit. Is this why he killed that man?"

"Your father? The Roman officer? He is your father?" The events two days prior gave them no indication of the relationship between the mother, the child and the murderous Roman.

"Quintus Flavius Scipio, Supernumerarius in the Legions of Caesar Galerius Maximianus?" Philip exclaimed, as if reporting to duty.

Slowly, the elder rose to speak, "Your mother is wise. Arise, all of you. Let us save this talk until this evening. Now, the sun is rising. Let us depart. Our journey continues."

II

The population of the Roman Empire reached its peak around 150 AD, two generations after the passing of Yesua's disciples. The estimated world population at that time was but 300 million. Conservative estimates placed the Empire's population at 65 million, although it is surmised to have possibly been as high as 130 million, representing between twenty to forty percent of the world's then-population. Of that number, no more than six to eight million were

Roman citizens. Rome itself was a city of one million people, over half of which were slaves. Alexandria boasted 750,000 people, whilst Carthage, Ephesus and Antioch all ranged from between 300,000 to 500,000. It was a world built on wealth for the select few, a world supported by extensive trade along favored routes, protected by an army of a half-million men, of which only 150,000 were career legionnaires.

Philip and the band of merchants were traveling to Antioch, once the Empire's third largest city. The previous two hundred years had reduced the population of Antioch considerably. A major earthquake convulsed the city in 115 AD. Fifty years later, plagues raked the entirety of the Empire, thus reducing the overall population. In the year 256 AD, a Persian raiding party captured the city and massacred citizens in the Roman theatre. By 303 AD, the citizen population had shrunk by a third. Even so, Antioch remained a teeming metropolis.

Ancient Antioch was located in the Orantes River valley in what is now southern Turkey, twelve miles inland from the eastern shores of the Mediterranean Sea. A mountain pass to the northwest of the city connected the region with the Euphrates river valley to the east. It was ideally situated along ancient spice and silk trade routes. The Romans understood its strategic importance. Numerous emperors built magnificent structures in and around the city. Octavian, Titus, Trajan and Hadrian made significant improvements, including roads, aqueducts, baths, temples, forums, villas and markets.

The seeds of Christianity were sown early and rooted deeply in Antioch. Early Christianity organized around three patriarchies: Antioch, Alexandria and Rome. Peter, Paul and Barnabas each conducted missionary activities in the city. Peter served as the first patriarch of Antioch from 37 AD to 53 AD. By 303 AD, the Antioch patriarchy included Syria, Palestine, Armenia, Georgia, Mesopotamia and India. The large Jewish community existing there predated the Greeks and Romans. Though Yesua's disciples quickly expanded their focus on gentile populations, their missionary zeal also included Jewish communities that had migrated to other parts of the world. Thomas was on such a mission to a Jewish community in India when he was martyred.

The journey from Rasafa to Antioch was 170 miles. Philip's camel caravan traveled much faster than did Miriam's foot soldiers. The journey normally took two weeks, allotting for a trading stop in Beroea. Each night, the journey ended with the same rituals. The camp was set, animals bedded and a prayer of thanksgiving offered to the 'Birther' before the evening meal. The previous night, Philip had bedded in early. Tonight, he was permitted to join the group at the camp fire for after-dinner conversation.

The conversation leader rotated nightly. The discussion revolved around one of Yesua's sayings, of the leader's choosing, which would then serve as a teaching lesson. Tonight, the youngest of the group led the discussion; he was the elder's nineteen year old nephew, who had begun his travels with the group when he was just Philip's age, ten years previously.

The young man spoke, saying, "Yesua says, 'I am the door; the person who enters by me will find Eternal bliss.'"

His two cousins spoke next. "Yesua says I am the bed; the person who lies on me will enter perpetual rest," responded the first cousin.

"Yesua said, I am the Light; the person who sees by me will view all things," said the second cousin.

"And where is Yesua?" the elder asked. A discussion ensued regarding the divine nature of Yesua.

Eventually, Philip himself spoke, "Yesua is in me and I am in him," offered Philip.

"How is he in you?" asked the elder.

"In spirit."

"And your mother taught you this?" the elder's brother asked.

"Yes," said Philip.

"So, young Philip. How did your mother explain to you your father's cruelty?"

"My father is under the spell of the demiurge that created him."

"And who created Yesua?"

"Yesua created himself," responded Philip.

The elder's brother was deliberately leading Philip with his questioning. In their decade of travel, the group had been exposed to many interpretations of the nature of Yesua's divinity.

Twelve disciples, each having direct personal experience with Yesua, took the messages to the far reaches of the Roman Empire and beyond, following long-established trade routes. For millennia, many riches were traded along these routes, not the least of which included the vast spiritual experiences of many diverse cultures.

Shunned by the religion that had birthed it, armed with the enlightenment of its Founder's Spirit and thrust into missionary exile by a murdering empire, Christianity exploded in all directions like the light from the birth of time. Viewed from many directions, the source of this Light was embraced from the relative perspectives of its viewers.

Had circumstances been different, perhaps with slower maturation in regional isolation, at the beginning of the 4th century, Christianity might have represented a more unified spiritual belief system. Such was not the case, however, particularly with regard to the patriarchy of Antioch. It was here, that for two hundred and eighty years, Christian beliefs had melded with Mesopotamian, Hellenistic, Buddhist and

Hindu concepts. For the vast majority of believers, these precepts were spread by word of mouth to illiterate populations.

Miriam, her parents and this band of Thomasine Christian merchants were all illiterate, taught solely in the oral traditions of their native regions. For the merchant, this translated into a Buddhist perspective of Yesua's divinity. For Miriam and Philip, the translation was made through Mesopotamian and Hellenistic lenses.

Fully aware of the different interpretations, the elder continued to question Philip, so as to gather the boy's perspective and to gauge the depth of his understanding.

"Philip. Tell me, who is the Demiurge?"

"He is the lesser God, who created this world. Not perfect himself, he created many imperfections, including my father and those like him."

"And Yesua? Who did you say created Yesua?"

"Yesua created himself. He is an Aeon." Philip's comment had an insolent air, reflecting his father's arrogance, suggesting that their ignorance underscored the stupidity of the question.

"And what is an Aeon?" asked the elder, knowing full well the explanation that Philip would give.

"An Aeon comes from the Light and is so pure and so good that it can create itself," replied Philip, adding, "like the 'Birther.'"

The younger cousins laughed, reinforcing Philip's perception of the group's ignorance. The elder rebuked them, saying, "Let him be. He is a child who was taught like a child. His spirit is pure. We have witnessed the death of a martyr whose blood has miraculously given this child sight. The Father has not revealed His intentions for this child."

Then rising, the elder said, "Enough for tonight. Our journey continues tomorrow."

III

On that fateful day in Rasafa, it was the elder who had responded to Quintus' search for a merchant. His quick thinking had saved the child. He had hoped that he could save the mother as well, but was foiled by Quintus' treachery. He had done this at great risk to himself and his companions, for he knew that none of them could deny Yesua, and that if pressed to do so, theirs would be a fate similar to that of the martyr Sergius.

Located in a waterless region of the central Syrian Desert west of the Euphrates River, Rasafa was anything but a barren Roman outpost. It was, in fact, an important juncture, teeming with the activity common along the ancient trade routes. The Romans built four immense underground cisterns in the city to capture the winter and spring rains. These rains were sufficient enough to supply not only the city, but also to provide year-round grazing pastures.

The Euphrates had long served as the eastern border with the Persian Empire. Conflict between Persia and western Mediterranean powers dated back to ancient Greece. The Euphrates valley was the site of numerous battles dating back to Alexander the Great. It was during the most recent battles against Persian Armies along the Euphrates that the fearless Roman officers, Sergius and Bacchus, had distinguished themselves with valor.

Because of the steep rugged terrain at the rivers' banks, travel along the Euphrates was at times exceedingly treacherous. Although the caravans followed the river's general course, quite often, their journey took them inland. Rasafa stood at the inland juncture of two major routes that led to the Mediterranean Sea, where a great coastal trade route extended from Antioch in Northern Syria to Alexandria, in Egypt. It was the same coastal trade route that Joseph, Mary and Yesua had traveled to Egypt so as to escape the jealous rage of Herod the Great.

Passage from the Euphrates to the coastal route at the Rasafa juncture had two paths. The first path was that of Miriam's fated journey south, across the desert to Palmyra, then west and on to Damascus. The second was northwest, to Beroea on the Euphrates, then west though a mountain pass to Antioch, the gateway to Greece and Rome beyond. It was the former path that the merchants should have taken to Egypt, yet it was the later route that they chose instead. The elder had misled Quintus so as to protect the boy. The merchants' true destination was Antioch. If fact, they had never been to Egypt, nor did they ever intend to do so.

The journey from Rasafa to Beroea is 110 miles. The journey took a week. Antioch lay sixty miles to the west. Inside the Roman walls of Beroea is a monumental citadel, rising high above the surrounding landscape. The citadel has been inhabited for six thousand years, serving as a key trading and military site for every civilization that would conquer the region. Legend has it that Abraham settled there briefly after leaving Ur. The city rivaled both Antioch and Damascus as a trading center.

Normally, this band of merchants would stop in Beroea to trade wares. Occasionally, the spices they brought from India could be traded for Chinese silks that fetched handsome prices in Antioch. Eastern merchants did not often venture deep into Roman territory, and Beroea was a perfect location for both the disposition and the acquisition of goods. The elder and his band often ended their journey in Beroea before returning to India. A sense of urgency, however, prevented him from entering the city to trade.

"We must deliver Philip safely to Antioch," the elder told his companions.

The caravan stopped outside the walls. Three of the group made a brief errand to gather supplies for the last leg of the trip to Antioch. Aside from this precious cargo acquired in Rasafa, the elder carried with him a letter from a missionary in India; it was addressed to Lucian the presbyter, a notable Christian teacher in Antioch. Something told him that these two possessions were far more valuable than all of their wares. He intended to deliver them to Lucian as swiftly as possible.

The elder was a close friend of the Indian missionary, a student of Lucian. The elder had met Lucian several times and often carried messages between teacher and student. On several occasions, Lucian had invited the elder, as well as his companions, to his own home for prayer services and communion.

Wending from Beroea toward Antioch, the road through the mountain pass was a wondrous feat of Roman engineering that rivaled Italy's Appian Way. The caravan's journey was swift. On the third day, they passed through the narrow passage on the stone highway as it hugged the southern edge of a deep ravine. Framed by towering mountain spires, there lay a magnificent view of the fertile Orantes plain, just north of Antioch. The caravan halted before reaching the city.

"Make camp here. I will return tomorrow," directed the elder, who left on foot, accompanied by young Philip.

Six centuries before, Alexander the Great had divided his conquest amongst his generals. The spoils of the Orantes valley became part of the territory gifted to his general, Seleucus I Nicator, who built a city there in 300 B.C.E., which was named for his father Antiochus. The Seleucid kings granted Jews free sanctuary in Antioch. It is estimated that by the time the first disciples began their missions there, 45,000 Jews resided in Antioch. "It was at Antioch that they were called 'Christian' for the first time," writes Luke in the Acts of the Apostles.

Lucian lived in a prosperous Jewish section of Antioch called Daphne. Philip and the tribal elder traveled quickly as dusk fell. Lucian greeted the elder's arrival with joy.

"The peace of Christ be with you, kind friend."

"And with your spirit,'" replied the elder.

"I pray you bring with you good news from India."

"Indeed," said the elder, as he handed the letter to Lucian, "and this young man Philip, who is Yesua's most recent miracle."

With his interest piqued, Lucian responded, "Please enter and tell me everything." As they celebrated the evening meal, the elder told Lucian of the miraculous events in Rasafa and the caravan's journey to Antioch. Lucian then quizzed Philip about his life in Rasafa with Miriam and Quintus. Miriam's Christian education of Philip was of particular interest. Finally, Lucian addressed them both.

"God's plan for Philip is to be a student of the Truth. You have heard the Word from your mother. Sergius' blood gave you sight, so that thus, you might see the Word."

Addressing the elder, Lucian said, "The child is not safe here. His father is well known in this region. I have seen the treachery of his deeds. I, too, fear his wrath. I am fortunate to have many Christian brothers who are soldiers in the Emperor's legions. They have risked their lives on several occasions to protect me from the wrath of this cursed persecution. I am planning to travel to Alexandria to visit Arius, one of my students. He can protect the child."

The elder countered, "Brother Lucian, Quintus believes that I am taking the child to Alexandria. From what we have heard, the persecutions are still worse in Egypt".

"Quintus believes that the child will be delivered to his Roman counterpart. His wish is to abandon the child so that he may continue his treachery in Syria without guilt. He will not pursue the child to Egypt. Our Faith is strong in Egypt. Alexandria is much larger than

Antioch. Egypt has many Christian communities; it is there that Philip will be safe. Arius will know what to do. Have faith, my son."

Lucian rose and walk purposefully to the corner of the room. He lifted a loose plank from the floor boards and retrieved a wooden box. Returning, he placed the box in front of them. He opened the box, revealing inside several leather bound manuscripts. He looked for a moment, searching for the treasure. With both hands outstretched, he handed the small manuscript to the boy.

"Your mother would want you to have this!"

"What is it?" Philip asked, surprised.

"The Gospel of Philip."

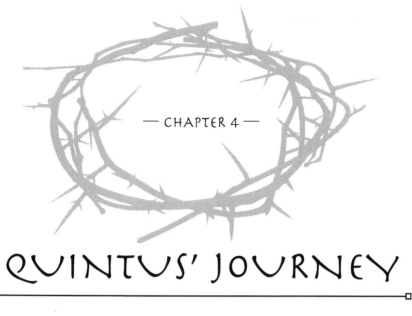

QUINTUS' JOURNEY

I

Quintus rose before sunrise the morning after he banished Miriam and Philip. Uncharacteristically, sleep had eluded him the night before. He troubled over nothing. His hardened ego had long ago evicted emotion from his psyched. Yet, he could not reconcile the odd happenings of the day before. Beheading a Roman officer did not disturb him. It was Sergius' fate alone that determined that he should die by the sword. It was Quintus' fate to be his executioner, yet he could not stop wondering, why would Sergius embrace this spurious belief that a lowly Jew was, in fact, a god, much less The God? Christians were weak. They consistently refused to fight. Quintus had fought beside both Sergius and Bacchus in the Persian campaigns. Both officers were fierce warriors. Yet, when confronted with treason, they refused to defend themselves. Even worse, they accepted death by torture and execution rather than to denounce their hopeless loyalty.

And what had happened to that boy yesterday? Did Sergius' blood cure his blindness? Surely not. The slave girl must be a sorceress. She cast darkness over the boy to punish Quintus for having raped her. She must have released the spell to punish him for beheading Sergius. What else could it be? He was feeling the same tangled uncertainty which he had felt the day that he raped her. How could she have this power over him? He was determined to stop thinking about all of it.

Quintus dressed and headed to the stable. The liverymen were not yet awake. He saddled his horse and walked him outside. Before mounting the steed, he patted its jaw saying, "Be one with me. Ride swiftly. Take us away." Eye to eye, they saw each other as equals.

Quintus was the best horseman in Galerius' Legions. He always preferred to ride the largest, fastest most powerful mount. When he was first given this horse, it had not yet been broken. Perhaps that is why its previous owner was willing to part with such an unruly but magnificent beast. Immediately, horse and rider coalesced, fused as one, a mythological centaur. Every movement of any sort was precise and graceful. In battle, the horse's legs were his. Together, they flew faster than any archer's arrow. Quintus believed his steed's conduct to be every much as courageous as his own, as if the beast shared the selfsame instinctive behavior which impassioned him.

With hooves barely touching the ground, they galloped away as free as the winds that tossed the stallion's great mane. They rode the sky at first light, raising each other's spirits, then galloped for less than a mile to the crest of a hill to behold the glorious sunrise. Quintus' angst dissipated at the mere touch, it seemed, of the sun's warmth.

When he returned to the villa, Quintus was greeted by another contingent of legionnaires, all commanded by a young stoic centurion. Wasting little time, the centurion delivered his message.

"Prepare for a journey. Plan not to return. This order comes directly from Caesar Galerius who requests your presence. I am to replace you here. With me is a satchel of denarii that is ample payment for your slaves and possessions".

"And what of my villa"? Quintus asked.

"You have no need of it now. That, too, shall be mine. Galerius himself will compensate you." Quintus thought. 'This one is steely cold. A fine replacement; it is time to leave this place. Jupiter has rewarded me."

"Where am I to meet Galerius?" Quintus demanded.

"Antioch!" The centurion handed the satchel to Quintus. The conversation was over.

Quintus ushered the centurion into the villa where he ordered the house servant to gather all of the slaves and livery men. Once assembled, he addressed them collectively, saying, "This is your new master. Prepare my horse and a donkey with supplies, for I journey now to Antioch."

With that, he retreated to his quarters to gather his possessions. By noon, he had departed, and by sundown, although he was quite unaware of the matter, he had reached a point just twelve miles behind Philip's Caravan. Deciding his horse had been exercised enough for one day, he stopped to make camp near a small ridge, near to the desert road. After unloading his supplies, Quintus groomed and fed the animals before bedding down for the night. The camp site provided a full view of the road and adequate protection from unfriendly travelers.

Unbeknownst to Quintus, however, that intentionally strategic decision failed to factor into his calculations the hostile desert horned viper. Its bite, comprised of more than thirteen different toxins, could be quite lethal. Its bulbous head resembles that of a toad. Closer examination reveals an uncanny resemblance betwixt the reptile and the fallen Lucifer. The serpent's resemblance rests in its sinister visage, replete with two crooked horns that protrude from its head just above its sinister, grotesque eyes. Some legends claim that Cleopatra herself chose to lose her life to just such a menace of the sands. Autumn evenings in the Syrian Desert can bring chilling temperatures. That night, drawn by the heat of sleeping bodies nearby, three of Satan's serpentine minions slithered forth and settled together beneath the right hind quarter of Quintus' own prize horse.

As day broke, Quintus awoke to a horrible commotion. Narseh, whinnying with fright, was trampling the three vipers to death. The bucking horse turned and galloped up the hill and across the ridge into the desert. Likewise, the frightened donkey galloped away, though in the opposite direction. Quintus grabbed his sword and scoured the camp, shearing off the heads of two vipers sheltered under his own bedding. He raced to the crest of the hill and surveyed both sides, looking for the animals. The horse had stopped running and was hopelessly hobbling in circles. The donkey was still galloping south. He turned back to the horse and saw the animal collapse, clearly a victim of multiple snake bites. Soldiers and their horses develop strong bonds. Under similar circumstances, most horsemen would end the horse's misery. But the bond betwixt Quintus and his steed was but a mere extension of Quintus' own being. The snake's venom severed that tie. Besides which, Quintus was an instrument of fate not of mercy. This was the animal's fate. There was nothing he could do for it now. He left the horse alone to die a slow death in the desert sun. Returning to his camp, he gathered a water pouch and a handful of oats for the donkey.

Quintus found the animal half a mile away, standing quietly in the new light. Steam rose from its body in the cool morning air. He approached the animal cautiously with an out-stretched handful of oats. Once calmed, he mounted the beast and returned to camp in order to gather supplies and continue the journey. A Roman supernumerarius mounted on a fully loaded donkey is not a regal site. Nevertheless, Quintus took a direct route east, reaching the banks of the Euphrates River late in the day. He was now a full day behind Philip's caravan.

The river below was a refreshing oasis. Quintus intended to take advantage of it. Although steep, the river bank was passable on foot and the donkey was ideally suited to make the journey down the slope. Quintus made camp at the river's edge. Disrobing, he waded into the water. The water tendered a welcome and refreshing climax to a dreadfully difficult day. As time passed, Quintus' mind began to drift. "Fighting heathen hordes would be a welcome change from torturing the pigheaded Christians," he mused. 'I will ask Galerius for an assignment in Gaul."

He waded deeper into the river and turned to watch the sunset. On the embankment above, silhouetted against the sun, he made out the figures of two horses. "A mirage!? A gift from Jupiter? No, there must be horsemen as well! But where?" Halfway down the embankment with lances in hand were two Persian scouts. A race for life ensued. Quintus waded furiously back to muster his sword. Naked and wet, he reached the camp as the marauders finished their decent. Hastily, he grabbed his sword and slipped onto his back as the skirmish began.

The Persians took aim at different targets; one at his throat, the other at his legs. Instinctively, Quintus rolled to his right and used his sword as a shield, deflecting the upper thrust which grazed his neck below his ear. The other thrust sliced into his calf. Rolling back, with his sword in continuous movement, he hacked at the right leg of one horseman who fell into the oncoming thrust of his companion's lance. Quintus was on his feet. The remaining combatant drew his sword, but did so far too slowly to defeat a Roman supernumerarius. As quickly as it had begun, the skirmish was finished.

Quintus' survival instincts leapt to the fore. He slit the throats of both men. Best to be certain they were both quite dead. He could not remain in this place. There would be more, many more, which would follow in the wake of these scouts. His victorious skirmish had left him extraordinarily vulnerable. Although not fatal, his wounds could prove significant. The six inch gash in his right leg laid open his calf. He wrapped the wound in a clean cloth torn from his least favorite garment. The neck wound below his ear, though superficial, was problematic in that it was difficult to cover. The combination of desert dust and oily sweat from his hair would make the wound difficult to keep clean. He tore a longer length of cloth and wrapped it about his neck.

He dressed quickly, and then gathered his saddle bag and only enough food to continue his journey to Beroea. He could re-supply and mend his wounds at the Roman Garrison there. Leaving the donkey behind, he ascended the slope to the horses. He unsaddled one of the horses and mounted the other, a staid roan. The unburdened horse, a chestnut, would serve as a reserve. Once again, he would spend his night in the shadows of the cold desert night.

II

5 00 years of Roman military conquest created one of the most efficient and sophisticated armies in history. As great assimilators, the Romans adopted, among other things, medical practices from conquered civilizations. From this assimilation, specialization and techniques developed that were closely mirrored by 18th century Western military medical practices. The Emperor Augustus had established the first Army Medical Corp over three hundred years before. Its officers were granted special treatment, including respectable titles and gifts. Eventually, medical professionals were required to train at an army medical school and could not practice unless they passed.

Although the connection between bacteria and infection was not truly understood, the Romans had a deep understanding of the circulatory system and the migration of blood through the body. Army surgeons routinely cleaned surgical instruments in boiling water between procedures. Medical practices also included a sophisticated holistic approach, incorporating plants and herbal cures for ailments. Quintus knew that the Roman garrison doctor at Beroea could treat his wounds. He also knew that the best treatment he might receive would be at the garrison in Antioch, but that journey was both longer and far too risky.

Quintus' cleansing ritual with Miriam was born from his instinctive obsession with corporeal purity. His battlefield experience had taught him the dangers of infections from untreated wounds. Quintus knew that the weak could succumb quickly to infections. Stronger men endure longer. The lurking uncertainty of Persian troops prevented him from doing anything other than covering his wounds. He knew he must reach Beroea before infection set in. Although Beroea was 140 miles away, Quintus was confident that he was strong enough to ward off septicity until he reached help.

He traveled north, following the stars long after midnight before stopping to rest. He slept for only four hours and departed prior to sunrise. The next day was longer than the day before, less eventful, but not without tension. He veered back toward the river late in the day so as to afford the horses with a brief respite. This time, he fully maintained his guard.

The laden horse would be spent in a few days, but as a victorious spoil, it could be sacrificed. On the second night, he passed an encampment silhouetted by an evening fire. He counted eight travelers as well as numerous camels. It was likely a merchant caravan, yet in this region, no travelers could be presumed to be friendly. He slipped by them quietly, altogether unnoticed. Had he stopped for help, he would no doubt be startled to discover his own son Philip amongst those eight fireside figures.

Quintus arrived in Beroea a day ahead of Philip's caravan. The first horse had perished. The second was near exhaustion when he finally arrived. Quintus' reputation as Galerius' favorite was well known within the Roman garrison. The garrison commander offered his quarters and also ordered that the best doctors attend to him.

Although they probably did not understand the mechanisms of disease and infections, the Roman fixation with personal hygiene and general obsession with cleanliness served them well. After a warm bath, the garrison's doctor washed Quintus' wounds with clean warm water that had been earlier brought to a boil. Because the Roman soldier was a highly trained and expensive commodity, military doctors developed a myriad of techniques to treat wounds in order to ensure Roman soldiers a much lower chance of dying from infection than did the combatants of other armies. These treatments included the use of honey, willow bark and even maggots.

Before applying clean dressings, the doctor applied a generous mixture of ground willow bark to Quintus' wounds. The chemicals contained in the leaves and bark of the desert willow affect oxygen uptake. Staph and other anaerobic bacteria cannot survive in the absence of oxygen. Consequently, any preparation that contains the chemicals in willow bark will fight just such microbes. An ancient Egyptian papyrus from circa 1500 B.C. states, when a "wound is inflamed…[there is] a concentration of heat; the lips of that wound are reddened and that man is hot in consequence…then you must make cooling substances for him to draw the heat out…[use] leaves of the willow."

The doctor also understood the benefits of diet in combating infection. Both the Egyptians and the Greeks understood the benefit of feeding laborers a diet rich in radishes, garlic and onions, all of which are extremely rich in chemicals that aid in building a stronger immune system. Quintus was fed a goulash mixture that featured a healthy dose of garlic and onions. Cleansed and fed, he fell into a deep sleep, waking only intermittently when urged to accept repeated feedings of the garlic and onion rich pottage. He slept soundly for two days. By the time he came around fully, Philip's caravan was one day ahead of him on their journey to Antioch.

"I must leave immediately for Antioch to meet with Caesar Galerius," Quintus told the doctor upon first waking. "My treatment of your wounds must continue another full week before you may travel," the doctor objected.

"Fate is with me," snapped Quintus. "Bring me clean clothing, as well as my armor!"

"You cannot leave," the physician insisted.

"I can and I must; now do as I command!" Although unsteady, he nonetheless rose to dress.

"I am ordered by the garrison commander to treat your wounds," the physician went on.

"Then bring the garrison commander to me," Quintus barked.

The ensuing conversation with the garrison commander was brief Attempts to sway Quintus were futile. By noon, he embarked on the last part of his journey, outfitted with a new horse and enough supplies to reach Antioch. Though weakened by his injuries, he traveled onward with the same sense of urgency with which he'd first set out.

III

Antioch was a city resplendent with Roman temples, markets and a full complement of entertainment venues including theatres, a circus and an amphitheater. The city lay on the eastern banks of the river Orantes. Its port was ideally situated at a cross-road linking the trade routes of the eastern and western Roman Empire. Adjoining Antioch's docks lay a large open market, teeming with trade.

Early one morning, Lucian met Philip, the elder, and his companions at the dock. Lucian left the group to secure passage for himself and Philip on a merchant ship traveling to Alexandria. The ship would embark in several hours. Lucian rejoined the group in the market, where the elder was bartering for silk cloth. The boy was mesmerized by the sights and sounds of the bazaar. He found the barter process, in particular, quite entertaining. Philip ran to greet Lucian as he approached.

"Brother Lucian! Look at the market! Isn't it exciting?" Philip exclaimed.

"Indeed. Indeed it is," Lucian agreed readily.

"I wish that I could trade for something, but the only possession I have is what you gave me last night."

"That is far too precious to trade," Lucian cautioned, "you must always keep that hidden and close to your heart. If the Romans were to find you with it, there would be serious consequences."

"What did you call it again? Why does it have my name? Why would my mother want me to have it?" Philip intoned. When the elder's trading was complete, the group rejoined Lucian and Philip. They walked northwest through the bustling crowd, back to the ship's berth at the dock.

As they walked through the crowded market, Lucian continued his discussion with Philip. "The book is written in the Greek language and contains many of Yesua's wise teachings. The book does not bear your name. It is you who bears the name of Philip, the messenger. The book, you see, also bears his name. Your mother named you in Philip's honor. I will teach you to read and write the Greek language so that you may come to know for yourself the witness of the Yesua's disciples."

"Tell me a wise teaching from the book, please?" Philip asked

Lucian began to speak. "Lo, the Gospel of Philips says,

'If I say, "I am a Jew," no one will be moved.

If I say, "I am a Roman," no one will be upset.

If I say, "I am a Greek, a barbarian, a slave, a freeman," no one will be troubled.

But if I say, "I am a Christian," they will tremble.

I wish I had that title. The world will not endure it when hearing the name.""

Lucian's quote brought a prideful smile to everyone, especially Philip. As the group made their way out of the crowd, however, their joyful expressions turned to shock. Before them, on horseback, was a soldier whose right leg and neck were wrapped in blood-soaked dressings… It was Quintus!

"Brother Lucian, take the boy!" shouted the elder, as he pointed back to the crowded market. Turning to his companions and pointing in the other direction, the elder then cried, "To the docks, now! Quickly!"

Quintus pursued the elder, shouting to legionnaires on the dock. "Seize those men!" Philip's band of liberators was quickly surrounded. Still on horseback, Quintus ordered a legionnaire to search the elder. The search revealed the satchel of denarii.

"I paid these men to deliver a slave boy, a boy I fathered, to the garrison commander in Alexandria. He was a favorite of mine. I fear that treachery has found the boy at the hands of these ingrates. Look in the satchel. You will find fifty denarii and a message bearing my seal."

It was unfortunate for all of them that the elder had not destroyed the message. The evidence was clear.

"What is your wish, sir?" the legionnaire requested.

"Imprison them. I will deal with them later," Quintus replied.

Hurriedly, he turned his horse and galloped to a road that traversed a hill north of the market, halting when he reached its crest. Facing the market, he raised his sword high up above his head. A cross-like image glistened from its surface, reflecting the rays of the southern sun.

Lucian and Philip made their way to the opposite corner of the marketplace. A Christian safe house sat three hundred feet away in a crowded neighborhood just east of the market. Lucian looked to the north before leaving the safety of the crowd. There, on the horizon, was the ominous horseback figure mounted below a glistening cross. The demon was watching, waiting for them to exit the market. To avoid discovery, they must walk cautiously across an open road that led to the neighborhood wherein lay the safe house.

Lucian and Philip slowed their pace as they walked down the open street. They were visible there for less than a minute. As they reached a side street, Lucian turned, looking north. The horseman was gone.

"Philip, we must run, quickly," Lucian said, grabbing the boy's arm.

They ran up the narrow side street as Quintus galloped down the hill from the north. He reached the street as Lucian and Philip turned down a side street. Quintus galloped to the intersection and spotted the duo stumbling into a courtyard. He raced after them and entered the courtyard, drawing his sword as he dismounted. He stumbled to his knees.

The garrison doctor in Beroea was correct. Quintus' wounds had not entirely healed. Infection, in fact, had now set in. That morning he was groggy and disoriented as he entered the city gates of Antioch. The path to Caesar Galerius' palace was well known to Quintus, but not on this day. Disoriented, he suddenly found himself at the edge of the dock's market, face to face with his son and the men who were to escort Philip to Egypt.

"Am I dreaming? Is this an illusion? No. It is them." Adrenaline surged as his instincts took hold. A chase ensued, but the rush was fading. He rose to his feet, stumbled to the door and slammed the butt of his sword against it. Again and again he pounded. Exhausted, he leaned against the door. Finally, the door opened and Quintus fell into the arms of a Roman officer.

"I am Quintus Flavius Scipio, Supernumerarius in the Legions of Caesar Galerius Maximianus," he muttered, "Bring me the boy."

"What boy?" the officer responded.

"My son, Philip. He entered this place with an old man," Quintus strove to explain as he tried to rise.

"With all due respect honorable Quintus, my name is Marcus. I too am an officer in the Legions of Caesar Galerius Maximianus. This is my home and I can assure you that no one, neither child nor old man has entered this place," the officer replied. "Tell me, what is your business here?"

"I have an audience with Caesar Galerius." Too weak to carry on, Quintus reclined on the stone floor.

"And so you shall." The officer replied.

Marcus summoned his servants and ordered them to make Quintus comfortable, saying "Find a cart to carry this man comfortably. Take him and his belongings to Caesar Galerius, announcing the arrival of Quintus Flavius Scipio. Stable his horse here until he is well enough to ride again."

Marcus watched Quintus and his escorts depart the courtyard. He turned back to his home. He entered an alcove off of the interior atrium where, unbeknownst to others, he had quietly hidden Lucian and Philip. "Brother Lucian, you must take the boy and leave Antioch immediately. You are not safe with that demon here."

"We have arranged passage on a ship to Alexandria. It will be departing shortly," Lucian replied.

"Then you must go now. May Yesua be with you!"

"And also with you, my son." Cautiously, Lucian added, "The child was brought to me by followers of Thomas. Quintus had them arrested on the docks. I am concerned that the same fate may await us."

"Then I will shadow you through the market to the dock. If there is any sign of trouble, I will arrest you myself. We will try another escape plan, but waiting is too dangerous. Quintus will regain strength and continue his pursuit. The legions will be on watch for you. If you are found, there will be no hope. It will be fatal, I am sure. If I am found out to be a follower of Yesua, the wrath of Caesar Galerius will lead to the sacrifice of many more Christians. Now is our best chance."

The morning's excitement changed Philip's perspective about the crowded bazaar. His senses were no longer attuned to the sounds, scents and sights of the marketplace. Marcus tailed the pair. Cautiously, they crossed the dock to the ship's berth. The walk proved uneventful. Marcus disappeared back into the crowd. They boarded the ship at mid-morning and were well away before noon. Soon afterwards, they'd left the brackish waters of the Orantes River and entered the clear blue waters of the eastern Mediterranean Sea.

Lucian and Philip huddled together on the ships aft deck. Resting now safely in Lucian's arms, Philip produced his prized manuscript and opened the book.

"Teach me some more, Brother Lucian," Philip asked, eagerly. He handed the open manuscript to Lucian. Lucian silently read the passage on the opened page and smiled. Softly, he read aloud.

"The Gospel of Philip says,

SOME ARE AFRAID

'Some are afraid that they will ascend from death naked,

And they will climb back to life in their flesh.

They are unaware that those who wear their flesh are naked,

And those who strip are not naked.

"Flesh and blood cannot inherit the kingdom of God."

What will we inherit? The flesh we wear on us.

But what then will we inherit as our own?

The body of Yesua and His blood. And Yesua said,

"Whoever will not eat my flesh and drink my blood

has no life within him." What does He mean?

His flesh is the word and His blood the holy spirit.'"

Lucian paused, for the passage was long. Seizing the moment, the ever inquisitive Philip then asked, "What does it mean, teacher"?

"It means to be one with Yesua, you must live by the Word and find the Spirit within you. I will teach you the Word. You must find the Spirit yourself."

"Enough for today!" he added. "Let us rest and be thankful for the peace we have found today."

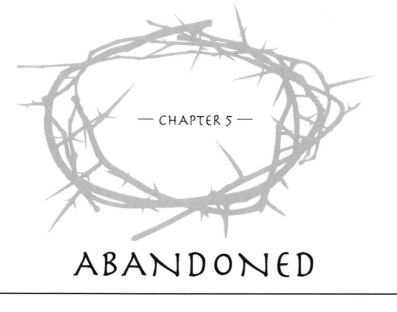

ABANDONED

I

She was designed for the night. Her legs were spindled with sinewy muscles. Her yellowish grey eyes balanced her grey face perfectly. Her nose was long and graceful. Her muscular jaws outlined a crisp wedge-shaped head capped by generous triangular ears. Her coat was thicker on the flanks of her hind legs, back and chest. Her mesmerizing stare reached deep into the soul. For her prey, the penetrating gaze was a precursor to death. For Miriam, it was a perpetuation of life. The only word that Miriam could utter to portray her perfection was Lupa, the feminized Latin name for her species.

"My sweet Lupa, lead us to Egypt," Miriam said as she escaped from under the city wall.

Miriam followed Lupa across a ridge to the safety of a wooded area. On the side of a hill, Lupa found a shallow cave. Miriam followed Lupa into the darkness. Exhausted, Miriam lay down to rest, yielding quickly to deep sleep. She awoke near midnight. Her eyes had adjusted to the darkness. The cave was half her height, twice as deep and four times its length. Lupa was gone, Miriam abandoned.

The view from the cave revealed a moon-lit night. Miriam crawled from the cave. She sat motionless at the cave's entrance. "I am lost and alone. What is to become of me?" she wondered, "and what of Philip? What is his fate to be? I love him more than life itself. Why has this happened?" Her mind raced, traversing her countless trials and she began to weep.

Since the moment she had been sold into slavery, Miriam had turned her whole self to Yesua. She gave Him her very life, body and soul. In return, He gave her the courage that enabled her to endure the atrocities of Diocletian's persecution and her life with Quintus. With clear self-understanding, she lived her life in the presence of God with perfect freedom and perfect love. Now she felt abandoned. For the first time, doubt entered her soul.

Miriam spoke aloud, "Yesua says 'you cannot be my disciple, unless you love me more than you love your father and mother, your wife and children, and your brothers and sisters. You cannot come with me unless you love me more than you love your own life. You cannot be my disciple unless you carry your own cross and come with me.' Is this my cross, to be abandoned? Have I not been faithful? My faith in You is without end, undying." Louder, she cried, "It was You who was crucified in that place, wasn't it? It was You whose face I cleaned, wasn't it? It was You who was abandoned by all but me, wasn't it? It was me who shared Your spirit as they killed You. It was me who held Your battered body close to me. I did not abandon You!"

Finally, she screamed, "Yesua, why have You abandoned me???"

Miriam wept copiously, falling into an exhausted stupor just hours before dawn. She woke to find Lupa asleep at her feet with a dead snake beside her. Lupa had brought Miriam breakfast. Wolves of this region are more akin to their close cousins, the coyote. They are relatively small, between 25 and 30 pounds and forage constantly for food. They eat snakes, small mammals and unlike their larger counterparts, will also eat fruit. Their large ears provide a keen sense of hearing and serve as a method for dissipating the heat generated in hot, arid environments. Because of their size, they forage in areas near water. Despite Miriam's doubt in Yesua, He sent her the perfect traveling companion.

Miriam rose. Lupa rose and followed, dangling the catch from her mouth. Miriam began searching for tools. She searched the cave entrance for a stone she could use as a mallet. With the stone, she hammered away at the soft limestone overhang until shards of rock began to crumble from the entrance ledge.

The debris generated several sharp edged options. She chose one, working its edges to a point until it was sharp enough to skin the snake. Then she gathered dead leaves, twigs and thorns for kindling. She found a dead branch the length of her arm and carved a channel, lengthwise in the branch with the newly fashioned shard of rock.

Placing the branch between her legs with the channel facing her, Miriam quickly rubbed a stick back and forth along the channel. The friction from the repetitive motion eventually created a black smoldering hole that grew to a hot, glowing coal that ignited the crumbled leaves that she had placed near the stick. Her hands were bloodied and blistered. The work was tedious, but successful, and soon Miriam was roasting the freshly skinned snake meat on a teeming campfire.

Thus, the odd partnership of survival between Miriam and Lupa was bound, with the hunter providing sustenance for the re-born woman. As they traveled together, Lupa would occasionally disappear, but always returned. Sometimes she would return bearing fruit, sometimes small rodents. Once she brought with her a chicken, obviously pillaged from some family's stock. On other occasions, she would return with nothing and would wait for Miriam to follow a path that led to fresh water. Along on their journey, Miriam carried the shard, the fire board and the snake skin. Once dried, she wore the skin around her neck as a remembrance of God's many gifts. Miriam's moment of doubt was replaced with an even stronger commitment to her faith in Yesua.

II

There were two trading routes to Egypt, a coastal route, the "Way of the Sea" and a desert route, "The King's Highway." The latter hugs the eastern edge of the Great Rift Valley, site of the Dead Sea. The highway crosses countless river beds and the availability of water made this a key trade route for over 5,000 years. From Damascus to the north, the highway travels south through the Biblical kingdoms of Edom, Moab, Amman and to the Gulf of Aqaba, where it forks across the Sinai to Egypt. Lining both sides of this 210 mile route were prehistoric villages from the Stone Age. A diverse ecology embraces the route, including forested highlands, open grazing plateaus, deep ravines, desert edges, and the warm tropical Gulf of Aqaba. Both Abraham and Moses traveled its path. Abraham's nephew, Lot, became the ruler of Moab.

At the half-way point between Amman and Petra, the highway traverses what some refer to as Jordan's "Grand Canyon." Until the end of the 1st Century AD, Petra, which means "stone or rock" in Greek, was the capital of the independent Nabatean Empire who used this highway as a trade route for frankincense and spices from southern Arabia. Petra's tallest mountain, Mount Hor, is believed to be the burial place of Aaron, Moses' brother. At its peak, Petra's population is estimated between twenty and thirty thousand people. In 106 AD, The Roman Emperor Trajan annexed Petra to the Roman Empire, and renamed the King's Highway Via Nova Traiana (Trajan's New Way), making it an imperial highway.

This was the route that Miriam and Lupa traveled to Egypt. They traveled southeast from Jerusalem through the desert wilderness, passing the ancient city of Jericho and crossed the river Jordan. There, they turned south into the ancient kingdom of Moab. The Moabites were a Semitic people closely related to the Hebrews. Ruth, the great grandmother of King David, was of the Moabites. In 303 AD, the capital city of Moab was known as Areopolis, City of the god Mars. According to an inscription on its walls, the Roman temple of Mars was dedicated to the emperors Diocletian and Maximian, who ruled jointly from AD 286-305. Moab was situated on an elevated green plateau ideally suited for its nomadic people.

Early one evening, Miriam and Lupa came upon a family of shepherds. In an open field below them sat the family, all gathered around their tent. No one was tending the sheep that were grazing in the field. Instinctively, Lupa halted and prepared to strike. The gaunt childlike woman traveling with a lone wolf startled the family. Miriam order Lupa to sit. The wolf stood down from her pose and sat peacefully at Miriam's side. Miriam rested her hand on Lupa's head. Several of the men took up their staffs and slowly approach the duo.

"Who are you woman?" inquired the father, obviously startled by the gaunt woman whose face bore a crescent-shaped scar, wore blood-stained garments and a snake skin necklace.

"I am Miriam of Egypt," she answered, softly.

"What are your intentions?" he asked her, still eyeing Lupa closely.

"I am traveling to Alexandria to find my son who was taken from me. We wish you no harm".

"Your traveling companion is no friend of ours," he noted.

"She was sent to me by Yesua as my guide and protector." Looking at the women huddled near the tent, Miriam said "What troubles your family"?

"Our youngest daughter is with a fever that has not passed. Her death is approaching. The women have begun to mourn."

Miriam spoke "Yesua said to his disciples, 'I am the resurrection and the life; those who believe in me even if they die will live.' Do you believe? Has the child been baptized in Christ?"

"We believe in the creator. If he wills her death, then so be it," he replied. "We have heard the story of Yesua, the prophet, who rose from the dead. But we have not seen him."

"Look into my spirit and know that He lives. If not, then believe that it is Yesua who has tamed this wolf, not me!"

The men gazed at Lupa, who amazingly had lost all interest in the flock. "Even if this is so, how can Yesua help her now?" queried the father.

"Let me baptize her in His name. Come pray with me!" Before they could respond, Miriam passed through them and walked toward the dying child. "Bring me fresh cold water," she ordered.

Miriam knelt at the girl's head. Gently, she removed the child's garments and lifted her body, placing the child's head in her lap. Then Miriam tore her robe, stained with the crucified man's blood. Dipping the rag in the pale of water, she tenderly bathed the child. As Miriam stroked the young girl, she prayed with calm and graceful gentleness.

"Yesua, You are the Light of Lights. Bring forth Your Spirit and save this child."

"Yesua, You are one with the Creator. Bring forth Your Spirit and save this child."

"Yesua, You died for us so that we might be saved. Bring forth Your Spirit and save this child."

With each incantation, she bathed the child. Then Miriam began to tell the stories of Yesua's miracles as they were told to her. She told them of the cripple whose Faith in Yesua had cured him. She told them of the blind man whose Faith in Yesua had given him sight. Then she told them of the story of Lazarus whose Faith in Yesua had raised him from death. All the while, she continued cleansing the child. Finally, she addressed the family.

"Yesua said to his disciples, 'I am the resurrection and the life, those who believe in me even if they die will live.' Do you believe now? Do you have Faith in Yesua?"

"We do," they replied.

"Then pray that your Faith in Yesua will give this child eternal life." Miriam's soothing voice calmed the family. Silence filled the night, interrupted only by the trickle of water as Miriam bathed the child. Peacefully, the girl's breath slowed to a halt. Miriam unfurled the rag and placed it over the child's face. All was still.

Finally, Miriam stood and turned to leave the family alone with their grief. As she walked away, the child's mother cried aloud. But the cry was not one of grief or fear. The child had gripped her mother's hand. The mother screamed, "My child is saved! She lives, she lives! Yesua has saved my child."

"No," Miriam replied. "Your Faith in Yesua has saved your child!"

Miriam returned to the ridge where she left Lupa, who greeted her with a surprising dinner catch, a small fallow deer. Lupa had ripped open the deer's under belly and was focused on its organs. Miriam started a campfire. While Lupa feasted, Miriam cut the back straps, skinned them and cooked them on the fire. From a distance, the shepherd family observed the duo silhouetted by the full moon. Was she an apparition, an angel, or a messenger from Yesua? The rebirth of the shepherd child through the handiwork of Yesua's messenger was strangely ironic. The two camps quickly succumbed to the exhaustion from the evening's events.

Miriam and Lupa were greeted at sunrise by the father and a teenage son.

"Greetings Miriam of Egypt, we come to thank you for your kind deed and to offer our assistance," the father said.

"Your place is with your family," replied Miriam.

"As is yours," the father replied. "The journey to Egypt is treacherous. We will accompany you to Petra. My other sons will tend to our family until we return. Yesua appeared to me in my dream and asked me to do this for you."

"So be it," Miriam replied with a smile. It was a strange sensation, for it had been months since she had smiled. "Before we depart, let us prepare the meat from this gift of God," she said. "We can share some with your family and take the rest for our journey. I would like to give Lupa respite from finding sustenance for me. She has been very busy on our journey."

"I have one other request," she continued. "I am in need of a walking stick. Can you use your knife to fashion one for me in the shape of a cross?"

"It would be an honor," the father replied.

Two days later, Miriam, Lupa and their two new companions continued the journey south on the Kings Highway. The three travelers departed with ample supplies carried by the family donkey. Lupa kept her distance acting as a scout. Miriam, with her tattered stained robe, snake skin necklace and new walking stick, bore resemblance to a disciple of John the Baptist.

III

The Romans established military defensive positions every 60 miles with the purpose to create a line of protection and control along the Empire's frontiers. There was the legionary fortress of Udruh, located just east of Petra, which housed the Legio IV Ferrata. A Roman Legion consisted of ten cohorts totaling 4000 to 6600 soldiers. The first cohort was the most prestigious, the tenth the least. At various times, a cohort consisted of six centuries of 60, 80 or 100 men, each commanded by a centurion assisted by junior officers. The most senior of the six centurions commanded an entire cohort.

As the crow flies, the trio's journey to Petra was 90 miles. The highway, though passable, was treacherous. Distance traveled varied from 6 to 15 miles per day. The trip would take 10 days and the trio would be susceptible to encounters with merchant caravans, bandits and Roman centuries that patrolled the highway. Lupa would wander ahead, always appearing to warn the group of oncoming visitors. Twice they encountered merchant caravans and once they avoided bandits due to Lupa's keen senses.

Miriam spent the evenings teaching her companions the sayings of Yesua that she had memorized and telling the fateful stories of the gruesome deaths of martyrs she had known.

As they neared Petra, they encountered the 10th cohort of Legio IV Ferrata. They were in a valley passage that offered no cover. Lupa watched cautiously from the ridge above. The young centurion halted his troops. He and two junior officers dismounted and approached Miriam and her companions.

The centurion addressed the father, asking, "And what have we here?"

Thinking quickly, he responded, "This is my wife and son. We are traveling to Petra to visit my wife's mother, who is approaching death."

"What is her affliction?" the centurion asked.

"Leprosy," the quick-thinking father replied.

The response dazed the junior officers. The centurion carefully studied Miriam and her walking stick. His next inquiry dispirited the father.

"Are you followers of Yesua?"

"Why do you ask?" Miriam replied.

"Your walking stick bears a striking resemblance to a cross," he said.

Now speechless, the father and son tensed as they awaited Miriam's response.

"Do you intend to crucify me as well?" she asked, her eyes now fixed with the centurion's.

He stared at her in a gaze of deathly silence. He drew his sword, placed it at her throat, pulled her near to him and whispered in her ear, "Peace be with you sister. I too am a follower of Yesua. These are dangerous times for us. Be patient with me."

Stepping back, he addressed the father, loud enough for all to hear. "We are in pursuit of highway bandits. We have no time to be troubled with the likes of you, or else we would grant your wife's wish. Continue your journey."

Rebuking Miriam, he said, "You will find your mother with the unclean who live in the caves south of Petra. I suggest that you hasten your travel through the city to avoid the fate you described. Christians are just as unwelcome there as are the unclean."

The trio waited in silence as the legionnaires vanished. Then the son began to cry. Consoling the boy, the father addressed Miriam. "Are you an angel or sorcerer? Why did you taunt him with crucifixion? If not for their pursuit of the bandits, we could all be nailed to a cross on this highway." It was a scene that the father had seen before; one he did not wish for himself or his son.

Miriam replied, "I cannot deny my Faith in Yesua. He died for me. I am willing to die for Him."

Convinced of her Faith, but nonetheless confounded, he asked, "What did the centurion say to you?"

"He confessed his Faith in Yesua, cautioned us to travel with haste and begged my patience," she replied.

He stood motionless with his son in his grasp, "Your Faith has saved us, Miriam of Egypt."

"How much further to Petra?" she inquired.

"Half a day's journey," the father told her.

"Our journey together ends tomorrow, then," she said. "Come let us find a place to rest for the evening." They spent the evening in silence each contemplating the events of their time together.

That night, Miriam fell into a deep sleep marked by a vivid dream in which she wandered through the deserted streets of Petra alone. The city bore no signs of life. At the edge of city, she saw a figure who was beckoning her toward him. As she approached, she recognized the battered and bloodied man who was crucified before her in Jerusalem. Before she could reach him, he turned and disappeared along a dark winding path cut through a deep, narrow ravine. Occasionally, she would catch a glance of him struggling before her. He left in his wake a blood-soaked trail. He appeared to be dragging a cross, the weight of which fell upon his hunched shoulders. Each time she approached him, he would disappear around a bend in the path.

Eventually, she reached a narrow opening with walls that extended hundreds of feet to a sun-lit oculus above. All signs of the man and the path that she had traveled vanished. She was trapped in a circular limestone tomb that had seven burrowed holes at the base of its wall. Suddenly, she heard a wolf howling. There, on the edge of the oculus above, silhouetted against the bright sunlight was Lupa, beckoning her onward.

She approached the closest burrow and began to scrabble. Eventually, the hole widened into a darkened passage way which led nowhere. Panicked, she scrambled backward into the opening. She tried again at the next burrowed hole. Again, she found a dead end. She tried one hole after another. Each hole led to a dead end. Exhausted, she sat motionless at the last hole and began to weep, too tired to try again. The oculus above was now moon lit. Silhouetted at its edge was the figure of a young child. Philip's voice cried to her, "Mother, come to me!"

Desperately, Miriam resumed digging. This too, led to a dead end. She dug some more. The tunnel opened. She crawled further to another dead end and more burrowing. On and on, she continued. At last, she broke through and crawled out into a wide cavern. Bright sunlight blinded her temporarily as she rose to her feet. As she regained her vision, Miriam could make out several caves along the wall of the cavern beyond. She counted seven in all. Then her eyes focused on several figures on the cavern floor below the caves. There, she saw the battered man flanked by two beautiful children, a boy and a girl. His arms rested peacefully on each child's shoulder.

Filled with hope, Miriam anxiously surveyed the cavern floor, looking for Philip. Dismayed, she could not find him. Then she heard the man say, "Bring the children to me!" She turned back toward his voice, only to find that he had vanished once more. The children stood silently gazing at her, their arms outstretched.

Miriam awoke from the dream. Its vividness kept her awake until dawn.

The trio broke camp and traveled the highway until mid-afternoon. Lupa had not appeared since the encounter with the Romans the day before. It was the longest period of separation since she and Miriam met in Jerusalem. Perhaps it was Lupa's sudden absence, or perhaps it was the eeriness of her dream, but suddenly Miriam's sense of abandonment and doubt fell upon her. They had returned.

As they approached Petra, their pace slowed to a halt.

"Miriam of Egypt, it is time for us to return to our family. Petra is very near. The highway will take you there. You have given us so much. Most of all you have left in us in the Faith of Yesua. May His peace be with you," the father said.

"And with your spirit," she replied. Miriam gave each a gentle embrace, grabbed her staff and continued her journey south.

"Wait," the son shouted. He ran to her with his hand outstretched. In it, he held the shredded garment that Miriam had used to bath his sister back to life.

"This belongs to you. You will need it again. Your work is not done," he said with a smile.

Returning his smile, Miriam accepted the stained cloth, her spirit renewed by the gesture.

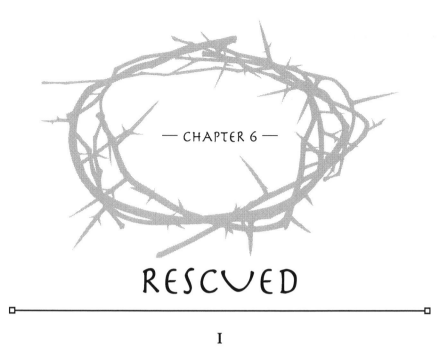

RESCUED

I

"**B**rother Lucian, tell me about Yesua," Philip implored.

"What did your mother teach you?" Lucian replied.

"That Yesua was an Aeon born from the God of Light and Goodness," Philip responded.

"Ah, yes, but you see, your mother was but partially right. There is much more to learn about Yesua, Philip!"

The happenstances of his journey found Philip in the presence of one of the most famous Christian scholars of his times. Lucian of Antioch was also a Hebrew scholar who corrected the Greek version of the Old Testament, expunging the errors that had found their way into the text over time. This highly esteemed Old Testament version was adopted by many of the churches of Syria and Asia Minor. He was also well versed in the numerous and disparate writings of early Christianity that evolved in the second and third centuries. Fifty years later, Saint Jerome used Lucian's work to prepare the Latin translation of the Bible known as the Vulgate.

Lucian's theological interpretations were often at odds with other teachings that were evolving at the time. He was excommunicated three times by different bishops because of his teachings. Nonetheless, his work was widely revered and respected. Lucian also studied a multitude of Christian writings that had evolved in the past two centuries. He concluded that among the eighty or so sacred writings that had been written since the death and resurrection of Yesua, the Truth could primarily be found in those writings that were attributed to those who witnessed the works of Yesua first hand. His findings and subsequent teachings were the basis for the body of scripture that defines the modern New Testament. No doubt this revered man had many disciples. Perhaps Lucian's most famous student was Arius of Alexandria with whom Lucian intended to leave Philip.

Lucian's explanation continued. "Your mother's story arises from a belief that the source of all being is the One God in which an inner being dwells. According to this odd tradition, this inner being emanates from the One God as a pair of male and female Aeons. This pair of Aeons, too, has inner beings, which in turn emanate in pairs. The emanation of inner beings thus continues sometimes to the number of thirty. These Aeons belong to the purely, intelligible, or ideal world known as the 'Pleroma.' But, alas, a flaw occurred in the last emanation by the passion of the female Aeon, Sophia, who emanates alone without her perfect partner. As a result, an imperfect creature emanates from her, one that never should have existed. This creature is the Demiurge who does not belong to the Pleroma. Alas, it is the Demiurge who created the world and humanity, along with all its flaws."

"My mother told me about the Demiurge. It is this spirit that lives in my father," Philip said.

"From what I know and have seen of your father, your mother speaks the truth," Lucian replied.

"Now back to the tradition of the Aeons," Lucian continued. "To save humanity from the Demiurge, the One emanates two savior Aeons, Christ and the Holy Spirit. Christ took the human form of Yesua, in order to be able to teach humanity how to achieve Gnosis. The ultimate end of all Gnosis is repentance, the undoing of the sin of material existence and the return to the Pleroma."

"Yesua was a man. Does that mean the Holy Spirit is a woman?"

"According to this tradition, some say that the Holy Spirit is the female Aeon partner of Yesua."

"What is Gnosis?" asked the ever-inquisitive child.

"Gnosis, my son, is the knowledge of spiritual truths," shared Lucian.

"So if I learn the knowledge of spiritual truth, then I will be able to go to Pleroma?" Philip asked.

"Knowledge alone is not enough. You must keep your faith pure. You must learn the holy Truths and learn to love them. Yesua is the Truth. Knowing and loving this Truth, you must act upon it."

"How?"

"Only through repentance will you undo the sins of humanity. You must learn to forgive and ask forgiveness in return."

"My mother taught me to forgive," said Philip, pausing. "Is material existence really a sin?"

"Yes," Lucian continued. "When I was about your age, I lost both of my parents. They left me with an abundance of worldly possessions, yet still, my spirit was empty. I therefore gave everything that I possessed to the poor and left my home in Samosata to live with a holy man in Edessa, a man named Marcarius. From him I learned the Truth through the study of Holy Scripture. He also taught me how to act upon this knowledge by practicing Christian virtues. Since that time I have dedicated my spirit to the priestly duties, to works of charity, and to the study of sacred writings."

"Is the Gospel of Philip a sacred writing?" Philip inquired.

"No, the Gospel of Philip is not a sacred writing. It is one of the many books that I have studied in my search for the Truth. It is popular in my country and was written only recently. The copy I gave you is written in Greek and is a simple book. I will teach you how to read it so that you may learn Greek. I kept this copy because I love the passage that I first quoted you. Do you remember it?"

"You said, 'People will tremble if I say that I am a Christian,'" Philip recalled.

"Yes," Lucian smiled as he quoted the passage again. "But if I say, 'I am a Christian,' they will tremble. 'I wish I had that title. The world will not endure it when hearing the name.'" Again, there followed a quiet moment of reflection by both Lucian and Philip.

Finally, the insatiably curious Philip broke the silence. "You said my mother was partially right. What did you mean?"

"Most certainly Yesua and the Holy Spirit came from the God of Light and Goodness. Most Certainly the God of Light and Goodness has existed for all time, but there was a time before Yesua when only God existed. God sent both Yesua and the Holy Spirit to reconcile mankind to Himself. It was the God of Light and Goodness who created all there is. There are neither Aeons nor a Demiurge who created the world we live in."

"If there is no Demiurge, why does evil exist?" inquired Philip, confoundedly.

"Evil exists because Adam and Eve, the first humans, disobeyed God and followed the temptations of Satan, the dark, evil angel who is jealous of God. God created Adam and Eve pure and without sin. This act of disobedience forever blemished their spirit and the spirit of all of their children. Evil exists because of this stain and mankind continues to succumb to the temptations of Satan."

"So who created Satan?"

"The God of Light."

"Why did the God of Light and Goodness create evil?"

"He didn't. The Angel of Darkness was created pure like Adam and Eve, but became jealous of God, who then cast him into the fires of hell." Lucian then told Philip the story of Genesis, of the creation, the Garden of Eden, Adam and Eve's submission to Satan and God's punishment of mankind for their original sin. He told of the prophets sent by God to warn the people of their evil ways and the punishments God inflicted on them for not changing. Philip listened intently and remained silent for several minutes after Lucian had finished. Philip asked no further questions, yet Lucian could see that the child was deep in thought, seeking to reconcile the two stories.

With a slight bit of his father's arrogance, Philip finally spoke, "I like my mother's story better."

"Why do you say this?"

"My mother told me that the One creates only goodness. Yesua and the Spirit came from the One to save us from the imperfect world created by the Demiurge, who is imperfect."

"The God of Light creates goodness in my tale."

"But how could all those people in your story be good, if it is also so that many became bad? That would mean that the One who is pure and perfect creates imperfect beings."

"Like who?" Lucian asked.

"Like Satan. Like the other dark angels, and like Adam and Eve's son, Cain, and all of the bad people in the world, people like, like my father.

Why, how, could a perfect God of Light create a world peopled with such evil as these? If the One is perfect, then how could He create such imperfection? Why would he create beings who could sin and who could be evil"?

"God gave us the will to choose between good and evil. Evil exists because we are weak."

"Why?"

"Because we are not perfect."

"Why?"

"Because, as I have told you, Adam and Eve were weak and chose to disobey God."

"Why?"

"Because they, like us, were not perfect."

"But you said that the One created Adam and Eve perfect, without sin. How could a perfect God create so many things that became imperfect? Only an imperfect God could create a world with so many imperfections. Only the Demiurge! The Demiurge must have created Adam and Eve!"

Again, the questioning stopped. Philip returned to an inner dialogue as he contemplated Lucian's responses. Lucian was amazed to find that he was discussing the nature of the Godhead and Christ's Divinity with an amazingly intuitive ten year old boy. He began to wonder how the campfire discussions with his merchant friends might have been. No wonder the Elder referred to Philip as a precious gift from God. Yet even though Lucian told the story as simply as possible and also answered Philip's questions with the same ease, the boy still remained skeptical.

The weather that morning was clear. The waters of the Mediterranean

Sea reflected the clear blue sky above. The ship had achieved a great distance from Antioch due to a strong downwind, but now the wind suddenly shifted, becoming a headwind, and the crew scurried to manage the sails, capturing the wind as the ship tacked forward. How magical it all appeared to Philip, who had certainly felt the wind before, but who had never seen it, nor proof of it. The mysterious vessel guiding them to safety was now capturing the wind to do so.

Lucian was suddenly struck by the fact that his young companion had miraculously been given sight only weeks beforehand. How many wondrous sights remained to be seen? He studied the child as Philip gazed at the sails. Lucian reminisced about his own boyhood, being abandoned by the death of his parents and reborn through the love of his teacher, Marcarius. Was Philip a gift from God to Lucian? Was this child a vessel to be cherished and molded as he had been? Was this, could this be God's plan?

If this was God's plan, he reasoned, it would have to wait. First, he would shepherd the child to safety with Arius, but then he must return to Antioch to save his friends from Quintus' wrath.

II

The ship was steered by two great paddles on each side of the stern that passed through two hawse holes, one on either side. The pilot steered the vessel with one rudder at a time. From his position at the oar, the pilot ordered the sailors to lower the main sail. After the mainsail was secured, they hoisted up the smaller foresail that was often used in storms. Lucian and Philip watched intently as the sailors scurried about. As was customary with most ships of this period, there were eyes painted on each side of the ship's bow, giving the ship a personality that came to life in the choppy sea. As the wind grew stronger, the ship's gritty personality faced headstrong into an oncoming storm. Lucian pointed out the storm that lay off on the horizon.

"A prayer for Yesua's protection is probably in order," Lucian said with a reassuring smile.

Hearing Lucian's comment, the pilot addressed the pair. Pointing to the shoreline on the horizon he said "Caesarea!"

Caesarea Palestina was a port city built by Herod the Great between 22 and 10 BC on the Mediterranean coast, 60 miles northwest of Jerusalem. Herod built the city to honor the Emperor Augustus. The political savvy Herod also erected a temple there, which was dedicated to the Emperor's divinity. For 600 years, Caesarea would flourish as the cultural center and capital city of Palestine. Both Peter and Paul visited the Jewish community there during their missionary journeys. It was the Roman mistreatment of Jews in Caesarea that led to the First Jewish Revolt and the consequent destruction of Jerusalem in 70 AD. By 303 AD, Caesarea had become a major center of both Jewish and Christian scholarship, which included a significant library founded there over a century before by the theologian Origen of Alexandria. As with other cities in the region, under Diocletian, it became the site of Christian martyrdom.

While the port was only three miles away, the ship struggled most of the afternoon to traverse the angry seas. Late in the day, the vessel reached safe harbor in the splendid port city. They had barely docked the ship when the storm's fury struck. Hastily, the crew pulled in the steering paddle and fastened ropes through each of the hawse holes at the ships stern. The ship, its stores, passengers and crew were all secured. Ship voyages in ancient times followed routes that kept shorelines within clear sight. Whenever ships were moored in port, passengers usually sought lodging for the night in the city. Tonight, the crew and passengers found sanctuary from the storm below deck with the dry stores. All dined meagerly on bread and olives, quietly waiting for the storm to subside. Philip surrendered to sleep shortly after supper.

"Kind sir," Lucian said, addressing the ship's pilot. "Please watch over the boy, for I must venture into the city."

"It is a terrible night to undertake such a foray! It is best that you stay here," responded the pilot.

"I must visit a friend who needs my counsel. I know the way. It is near."

"For you, old man there is more danger about you than just this storm. I overheard you speaking with the boy today. You are a believer?"

"A believer?" Lucian asked. The question took him by surprise.

"Of the One who died for us, Yesua," said the pilot.

"Yes, I am a Christian," spoke Lucian, proudly repeating his favorite sentence, the same words that the pilot had overheard Lucian recite to Philip earlier that day.

"Caesarea is not safe for Christians. I traveled through here months ago and heard terrible stories of torture and murder!"

"If that be my fate, I can wish for no greater gift. But, you see, my work with this child is not done. I shall be cautious, and return before the break of day."

"If the sky is clear, we sail at daybreak."

"If fate finds me elsewhere, please take this child with you to Alexandria."

"And what do you wish for me to do with him in Alexandria?"

"Do you know of Arius of Alexandria?"

"Yes, I have heard of this holy man."

"If I do not return, find Arius and tell him of my fate. Present this child to him and tell him that the boy is a student of Lucian of Antioch. He will know what to do."

"You are Lucian of Antioch?"

"I am."

The pilot dropped to his knees, grabbed Lucian's hands and kissed them. "Bless me brother, and may God be with you."

"And with your spirit, my son," Lucian said, shrouding his head with his cloak and vanishing into the dreadful, stormy night.

The city was difficult to reconnoiter. Lucian had underestimated the challenge the storm presented. Lucian questioned his aging memory as he struggled to discern familiar landmarks. He was in search of a Christian safe house where followers met to pray and to worship. He knew of several in the city, but hoped to find the one nearest to the docks lest he be delayed; he hoped to keep his journey back to the ship as short as possible. The task became more daunting as the storm grew still worse.

He soon found that his garments were soaked throughout, the wind chilling him to the bone. Shivering, he whispered aloud. "Is this the street? No. It is too broad. Perhaps it intersects this one. Yes, midway down the hill. This seems right. Now where is the street? I should have found it by now. To the left? No. To the right? Ah! There, that narrow passage on the right. Yes. This is it. The house is at the end."

Cautiously, he knocked on the door, still a bit uncertain. A young girl's voice cried out. "Who calls at this hour?" If this was the safe house, then surely his name would be recognized here.

"Lucian of Antioch."

"Can you wait please?" the girl asked.

The rain intensified. The wait seemed too long for a visitor whose name should be known at once here. He must have made a mistake. He turned back into the night and started up the hill. A voice shouted to him from the house. "The Lucian I know would never turn his back on a friend!"

"Eusebius!" Lucian cried, turned and raced to his friend's embrace.

"Sweet man, you are soaked to the bone. Come in. Come in. Please accept my regrets. The child and her family are new to our community. We have just finished evening prayers. What brings you to Caesarea on this frightful night?" Eusebius inquired.

"I am traveling to Antioch as the guardian of a young companion whom I hope to leave in the care of a friend. We docked in Caesarea just as the storm arrived this afternoon. I come seeking news of our brothers and sisters here. We have heard rumors in Antioch. Talk of loathsome persecutions in Caesarea, especially concerning our good friend, Procopius. Is this true? What can you tell me?" Lucian asked, his anxiety palpable.

"First let us find you some dry clothes while your cloak dries by the fire." Eusebius directed the girl to stoke the fire and to make a place for Lucian. After Lucian had changed gratefully into dry clothing, he assumed the fireside place prepared for him.

Procopius, the subject of Lucian's inquiry, was a morally strict man of pure habits. His godly discipline was notorious. It was rumored that he subsisted only on bread and water, often fasting a whole week, abstaining from food altogether. His given name was Neanias, born in Jerusalem to a pagan mother and a Christian father. When he was just a boy, his father died. Subsequently, his mother raised him in the spirit of Roman idolatry. As a young adult, he persecuted Christians, much like Saul of Tarsus and like the disciple Paul before him, Neanias was confronted by a vision of Yesua on one of his journeys, whereupon he passionately repented and accepted Yesua as his savior.

As a devout Christian, he took the name Procopius and went to live in Scythopolis, where he held three ecclesiastical offices. He was a fluent reader and interpreter of the Syriac language. He was also a renowned exorcist, curing many who were possessed by evil spirits. Diocletian sent the Governor of Caesarea to investigate Procopius and to handle his capture. When the Governor brought him to Caesarea, Procopius confessed his faith in Yesua, whereupon he was horribly beaten by Roman hands, narrowly escaped death, so severely had he been brutalized. He was then cast into prison.

After Lucian had settled, Eusebius spoke. "Our good brother, Procopius, was martyred on July 7th past. He was imprisoned by the Governor and tortured by his captors. One day, twelve women appeared at his prison window, each of whom professed her faith in Yesua. They, too, were exposed and captured. When Procopius was led to his execution, he raised his hands, praying to God for all who are poor and unfortunate, professing a last wish for the continued spread of Christian beliefs. He was then decapitated and those twelve women were brutally tortured to death."

Softly, Lucian spoke. "But if I say, 'I am a Christian,' they will tremble. I wish I had that title. The world will not endure it when hearing the name." The rest of the evening was spent in prayer, honoring the martyred champion and his companions.

Numerous legends and stories of Procopius' visions of Christ arose in the wake of this holy martyr's death. One such legend styles Procopius as a soldier prince of Alexandria who is confronted by a stranger on the road. When Procopius confronts the stranger, a glowing, crystal cross appears in the air and from the cross, there comes a voice saying: "I am Yesua, the crucified Son of God. By this sign that you see, conquer your enemies and My peace will be with you."

In Procopius' honor, this Hymn of Praise ascends.
When it is the will of the Omniscient God,

Persecutors become His servants,
Haters, wonderful apostles
Pagans, zealots for the Faith.
By God's will, Saul became Paul
Neanias, Saint Procopius.
Procopius, against Christ went,
As a Christian, to his mother came.
Tortures prepared and himself received tortures,
All of a sudden, the truth he recognized
Before the Son of God, bowed down,
The earthly king, ceased to serve
To the heavenly King, a servant became.
The King of Heaven to him a gift bestowed
The gift of might, the afflicted to help
As at that time, so it is today:
By Procopius, the afflicted are comforted
For today as one time, he helps.

III

The next day dawned with a glorious sunrise and clear sky. With Lucian safely aboard, the crew cast off. Steady tail winds favored the remainder of the voyage. Each day of the journey, Lucian taught the boy how to read the Gospel of Philip in Greek. Each day, the boy's passion for the written word grew. The journey to Alexandria took eight days in all. Before arriving, the ship made port in many ancient cities, including Sidon, Caesarea, Gaza, Pelusium and finally, Alexandria.

By the autumn of 303 AD, the dismantling of the Christian church in Alexandria by Diocletian was noteworthy. Locating Arius proved difficult, for he, too, had gone into hiding. As the search for Arius continued, Lucian's anxiety intensified. Travel by sea after September 1st became increasingly dangerous. It was already late fall and the winter storm season would limit the possibility of any return to Antioch ventured by sea. The delay of Lucian's return put the lives of his imprisoned friends in great peril.

Their search for Arius was focused in the Jewish quarter east of the great harbor. The Jewish community of Alexandria had been nearly destroyed by the Emperor Trajan's army during a revolt in 115-117 AD. An estimated 50,000 Jews were slaughtered. Since then, many of the remaining Jews had become Christians. Lucian and Philip finally met a Jewish Christian named Jacob, who revealed that Arius had left the city and taken refuge at a farm south of the city on the banks of Lake Mareotis. Jacob offered to take them to Arius. They left the city through the Gate of the Sun and traveled south, crossing the ancient Nile canal. True to his word, Jacob delivered the pair to the secreted safe house where Arius now dwelled; their meeting took Arius completely by surprise. The passionate reunion was like that of a father and a son greeting each other after a long and difficult absence.

"Lucian, my teacher, you are here! Ah! You are here! What miracle is this? I have prayed so very often for this reunion, and now, my prayers have been answered in a most surprising way," proclaimed Arius.

As they approached the farm, Philip had noticed children playing along the water's edge. Now he stood at the window, entranced by their merriment. Lucian then began to explain to Arius the purpose of his visit, but then noticed that Philip had remained standing nearby.

"Young philosopher, Philip! Go join the others in their games. You have spent enough time with this old man discussing the mysteries of life. It is time that you have fun and rejoice in the safety of your new friends." Philip burst from the room and sprinted to the water. In Rasafa, he had only sensed the raptures of youthful play as but a blind bystander, who silently pined to participate, to join with his fellows, and here now, his dream was about to come true. Lucian smiled as he watched Philip sprint off.

"I have brought you a gift from God. That young boy is the handiwork of Yesua," he told Arius.

"How so?" Arius asked, probing.

"Come. Sit. I will tell you his story," responded Lucian.

As Philip drew closer to the shore, he slowed to a walk, taking note of the children. 'What an odd game!' he thought. The children, six in all, were young boys, very near to his age. Four were in a single file line at the water's edge. The pack leader stood in the water. Philip watched as he dipped another boy into the water, and then lifted him out. As Philip approached, the leader pointed to him and spoke to the others.

"Behold ! After me comes one who is more powerful than I, whose sandals I am not worthy to carry. He will baptize you with the Holy Spirit and fire." Addressing Philip, he said, "I need to be baptized by you, and do you come to me?"

"Who are you?" Philip asked, perplexed.

"I am John, the Baptist," the leader answered.

"No! You are not! John the Baptist was beheaded centuries ago. Who do you think I am?"

"God has spoken to me, 'This is my Son, whom I love; with him I am well pleased.'"

"You think that I am Yesua?" Philip queried.

"You must be. We are proclaiming the baptism of Yesua and suddenly you have appeared to us!" the leader replied. The other children, awed by this strange boy's appearance, dropped to their knees in veneration.

Philip laughed, "Get up! Get up! My name is Philip. I am the son of Miriam, a slave girl. My father is a Roman soldier. I came here with my friend Lucian who is Arius' teacher."

Embarrassed by his erroneous rapture, the leader was momentarily dumfounded. Then he bent to gather a handful of mud.

"Well then Philip, son of a Roman soldier and the slave girl Miriam, you must announce yourself properly next time," he said, flinging the ball of mud at Philip. Philip, in turn, raced into the water and the others followed closely behind him. A reenactment of Holy Scripture soon turned to a friendly, frolicking, mud-slinging wrestling match that eventually ended with proper introductions all around.

"My name is Barnabas and you, Philip, baptized in mud, will be my friend for life!"

As the boys played, Arius listened intently as Lucian told Philip's story in great detail. When Lucian outlined his conversations with Philip aboard ship, Arius interrupted. "Obviously, the mother's family were followers of Valentinius."

Valentinius was a second century Christian theologian who claimed to have received mystical teachings from a secret disciple of the Apostle Paul. He was born in the Nile delta and educated in Alexandria. At one time, he had been a serious contender for bishop of Rome and taught that there were three kinds of people: the material, the psychical, and the spiritual. Material people were pagans and Jews who were destined to perish forever. Psychical people were ordinary Christians who could only reach a lesser form of salvation, and Spiritual people only, were those who received gnosis and could return to the divine Pleroma and eternal union with God. Valentinius' teachings gained widespread acceptance in Egypt and Syria. It was Valentinius who developed the elaborate matrix of Aeons that Lucian had explained to Philip whilst they voyaged.

Lucian continued, "I am certain that your assumption is correct. But the boy's mother was Philip's age when she was separated from her family. She only understood those teachings with a child's comprehension. I am also certain that his freedom from blindness was a miracle given to him by the blood of a martyr possessed of undying faith. He is most eager to learn. I wish to teach him, as I have taught you, but he must remain safe from his father's wrath until I can return to retrieve him from your care."

Cautiously, as to not offend his mentor, Arius replied, "I am honored that you would entrust him to me, but Alexandria is not safe. The children with whom Philip is playing are all orphans of their martyred parents. They are gathered here for a journey to a distant desert community on the Nile where they can practice spiritual works in solitude and peace. Young Barnabas is the oldest. He is twelve years old and a natural leader who is literate in Greek. He will befriend Philip and can continue to educate him in the Greek language. Let Philip enjoy the friendship of these youthful companions. When all is safe, we will send for him upon your return."

Lucian thought for a minute. "And will you accompany them?"

"No. I cannot. I must continue my ministry here."

Pleading, Lucian said, "But you have said yourself that Alexandria is not safe. The Emperor is aging. This persecution will pass. We will prevail. Be exiled with him. This boy, this miracle of God, has been given to us for a purpose."

"There is a far greater threat to our Faith than the Romans," Arius continued. "Many scholars are mistakenly teaching our followers that Yesua and the Holy Spirit have been one in being with the Father forever. As we have often discussed, this teaching is false. First, there was the Father, then the Spirit as seen through the prophets, then the Son. The Father is the greatest of all, The One, the only God of Goodness and Light. I must continue my ministry here. I must teach this truth."

"As you know, I have struggled with understanding Yesua's True Godhead. Beliefs of misinterpretations have led many to erroneous teachings such as those of Valentinius. I have not reconciled my struggles as yet, but you are resolute. So be it," Lucian said with a smile. "We shall follow your plan."

Just then, their conversation was interrupted by the boys. "Lucian, meet my new friend, Barbanas!" The boys were arm in arm, soaking wet, muddy and smiling from ear to ear.

Lucian rose to his feet, laughing, and addressed the boys.

"Barnabas, I am leaving my friend Philip in your care until I return. He is now your little brother. Philip….," a melancholy tone entered his voice. "Philip, rejoice in the joy of your new friends. Learn all that you can until I return to teach you more." Addressing everyone, he said, "Now I must go. The vessel that brought us here is preparing to return to Antioch. It departs tomorrow. With God's grace and Jacob's guidance, I will be aboard by daybreak. May the Spirit of Yesua be with you, and may your Faith keep you strong."

Arius, Philip and Barnabas watched the pair's departure until they disappeared over the horizon. As they vanished, Philip whispered softly, "May the Spirit of Yesua be with you, teacher." Arius and Barnabas replied quietly, "Amen, Amen."

Philip's dreams where increasingly visual. The child who could only dream in sounds and tactile memories had begun to add visual impressions to his recollections, particularly his memory of faces, which included those of his merchant friends, as well as Lucian, Arius, Barnabas and, of course, his beloved mother, Miriam, petite and lovely, her visage distinctively stamped with its crescent-shaped scar. He had traced its shape with his fingers every night before sleep.

Regrettable also was the nightmare face that had first woken him to reality, the enraged face of his father, Quintus, standing over his mother, sword raised high. He had not shared with anyone that his dreams always ended with that vision.

This night he prayed to Yesua for his face not to appear. Alas, sadly, his prayer went unanswered. In life, Quintus' enraged, manic face had been his first sight. In the illusive realm of his dreams, it was his last.

IV

By the time Lucian returned to Antioch, nearly a month had passed since his friends were imprisoned. He prayed daily that they had not met a martyrs' fate and if so, he prayed that it was swift. To Lucian, there was no greater gift than to die for Yesua, as He had died for mankind, but the Romans had perfected persecutions into a sport, altogether literally. Torture was an art and death a spectacle. Lucian hoped to spare his friend's lives to avoid the horrors of both. As soon as Lucian disembarked, he raced to Marcus' home in the shadows of the afternoon sunset. Surely, he thought, Marcus could help him to devise a plan to rescue the merchants.

Awaiting a response to his knock, Lucian was greeted at the door by an unfamiliar centurion. "Welcome back to Antioch. Your return has been expected!"

Something was dreadfully wrong. Lucian turned to run. He was surrounded immediately by a half-dozen legionnaires, their lances drawn. The first thrust the butt end of his lance into Lucian's torso, just beneath his rib-cage. Breathless, Lucian fell to his knees.

"Foolish old man! It is Quintus who awaits your return!" The centurion barked.

"Where is Marcus?" Lucian gasped.

"You will see him soon," the centurion said, grinning. The others laughed.

The days were growing shorter as the year was ending. The October sun was setting low in the west. Long shadows traversed the road as the entourage marched toward the Imperial Palace, which was situated on the East Bank of the Orantes River. As the road exited the city's forum, the street broadened and turned due west. Corinthian columns, twelve feet tall, lined either side of the street at twenty feet intervals. The setting sun projected shadows twice the columns' length along the pavement before them. The shadows of the columns' capitals projected an odd shape at their tops. Lucian looked atop the columns, but was thwarted, blinded by the setting sun. As they passed the first pair or columns, the mystery was revealed as Lucian turned to his right.

To his gasping horror, on top of the column, was the head of Marcus' youngest daughter. To his left was the head of the Elder's youngest son. Column by column, to the right and to the left were the gruesome horror of the heads of his dearest friends. Column by column on the right, were the heads of Marcus' family. Column by column on the left, were those of the merchant's family. At the end of the colonnade, stood a familiar and ominous figure, Quintus Flavius Scipio; a runner had been dispatched to inform Quintus that his prize catch had arrived.

"Welcome back, old man. Alas, you have missed our festivities." Quintus made a sweeping gesture with his outstretched arm, motioning toward the martyrs' heads. The last of these, one on each side, were those of Marcus and the Elder.

Undaunted, Lucian replied. "You have sent them to the Father. You have granted them eternal happiness, in spite of your attempts to deliver misery."

"I have heard this myth many times before, old man." Smiling sardonically, he continued. "I can assure you that based on the generous dose of misery we dealt them; no doubt they are now indeed much happier!'" His grin was for him a peculiar gesture, for while Quintus enjoyed his work, he seldom, if ever, displayed even the slightest emotion.

"Where is the boy?" Quintus' question was direct, his face stern.

"He is in the grace of God, filled with the spirit of Yesua," Lucian replied.

"Never mind!" Quintus knew that Lucian would never divulge his secret. "You are lucky old man. I have convinced Caesar Galerius that your life should be spared. Better you should die in prison of old age than that you should enjoy a martyr's fate."

"You will deny me that honor?"

"I have," he said, again with that same, derisive smile. "I have also convinced Caesar Galerius that my days of killing stubborn Christians have drawn to an end. You have beheld now, my final kills. Galerius has at last granted my wish to join the legions is Gaul. Get a good night's rest, old man. I leave at dawn. I shall take you with me as far as Nicomedia. The journey will, no doubt, be long for you. Your life as a teacher is over. Lucian's Antioch School of Christianity shall be no more."

Lucian now understood the nature of Quintus' mocking grin. Quintus' life as the "Christian Murderer of Syria" was finished. As promised, Quintus would deliver Lucian to a prison cell in Nicomedia. As predicted, Lucian's career was over. He would spend nine years in that prison, where he died at last, on January 7, 312 AD. Like most of his martyred counterparts, there are many legends about the circumstances of his death. One legend reports that he was starved to death. Another claim holds that he was beheaded. Still another says that he died after twelve days of brutal torture. With each variation, though, all narratives conclude that Lucian's proudly proclaimed last words were these; "I am a Christian!"

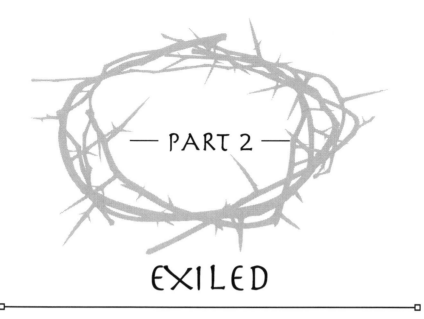

— PART 2 —

EXILED

After wresting free of Egypt's grip, Moses and his people endured a forty year exile in the desert whilst searching for the "promised land." This exile was as much a search for cultural identity and a place in history as it was a search for a place to live. So too, Miriam, Philip and Quintus were exiled. All were scattered. Each was searching for a new identity, a life restored, a life reborn and a life renewed. As they searched, howling winds of change rumbled through the Empire.

On 27th of February 272 AD, he was born in what is now modern Serbia. He was eighteen when Diocletian proclaimed Christianity as an enemy of the state. Like Philip, Miriam and Quintus, this child was raised in the Age of Martyrs. He was the son of a Roman commander, Constantius Chlorus and his mother, Helena, a woman of lowly stature.

Legends paint Helena as his father's concubine or perhaps a "favored" bar-maid. At the time of the boy's birth, his father was one of Emperor Aurelian's Imperial bodyguards serving in Syria. Under Diocletian, Constantius Chlorus rose to the rank of Praetorian Prefect. As Diocletian finalized the Tetrarchy structure that would rule the Empire, he hand-picked the commander of his Praetorian guard to serve as Caesar under Maximian in the West.

From Nicomedia, Diocletian ruled the Eastern Empire as Augustus with Galerius as his Caesar. From Rome, Maximian ruled the Western Empire as Augustus with Constantius Chlorus as his Caesar. The Tetrarchy would be further entwined by marriage. Constantius divorced the boy's inconsequential mother to marry Maximian's step-daughter, Theodora. Galerius married Diocletian's daughter, Valeria, who in turn adopted her husband.

Constantius was given Gaul as his to rule. Galerius was given the countries of the Danube. Of these four rulers, Galerius was the most politically insignificant. He was raised as an illiterate shepherd, but became an efficient soldier intensely devoted and loyal to Diocletian. Immoral and violent by nature, he was Diocletian's lawless goon. Throughout his career, he was viciously diligent in the Eastern Empire both in battle as well as in the persecution of Christians.

While the division of the Empire brought stability and strengthened Roman authority, Diocletian's ruling Tetrarchy was not built on trust. With political savvy born years before in an age of tyranny, Diocletian understood that other "collateral" was also essential to the survival of the Tetrarchy. The last bauble of "collateral" was Constantius' son, the child born to the trivial "bar-maid." As a condition of Constantinius Chlorus' elevation to Caesar, the child was not permitted to accompany his father to Gaul. Instead, he remained in Nicomedia, some say as a hostage, to be raised in the court of Diocletian. The boy was born Flavius Valerius Constantinus but is known to the ages as "Constantine the Great."

CHAPTER 7

JOURNEY TO HELL

I

If Galerius was Diocletian's henchman, then Quintus was Galerius'. When the delusional Quintus was delivered to Galerius at the Imperial Palace, he received the undivided attention of Galerius' personal physician. Healing his wounds was a relatively quick fix. Infections from wounds induce enzymes, which in turn induced a progressive degradation of tissue cells. This process is called necrosis. While necrotic tissues are harmful to humans, they are also a culinary delight for maggots. In fact, a large number of small maggots can quickly remove necrotic tissue far more precisely than can most surgical procedures. Typically, the maggots will molt twice and quadruple in size within a three to four day period. While the wounds are cleansed in a matter of days, the wound's surface size increases due to the maggots' voracious appetite. If they stay too long, or if too many are used, healthy tissue is removed as well.

Galerius' favorite butcher was now under the care of his favorite surgeon. Quintus' fever was particularly troublesome. The physician knew that Quintus' life depended upon an aggressive application of ancient therapies. His pugnacious approach was successful. Within a week, Quintus was on his feet seeking vengeance. Galerius was pleased. So was Quintus, in spite of the fact that he would permanently bear grotesque scars on his neck and calf. For him, they would serve as symbols of life's conquest over death.

When he was well enough, he spent a morning with Galerius, retelling the story of his journey from Rasafa to Antioch. He began with the beheading of Sergius and the miraculous healing of his blind son. He told of the separation of mother and child and how he had paid the deceiving merchants to deliver the boy to the Roman Garrison in Alexandria. Galerius was humored by the encounter with the desert vipers and proud of his protégé's defeat of the Persian scouts. The vision of Quintus Flavius Scipio crossing the Syrian Desert on a donkey brought them both to heel in gut-wrenching laughter. The laughter ceased, though, as Galerius continued to listen intently as Quintus told of his daydream of fighting barbarians in Gaul and his fill of murdering belligerent Christians.

Galerius changed topics, "Enough of this Quintus! Your story exhausts me. Come, let us soothe our aches together in a hot bath. They then spent nearly an hour submerged in the silence of the Imperial baths.

Finally, Galerius spoke, "tell me more about the girl!"

Quintus began his story with the bathing ritual and a vivid description of the girl's beauty, which had grown as her pristine body matured. He described his taunting and how her body had trembled at his touch. He explained in detail the exquisite feel of her perfect skin and the intoxicating smell of her hair. He told Galerius of the incident with the mother and her crucified son. Finally, he confessed his moment of weakness and his naked exposure to a strange inner vulnerability.

"'Yesua will forgive you,' she said!" he shouted. "Yesua will forgive... Me?! My first reaction was to kill the bitch by drowning her in a bucket of water. Instead, I chose to violate her spirit. Not just her spirit, but the spirit of her Almighty Yesua." Then he told Galerius how he had forced her to watch as the young boy slave continued the cleansing ritual. He paused for a moment. With a hollow stare, he concluded his confession, "Then I made her watch as I violated the boy."

Galerius' ravenous addiction to carnal pleasure was notorious and he began to stroke himself as Quintus told the story. Finally, he ordered the servant who was tending the bath, "Come here and listen intently to what my friend is about to tell you."

Turning to Quintus, he commanded, "Describe again, in detail, both the boy and the girl."

His breathing grew heavy as he ordered the servant, "Bring us my finest wine and a boy and girl matching his description. Quickly!" Galerius was no longer content with having a purely vicarious experience.

The servant promptly returned with wine, and both a girl and a boy as he'd been commanded. Quintus perused the boy and nodded yes. He shook his head no after inspecting the girl, "She is too tall altogether!"

"Now pay attention, fool, and hurry!" Galerius shouted.

The servant returned, this time with a suitable replacement. The boy and girl were both about fifteen years old. He ordered the pair to stand in front of him waist high in the bath water. With his left hand, he fondled the boy's genitals. With his right, he stroked the girl's nipples to erection. Then, using both hands, he squeezed her nipples as he fixated on her young breasts.

"Tell me Quintus, do these match the pair possessed by your little bitch?" Galerius was referring to her breasts, but Quintus was staring into her eyes, sensing the fear that had gripped Miriam on so many occasions.

"Perfect," Quintus replied.

The servant poured the wine. Galerius took a healthy swallow. "Ah, Bacchus is generous with his gifts." He waved the goblet in a broad motion. "Alas! I haven't hands enough to enjoy all of these pleasures at once. This wine is too delightful to put down. What now? Hmm…?"

Galerius addressed the couple. "Give us a show my dears." Then he instructed them to pleasure each other as he and Quintus watched. The servant poured another serving of wine. The men watched in silence. The silence was broken as Galerius directed step by step instructions for the pair. Each man finished his wine.

Galerius addressed Quintus, "Shall we?"

Quintus did not share Galerius' core of debauchery. He was one who found pleasure in sadistic dominance and fear rather than carnal lust. This pleasure would require great discipline, which had eluded him only once. He had no desire to re-enact that moment. He hungered to erase forever his memories of Miriam and Philip.

Pointing to Galerius' erection, he noted, "Oh Great and mighty Caesar, we both know that I am no match for you in a contest like this. Besides, the wine is having quite the opposite effect on me. I must still be weak from your surgeon's handiwork. I find that I must retire now and rest some more."

"Join me for supper, then," Galerius barked, preoccupied.

"Certainly, but do not expect me to compete then, either. Surely you will be ravenous once you have finished here."

Both men laughed as Quintus rose to leave. As he left the room, he stopped to question the sentry who was stationed at the portal. The topic concerned the whereabouts of the captured merchants.

"Still alive. Chained in the prison," the sentry reported. The retelling of his story to Galerius had aroused his insatiable lust to dominate, to inflict terror, and Quintus was determined now to slake his licentious thirst.

When Quintus arrived at the prison, he questioned the guards about the events that had occurred during his altered state. The conversation disclosed Marcus' secret. As a sign of gratitude for Quintus' safe return,

Galerius arranged for a sacrificial offering in the temple of Jupiter. As a reward for saving his friend, Galerius invited Marcus and his family to join him at the temple, and then at an ensuing celebration. Marcus had tried to beg off, claiming that his youngest daughter was far too ill. Galerius insisted that her attendance would be favored by the gods, thus insuring her good health. Marcus had no choice. Any further reluctance would create suspicion and endanger his family.

The story continued. As the family entered the temple sanctuary, the youngest daughter stopped short of the entry portal and began to cry. Concerned about the commotion, Galerius had knelt before the girl and said, "Hush, child! This sacrifice to the gods will heal all that pains you." In reply, the girl stammered and cried, murmuring plaintively, "But will Yesua forgive me?" The intended ceremonies were terminated immediately. Marcus and his family were beaten and dragged off to prison.

The combination of the hot bath and wine had rendered Quintus too weak to deliver the punishment that he yearned so dearly to administer. When the centurion finished the story of Marcus and his family's demise, Quintus ordered. "Deliver them and the merchant prisoners to the harbor market at dawn where I will give Jupiter a proper sacrifice."

Then he returned to his room at the Imperial palace where he instructed the chamber servant to wake him for dinner. He slept soundly until the servant roused him for the evening feast. He was the last guest to arrive. Galerius stopped the festivities to greet his friend and to introduce him to the other guests. The evening was abundant in every respect, food, wine and entertainment. As the guest of honor, Quintus sat beside Galerius.

As the celebration subsided, Galerius leaned toward Quintus. Speaking softly, he addressed him, "Dear friend, was your thought of fighting barbarians really a day dream? Is it true you've really had your fill of killing Christians?"

"Yes," Quintus replied.

"What about those who betrayed you, those who now wallow in my prison?"

"For them I seek only vengeance. With your kind permission, I will deliver it in the morning."

"You have both my permission, as well as a gift."

"A gift?"

"Your wish is granted. I shall arrange for you to join the legions in Gaul. You are right. Killing these pugnacious Christians is beneath the honor of a valiant warrior such as you. I must voyage to Nicomedia. Diocletian expects my return. You will accompany me. We depart with the next full moon. I will arrange an audience with Augustus so as to properly reward your loyalty."

Quintus smiled.

II

At dawn, Quintus entered the harbor market on horseback, and was accompanied by two centuries of legionnaires. Addressing the senior centurion, he ordered, "Take the prisoners to the docks! The rest of you! Close the market and bring everyone to the quay so that they may witness today's lesson. Let no one escape. " Finally, he addressed several legionnaires. "Scour this market and bring me as many serving platters as you can find. You will pile them in a heap at the gathering."

At the docks, Quintus found the prisoners chained and huddled together. The youngest wept.

Addressing the crowd, Quintus said, "Today we will have a history lesson about the story of Yesua the Nazarene. Our friends here have been recruited to serve as actors in our little drama!" He paused for a moment. "Ah yes! The tale begins with a virgin!" Turning to the prisoners, he mockingly inquired, "Is there a virgin amongst you?"

Marcus' wife began to wail without cease. "No, no, no, woman! Fear not, for clearly you are no virgin!" The legionnaires and some of the crowd sniggered and jeered.

"Well, well. It appears that we have the great pleasure of considering not one, but three candidates," he said, gesturing as Marcus reached out toward his daughters.

Quintus snapped, "Stop whining, Marcus. I will play the role of the Angel who shall choose the virgin. That is not your task! Now, she must be capable of bearing a child, so let us see, hmmm. This one is too young! Perhaps one of these two might do."

Grabbing the older daughters by their hair, he unchained them, dragged them to the center of the gathering, and hastily stripped them both naked. He groped the youngest. "Ah! This one is budding. Yes. Let me feel these breasts. Hmm. How succulent! How sweet! A pair of perfectly ripened pears, these are!"

Several women in the crowd began to wail. Those who had jeered earlier began to laugh.

Marcus shouted, "Stop this, you sadistic butcher!"

"Oh? And now he elevates himself! He is God, and is now commanding this Angel!" Quintus replied, thumping his chest, clearly amused. The pitch rose to a frenzy, exceeded only by Quintus' manic antics. His lust to intimidate, to solicit fear, which had so frustratingly eluded him the afternoon before, now detonated before the crowd. Addressing them, he shouted, "Pay attention! Yes, you, Marcus! I have told you that I am playing the Angel, but not really, for I AM the Angel. The Angel of Death!!"

Quintus grabbed the oldest girl, wrenching her hair at the scalp. She cried out, screamed, writhing, collapsing into a torrent of tears. "The Angel of Death chooses you! And now, oh yes! Now we need the Holy Spirit." Arching a brow, he began perusing the crowd, then pointed, abruptly, to a teenage boy and said, "You! Come here! Now, I say! I appoint you to be the Holy Spirit!"

The gangly boy looked about, and then nervously approached Quintus. "Show us your spirit, boy," Quintus taunted, raising the boy's robe and exposing the frightened youth's slight and flaccid penis. "Well, now! He may be holy, but I see he does lack spirit!" Quintus scoffed, drew himself up, and then struck the boy across his face, enjoying himself immensely. As the boy staggered and fought to right himself, the impatient Quintus seized him by the throat, brusquely dragged him to the wharf's edge and hurled him into the river, as if he were disposing of a sack of vermin.

Returning to the crowd, he pranced back and forth, his arms stretched high, shouting, "Surely there must be at least one amongst you who has some spirit, so who is it? Who has the spirit? Who has the spirit?"

A toothless middle aged man broke from the crowd, hoisted his robe abruptly and thrust forth his pelvis, erection in hand for all to see. "I do, oh Angel! I have the spirit, I do!"

"Then, give it to her. Give her the spirit," ordered Quintus.

The clearly addled man was half-drunk and needed no encouragement. He seized the thrashing young girl, who at half his size and in mortal fear for her life, he pinioned with ease. He eagerly leapt upon her while she screamed, writhing in the hot sun. As she lapsed into shock, he proceeded to rape her, seemingly delighted that she'd finally ceased fighting him, for out of pure terror and shame, she'd lapsed into unconsciousness. "Noooooooooooooooh!" Marcus cried out in mortal anguish, as the lecher went on ramming the girl's tender flesh with brutal abandon, slavering as the legionnaires all chanted, "Spirit, Spirit, Spirit......," the buffoon's grunting strokes now timed to the rhythm of the chant. The grotesqueness of the scene was amplified by its endlessness. The drunk went on and on, not so much as a feat of stamina as an inability to climax. Not ashamed in the least, a born exhibitionist, he played to Quintus and the crowds' direction and only stopped at last upon Quintus' explicit order that he cease.

Throughout the morning, Quintus directed scene after heinous scene. Most of the crowd jeered and laughed. Those who did not, and especially those who sought to flee, were instead trapped by a cohort of Roman legionnaires.

Quintus forced the elder merchant to play the role of John the Baptist, ordering him to baptize his son in the river.

"Well, is God pleased with his Son? No? No. Not satisfied, not yet. Let us remember the story. Ah.Yes! The Son must first die and then be raised up again!"

Quintus jumped into the river, sword in hand, swiftly decapitating the elder. After flinging his head onto the dock, he mercilessly drowned the boy, screaming, "Behold! The Father will now raise the Son!"

As the motionless body drifted away, he guffawed, "Well at least we all know this miracle shall require of us three full days for its magnificent manifestation!"

Back on the dock, Quintus grabbed the decapitated head and placed it on a platter, which he thrust into the hands of a reluctant girl in the crowd. He shouted, "I will now play the role of King Herod and you will be my daughter, Salome! Dance for me now, my child! Dance with the head on this platter."

The legionnaires were now rhythmically pounding their swords and lances on the dock. Quintus shouted again, "More heads.... more platters.....more dancers....more...more...more!" The legionnaires pounded on with the rhythm shouting, "more...more....more..."

Then he beheaded all of the remaining prisoners. With each thrust he shouted, "More!"

Marcus was beheaded last. When it was done, Quintus commanded the legionnaires, "More, damn you. Surely, there must be more Christians here. Kill them all, as well as anyone who dares try to protect them!"

For the Christians present that day, Satan manifested himself in copious forms, not the least of which was the person of Quintus Flavius Scipio, Supermunerarius in the Legions of Gaius Galerius Valerius Maximianus, Caesar of the Eastern Roman Empire. By noon, Christians and sympathizers in the crowd, totaling over one hundred souls, were martyred. Among them were twelve legionnaires who that day defended their Faith with a martyr's death.

III

Founded in 268 BC, Nicomedia lay 500 miles northwest of Antioch and 50 miles east of the Bosporus which connects the Black Sea with the Sea of Marmora then to the Aegean Sea beyond. Across the Bosporus was the ancient city of Byzantium (now modern Istanbul.) Nicomedia bears the name of its founder, a local king named Nicomedes, who made the city his capital and adorned it with monuments. The city's growth was later affected by Roman expansion. The Emperor Trajan built several public edifices in the city, including a senate house, an aqueduct, a forum, and several temples. Trajan also proposed an elaborate canal system to create another route from the Black Sea to the Sea of Marmora at the Gulf of Astacus.

From the first, Nicomedia was cursed with what became a tradition of treachery. Upon his father's death, Nicomedes seized control by murdering two of his brothers and exiling a third, who later waged an unsuccessful revolt. Sixty years later, rather than surrender at the end of the 2nd Punic War, the illustrious Hannibal chose exile in Nicomedia. When extradition to Rome became imminent, Hannibal committed suicide there.

For Christians living in the early Fourth Century, Nicomedia was the nearest place on earth to Hell. The treachery of Diocletianic persecution was especially gruesome in Nicomedia, where a great many Christians were martyred. Fully half of the city's population was Christian; indeed the palace itself was rife. Legends of Saints and Martyrs in Nicomedia during this period flourish in Church history and folklore.

December 4, 286 AD marks the death of a popular saint revered by Eastern and Western rite churches. She does not appear in the chronicles of the period, nor is she listed in St Jerome's martyrology, the oldest surviving list of Christian martyrs. Some say she lived near Nicomedia. Others say Egypt. Because of doubts about the source of her legend, she was removed from the liturgical calendar of the Roman rite in 1969 by Pope Paul VI.

She was the daughter of a rich pagan who kept her locked up in a tower in order to preserve her from the outside world. The girl, however, had secretly become a Christian. Her father orchestrated a marriage offer to a non-believer. When the girl spurned her father's offer, suspicious servants revealed her secret. A chain of intrigue ensued, including her escape, betrayal by a mountain shepherd and capture by her father. Finally, in a public display in Nicomedia, she was tortured and condemned to death by beheading. At his own request, her father executed the sentence. God's vengeance was swift. On his way home, the father was struck by lightning and his body consumed in flames. Until 1969, the Roman rite celebrated December 4th as St. Barbara's

Feast Day.

In December 302 AD, a mass murder of Christians occurred in Nicomedia on the feast day of the Nativity of Christ. About 20,000 Christians crammed the assembly to celebrate. The emperor sent his legions, who ordered the premises vacated and commanded the assembly to offer sacrifice to idols. If any were to refuse, the legionnaires had been ordered to burn the entire complex along with all who had resisted. The Bishop baptized the catechumens who were present, then communed with the congregation as their tormentors set fire to the church precinct. Legends vary as to the number of those who perished that day from 10,000 to all who were assembled. Regardless of the number, the event unbridled Diocletian's wrath. No longer content with eliminating Christians from the ranks of his Legions, he resolved to eradicate the faith entirely from the Empire. All Christians were fair game, especially the clergy.

In February 303, a series of edicts were issued throughout the Empire rescinding all legal rights of Christians and ordering universal compliance with traditional Roman religious practices including sacrifice to the Gods. Now, in the waning days of 303 AD, the legendary Lucian, Patriarch of the Antioch School, traveled to Nicomedia chained in a cart as Quintus' prize prisoner.

Over the next ten years, countless martyrs traveled to their deaths in Nicomedia, many of their own free will. The year before Lucian's execution, Archbishop Peter of Alexandria was martyred in 311 AD. Inspired by the death of their patriarch, 3,628 Christians of Alexandria traveled to Nicomedia to pronounce their faith and accept martyrdom. Their feast day is commemorated on September 2nd. The city that Diocletian envisioned as Hell on Earth for Christians was transformed instead into a Gateway to Heaven.

Diocletian's persecution was to be the last and most brutal persecution of Christians by the Roman Empire. The period from 303 AD to 313

AD was by far the most violent. By the end of the first year, even Quintus had had his fill.

With his prisoner in chains, Quintus entered Diocletian's court following Galerius' lead. He surveyed the gathering. Seated in the center of the entourage was an older man whose grey hair, beard and wrinkled complexion revealed an aging ruler, the Emperor of the Roman Empire, Caesar Gaius Aurelius Valerius Diocletianus Augustus. In stark juxtaposition, standing behind Diocletian was a youthful man of regal posture. His curly, sandy hair was close cropped, his skin pristine. His wide piercing eyes lay below a firm brow, flanking a prominent yet stately nose. The regal face was outlined by broad jaws and a cleft chin.

"That one looks more like an emperor than the old man!" thought Quintus.

Little did he know how prophetic his thoughts would prove. The 31 year old man standing behind Diocletian was indeed a future emperor, Flavius Valerius Aurelius Constantinus Augustus, the 57th Emperor of the Roman Empire.

Diocletian's robes were crafted of silk and gold. His shoes were studded with precious gems. Galerius knelt and kissed the hem of the emperor's robe. Quintus followed suit. After formal salutations were exchanged, a surprised Diocletian addressed Galerius, "Dear Caesar, I summoned you here for a private audience, but you do not come alone. Who, or what, pray tell, is this odd couple I see before me?"

"Dominus, before you is a loyal servant and a prize catch. Quintus Flavius Scipio is a Supernumerari in my Legion. Per your command, he has been faithfully purging Christian traitors from our Legion's ranks. Most notably, he executed a notorious officer, the traitor Sergius. He also captured the wretch who stands before you, the infamous Lucian of Antioch."

Galerius turned to Lucian, who was staring intently at Diocletian. "Foolish old man, do not look at the Emperor. Kneel and pay homage to the lord god before you!" Galerius commanded. Quintus kicked Lucian in his back, splaying him face down on the floor.

"I cannot," Lucian replied. Raising his eyes again to Diocletian's, he continued, "I am a Christian!"

Quintus struck a blow to the back of Lucian's head. "Enough of this, old man! You must do as you are ordered!"

"I cannot. I am a Christian!" Again he raised his eyes to those of Diocletian.

Before Quintus could strike again, Diocletian raised his hands and spoke. "Enough indeed!"

Turning to his praetorian guards, Diocletian commanded, "Imprison this insolent prize. No swift death for him. Let him rot, so that he may endure great anguish as he so lusts for glory. Find suitable quarters for this valiant Supernumerarius. Let him bask in the triumph of rewards for his faithful duty."

Standing, he ordered, "Be gone. Now. All of you. I wish to speak to Galerius in private." When they were alone, Diocletian motioned to Galerius, "Come. Let us walk in my garden."

Soon they were amidst a large vegetable garden. "Ah. Look at these sweet darlings." Gathering an armful of cabbages, Diocletian queried, "Far more regal than my robes don't you think?"

"I think not, lord," Galerius replied with a smile.

"Tell me. How shall I reward your loyal liege?"

"He has shared his wish with me."

"Go on." The comment piqued Diocletian's curiosity

"He wishes to return to battle."

"We have quieted the Sarmatians and Persians." Diocletian was even more inquisitive.

"Not Persia. He wishes to fight barbarians in Gaul."

"You would let him go? Is he not loyal to you?" Now, Diocletian's ire had been roused.

"He is my most trusted officer, almost to a fault. But he is a born warrior." Galerius recapped Quintus' Calvary exploits, his dedicated purge of Christians from the Legions' ranks and finally his encounter with the Persian scouts on the banks of the Euphrates. "Murdering Christians is beneath him. He is a warrior who wishes to die a warrior's death."

"Alas, I am an Emperor who wishes to die a farmer's death," Diocletian quipped, clutching the cabbage closer to his chest.

"Lord?" Galerius was astounded by the response.

Diocletian placed the cabbages on the path. "An Emperor's death is by the sword, most often by those closest to him. I have divided the Empire by choice so that I may retire by choice. Better to die as a farmer than through an act of betrayal. The time grows near. I plan to build a palace with a magnificent garden over-looking the sea in my homeland of Dalmatia. By design, you will succeed me and Constantinius Chlorus will succeed Maximian."

The shock left Galerius dumbfounded. Finally, he spoke, "Does Maximian know?"

"No. Only you. I summoned you here so that I might tell you first. Will you grant me my wish?"

Galerius paused, then dropped to his knees and kissed the hem of Diocletian's robe, "With honor, Dominus."

Pulling him to his feet, Diocletian said, "So be it then. Now, I will grant Quintus his wish. When I retire, young Constantine will be free to join his father in Gaul. It will be vital then to have servants loyal to you in key positions. I will assign your friend to Constantine's personal guards. Instruct him to stay very near to the young minion. This buck is a skilled commander with canny political instincts and must be watched."

He continued, "I leave in three days by ship to Rome. Maximian is preparing a grand celebration in December to celebrate the anniversary of the Tetrarchy. I will share my dream with him. You must stay here and prepare yourself".

"When lord?" Galerius asked.

"In due time. Today, I plant the seeds. The vines must ripen before the fruits might be harvested."

On 20 November 303 AD, Diocletian celebrated with Maximian the twentieth anniversary of his reign and the tenth anniversary of the Tetrarchy. Diocletian found the deference of Rome's populous lacking and cut short his stay. Perhaps their irreverence ratified his resolve.

The seeds of his reign had been planted on a hill three miles outside of Nicomedia, where he was first proclaimed Emperor. In May 305, on the same hill, his vine was harvested in the presence of his generals and troops in a ceremony where he passed the reigns to Galerius, becoming the first Roman Emperor to voluntarily abdicate his title. He traveled to a picturesque new palace he'd constructed for his retirement. It lay in a small harbor overlooking the Adriatic Sea. That same year, Quintus traveled to Gaul as Constantine's personal body guard. Both wishes had been fulfilled.

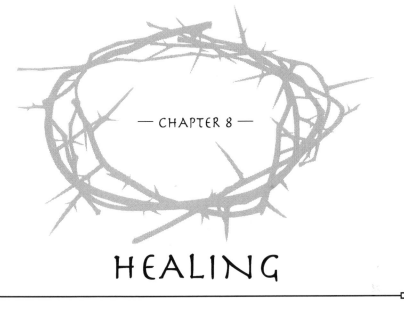

HEALING

I

Alone in the haze of dawn, Miriam entered Petra through the Roman Triumphal arch that spanned the entrance to the city. Petra was awakening for the day. Over the years, the Romans had built many free standing structures and buildings in Petra, but the city was marked by numerous unique structures that had been carved into it limestone cliffs since the city was first settled over nine centuries before. Each successive culture had built elaborate mazes of cisterns. The Romans continued the rock carving tradition, which included a theatre that could house 3000 spectators, as well as the Roman trademark of improved public water systems. In spite of Roman control, the city had a distinct Nabataean style. Although their influence was declining, the Nabataeans still maintained a degree of political independence. For most of its citizens, life in Petra went on unchanged.

Local Arab lore purports that Petra was the site where God gave the Israelites water when Moses struck his staff against a rock. Unbeknownst to Miriam, the site was also reputed to be the burial place of her namesake, Miriam, Moses' sister. She had arrived in a city teeming with varied cultural influences, but Miriam was inattentive to the uniqueness of her surroundings. Lupa had gone. Nothing remained to guide her, save for the unnerving nightmare she'd had the night before, about the crucified man, the seven caves and the children. It was the vision of the children that was most vivid.

Hastily, she passed through the city in search of a path that would lead her to the children. Just as the Roman centurion had described to her the day before, she found one; it was cut into a tight ravine as she exited the city. As in her dream, the ravine wound about and began to narrow. The walls on either side grew taller the further she traveled along. She prayed aloud to Yesua as she journeyed onward. Finally, the ravine opened, revealing seven caves in the hill beyond. She paused in the opening, searching for signs of life.

As Miriam surveyed the caves, she barely discerned two small figures in the shadows of one of them. With her walking staff in her right hand, Miriam outstretched both arms in a welcoming gesture. The two small figures emerged from the shadows, hand in hand. They made their way down the hill and across the opening and approached Miriam. A boy and a girl, both about Philip's age, greeted her.

"Welcome to our community, sister. What ails you?" asked the boy.

Miriam was dumbfounded. They two were identical to the pair she'd envisioned in her nightmare. A slight tremor gripped her body, raising the delicate hair on her arms and neck. She had not felt such a curious uneasiness since the day when the bloodied and confused Quintus had entered the bathing chamber.

Finally, she answered, "I suffer from a broken heart."

"In our community, we all suffer from a broken heart," spoke the girl, who continued, asking "but what ails you physically?"

"Only the pain of my heart, that alone."

"Then you should leave, lest you become like us. This is the community of the unclean."

Although their clothing was dirty and tattered, their skin appeared unblemished and pure. Miriam replied, "But you are not unclean."

"We will be."

"How do you know this?"

"Our parents told us. When they were young, they too were clean."

"And where are your parents now?"

The children turned and pointed to the cave from which a shrouded pair emerged. "We are the greeters. Our parents send us down here to warn the clean and to welcome the unclean. You must leave and find a cure for your ailment somewhere else."

"I think I shall search for it here. Take me to your parents. Please."

The modern day clinical name for leprosy is Hansen's disease. The book of Leviticus refers to it as "sara't," prescribing social banishment as both a hygienic precaution and a means of religious cleansing as well. For the Hebrews, it was not only a form of skin disease, but also a condition that could affect clothing and homes as well. The Greeks called it elephantiasis graecorum. St. Jerome's Vulgate translated the Old Testament word as "lepra."

Today, it is widely held that a genetic defect in the human cell's ability to mediate and neutralize opportunistic infections causes susceptibility to the disease. It is estimated that 95% of human beings are naturally immune. Contemporary research has also linked it to a region of DNA that involves Parkinson's disease, which suggests that the two disorders might be biochemically related. In developing countries, severe malnutrition in children has been linked to the degradation of this cell-mediated immunity, increasing the success of opportunistic diseases. Perhaps exacerbated by the effects of malnutrition, children are more likely to contract the disease than are adults. "Sara't" is not very contagious and has a long incubation period. Nevertheless, this mysterious disease was greatly feared in ancient times, when it was also thought to be highly contagious. Untreated, the disease's cruel progression leads to horrific disfigurement and prior the development of drug therapy in 1941, had been altogether incurable.

The primary symptoms are localized skin lesions. These lesions can be flat or raised, light or heavily pigmented. There is sensory loss in the area of the lesion and the peripheral nerves thicken. The final primary symptom is that the lesion is filled with acid-fast bacilli. Bacterial organisms that are not readily decolorized by acid staining are referred to as "acid fast." No such tests existed in Roman times. There were no herbal remedies or therapeutic measures. Nor were there any efforts to determine whether the disease was communicable. At various times throughout history, bathing in blood as well as the drinking of blood-based beverages enjoyed some popularity, as these were considered to be therapeutic. The blood of virgins, children, dogs and lambs in particular was used by various cultures as late as the 18th century.

Because no definitive test existed, other dermatological and neurological ailments such as psoriasis and elephantitis were often confused with sara't. To be outcast as "unclean" was condemnation to a forsaken life. Entire families were exiled, including those who were perfectly normal. Castaways had no means of livelihood. Healthy children were forced to beg. Communal living increased survival and provided the only grains of human dignity and kindness permitted.

Sixty-six souls communed together in the seven rock cliff caves on the outskirts of Petra. The community was multi-generational, with grandparents, parents and children. Ten families lived in the seven caves. Among them, only seventeen had leprosy. Another ten had a disorder that was confused with the disease. Six community members had no family members, but were welcomed and adopted by other families. Her life as a slave, although humiliating, had been sheltered. Miriam had never seen a leper, much less a community of unclean. Trepidation filled her spirit as she followed the children.

Miriam prayed silently over and over as she climbed the hill, "Yesua said, 'when you walk through the countryside and people receive you, eat what they serve you and heal the sick among them.'"

At the face of the cave, Miriam was greeted by the children's father, mother and paternal grandmother. The father suffered from symptoms of the advanced stages of the disease. The mother was still pure. The grandmother was blind and suffered from psoriasis. Her blindness was caused by a chronic infection of the eyelid named trachoma. Constant rubbing of the eyelid results in blindness over time. Both Horace and Cicero were blinded by this chronic disease. The grandmother's maladies were confused with that of her son's. Thus, their entire family had been banished from Petra. The girl, named Puella, was the same age as their son. Puella had been adopted by the family shortly after they first arrived at the community. She was the daughter of a single mother who had perished a year prior to their arrival.

The trio remained in the shadows of the cave. As Miriam and the children drew nearer, the father spoke. "Come no further, lest you be cursed by this affliction."

Without hesitation, Miriam responded, "Yesua says 'When you strip naked without being ashamed and take your clothes and put them under your feet like small children and trample them, then you will see the child of the living one and you will not be afraid.'"

She approached the father, placing the palm of her hand on his chest saying, "Be not afraid. Yesua is here."

Placing his hand, a three digit stump, over hers, the father replied, "I cannot find him. My spirit is cursed by this affliction."

Undaunted, Miriam replied, "Yesua says, 'Whoever blasphemes against the Father will be forgiven, and whoever blasphemes against the Son will be forgiven, but whoever blasphemes against the Holy Spirit will not be forgiven either on earth or in heaven.'"

Addressing the group, she continued with her lesson, "It is the Spirit of the Father and Son that is within you. It is sacred and holy. It is one and the same as the Father and Son. If you blaspheme the Spirit within, you will always be lost. Find peace with the Spirit within you, and all will be yours and the Father and Son will forgive you."

This strange young woman with the crescent shaped scar wearing tattered, blood-stained clothing had suddenly calmed all of their fears. Puella was immediately drawn to her, sensing the same motherly love that had been swept away from her years before. The two would soon form a lasting bond.

Later that day, the entire community shared the evening meal with Miriam. The servings were meager, but this caring young stranger filled the hunger within their souls as she shared her stories. Miriam's faith in Yesua was the most satisfying course. That night, she bedded with Puella's adopted family. It was only the second time that she had slept in a cave. The first had been the night she'd felt totally abandoned after her escape from Jerusalem. She'd shared the cave with Lupa. It was on that night that she had doubted Yesua the most. The memories of abandonment she felt that night kept her from sleeping. Quietly, a small body lay down beside her. It was Puella. Miriam rolled onto her side to face the girl. The two embraced. Peace was with them both as they slept together that night.

II

Nearly half of Petra's sixty-six was comprised of children, a quarter of whom had the disease. The healthy children who were old enough all left each morning to spend their day begging in the streets of Petra; there were sixteen in all, ranging in age from six to twelve. The blossoming adolescents remained in the community to assist the elders less out of duty than for protection, lest they be kidnapped and forced into prostitution.

Most often, the sixteen would split into groups of four. No more than three groups were ever in the city at one time and then only on the busiest of trading days. The children not only rotated days, but also rotated groups.

Rotating in groups increased their anonymity. Begging in groups afforded protection. Creating diversion was easier with a group. When their begging was unsuccessful, as sometimes happened, they would steal. Stealing, however, was much riskier. Artful diversion increased the odds of successful theft. On occasion, a child would fail to return to camp; such loss was always devastating to the community.

The children never begged for money. A homeless child with money had little purchasing power. Primarily, they begged for food. Occasionally they received rotting fruits, vegetables and stale bread. Most often, the richest cache was found at the end of the trading days, rummaging through discarded trash in competition with roaming packs of wild dogs. When they chanced upon anything of value, they would trade it for more food. Quantity was often more precious than quality, for many mouths needed feeding in the commune. Any money collected was saved for purchasing fresh water from public cisterns, one bucket at a time. The eldest children rotated this task. Good water was a limited commodity in the leper colony. The limited supply was usually spring fed and always scarce in the dry seasons.

The next morning, Miriam awoke to find Puella gone. Today was her rotation in Petra. Miriam spent the morning talking to others in the community. The more she learned, the greater grew her desire to help. She quickly determined that not unlike the children, her anonymity might prove valuable in finding resources within the city. What those resources might be remained unclear and could be determined only by spending time in Petra.

Around mid-day, she left the commune and returned to the cavernous path that she had traveled the day before. The path from Petra to the commune appeared to be straight forward. The return journey, however, was confusing, and branched into several alternative paths, making it unclear as to where the original path lay.

Invariably, Miriam made the incorrect choice at the first juncture. Another choice presented itself further down the path. Again, her decision drew her further and further away from the main path. As the caverns on either side of the path grew taller, darkness shrouded her view. Her footing became uncertain. She tapped the ground with her cruciform staff as she walked. She moved to one edge of the cavern wall to feel her way along as she stumbled forward. She anxiously tapped the path in front of her. She reached a low spot in the path. Suddenly, the sound of her staff against the canyon floor varied in its sound. Tapping again, she discovered what seemed to be a hollow spot beneath her feet. The overhanging ledge of the canyon walls made it impossible to see the ground below her feet.

She backed up slowly tapping as she retreated. The hollow tone changed to a thud. She moved forward again more cautiously than before, tapping left and right a she proceeded. She backed up again. Dropping to her knees, she hastily cleared the dirt path below her and revealed a stone lid about three feet square. The grooved lid was rife with debris. She tried, unsuccessfully, to clear away the debris. It was simply too dark to ascertain precisely what she had found, but it was clearly man-made and clearly too heavy for her to dislodge. Miriam sat back on her haunches. She started ripping her garment into a handful of small strips. Standing, she turned to retrace her steps. As she did so, she dropped the garment scraps along the ground. On her return trip to the commune, she retraced her steps, dropping a scrap of cloth at each junction in the path so as to mark the return trip. She would need Puella and several other children to remove the lid to the vault below.

The children returned after sundown. They always waited until dusk to return, and never did so via the main path. There were several less direct routes back. It seemed unlikely of course that anyone would want to visit a commune of the unclean. Everyone knew of the main path. Everyone knew where the journey ended. The alternate routes help the children maintain the veil of deception that they were homeless children who lived elsewhere. City dwellers had little interest in interactions with anyone from the commune, clean or unclean.

Life in leper colonies, although isolated, was often organized to an extent, particularly near larger population centers. In the more sophisticated colonies, governance structures existed to control trade and social interaction within and without the colony. Evidence suggests that some colonies even had their own currency. The Petra sixty-six was governed by a six member council comprised of the male elders from each family. Four of the families were fatherless and relied on the council for guidance. Each evening, the council would convene after a communal meal to divide the beggars' cache and discuss other communal business, including care for the sick.

Miriam's observations of the people she beheld, their spirits humbled, moved her deeply. That night, after the daily cache of food had been distributed, the senior elder rose and addressed Miriam.

"Before we discuss care for the sick, the council has asked me to speak with you on behalf of the community. Sweet woman, it is rare indeed that we find ourselves with a guest in our midst, especially one so kind and caring and this is why we must insist that you leave - tomorrow. This place is unclean. We are unclean. You must leave right away, before you, too, become unclean. It is not safe for you to be here," he said, his eyes beseeching hers.

Yet Miriam looked not at him, but instead she addressed the gathering as a whole. "I have spent most of my life in the cleanest of places, bathing an evil one who desired to wash from his flesh the sacred blood of martyrs. Although his flesh was clean, his spirit was not. Yesua says, 'Blessed are the pure in spirit, for they will inherit the kingdom of God.' Your spirits are clean, though your flesh is not."

She rose to her feet and stared intently at the council members. "I have lived most of my life in hell. I was raped by a demon. My child has its blood. Everyone I loved has been taken from me. Everyone who loved me has vanished. You look at your flesh and see filth. I look at your spirits and I see purity." Now louder, and at slower pace, she said, "You say this place is unsafe. I say this place…" she paused, bent to the ground and gathered a handful of soil, "this place," now pouring it out, she now shouted, "this place IS the kingdom of God! How could it possibly be unsafe for anyone?"

With that, she fell to knees, crying, then wailing. Everyone was silent for what seemed like an eternity. Finally, Puella knelt beside Miriam, gently molding her body to hers. Using the Latin name for mother she then whispered, "You are safe here, Mater! You are safe here with me."

No more was spoken that evening. The council leader waved his hands to dismiss the community. Puella and Miriam remained alone together, seated near the council fire. Overwhelmed by the memories of her life's tribulations, Miriam cried herself to sleep in Puella's embrace. There would be no more discussions concerning her departure.

III

Miriam woke Puella the next morning, whispering in her ear, "Puella, Puella, yesterday I found a treasure. Find three strong boys and meet me at the head of the path that leads to Petra." Puella and the three boys she'd invited, soon joined Miriam. "Come!" Miriam turned and hurried off, the four children in close pursuit. At the first junction, she stopped and picked up the scrap of cloth she'd purposefully left the day before. Following this pattern, the small group finally reached the destination of Miriam's discovery.

"This is a stone cover," Miriam said. "If we are able to clean these grooves, we should be able to grip it."

Frantically, all five crouched down and together scratched and clawed the dirt out of the furrows, which revealed four ample openings at its corners. Puella ordered her companions in a synchronized lift. It took several tries for them to dislodge the cover. The darkness of the cavern prevented them from seeing into the pit below. Puella dropped a stone into the pit. A splashing sound soon followed. Excited, they all exchanged hopeful looks. Miriam approached the pit and dipped her staff into the darkness. She rotated her staff as if stirring a pot. She dropped to her knees at the pit's edge. Cupping both hands, she reached down and brought a handful of water to her face. First, she smelled the water. Then, she tasted it.

"Water! This is fresh water!" she exclaimed. "We have discovered an ancient cistern with clean fresh water for the commune. Fresh water to drink. Fresh water in which to bathe. Fresh water to wash unclean flesh. My prayers have been answered."

Speaking as if she were alone, she said aloud, "Yesua, you sent me here to cleanse their bodies while their faith in You cleanses their spirit." Addressing the boys she said, "Your burden has been lightened by this gift from Yesua. No longer will you have to fetch and pay for fresh water for our community!"

Petra is sited in the midst of inhospitably arid land. It rains only in October and March, coming then only in torrential downpours. Before the Romans, Nabataean ingenuity created a system of riverbed dams, piping and cisterns to capture the water for re-use. The system incorporated terrace farming. After the Roman Emperor Trajan annexed the region in 106 AD, the Romans expanded dam construction to the north of the city, which subsequently developed even greater expanses of terraced farms, producing crops such as olives, grapes and wheat. Roman armies needed to be sustained and the Roman appetite for wealth and comfort often spawned corresponding prosperity in its garrison locations.

Such was the case for Petra, the southeastern-most outpost of the Empire. The extensive farming not only fed the Legions, but expanded trade in Petra as well. Agriculture and trade flourished for several centuries until a severe earthquake in the late 4th Century AD, from which Petra never recovered, decimated the region. On May 18th and 19th, 363 AD a series of earthquakes in the Dead Sea Transform Fault System wreaked havoc from Jerusalem to the Gulf of Aquaba. Bishop Cyril of Jerusalem chronicled that the earthquakes thwarted an effort to rebuild Solomon's Temple in Jerusalem and destroyed half of Petra.

Miriam had arrived in Petra at its zenith, sixty years prior to its catastrophic demise. She and the children had uncovered an ancient cistern, still active but unused. Miriam instructed the children to tell no one. Instead, she outlined a plan for how the water would be used. The children were to no longer bring fresh water from the public fountains, but to instead use this source solely for the community. Next, other than food, anything of value that they received would be given to Miriam. She would trade the valuables for materials to build a water system for collecting and routing water. The water would be channeled to a bath, which would also have to be constructed near the well.

"We will need lumber, ropes, clay pipes, fresh linens, oils......" she rambled. The one and only skill which she had learned in her life would now be put to the use of God's own work. The plan was launched that afternoon.

Before returning to the commune, the four children rendezvoused at the well site and gave Miriam everything of value that they had collected that day.

"What will you trade for first?" asked Puella.

"I will buy myself a new robe made of pure white linen," Miriam replied. The children laughed at the response, but their laughter quieted as they studied Miriam's expression. They realized that she was serious. Sensing their uneasiness, Miriam went on to explain. "My garments are stained with sacred blood." She continued with the story of the crucified man, of Lupa, of the mysterious footprints and how the dying shepherd girl was saved after being bathed with the cloth torn from her garment.

The children were stupefied by her stories. "We will divide this sacred garment into wash cloths to cleanse the community and shall teach them about Yesua's spirit. Just as my parents left in me the Faith, so too we will leave in them the Faith. That Faith will heal them. "

From that moment forth, the children accepted this mission as their sole purpose in life. One hundred yards below the well, the path took a sharp turn and opened into a small valley. Over time, under Miriam's direction, a small heated bathing pool was built there. Water was siphoned from the well into a clay piping system that not only fed the bath, but provided irrigation to a small vegetable garden. In her white linen robe, she would bathe each member of the commune with the sacred blood-stained rags. Repeating the chorus she had used as she'd gently cleansed the dying shepherd girl, she prayed again now, carefully tending their ravaged bodies. She retold Yesua's sayings and the stories of Yesua's life and works, his death and resurrection, just as her parents had taught her. At first, the baths were organized each morning for groups of ten. Saturday was preserved as the Sabbath, a day of solitude, contemplation and rest.

Every afternoon, Miriam would go to the public square in Petra. From the wooden shoulder harness that Puella had crafted for her, dangled two buckets of water, each drawn from the sacred well. In the square next to the public fountain, Miriam would kneel with the water before her and the sacred cloths drooped from the buckets' handles. The shoulder harness served a dual purpose. A hole was carved in the center to hold Miriam's cruciform staff. Puella worked the crowds searching for souls willing to have their feet washed in the sacred water.

Silhouetting a cross, dressed in pure white linens, customers were mesmerized by the aberration of an angel with a cherubic face marked with a crescent shaped scar. Her small hands gently massaged their feet with the water soaked sacred cloths. She always finished with a prayer, "Sweet Yesua may this kind soul find your spirit within him." Then, addressing the patron, she would say, "Kind sir, I care for the poor. Might you spare a coin to help me?" Her modest request was never denied.

The legionnaires left her alone, some out of respect, some out of indifference and some out of fear. Those most fearful were the secretly Christian legionnaires who dreaded inadvertent exposure should they associate with her. Accompanying this fear was their tremendous respect. As her popularity rose, Puella fashioned another shoulder harness for herself. Always addressing her as Mater, she never left Miriam's side. As time passed, lines formed in front of the pair as soon as they set up their wares. No matter how busy the day, miraculously, the buckets were never depleted.

The donated coins multiplied and Miriam used these funds to purchase seeds for the communal garden, for fresh-baked bread and new clean linen robes for all members of the commune. Over time, the health of the commune improved. Several souls were cured of their afflictions. Perhaps it was from the improved hygiene, or perhaps the improved nutritional value of their meals. Miriam attributed it to their Faith in Yesua. Just as Yesua told those whom he cured, she also told them, "Your Faith has healed you."

Through the years, her reputation grew. She became known to those who met her as Mater Miriam. The quiet Sabbaths transformed into a weekly ministry reserved for the city's sick, who would travel to the secluded valley to be cleansed physically and spiritually. Those unable to travel were brought there by friends or relations. The ritual Sabbath bathing of those who were unwell would be followed by a spiritual lesson; these were taught by Miriam. Although the clean and unclean remained physically segregated, Miriam's work opened the path to a spiritual bond that encompassed them all.

Puella and Miriam shared a bond as close as if they were mother and daughter. Their spiritual discussions were reminiscent of her talks with Philip, whose memory she held close to her heart. Each day she prayed for his safety. What was his fate? Were the merchants heartless enough to deliver him to that Roman garrison in exchange for another share of the blood money? Was he in contact with his demon father? Would his life without her lead to corruption? Would he stray from the path?

Mater Miriam prayed and wondered.

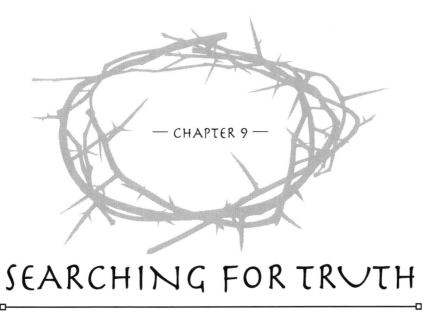

SEARCHING FOR TRUTH

I

Philip, Barnabas and the other children traveled south by caravan for two weeks along the Nile, where they encountered a canal that branched off to the west. They followed this canal until it terminated at a lake. To the boys' amazement, they had reached a teeming city known in ancient Egypt as Pr-Medjed. Astonished, they passed many public buildings, including temples to various gods. The city housed four public baths, a theater with seating capacity for 11,000, a hippodrome, a gymnasium, and two small ports on the canal.

After Alexander the Great's conquest of Egypt in 332 BC, the city was renamed Oxyrhynchus or "town of the sharp snouted fish." Under Greek and Roman rule, the city grew to be the third largest city in Egypt. Virtually no rain falls west of the Nile Valley in this region. The great Western Desert of Egypt abuts this oasis city. Over the centuries, its inhabitants used the arid desert land to the west as waste dumps. Wind-blown desert sands and the dry desert climate preserved these dumps, which have become one of the most significant archeological sites ever unearthed.

Nearly 70% of all papyri documents from antiquity ever discovered are from these well-preserved dumps. Because rule under the Greeks and Romans was extremely bureaucratic, most of the discoveries were of public records, census documents, certificates and licenses of all kinds. Periodically, the public records were purged of aging documents, which were gathered in wicker baskets and deposited in various desert waste sites.

Although most of the discoveries there have proved insignificant, nearly ten percent of the papyri yielded important archeological documents, including plays by Menander, fragments of Euclid's Elements, fragments of the Gospel of Thomas, as well as other early Christian writings. After the conversion of Egypt to Christianity, the city became famous for its Churches and Monasteries. To the Christian community, the city was known as Pemdje.

"What town is this?" Philip asked.

"Pemdje," replied the caravan leader.

"Pemdje? Pemdje? My mother was born in Pemdje!" Philip exclaimed.

"Do you have family here?" the leader asked.

"I don't know. My mother was an only child. My grandparents were martyred in a public display and she was sold into slavery."

"Let us settle at our destination. We will then try to help you find your family. If your grandparents were martyrs, their story will be known to many."

While it takes the brain a fraction of a second to process input from our senses, it takes nearly twelve years for our brain and central nervous system to develop fully. Learning is continuous from birth on. In a normal child, the processing of visual input begins immediately in the visual cortex. This region is one of the most powerful parts of the brain with over forty modules. On the other hand, the brain's other sensory processing region has twenty. From the very beginning, the brain begins to learn by associating memory tags to visual images, including colors.

In blind children, no such association takes place. While a blind child can recognize its hand through touch, there is no visual memory tag associated with it. With colors, the effect is acute. A blind child may hear the word, "white," but there is neither a sensory nor visual memory tag associated with the word.

The brain, however, is also amazingly resourceful. As a blind child develops, the brain adapts unused modules in the visual cortex to enhance input from other senses. Consequently, for those who are blind from birth, the non-visual senses are superior, enabling them to better spatially navigate in a non-visual world than those who might later become sightless. The non-visual senses develop to a much higher acuity in blind children, which is further stimulated by rocking motions of the body and head, giving the blind child greater spatial awareness regarding the location of where a sound or smell originates.

Philip's visual cortex had been dramatically roused. His visual learning process awakened. At times during his journey, this new stimulation was overwhelming. Often closing his eyes, he would retreat to temporary blindness for comfort, in particular, to memories of his mother.

Philip's mind raced. "Mother was an only child, yet she did mention cousins, some childhood friends. What were their names? What were their names? I can't remember. Please, Yesua, help me remember. Please."

As he prayed, Philip closed his eyes and began rocking back and forth, back and forth. As he rocked, he rubbed his eyes. These were habitual activities formed during his years of blindness. His father refused to tolerate this behavior, often commanding Miriam to remove the child from the bathing chamber when Philip exhibited such behavior. In her presence, Miriam tolerated this activity. Sometimes, Philip would lean his head backward, rolling it from side to side as he listened to the sound of his own voice. Her motherly instincts told her that this odd behavior somehow helped Philip cope in a sightless world.

As he rocked, Philip began to daydream of her. He could hear her soft voice speaking, "Philip, although you cannot see, there is yet a sixth sense that you possess that is the strongest of all. It is the Spirit within you. And when the Spirit of Yesua and your spirit are One, then you are One with all that there is; with God the creator, with the world around you, with those who believe. Before he was given up in the garden by his betrayer, Yesua prayed to his Father,

'The glory you gave me I gave them

So they may be One as We are One,
I in them and You in Me
So they may be made perfect as One
So the world may know that You sent Me
And loved them just as You have loved Me.'

"Yesua loves you. I love you," he heard her say.

Whispering aloud, Philip said, "I love you Mother. May the Spirit of Yesua be with you."

The caravan traveled with several mule drawn carts that afforded the boys the luxury of rotating between walking and riding. During this calming trance, Philip was sitting on a cart with Barnabas and three of the boys. The trance was broken when his auditory senses told him that his fellow travelers were staring at him. The quiet around him woke him. He stopped rocking and slowly opened his eyes to find Barnabas and the others staring at him. He sensed in them emotions of pity, curiosity and fear.

"Why do you do that?" one of the boys asked.

"What?" Philip replied.

"Rocking back and forth with your eyes closed."

"I used to be blind. I used to do this when I was nervous. It calms me down."

"Why are you nervous?" Barnabas asked.

"My mother told me that my grandparents were from Pemdje and they were martyred by Romans because they were Christians."

"Were they crucified?" another boy asked.

"No. My grandmother was tortured to death and my grandfather was beheaded."

"Is your mother here in Pemdje?" Barnabas asked with a curious smile.

"No. She was sold into slavery and sent far away into the desert. Her master was my father. My father separated us before this journey began. He sent her to a place I had never heard of before. He sent me to Alexandria."

"To be with Christians?" the first boy asked.

"No. I was rescued in Antioch by Brother Lucian, who brought me to you."

"Did your mother see her parents die?" Barnabas asked, this time more sullen.

Philip paused. "She saw her mother die, but not her father."

"How horrible!" Barnabas thought aloud. "Yet, how did she know that her father had been, er, well, decapitated?" He spoke this last softly, wincing as he said it.

"She heard it as she was being carried away by the Romans."

"She heard it?" another boy exclaimed. "What did it sound like?"

"Just like that day."

Barnabas leaned forward, then asked, both quietly and gently, "What day?"

"The miracle day. The day that … finally, I could see."

The boy's stopped their quizzing. The collective curiosity that had initiated the conversation had now given way to fear. As they had questioned him, Philips's voice had grown increasingly more monotonous and deliberate. Goose bumps had raced up the boys' arms. Philip closed his eyes and started to rock again. They watched him for what seemed an eternity. Within a short time, the rhythm of his rocking was in sync with the creaking of their wagon's wheels.

He went on rocking, but then spoke quite suddenly, although his voice, just barely above a whisper, was difficult to discern. "She told me, she told me that there'd been an eerie silence, and then she heard the sound of a cold metal sword, pulled swiftly from its sheath….. shwoosh…...a gruesome slapping sound as steel sliced flesh… then a slight thud…. and then a louder one."

He paused. "Just like that day. I could hear my father's sword slide from its sheath….the slapping sound of steel against flesh…just like she told me…..the slight thud followed by a larger one….just like she told me….just like she told me."

Stillness overcame the boys; it swallowed every noise. They had ceased to hear even the churning, clunking beat pounded out as the cart's wheels plodded on across the dirt road.

"Something rolled into my lap. Warm liquid sprayed my face, my shoulders and chest. I reached up immediately to rub my eyes, trying to clean them. When I opened them, I,… I could see. I could see! I turned to my mother and he was right there, standing above her, his sword drawn above her head. Panic swallowed me. Instantly, I knew, he was about to behead her! I leapt up, then raced between them, holding my hands high! 'I can see!' I screamed. 'Father, I can see!' My mother pulled me toward her, trying to protect me. She wiped my face clean. I saw her face only for a moment. The crescent scar she bore on her cheek, a scar she'd earned through her devotion to Yesua. She was a beautiful vision! Just as she felt beautiful to my touch, only more so! Then he yanked us apart, roughly, separating us.....intentionally, wanting to punish her.........to punish me.......to punish us both for our love of Yesua."

Silence reigned. Philip moved off to the nearest of the cart's corners, where he lay down in the fetal position amidst the dry straw scattered over the wagon bed. He pulled his robe up, over his head. Barnabas moved to be near him. From that moment on, Philip's withdrawal into himself was complete, with the exception of Barnabas. Philip rarely spoke to any of the other boys or to his elders, reserving his speech for Barnabas alone. Almost as it had been between Philip and his mother, Miriam, now Philip and Barnabas forged a singular bond and became near-constant companions to one another.

II

The caravan's destination was a Christian community situated on the outskirts of the town at the edge of the great western desert. The western desert had long been a favorite destination for hermits and religious zealots who pursued a life of self-denial and seclusion. The concept of religious communal living was rooted in Jewish traditions established several centuries before the birth of Yesua. The most notable of these groups were the Essenes, Nazarites and Therapeutae.

The Essenes were associated with Jewish aesthetical communities located in Qumran near the Dead Sea. Their communal society lasted from 200 BC to the first Century AD, which corresponds with the

Roman razing of Jerusalem and the subsequent great dispersion of the Jews throughout the Roman Empire. The Essenes were a mystical community who lived a ritualistic life studying mystical and apocalyptic Jewish writings of the period. Scholars attribute the authorship of the Dead Sea scrolls to the Essenes.

The Nazarite practices were prescribed by Moses in the Book of Leviticus and were very popular during the time of Yesua; these were segmented into two groups, those who practiced the Nazarite habits for life and those who vowed to the practices for limited, but intense periods of time. Their disciplined lives included strict rules for prayer, ritual sacrifice, punishment for defilement, refusal to cut their hair and abstinence from grapes and wine. Some believed that Yesua's cousin, John the Baptizer, had dedicated his life to Nazarite vows and that Yesua's 40 days and nights in the desert prior to His ministry exemplified the limited, but intense practices.

The Therapeutae were 1st Century Jewish aesthetics living in Egypt as hermits or communally in contemplative existence, practicing solitude, prayer, fasting and ritualistic cleansing. The earliest Christian monastics, "the desert monks of Egypt," sustained these esthetic traditions in both eremitic (solitude) and cenobitic (communal) lives. Not surprisingly, the father of Christian monasticism was an Egyptian holy man who pursued an eremitic life. Anthony the Great, also known as St. Anthony or Anthony of Egypt, is considered the Father of All Monks.

Anthony was born in 251 AD in Koma, just 35 miles north of Pemdje. His parents were wealthy landowners who died when he was eighteen years old. Orphaned along with him was his unwed sister. Anthony's conversion to Christianity soon followed, and the young man accepted Yesua, literally. He sold all of his earthly possessions, giving the proceeds to the poor. He placed his sister in a group home for Christian virgins. Anthony then became the disciple of a local hermit, dedicating his life to a primitive existence, seeking oneness with the divine Yesua.

Anthony's life was chronicled in 360 AD, four years after his death, by St Athanasius, bishop of Alexandria. Fourteen years later, the biography was translated into Latin by a Christian scholar in Antioch. As Christianity grew, this biography became one of the most renowned pieces of Christian literature and monastic lore. Athanasius depicted Anthony as an illiterate man wholly dedicated to a life of self-denial in barren, hostile environments, searching for complete oneness with the divine truth. Constantly beguiled by the devil, he lived alone in the Libyan Desert west of Alexandria for thirteen years, not as a nomad, but as a hermit living in deserted structures, caves and even a tomb. Anthony's longest period of isolation was in an abandoned remote Roman desert fort where he survived on meager sustenance brought to him by his followers. His only communication with the outside world was through a crevice in the fort's walls which his followers used to share food and listen to his advice.

The stories he shared of his tribulations with the devil were so heinous that many believed that he had gone mad. After years of reclusion, Anthony emerged from his self-imposed cell, sane, wise and revered. His legend, secured by his will and faith in Yesua, became a model for all, Anthony of Egypt, the Father of all Monks.

Anthony's biographer, Athanasius, was also an arch rival of Arius. The dispute between the two would become the most controversial Christian theological challenge of the era. Known for all times as the Arian controversy, this dispute ultimately defined the orthodox nature of Yesua' s divinity with the Trinity as the true nature of the Christian Godhead. Not surprisingly, Athanasius recounting of Anthony's life depicts this illiterate hermit's theological views in complete harmony with Athanasius' views. Athanasius' biography of Anthony recounts an occasion when Anthony returned to Alexandria to publicly renounce Arius' views as false.

Not all Christian communities shared Athanasius' view of Yesua's divinity. The Arian interpretation was widely accepted in Egypt.

Additionally, traditions and remnants of the Valentinian model of the godhead, complete with legends of the Aeons and the Demiurge, remained popular with the general Christian population.

Philip's new community was one that practiced the search for truth or "Gnosis" as the Greeks described it. These groups had no formal priesthood, or even leadership for that matter. Their cyclical lifestyle was one of contemplation, discovery, discourse and more contemplation. The responsibility for spiritual leadership rotated frequently within the group. Their search for truth was all-consuming. Ignorance replaced disobedience as the original sin. Personal interpretations of the meaning of Yesua's sacrificial life varied greatly from what was soon to become modern Christian Orthodoxy.

These groups were also keepers and scribes of popular Christian writings, including the written stories and sayings of Yesua. Eventually, these writings made their way to monastic communities brought there from the various regions of the Christian world that stretched from Britannia to India. As with any oral tradition that is transcribed over a long period of time, the perspective of the author, and the influences of local customs and culture, eventually steal their way in. Such was the case with the story of Yesua. Hellenistic, Hindu, Hebrew and nomadic traditions found their way into the stories. At no time in history was the story of Yesua and its meaning more diversely interpreted than in Philip's own.

Every disciple, including Mary Magdalene, had a gospel penned in their name, describing a uniquely personal relationship with Yesua. These gospels frequently twisted the story in favor of its namesake. The Gospel of Mary Magdalene depicts Peter as a bit of a buffoon and Mary as Yesua's favorite, whom he would often kiss on the lips. The Gospel of Thomas, a compilation of Yesua's sayings and teachings, was an early contender with the Gospel of John for the overriding spiritual interpretation. The story of the doubting Thomas is found only in the Gospel of John and nowhere else.

There is even a Gospel of Judas, which ends not with the crucifixion and resurrection, but with the betrayal. Judas is portrayed as Yesua's most beloved and trusted friend, so beloved that only Judas could be trusted to set in motion the fulfillment of Yesua's purpose Two Gnostic Gospels report that Judas did not commit suicide, but instead used the blood money to purchase a farm, where he later broke his neck in a farming accident. A Christian sect named the Sethians, adopted the Gospel of Judas as a favorite text, complete with the depiction of Yesua as an Aeon and the creation of the world by the Demiurge. This sect was named after Adam and Eve's third son, Seth, whom the sect believed was Christ himself and that Yesua was Seth reincarnate.

This was the world that Philip and the boys were entering as they passed through the gates of the compound. They were entering a loosely organized Gnostic community, whose members dedicated their existence to transcribing the mysterious and sacred teachings of Yesua.

Philip felt safe here in his ever deepening seclusion. As much as he tried to forget the nights sprouting fits of terror, Philips dreams morphed into constant nightmares, nightmares of visual flashes devoid of any continuity: flashes of colors, people and noises from the market; visions of his father, enraged, looming over Miriam with his bloody sword; flashes of wind-blown sails and raging winds from an angry sky; visions of strange hump-backed desert beasts, mules, carts and a blinding hot sun. His hyper-stimulated visual cortex dominated even his nights.

Rarely did he sleep through until dawn. It was only in the darkness of his cell, awake, or in his rocking trance, that he could recall his mother's gentleness, her touch, her sweet smell, her calming voice, the words she spoke. Words of love, of her love for him, of her love for Yesua. Yesua's love for them both, a love patient, gentle, forgiving and sacrificial. This is how she endured the cruelty in her life. Even though she feared Quintus' wrath, she prayed that Yesua would forgive him. Ironically, it was this thought precisely that she'd spoken aloud to Quintus during that ephemeral moment of weakness and need, which had triggered Philip's conception. It was almost as if Philip's conception had made incarnate the forgiving spirit of Yesua's love.

As time progressed, Philip's thirst for Yesua's words drove his daily life, searching for a spiritual connection to Miriam through the stories and sayings of Yesua. For Philip, this was a rebirth into a lifelong quest for the truth. With it came the greatest gift with which his sight had bequeathed him, the ability to read and to write the word of God. His hectic sighted journey from Rasafa to Pemdje brought him to the ideal place for his quest. As Miriam searched for water to cleanse the spirit of the Petra lepers, Philip searched for words to cleanse his spirit.

III

Its green triangular stem grows as high as fifteen feet, with sharp leaves and foot-long flowering clusters blooming at its tip. It is an aquatic plant that grows in abundance along the banks of the Nile River. Its stems were used to create mattresses, chairs and even light boats. The plant is named Cyperus papyrus. Its most famous product, as its name suggests, is papyrus, the choice writing material of antiquity. The addition of ink in the form of the written word, transformed the blank, plant-based papyrus into "papyri."

Under the watchful eye of a toothless elder, the boys were taught how to make papyrus. Only after mastering this essential craft would they learn both to read and to write. Philip and Barnabas worked together as a team. The other boys were likewise paired with one another. Between them was a long flat board. First, the boys removed the outside layer of the stem. They then sliced the inner layer of the plant into long strips which they squared at the end. The best pieces the stem yielded were those nearest to its center. Together, they placed these sections side by side with great care, striving to minimize gaps or overlays. When the first layer was complete, they carefully repeated the process, placing a second layer at right angles atop the first. The multilayer arrangement was then soaked in water and pressed under a flat, heavy rock for three weeks. Natural juices secreted by the plant congealed into a unique kind of glue, which served to tightly bind the layers together. The pressed sheets were then dried in the sun.

Once dried, the boys worked in silence on the painstaking process of preparing the papyrus for writing. They smoothed the rough spots out with shells. If the papyrus was rubbed excessively, the result would be a shinier and less absorptive surface, which would cause the ink to run. Lumps developed if the strips were poorly laid, or if too much liquid was absorbed by the papyrus. These irregularities were beaten smooth with a mallet. Unsightly spots were repaired by inserting repairs strips using a common paste. This repair process was tricky. Although invisible to the naked eye, if not executed precisely, patches were susceptible to runs of ink. Crafting papyrus was serious work, and far from a merely menial task. Few other teams of boys were able to replicate the excellence that Barnabas and Philip were able to achieve consistently. Philip and Barnabas achieved mastery learning a craft at which they both excelled.

For centuries, the Egyptians, Greeks and Romans produced a papyrus that had a superior writing side, and an inferior side, which while unsuitable for writing, was sturdier, and served to protect the document when rolled into a scroll. Yet in Coptic Egypt, process improvements resulted in a product that could be transcribed on both sides. The papyrus used for the transcription of sacred texts was folded and bound in leather or cloth for protection. This type of document is called a Codex.

Each night, the boys also assisted in preparing and serving the communal meal. After supping, the boys were permitted to remain and participate in communal prayers. Following these prayers, the elders would then discuss the spiritual and aesthetic mysteries of creation, Yesua and the sacred Spirit of God. Children were not allowed to participate in these discussions, but the most perceptive were able to move beyond merely understanding what the words meant, to a complex and nuanced appreciation of the narratives. Again, Philip excelled, with Barnabas closely behind. They had not yet, however, gone so far in their accomplishments as to read and write in Greek.

The most experienced scribes were fluent in other languages to varying degrees, and would translate writings penned in other languages, such as Greek or Syriac. Greek translation was the most complicated, since Greek words have multiple meanings that required contextual understanding for proper translation. The Greek word for love is one such example. The story of Yesua was one of complete sacrificial love, a nuance that could be captured in Greek, but could be misinterpreted when translated into other languages.

Depending on the scribe's prowess, these subtle nuances either might or might not be captured when translated into Coptic. Depending on the community, such as this Gnostic group, the search for truth discussed in their ritual discourses would also find its way into the interpretation and translation of phrases and concepts. Verbal traditions, especially about the nature of creation, also influenced interpretations.

Philip had fashioned a cloth pouch and necklace to keep his Greek Codex of the Gospel of Philip close to his heart. He leafed through the leather bound book each morning before prayers, and then again, by candle light, each night before sleeping. He wondered if he would ever understand the meanings of the words. This activity he kept very private, and was known only to Barnabas.

One morning, an elder entered the children's sleeping chamber and noticed Philip leafing through the leather bound Codex. Presuming that the boy had stolen a scared book, he snatched the precious text from Philip's desperate hands.

"Where did you get this?" The elder demanded.

Panicked, Philip was mute.

Again, he asked, "Who gave this to you?"

Again, there was no response. Philip had by now, though, scrambled to his feet, his arms outstretched, his hands trembling, in a supplicant and pleading gesture that anyone could discern clearly; "Return it. Please."

Barnabas raced swiftly to Philip's side. "It was given to him as a gift by Lucian of Antioch."

Stunned, the elder opened the Codex and saw that it was written in Greek. Addressing Philip, he asked, "Do you know the meaning of these words?"

The sniffling and teary-eyed Philip finally stuttered "Nnn….Nnn… No."

Abruptly, yet softly, the elder summoned them, "Walk with me now, both of you."

The trio found their way out to a courtyard. The boys followed the elder, walking arm in arm. Try as he might, Philip could not stop crying. Others were scattered individually throughout the courtyard, practicing morning devotion and meditation. Striving not to disturb them, the elder led the boys off to a more secluded area.

Again, the elder attempted to question Philip, yet to no avail. The boy could barely catch his breath between his sobs and sniffled tears. Turning to Barnabas, he asked him to relate his knowledge of the origins of the Greek Codex.

Barnabas recounted everything that he could recall of Philip's miraculous cure and journey to Pemdje from Rasafa. The elder listened intently, occasionally asking Barnabas to repeat parts of the story.

"So, ... Lucian of Antioch saved this boy from his murderous father?"

"Yes," Barnabas replied, as Philip nodded through his tears.

"Lucian of Antioch!" he said with awe. "That is something indeed. My, my, my."

Addressing Philip, he asked, "Did Lucian explain its meaning to you?"

It took a few minutes, but Philip mustered a deep breath, then answered, "He read passages to me every day as we voyaged. He read the entire story, yet I, ... it's difficult to remember most of it. And I can't, alas, I cannot read the words. I have been praying for a miracle, so I might read it."

"My son, your prayers have been answered. I am learned in Greek; I can translate it for you."

"But Brother, I don't want you to read it to me. Really, what I want is to be able to read it myself," Philip explained, surprising himself with this blunt assertion.

"And so you shall. If you would trust me with your precious gift for a few days, I will transcribe the codex into Coptic for you. Like the original, I will bind it in leather and return it with the original. You are beginning to understand Coptic, yes?"

Philip nodded.

The elder continued, "As you progress with your learning of our written language, you will be able to understand better the meaning of this book, its significance. As you read the translation, do come and see me if you have any questions, or if you wish to discuss what you've read," he offered, secure in knowing that Yesua, that God, approved.

He smiled, pleased to help the boy, and asked in conclusion, "Do you find this satisfactory?"

Philip smiled broadly in return, nodded, and uttered a barely audible, "yes."

"Now, do hurry my boys; we are late for our morning prayers. Off, now! You are both young and swift. I'll catch up! Now off!"

CHAPTER 10

TURNING POINT

I

History belongs to the future. Those who look back often cloud the truth with their beliefs. Even as life unfolds in the present, history is clouded by its backward looking participants. It has been said that history belongs to the victor. More accurately stated, "recent" history belongs to the victor. Over time, the story of what actually happened may be corrected, but never perfectly, for the past is forever viewed through the future's lens.

The Roman world was, in a sense, a form of militaristic capitalism for the few. With it came a materialistic thirst with all of its consequences, some good, some bad. In the Greco Roman world, the good was prolific. The foundations of literature, art, architecture, science and philosophy were all built by the Greeks. Upon this foundation, the Romans overlaid marvelous feats of engineering, robust urban development, international trade, and a codified legal system.

And the bad? Well, the bad was not uniquely Roman. It belonged to all cultures. The sins of the "flesh" have always been and will always be universal. What was uniquely Roman is that as they conquered, the Romans, for the most part, left intact the moral, ethical and religious beliefs of the conquered cultures. Aside from an allegiance to the

Empire and the certainty of tax collection, there was no evangelical attempt to "convert" the conquered. There was, however, a practice of extinction when a belief system threatened the peace and stability of the Empire. The destruction of Jerusalem after the Maccabean revolt was one such political act by the Romans against an unruly and troublesome culture at the edge of the Roman Empire.

In a purely historical sense, what was unique about the spread of Christianity was that, although rooted in Hebrew traditions, it quickly crossed all cultural boundaries, threatening to become a universal belief in the Roman Empire. Like all religions at the time, it delved deeply into the understanding of the spiritual realm, but as a spiritual overlay, it challenged the need for the material world that the Romans built and ruthlessly defended. Hence, the sporadic attempts at the extinction of Christianity across the span of three centuries.

The word "pagan" in contemporary theological circles paints an image of wayward souls practicing hedonistic life styles. To assume that all pagan believers lacked a sense of morality and spirituality clouds history through a Christian lens. The only broad assumption that is certain is that pagans were not true believers in Yesua. What are now deemed ritualistic pagan superstitions were in fact serious attempts by human beings to connect with the power of the spiritual realm. This distinction is a critical ingredient to understanding the lightning bolt that was about to strike the world of Yesua's believers.

Diocletian retired in 305 AD. By 311, Maximian, Galerius and Constantius were all dead. In less than a decade, the orderly succession from Caesar to Augustus that Diocletian planned had dissolved into the "Civil War of the Tetrarchy." The battle for the Western Empire took place on a late October day in 312 AD between the two competing Emperors, Constantine and his brother-in-law, Maxentius, at a strategic crossing of the Tiber River at the Milvian Bridge near Rome. What happened prior to the ensuing battle has been chronicled by several historians. The most famous account was that of the Christian historian, Eusebius of Caesarea, who described the event in his Historia Ecclesastica, the same Eusebius that Lucian visited on Philip's voyage to Alexandria. What Eusebius recounted would change the course of history, and concomitantly, Christianity, forever.

Some versions of the event report that it happened at sunset, others at sunrise. The recollections of what was seen in the sky also vary, but the outcome is consistent in every version. It has long since been debated whether the bond that was fused that day was political or spiritual, particularly from a Christian perspective. The Triumphal Arch that was constructed near the Coliseum in Rome to memorialize the events of the Civil War's victories indicates that an act of divine intervention was instrumental in the outcome, although the intervention of which deity is unclear. Through the lens of a pagan Roman general looking for a sign, a lasting union was nevertheless consummated.

The general's legions were in full battle order an hour before sunrise. Carefully perusing the sky, the augur traced a square on the ground and pointed slightly northeast above the rising sun and stepped away. It was the augur's duty to mark the spot for viewing, but not to interpret the signs. That responsibility belonged to the general. Constantine stepped into the square and studied the sky. Just above the rising sun, wispy clouds formed into an image of a cross. No doubt his adversary was studying the same sky.

Constantine turned to a Roman high priest standing behind him.

"What does that mean?"

"Death," replied the priest.

"Rather obvious isn't it," Constantine snapped, "Death for whom? Is this a good or a bad omen?"

The priest hesitated before proclaiming, "This is the sign of an impending battle. But it does not predict the outcome. It is neither a good nor a bad omen. It is merely a sign of things to come."

Just then, a horseman galloped into the group. It was Quintus. He had been out early, scouting the river and the position of Maxentius' army. As he dismounted, Quintus was shouting excitedly.

"Sire, the enemy has left their defensive position and is massing on this side of the river. They have partially destroyed the bridge behind them. The battle is here."

Maxentius was bringing the battle to him. It would prove to be a fatal decision. Still standing in the augur's square, Constantine turned back to the sunrise. The wind had changed the shape of the cross into what appeared to be letters.

Keeping his gaze on the sign, he shouted, "Can anyone tell me what this means?"

The Roman high priest was mute. A moment passed. Finally, a cohort commander spoke up. "Sire, that is a Christian symbol."

Knowing that many of his troops were loyal Christians, Constantine commanded, "Find a Christian priest who is traveling with the legions and bring him to me, quickly."

Constantine and his entourage of commanders stayed fixed on the sunrise, motionless for nearly twenty minutes. Finally, the messenger arrived with a local bishop who had been traveling with the camp followers.

Constantine glanced at the man briefly then said, "Tell me what that means," pointing to the wispy letters.

Without hesitation, the bishop replied, "Chi, Rho. Those are the first two Greek letters of my God and Savior, Yesua, whom we call the Christ. "

"And when you see that sign what does it tell you?"

"That all who believe will conquer death."

Constantine turned instantly and ordered the bishop, "Drop to your knees!"

Instinctively, Quintus grabbed the handle of his sword.

Constantine addressed the bishop, "Believer in Yesua, stay here and pray to your God that victory is ours." As he walked to his steed, Constantine pointed to the sky ordering his commanders, "Have that symbol painted on all of the men's shields and each cohort's labarum. Prepare the legions for battle."

II

Constantine's journey from being a hostage in the Emperor's court to being declared Emperor by his Legions was swift. Being raised as a hostage in Diocletian's court had its benefits. He received an education in Latin and Greek literature, as well as philosophy. His also witnessed first-hand the fury of the Diocletian persecution against the followers of Yesua. It was rumored that Constantine was an eye witness when the newly constructed Christian Church in Nicomedia was burned on February 23, 303 AD.

Undoubtedly, his most valuable education was learned in battle. Constantine fought in the Persian Wars in Syria under Diocletian and later in the Mesopotamian campaign under Galerius. He campaigned against barbarian incursions across the Danube. The student's military education was faultless. Constantine became one of Roman history's most noteworthy military geniuses.

According to some reports, after Diocletian's retirement seven years earlier in 305 AD, Constantine's father, Constantius, visited Galerius' court in early summer under the pretense of a courtly gesture and of respect for Diocletian's successor. Constantius was now Augustus in the West. Galerius was Augustus in the East. Realizing his son's perilous position in Galerius court, Constantius convinced Galerius to release Constantine to his father. Galerius granted the request after a long evening of drinking. Obviously, Constantius was aware of Galerius' lurid side and took advantage of it. Quintus and Constantine were among those present when the topic was raised by Constantius.

Turning to Constantine, his father asked, "What were the barbarians like on the Danube frontier?"

"Fair-haired and furious, father," Constantine answered.

Addressing Quintus, Constantius asked, "And you, what barbarians have you been slaying?"

Before he could reply, an amused Galerius wailed in reply "He has been fighting the worst kind. Christians. Those who refuse to fight back and then forgive him for death by his sword! He is so disturbed by them that he wishes to fight barbarians in Gaul!"

"This can be arranged," Constantius said. "There is an uprising by the Picts in Britannia."

The drunken Galerius leaned forward and slurred, "and what are those bastards like?"

Constantius replied, "Hairy, dirty and ferocious, part bear, part wolf. They paint their faces and bodies. When the engage in battle they howl like a pack wild beasts, hungry for blood. They most certainly will fight back and grant no forgiveness. I have seen them eat the beating hearts of their victims."

Intrigued, Galerius asked Quintus, "Are these the worthy opponents you seek??"

Quintus replied, "Perfect, but I prefer the taste of fresh liver."

This roused the group to a bout of infectious laughter.

Constantius mustered a comment between laughs, "What say you Galerius? How about these two returning with me to get a "taste" of the Picts?"

This brought another round of infections laughter. Almost in tears, Galerius rose to his feet, waiving his chalice and showering all with wine, "I, Augustus Galerius Maximianus hereby grant the release from my service the youths, Quintus and Constantine, to your servitude so that they may have a "taste" of the barbarians in Britannia."

With that, he stumbled out of the room to his sleeping chamber, laughing as he departed.

The next morning, before Galerius awoke, Constantius, Constantine and Quintus departed for Ebaoracum, modern day York in Britain. Their destination was built originally as a Roman Garrison in 71 AD, when the Roman IX Legion conquered the Brigantine tribal areas. The Legion constructed a wooden fort on flat ground near the confluence of the River Firth and River Ouse. It was eventually replaced by a stone structure that garrisoned the 6,000 strong IX Legion on a land area of fifty acres.

Over time, this proved insufficient in controlling the northern barbarian incursion. In 117 AD, the entire IX Legion mysteriously disappeared on a northern campaign to quell an uprising. The mystery of the IX Legion had a profound effect on Rome's strategy in Britannia.

In 122 AD, the emperor Hadrian ordered the construction of a defensive structure 90 miles north of Ebaoracum, which stretched 73 miles from east to west. The project took six years to complete. The structure was comprised of a series of berms and ditches capped by a tall wall. The Romans used indigenous materials to construct the wall. In the east, the wall measured 10 feet wide by 16 feet high, and was constructed of square stones. As the wall snaked further west past the River Irthing, turf replaced stone, and the wall thickened to 20 feet wide by 11 feet tall. As the Romans pushed further north, another wall was constructed across the middle of Scotland in the year 142AD. Its construction was commissioned by Hadrian's successor, the Emperor Antoninus Pius. This structure stretched 39 miles across Scotland at a location 100 miles north of Hadrian's Wall.

Both walls served several purposes: a deterrent for barbarian raiding parties, a means of toll collection and an awesome reminder of the power of Rome. To the northern tribes, however, these walls symbolized victory over the IX Legion and Rome's ensuing fears. Over the years, Roman Legions were pushed back to Hadrian's Wall, which fell into disrepair and required rebuilding under various emperors. Constantius rebuilt the walls to ward off the Picts.

This trip with Constantine and Quintus to the northern reaches of the Empire was Constantius' second campaign against the Picts, whom he pursued as far north as the Antonine Wall. Skirmishes had been occurring for several months along a 10 mile stretch of the wall, which was protected by 16 forts with a series of gated milecastle fortlets at regular intervals. An internal road paralleled the wall to support rapid troop deployment. Constantius deployed two legions, each 6,600 strong, along the 10 mile stretch. Constantius gave his son command of the elite First Century of the VI Legion. Constantine commanded sixty crack troops, which were deployed to the western-most fortlet, protecting the left flank.

A half mile north of the fortlet was a forest beyond a ravine that was hidden from view by the rolling terrain. This particular location had been the target of frequent raids by the Picts. Constantius was in search of the main Pict force and considered this forest a prime location. Each morning, a cavalry contingent of 10 to 12 men sortied into the forest to search for signs of the main force.

The enemy for which they searched was a confederation of Scottish tribes that lived north of the Forth and Clyde Rivers. The name "Pict "comes from the Latin word "pingere" which means "to paint," the

Roman term related specifically to barbaric tribes who painted their faces and bodies. The Picts mysteriously vanished from history in the early middle ages. What they called themselves and even their language remains a mystery. The sparse evidence of their culture has left them as the most enigmatic lost tribe of Europe. Nevertheless, Roman Emperors from Claudius to Constantius considered them a serious threat to the northern borders of the Roman Empire, regarding them as fiercely independent savages who refused to embrace the civilized world.

This day, accompanied by Quintus, Constantine led the scouting party. The group crossed the ravine and rallied at the edge of the forest by a large oak tree. Constantine divided the men into three squads. Quintus' squad headed west with orders from Constantine.

"Go to the edge of the horizon where I can still see you. Wait for my signal. Spread out as you look for signs of the enemy. As you search the forest, keep each other within view. Keep the sun in view. When the sun is highest, all will return to the forest edge. Make your way to this rendezvous point."

The forest was a jungle with limited paths. The squads moved as quietly as possible. On several occasions, the legionaries dismounted, leading their horses on foot. Constantine's squad was the first to return to the oak tree at the forest's edge. Ten minutes later, the eastern squad exited the forest and made their way to the rendezvous point. Eight of the twelve had returned safely without evidence of the enemy's whereabouts. The eight waited patiently, watching the forest edge on the western horizon. Twenty minutes passed. Constantine became uneasy.

Suddenly, the forest erupted in a mass exodus of birds that was followed by stands of deer and elk. There followed the unmistakably shrill battle cries of a large force on the run. A lone figure penetrated the forest edge and raced across the field toward the ravine. It was

Quintus. Close behind, in full battle paint, were a dozen Picts in hot pursuit. Constantine looked back to the edge of the forest. Sunlight glistened off of spears and battle axes like fire flies in the forest.

"Quickly, all of you! Back to the fort! Warn the First Cohort that the main force is here. Send a messenger to my father that the enemy is upon us," Constantine ordered.

Without hesitation, he turned his horse toward the ravine to save Quintus. Halfway there, Constantine saw Quintus disappear over the edge of the ravine. The pursuing barbarians were forty yards behind. As Quintus vanished, the Picts instinctively split into two groups, one west, the other east, so as to cut off his path. The odds were now improving.

Constantine had spent enough time with Quintus to know that he was a cunning warrior with sharp instincts. Quintus would come to him in hopes that someone was coming to his rescue. Constantine turned to the east. When the Picts breached the edge of the ravine, he chose a spot about 40 yards upstream and entered the ravine. As he galloped west through the stream, he saw Quintus, surrounded, flailing a long piece of timber to ward off the Pict's blows.

"Down, Quintus, down! Down, down, down..." he kept shouting as he galloped into the fray.

Quintus caught sight of the horseman and immediately dropped face-down into the stream bed. Constantine galloped over him, splaying the Picts as he passed. Instinctively, Quintus was on his feet in pursuit of the horseman. Constantine raced back toward Quintus and turned again as Quintus came along side, and pulled him up on the horse. The two breached the far side of the ravine just as the main force swarmed over the other side. The race for safety was on.

"Thank you sire! Those were some very hairy bastards indeed!" Quintus shouted.

Racing through the compound's gate, Constantine was off his mount before stopping, leaving Quintus with an awkward dismount. The moment he passed through the gate, Constantine was barking orders.

"Barricade the gate quickly! Waste nothing! It's a huge force! Archers, to the ramparts! Build fires to boil oil! Quickly! Quickly! Man the ballistae!"

The well-disciplined Roman legions anticipated his commands and most were already in action when Constantine arrived at the fortlet. He raced to the highest parapet with Quintus fast behind. The mass of Picts moved like an ocean wave, disappearing into the ravine and swelling up onto the field from the trough below. Constantine estimated that least a thousand men where charging the position.

Like its political and legal systems, Rome's military was highly structured and very successful. From the earliest days of the Republic, the army had followed the same tactical handbook for centuries; deviation was seldom exercised, let alone tolerated.

But success breeds success only if rewarded and rewarded behavior is self-reinforcing. Strict adherence to the army tactical handbook resulted in an exquisitely disciplined and loyal soldier who was rewarded with land and a pension for years of dedicated service. Compliance also increased the likelihood of survival. Survival in battle resulted in rewards from a grateful Empire.

The Romans preferred open field battle or long siege affairs. They excelled at both, but the Picts would engage in neither. For the most part, they avoided major engagements, preferring raids or guerrilla fighting in the forest. For Constantine, the trick would be to have them believe that his much smaller force could be annihilated. His goal was to keep them engaged for as long as possible. Constantine's mission that day was well rehearsed with his father. Hopefully, the ruse would work. It had thus far.

Constantius' army was 12,000 strong, consisting of two Legions. Each Legion was comprised of one hundred cohorts of sixty men each. Generals commanded Legions. Tribunes commanded cohorts and Centurions commanded centuries. Two hundred centuries were spread across a ten mile stretch of the wall. The strongest concentration of men was in the center, the weakest on the extreme flanks. Constantius hoped to lure the enemy from their forested lair toward either flank. Depending on the size of the enemy force, the flanks could be quickly reinforced. If overwhelmed, the Antonine fortlets offered protection for a swift retreat back to the main Roman force.

With the enemy engaged, Constantine faced a conundrum. Stay and fight, or retreat to safety? Sixty versus a thousand? They were not good odds, but if he retreated, so might the Picts. If he stayed, his position could be quickly overrun. Yet he was born to fight and so were the men of the elite First Century of the VI Legion. He knew that his father was near. If he could keep the Picts engaged long enough, Constantius would outflank the Picts and victory would surely be Rome's.

Constantine ordered, "Quintus take a messenger with you and instruct him to bring reinforcements from the forts to the east. You race on. Find my father and tell him what you've seen here and this morning in the forest. We will keep the Picts engaged."

"I cannot leave your side, sire!"

"Do as you are commanded! Hurry!"

Within minutes, the two horsemen disappeared over the Eastern horizon. Smoke from the fires at Constantine's camp alerted the fortlet to the east that the enemy had engaged. This spurred other battle fires, one after the other at other fortlets all along the wall. By now, the messenger sent earlier by Constantine at the forest's edge had reached the next fortlet to the east. The Second and Third Centuries manned this fortlet. The senior Centurion commanded the Second. He ordered legionnaires to battle stations and waited for further instructions from Constantine. The scout continued on so as to warn Constantius.

When Quintus and the second messenger arrived, the senior Centurion ordered the Third's Centurion, "Stay here and defend this position in case this is a feint. The Second will reinforce the First and Constantine. Join us when this position is reinforced."

With that, sixty legionnaires were quick-stepping west to the fray. The entire west flank was soon alive with battle fires, legionnaires quick-stepping west and messengers racing east. Quintus sprinted east, stopping only to change horses at every milecastle, passing quick-stepping troops as he raced ahead. The legionnaires running west replaced the fresh troops who remained behind. Two centuries relieved one, three relieved two and so forth, as the size of the reinforcing force grew.

Using the parallel road system, quick-stepping legionnaires in full battle gear could cover a mile in twenty minutes. Constantine would be reinforced by three cohorts of the most elite legionnaires in twenty minute increments over the next hour. Two hundred and forty legionnaires with superior weaponry could defend this position of the Antonine Wall for days.

As luck would have it, when Quintus arrived at the third milecastle, he met a scout sent there by Constantius who saw the smoke from the battle fire along the wall. The scout explained to Quintus that Constantine's father had crossed the ravine with two cohorts and two hundred cavalry this morning. They marched west toward Constantine's position. From earlier reconnaissance, the general was convinced that the Picts were somewhere between his position and Constantine's.

"Take me to Caesar, Constantine is engaged with the main Pict force. He is outnumbered by twenty to one and has barricaded himself at the fortlet."

The first scout sent at noon by Constantine had found Constantius earlier. By the time Quintus caught up with Constantius, his cohorts were already marching to the battle. Quintus' arrival was no surprise. Aware of the enemy's position, the general was expecting another messenger to inform him of the enemy's strength.

Constantius' strategy was to lure the enemy to the weakened unbalanced western flank, allowing a much stronger force to the east to outflank and surround the enemy. This was a tactic similar to that used on an open field battle, a maneuver referred to as "rolling up the line." To succeed today, Constantius had to commit the main force early, then move quickly to surprise the Picts.

Quintus found Constantius and detailed the morning's events. Quintus' scouting party discovered the main camp in a forest glen. The Picts were marshaled in battle formation. Quintus was surveying their strength when his party was discovered by roaming sentries. A skirmish ensued and his companions were killed. Quintus sprinted on foot to the forest's edge.

"Were you able to get an idea of their strength?" Constantius asked.

"At least twelve hundred. Maybe stronger," Quintus replied.

"Where is Constantine?"

"He and the First Cohort have barricaded themselves in the western most fortlet. At least three centuries are moving west to reinforce his position."

"What is the size of the attacking force?"

"At least one thousand. They move like a wave across the field." Quintus described their charge across the rolling terrain and the hidden ravine.

"Did you see reserve forces?"

"We could tell that some contingent remained at the edge of the forest, but we couldn't determine their strength. Based on the size of the first encountered, I would guess that there are several hundred men hidden within the forest in reserve.

"How close can we move to their position before being discovered?"

"Very close, sire. There is a steep hill that cuts off the enemy's view from the forest just to the east of the fortlet. The hill stretches across the field to the forest, but the enemy will have scouts to warn the main force."

"How well-traveled is the forest?"

The first scout asserted, "Sire, we surveyed the forest east of Quintus and Constantine. About one hundred yards into the forest, we crossed a path that paralleled the forest's edge. The forest and path continued east over the ridge, following the terrain."

"We also crossed the same path further west," Quintus added.

Addressing the cavalry's commander, he ordered, "Centurion, take your men into the forest as far east of the hill's crest as necessary to avoid detection. Find this path. Eliminate the scouts, then attack the reserve forces. Take these two scouts with you."

As Quintus prepared to leave, Constantius shouted, "Wait! Quintus! How did you escape?"

Quintus halted his mount and turned to reply, "Your son rescued me!" He then he galloped off to join the others.

At the fortlet, Constantine and the Picts were maneuvering for battle. The Picts massed at the crest of a large berm on the other side of a deep ditch that paralleled the wall. Constantine's First Cohort manned the ramparts with archers, cauldrons of hot oil and ballistae, which are large cross bow devices capable of projecting heavy, spear-length arrows over long distances.

The Picts stood on the opposing berm and were howling and beating their square wooden shields, all exquisitely adorned with carved Celtic symbols. They were excellent horsemen and often used two man chariots in battle, but the chariots had little success in early engagements with the Romans. The enemy before him was an infantry contingent armed with lances and a variety of short arms, including knives, daggers, short swords, and axes.

Constantine opened fire with six ballistae at the horde of screaming Picts, who responded en-masse by squatting low and raising their wooden shields above their heads. The shields offered no protection. In a moment, silence eclipsed the warrior's howls, and then deadly missiles shattered wooden shields. Unnerving screams of mortally wounded combatants filled the air. In a flash, the Picts retreated to the far slope of the berm, where they hugged the reverse incline. Twenty of their brethren lay dead or dying on the berm.

Twenty Roman archers launched a continuous barrage of high arcing arrows over the berm. Occasional screams followed. Constantine turned his attention to the boiling cauldrons positioned above the main gate.

"Stand ready at the gate. Archers stand ready. Prepare to repel," Constantine ordered.

No sooner had the order been given than the berm erupted with a hundred infantry with lances, all charging through the ditch and followed close behind by hundreds more with ladders and small arms. The lancers hurled their weapons at the archers hoping to delay their effects. A contingent of Picts protected by shields trudged a battering ram toward the main gate. The small armed infantry followed close behind, the lancers bracing their ladders against the walls. Weapons of all sorts were flying to and from the wall.

For the Picts, victory would be achieved by swiftly overwhelming the outmanned Romans along Constantine's defensive line. One thousand fearless warriors were in the ditch and now charging the wall. For Constantine, success could be achieved by continually reinforcing his troops. The Second was still in route. He ordered the ballistae fired at the turtle-like ramming contingent. Splintered shields went flying. The entire contraption fell to the ground. Before the ballistae could re-arm, fresh troops replaced the injured Picts. The turtle was back to life, inching toward the gate; this sequence continued until the ballistae lost their field of fire. The ram began rhythmically pounding the gate.

Legionnaires on the wall hurled back the enemy's lances at the Picts, who were trying to breach the wall. Several Picts had breached with little success against the elite First infantry, being tossed from the wall back into the trough below. More breached the wall on either flank. Hand to hand skirmishes whittled the defender's numbers.

The First was reduced to forty able legionnaires when Constantine ordered the boiling oil showered on the battering ram. Archers followed with fire-tipped arrows. The turtle like contraption, Picts included, erupted into flames. The smell of burning flesh filled the air. Flaming figures scurried around the base of the wall, screaming in pain, the acrid scent of seared flesh tortured the defender's nostrils.

From the forest came the warning sounding of horns signaling retreat, followed by Pict horsemen scattering onto the field in all directions. Quintus and the cavalry had successfully neutralized the scouts. Using the forest path, they rallied behind the Pict reserves and were routing them from the forest.

From the ramparts, Constantine watched the entire battle field erupt before him. The fleeing Pict reserves scattered into two groups, one west, one east. Flying from the forest in unison, the Roman cavalry galloped west in pursuit. The main tide of the Pict force was retreating back into the ravine toward the forest. No sooner had the eastward Pict cavalry disappeared over the hill's ridge than he caught sight of them sprinting back, followed by tightly organized double timing cohorts of Roman legionnaires. His father had arrived.

Constantine turned back to the southeast, looking for his reserves. The Second had just arrived. The Third appeared on the horizon. On the crest of the berm in front of the wall, a hundred Picts rallied to protect the main force's retreat.

Constantine shouted commands. "Open the gate! Open the gate! Ballistae on the berm. The rest of you, abandon the wall. Engage the enemy on the berm!"

The quick-stepping Second double timed as they passed through the gate and into the ditch, with Constantine and the remaining contingent of the First close behind. Spear-sized arrows from the ballistae whistled above them toward the Picts defending the berm. A fierce hand to hand skirmish ensued. While the Picts wielded axes, daggers and swords, the Romans conducted an ordered sweep of the crest behind a tight-knit wall of shields. Protected by this wall of shields trooped the most disciplined killing machine yet invented, the battle-hardened Roman legionnaire with his trusted sword, the glatti.

The Third Cohort's arrival spelled doom for the Picts on the berm. Total annihilation followed. Constantine regrouped his troops in tight formation and double timed to the ravine. One hundred twenty unscathed legionnaires advanced to the slaughter.

While Constantine was skirmishing on the berm, the first wave of retreating Picts breached the opposite side of the ravine, only to be greeted by a wall of shields and crimson clad cohorts. The ravine itself was blocked by Roman legionnaires to the east and the Roman cavalry to the west, which had turned to trap the main Pict force. The noose was tightening. As Constantine reached the ravine, he turned back to the wall to see more reinforcements spilling through the gate.

Confident that his position would soon be reinforced, Constantine grabbed the First Cohort's colors, hurled them into the ravine and chased down the slope. One hundred and twenty legionnaires under his command broke ranks, following his lead down the slope into the trapped barbarian horde. The emperor's son was in grave danger, and fighting ferociously. His father's cohorts broke ranks, swarming into the ravine from the opposing side. Amidst the bedlam, Constantine rallied troops to his side. Quickly, a crimson tide massed about him.

"Form up! Form up!" he shouted. "Push the enemy to your brothers at the ends of the ravine!"

As quickly as they had evaporated, two walls of tightly knit shields formed, methodically pushing the enemy east and west in the ravine as the vise closed. Reinforcements flanked the banks to prevent escape. The Pict force was trapped in the ravine. Constantius and his son could have slowly whittled their numbers and captured a large contingent, yet Constantine would have none of it. His resolve was for total annihilation, revenge for the lost IX Legion.

Victory this day was one of many that Constantius' Legions would inflict on the Picts during his second campaign against them. His son's calculated heroics won the day. The two pressed north after the Picts declaring final victory on 7 January 306. Constantius' Legions retired to Ebaoracum for the winter, but the winter was unkind to Constantius, who fell suddenly ill. At age 56, just 14 months after becoming Augustus, Constantius died on 25 July 306. The VI Legion of the Roman Empire proclaimed his son, Constantine, as Emperor.

III

Six years later, at the Milvian Bridge, as he walked to his steed, Constantine pointed to the sky and ordered his commanders, "Have that symbol painted on all of the men's shields and each cohort's labarum. Prepare the legions for battle!" The labarum was the Roman Legion's equivalent of a modern day flag. Draped over a cruciform stanchion crested by the Roman Eagle, it carried each cohort's colors into battle. Roman officers would frequently thrust the labarum into the midst of the enemy to rally the troops in battle, just as Constantine had done that day at the ravine.

Proclaimed Emperor in 306, it would take eighteen years for Constantine to consolidate the Roman Empire under his sole rule. There would be many battles on land and sea, consolidating first the West, then the East. For Constantine, the battle at the Milvian Bridge was no more crucial than any other battle necessary to consolidate the Empire. The outcome, however, was crucial in cementing the orthodox beliefs that define modern Christianity.

Just as the political events of Diocletian's persecutions in 284 AD marked the beginning of the Coptic Church in Egypt, the battle of the Milvian Bridge in 312 marked the Romanization of Christianity and for all intents and purposes, the beginning of the Roman Catholic Church.

On October 28, 312 AD, for the first time in history, an army marched into the battle under the banner of Christ with the belief that Yesua was on its side. For the first time in history, Christians were willing to kill in defending their faith. The Age of Martyrs was over. The hunted became the hunter. Conversion by the sword augmented conversion by the cross.

After crossing the bridge, Maxentius' Legions regrouped into a wedge formation with a strong center and weak flanks. His strategy was to break through his enemy's outmanned forces, turning Constantine's flanks toward the river. Constantine countered by strengthening his flanks and weakening his center. Each strategy was risky, depending on either line to hold their weakened positions as long as possible. Constantine entrusted the center to Quintus, who was now the commanding Tribune of the vaunted First Cohort of the VI Legion. The battle at the Antonine Wall six years earlier had established a lasting bond of trust between the two.

"Quintus, I will double our flanks and force the enemy to the river. The First Cohort will lead the center. You must hold the line until their flanks are destroyed. Victory is in your hands." Constantine galloped to the left flank to lead the charge. Rome and control of the Western Empire was the prize.

The armies began their assault with light skirmishes, hoping to force fatal movements by the other. Maxentius positioned his cavalry on the ends of his line to prevent outflanking by Constantine, who positioned his cavalry on the flanks to counter Maxentius. The gap between the armies closed slowly. Missiles from bastillae crisscrossed the lines as the opposing legions closed. Heavy infantry double-timed toward each other. The front ranks hurled their pila at the opposing line as legionnaires drew their swords.

Discipline prevailed on both sides as the opposing troops melded together. Great care was exercised in staying behind shields, stabbing thrusts from its protection when the enemy exposed himself. Both sides moved their lines in a checker board pattern, filling the gaps penetrated by the enemy with fresh reserves from the rear.

Quintus raced up and down the rear of his line, ordering troops into the gaps. "Hold the line, hold the line! Maintain your formation. Move back slowly. Move up. Fill that gap!"

Maxentius' main force was pushing Quintus' line slowly backwards. The thinning ranks were fighting hard to prevent a break through. As Maxentius pressed hard in the center, Constantine was overwhelming Maxentius' flanks, whose only retreat was to the river. The battle reached a crucial moment.

"We must hold! We must hold!" Quintus was frantic. His line was breaking. He could see Maxentius' flanks collapsing. "Hold the line! Hold the line! Maintain your formation!" The line was crumbling.

"I must do something," thought Quintus. He remembered the battle at ravine and Constantine's heroics. Galloping down the line, he grabbed the First Cohort's labarum and charged into the enemy's ranks.

"First Cohort! Follow me! Follow me" With labarum in hand, he raced through his ranks into the enemy's line. The First Cohort followed in a ferocious charge. At the same time, Constantine eliminated his opponent's flanks and was now attacking Maxentius' forces from both the left and the right.

The rout was on, led by Galerius' murderous henchman, Quintus Flavius Scipio, carrying the banner of Christ to victory, the irony lost to all who followed him!

Maxentius' forces collapsed in chaos. The center of the battlefield parted as Quintus galloped to the bridge. Maxentius was on the bridge, trying to retreat to the other side. Destruction of the bridge was intentional to prevent his Legions from retreating. The destruction, however, was incomplete. Scorched portions of the bridge remained, making passage treacherous. Maxentius' horse slowed to a cautious walk. As he sprinted onto the bridge, Quintus dropped the labarum. Drawing his dagger, Quintus leapt from his horse at Maxentius, knocking him from his perch onto remnants of scorched bridge decking. Maxentius' mount fell precariously between the decking and a cross beam. Quintus' mount was less fortunate, falling into the river below.

Maxentius lay dead with Quintus' dagger deep in his throat. Quintus' shoulder was dislocated. Disoriented, he rose to his knees, just as Maxentius' horse struggled to gain its footing. The horse reared back, falling on Quintus and breaking his arm, whilst destroying the fragile decking. Quintus, the horse, the decking and Maxentius' corpse fell together into the river below.

The horse broke its neck in the fall. Survival instincts took over as Quintus struggled to pull himself atop the dead horse. Successful, the living man and the inert horse floated down the river. Fractured in three places, spiked bone fragments protruded from Quintus' right arm. The pain was excruciating. Quintus passed out.

He woke in a haze of soft light filtered by tent fabric. The pain was still unbearable. He reached across his body to hold his right arm. It was gone, removed by a skillful Roman surgeon. The guard saw him wake and left the tent. When he returned, he was accompanied by Constantine, as well as an elderly woman.

"Am I alive?" Quintus asked.

"You, my friend, are alive. Your right arm, alas, is dead. It could not be saved," Constantine answered.

He continued, "Your bravery saved the day, Quintus. The First Cohort held the line. Your charge broke the enemy. The pretender, Maxentius, is extinguished by your hand. Thank you, brave Tribune, Quintus Flavius Scipio, commander of the First Cohort of the VI Legion of the Roman Empire!"

The haze cleared around him as he tried to remember the battle's events. Now he recognized the woman, whom he addressed, "My lady, how are you here?"

The woman replied, "We are in Rome. You have been unconscious for many days. Constantine entered the city in a triumphal march last week. I arrived yesterday. Rest now. Your recovery is most important."

The two left the tent, arm in arm. "He must be a very brave man," the woman said to Constantine.

"Brave indeed. Also cunning and vicious," he said.

"What will become of him now?" she asked.

"He will be your personal body guard," Constantine answered.

"Can a man so brutal and cunning be trusted?" she inquired.

"He is loyal to a fault. We are targets of much tyranny, and he knows how much I love you. He will protect you with his life."

"Do you know this for sure?" she queried further.

"I saved him in battle, personally. He owes me his life!"

The woman was Constantine's pious mother, Helena, who had been living in obscurity in Nicomedia. In spite of Constantius divorcing her, Helena never re-married. Constantine remained quietly devoted to his mother throughout the years. With his elevation to Augustus of the West, Constantine summoned her to his side and to public life in the imperial court, where she was appointed Augusta Imperatrix. With Quintus by her side, she would use her powers to unearth relics and holy places of Christian history.

Quintus slipped back into a deep sleep. In his dreams, he returned to the days he'd devoted to persecuting Christians. The dreams were vivid reprisals of the past. The dead returned to life: the beheaded woman; her crucified son; those slaughtered in the market square, and also Sergius. They were all together, crowded behind Miriam and Philip, who sat together before him, arm in arm, bloodied and trembling. Next to Quintus stood his elegant white Persian horse with its blood stained legs.

The beheaded stood with their heads in their hands, eyes fixed on Quintus. They spoke in unison. "I forgive you. I forgive you. I forgive you." At first they whispered. Their voices grew louder until they were chanting, "We forgive you. We forgive you. We forgive you!"

Out of the crowd raced the toothless troll with his robe raised, erection in his hand. He jumped up and down as he circled Quintus, laughing and singing, "They forgive you, They forgive you, They forgive you! Hahaha!!!!"

Quintus closed his eyes and covered his ears, yet the visions persisted and the voices grew louder. In hopes of escaping, he mounted his horse and galloped away. He was in a city. The faster he rode, the louder the chanting. He turned his stallion onto a cobbled street and climbed a steep hill. In front of him was a procession of soldiers, guarding a man bearing a cross and followed by a solitary woman. As he galloped toward them, he drew his sword. Using the flat side of his sword, he swatted the back of the man's head, driving him face down onto the road. As part of the man's torture, the soldiers had outfitted the man with a crown of thorns. The blows drove the thorns through the man's eyebrows, just above his temple.

Quintus stopped at the top of the hill. Turning back, he reared the stallion on its hind legs and thrust his sword to the sun. The sun's reflection cast a brilliant cross down the gabled street below and across the bloody scene.

The man was on his knees with arms outstretched, pronouncing, "I forgive you, I forgive you, I forgive you!"

Beside the man and on her knees was Miriam, who was cleaning the man's bloodied face. As she turned to Quintus, she pointed to the man and said, "Yesua forgives you! Yesua forgives you!"

Quintus awoke from the nightmare in a cold sweat, completing her chant, "Yesua forgives you!"

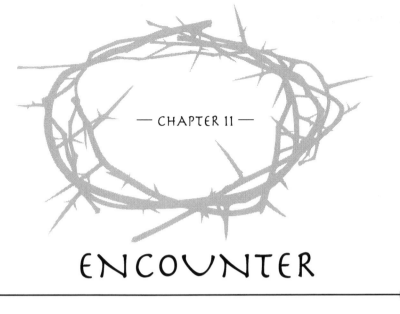

CHAPTER 11

ENCOUNTER

I

The hill was silent that day. Miriam woke to a bright sunrise. The sky was clear. Miriam and Lupa were alone. They were on the hill crest where the man was crucified. Lupa was on her feet, nudging Miriam to rise. Lupa turned and trotted down the hill toward the temple. Miriam rose to follow. The bloody scene was washed clean by an earlier storm. She saw no evidence of the fallen man as she followed Lupa down the street. When they reached the temple precinct, Lupa raced ahead up the stairs leading to the entry portico. Sniffing the ground, she paced excitedly around the portico landing.

Miriam followed her up the steps to the entrance. There, on the portico floor, were bloody footsteps. A burst of energy charged through Miriam as she hurried her pace in search of the man. The footsteps led beyond the center of the sanctuary to a dark alcove. Miriam stared into the darkness where she could see a faint outline in the shadows. It was the man.

Miriam spoke first, "You abandoned me after I cared for your broken body."

A voice said, "I will never leave you. I am in you and you are in me."

It was her father's voice. Trembling, she thought, "It can't be." She had watched as the man was beaten and murdered. She'd held his bloodied body in her arms. That man was not her father.

"Are you Yesua, the Christ?" she asked.

"You have said it," the man replied.

"My parents and my son have been taken from me. I gave you my whole life, my very being, body and soul. Why do you keep abandoning me?"

Deep from the shadows, the man spoke, "You cannot be my disciple, unless you love me more than you love your father and mother, and your child. You cannot come with me unless you love me more than you love your own life. You cannot be my disciple unless you carry your own cross and come with me."

"When will this all end?" she cried.

"You cannot deny me, for I am in you and you are in Me, just as I am in them and they are in Me. Our Spirit, Our Love is eternal. To deny Me is to deny eternity. The journey ends where it begins, with Me. With them, One in being together."

From the shadows the man's silhouette illuminated into a pure, white, incandescent aurora and then vanished, leaving only darkness.

"The journey ends where it begins." She repeated his words over and over. "The journey ends where it begins." She wondered, "What does that mean? What am I to do? Where am I to go?"

She turned toward the portico. There, silhouetted against the morning sun, was Lupa. The animal stood patiently, waiting instructions.

"My sweet Lupa, lead us to Pemdje." Lupa turned and disappeared down the steps.

In her exile, Miriam was haunted by dreams of the crucified man, which invariably shook her from sleep. Tonight was no different. At the exact moment that Quintus was shaken from his nightmare, Miriam was roused from hers. As she oriented herself to her surroundings, she was haunted by the dream.

"Where does the journey end?" she thought.

"It ends where it begins. It ends where it begins," she whispered.

The night was dark and clear. The sky was star-filled. A full moon rested on the cavernous crest above. A lone wolf trotted on the crest toward the moon. Perfectly silhouetted in front of the moon, the wolf sat on its hind legs, stretched its head to the sky, and began to howl.

Miriam studied the scene, then whispered, "My sweet Lupa, lead us to Pemdje." As if the wolf could hear her voice, it disappeared over the horizon. Miriam lay awake throughout the night.

The next morning, Puella and Miriam went into the city. They walked in silence. Puella could feel Miriam's tension. When they reached the square, Miriam set up her bathing station while Puella worked the early morning crowd. For nine years, Miriam bathed the feet of strangers and ministered to the lepers. At age nineteen, Puella was now a woman.

Many of the strangers were merchants who regularly traveled the King's Highway. Over the years, her reputation grew as Mater Miriam "guardian of the traveler." Her foot baths and spiritual blessings were considered essential for good luck, making Puella's work of finding customers nearly effortless.

One of Miriam's regular customers was a Christian merchant from Petra who frequented Jerusalem in his travels. Whenever he traveled, he would visit Miriam, receiving her blessings both before he departed and after he returned.

"Where does your journey's take you this trip, sir," she asked as she gently washed his feet.

"The Holy City."

"Do you know the City well?"

"Very well."

Miriam described the cobbled road near the temple leading to the hill where she saw the man crucified.

"I know the place. Why do you ask?" Curious question, he thought.

"Can you take my companion with you and leave her there?"

Strange request he thought. "Again, may I ask why?"

"It is time for her to start her journey. I can think of no better place from which to begin."

"My caravan leaves in an hour. Have her meet me here." He smiled lovingly.

Twenty minutes later, Puella returned with several customers. Praying for their safety, Miriam bathed the travelers' feet. A lull in activity followed. Puella and Miriam were alone. Puella could feel Miriam's tension even more acutely now than she had earlier.

"Mater Miriam, what bothers you?" Puella asked.

Miriam broke her silence, "Do you know the man named Simon of Petra, the merchant who visits me frequently?"

"Yes, has he done something to you?" The bond between the two, as strong as between mother and daughter, had grown still closer as the years had passed.

"No, my child. He is a kind, generous, Christian man. He has been our most loyal benefactor, rewarding us handsomely upon his safe return to Petra. From his generosity much good has come to our commune." Miriam's voice revealed a touch of melancholy.

"What then? What makes you so sad?"

"I must leave this place."

"Why? What has happened?"

Miriam described her dream to Puella. Puella knew the story of the crucified man well. She knew also that the rags that she used to wash the feet of the weary and the souls of the sick were soaked with the man's blood. She knew the event held a powerful influence over Miriam.

"What does this mean?" Puella thought to herself.

As if reading her mind, Miriam said, "I must finish my journey where it began. I am leaving today for Pemdje."

"With Simon, the merchant?"

"No, he is going to Jerusalem. I will find another merchant caravan that is traveling to Egypt."

"I will go with you."

"No. You will go with Simon to Jerusalem."

"What? Why? No. You are the only mother I have ever known. My brothers and sisters are here. Why must we be separated? Why?" she pleaded.

Miriam quoted Yesua, saying, "You cannot be my disciple, unless you love Me more than you love your father and mother, and your brothers and sisters. You cannot come with Me unless you love Me more than you love your own life. You cannot be my disciple unless you carry your own cross and come with me."

Continuing, she told Puella, "Go to the Holy City. Go to the place where I held the crucified man. Find your cross. Take it up. Begin your journey."

"But…" Miriam interrupted her by raising her palm, saying nothing aloud, but conveying everything.

By sundown, each was on her way. Before parting, Miriam gave Puella a handful of rags from her blood soaked garment.

"Heal the sick!" were her parting words.

Miriam found safe passage on a caravan destined for Alexandria. During her journey, the cruel words Quintus had spoken nine years earlier scorched her memory.

"Take this boy to the military commander of the Roman Garrison in Alexandria. Here are 50 denarii for your trouble. This note bears instructions to give you another 100 denarii when you deliver the boy. The commander is a friend of mine. He knows my seal. He will honor my word."

"Did Philip arrive safely at the garrison? What had become of him? Slave, or soldier? Had they turned him into a murderer, like his father? Worse yet, had the demon father found the child?" she wondered.

As she traveled, thoughts of Philip consumed her. Her life with Puella had eased the pain of separation, but now Puella was gone, too. Throughout the trip, her mind was pummeled with words from the past.

"You will never see your son again. My Roman brethren in Aelia Capitolina will be far less tolerant than I have been."

"You cannot be my disciple, unless you love me more than you love your father and mother, and your son."

"God's love will save you. Yesua says, 'Ask for forgiveness and you shall receive.'"

"You cannot deny me for I am in you and You are in me."

"Father, father……I can see!"

"Take this boy to the military commander of the Roman Garrison in Alexandria."

Her inner dialogue raced. "Was Pemdje where it all started? Is this where the end meets the beginning? Or was it Rasafa? No, not Rasafa. There is nothing there. What did the dream mean? He speaks to me in dreams. What he says comes to be. Why can't I understand? It ends where it begins. Whose beginning? Whose end? Mine? Philip's? Is Philip looking for me? Should I have gone to Jerusalem?"

Her faith was riddled with doubt. Doubt, Faith's cancer, was consuming her soul. "I am abandoned again. Send me a sign. Send me Lupa to show me the way. There must be a sign in Alexandria. Philip is there. Will we be reunited there? Shall we end as we began, one in being? Yes. Yes. He must be there."

II

Miriam's journey led to a Christian community that was still recovering from the Martyrdom of its beloved bishop, Pope Peter of Alexandria. Peter became the 17th Pope and Patriarch of the See of St Mark in 300 AD. As he devoted his life to protecting his flock from the physical scourge of Diocletian's persecution, Peter staunchly defended them from spiritual controversies that had been festering amongst Christian theologians for decades.

More than once during his papacy, Peter had fallen victim to imprisonment. Legend reports that he was once imprisoned with Bishop Meletius of Lycropolis. During their imprisonment, Peter and Meletius descended into a violent argument over believers who compromised their Faith to save themselves by offering pagan sacrifices or surrendering sacred books to their persecutors. Peter favored forgiveness, but Meletius argued that those followers had strayed and therefore, must be re-baptized. The argument ended abruptly when Peter hung a sheet between the two for the remainder of their captivity. But the most controversial spiritual teachings confronting Peter were those of Lucian's student, Arius, concerning the nature of Yesua's divinity. It was in Alexandria that the controversy brewed hottest. In 311 AD, Pope Peter of Alexandria excommunicated Arius.

In the fall of that year, the beloved Pope Peter was captured again by the Romans. A large crowd of believers stormed the prison, hoping to save their Patriarch. Riot and an impending massacre loomed. To save his followers from a similar fate, Peter arranged a secret pact with his captors to fake an escape and thus disperse the crowd.

Still captive, but secluded from the crowd, Pope Peter willingly accepted his fate. Kneeling, he removed his shoulder vestment and said peacefully, "Do as you have been commanded." His calmness troubled the soldiers. None were willing to serve as executioner. Knowing this was not an option, a member of the group suggested that they each contribute five denarii to a pool so as to entice one among them to perform the deed; there were then six legionnaires present. The scheme of offering a reward had worked. Executing their orders, the beloved Patriarch of Alexander was beheaded for 25 denarii in blood money.

On 29 November 311 AD, Pope Peter of Alexandria became the martyred St. Peter of Alexandria. When his flock heard the news, 3,628 Christians from Alexandria traveled to Nicomedia to pronounce their faith and accept martyrdom. Their feast day is commemorated on September 2nd. They accepted martyrdom one month before Constantine's conversion at the Battle of the Milvian Bridge.

When Miriam reached Alexandria, she abandoned the missionary zeal she had exercised in Petra, replacing it with an obsessive search for her lost son in a teeming city of 700,000 inhabitants.

"Where shall I begin?" Her only knowledge of Alexandria came from the story of St. Mark, as told to her by her parents.

That oral tradition taught her that Mark was born in Libya and moved to Jerusalem, where he and his cousin became disciples of Yesua. His given name was John Mark. His cousin, later named Barnabas, was also a disciple. Barnabas was a Cypriot Jew named Joseph who migrated to Jerusalem, sold his farm and belongings, and followed Yesua. Mark's mother, Mary, lived in a home near the Garden of Gethsemane. As one of the seventy disciples, Mark knew Yesua well and may have been present when Yesua was betrayed. Miriam remembered a story told by her mother that after His Resurrection, Yesua appeared to a gathering of disciples at Mark's mother's home, which was a frequent gathering place for Yesua's followers after the crucifixion.

Miriam learned that Barnabas introduced Paul to the other disciples after Yesua appeared to Paul. As the disciples crafted their missionary strategy, Barnabas, Mark and Paul agreed to convert the Gentiles. Paul and Barnabas established many churches in Asia Minor. Barnabas established the Church in his native Cyprus. Sometime around 50 AD, Mark established the first Egyptian Christian church in Alexandria, one of the three original episcopal sees of Christianity.

After his successful missions in Egypt, Mark traveled with Peter to Rome as a companion and interpreter. The Christian converts in Rome urged Peter, their first Bishop, to memorialize in writing his inspiring stories of Yesua. While in Rome, sometime between 60 and 63 AD, St. Mark the Evangelist wrote his Gospel in Greek, which is generally considered Peter's story of Yesua's life.

While Mark was authoring his gospel, Barnabas returned to Cyprus, where he was martyred by pagans in 61 AD. Three years later, on a hot, windy summer night in July 64 AD, a fire broke out in a merchant district in Rome. Fueled by the summer winds, the fire burned six days and seven nights, destroying seventy percent of the Imperial City. The angry citizens of Rome blamed Nero.

Looking for a scapegoat, Nero blamed the Christians, launching the first of ten persecutions by the Roman Empire. After the fire, Nero rounded up a band of Christians and literally fed them to lions as a public spectacle in the city's only remaining amphitheater.

This tragedy started a 249 year cycle of concerted persecutions by the Roman Empire. During that period, the Christians experienced 129 years of horror with 120 years of intermittent, but fragile peace. During the same time, no less than 50 Emperors ruled the Empire.

Had it not been for the tenuous state of the Imperial government, the persecutions could have been more devastating. Being a Roman Emperor proved almost as treacherous as being a Christian.

For Miriam, the history of Christianity was dominated by violence, most of which she experienced firsthand. Nero's vicious persecution of Christians lasted four years, from 64AD - 68AD. With nowhere to live, Rome's Christians, hunted by the pagan population, resorted to hiding below ground in the earth's bowels. Mark returned to Egypt to protect his flock in Africa. Peter and Paul were captured in Rome.

At his insistence, Peter was crucified upside down. The ordeal lasted three days. On Peter's last day, Paul was beheaded in the streets of Rome. The Apostles Peter and Paul became martyred saints on 29 June 67 AD. The faithful retrieved the bodies and hid them together in a temporary grave in the Catacombs.

In his absence, grateful Christians in Alexandria erected a church in the Baucalis district in Mark's honor. On 25 April 68 AD, Mark was celebrating the Liturgy in the Baucalis church, when the ceremony was interrupted by a crowd of pagans. They dragged Mark from the Church and beheaded him in the street nearby.

Like Yesua before him, he accepted his fate willingly, begging Yesua to forgive them for their act. As with the aftermath of Yesua's death, a violent thunderstorm erupted, and was then followed by an earthquake.

The frightened crowd dispersed, allowing Mark's followers to recover his body, which they buried in a crypt under the Church.

"The Church," Miriam thought. "I will find the Church. If Philip survived, someone there will know the story of the blind child who was miraculously cured by the blood of a beheaded martyr."

III

Finding the Church was easy. Finding people willing to listen to her story proved more difficult. First, she tried questioning people as they left the church. Few stopped and still fewer listened. Those who bothered to hear her out thought her story a bit far-fetched. Several kind and patient followers stopped to listen to her story every time they left the Church. The story was always the same. Miriam's resolve had now morphed into obsession. Thinking she was a beggar, some donated money to her, which she used for sustenance. Others thought she was possessed by demons and prayed over her.

Her story ended the same way every time. "Tell as many as you can; someone will know him. He can find me here waiting." For six months, she stayed at the Church day and night, existing on meager donations of food from Church members. During the day, she sat at the entrance of the Church. At night she slept beneath the entry portico. It had been nearly ten years since she and Philip had been parted. Her complexion, once a silky olive, was now wrinkled, dark, and weathered by the sun. Her sparkling hazel eyes and white pupils were milky and yellow. Her teeth were worn and dark. She was in her late thirties, but looked much older. Years of suffering, separation and searching had taken their toll.

She rarely prayed anymore, choosing instead to perseverate about

Philip. Before his death in 311 AD, Galerius ended the Christian persecution, too late for Pope Peter of Alexandria and his faithful followers. By 313 AD, Constantine secured his position as Emperor of the West. Another General, Licinius, followed a similar path, becoming Emperor in the East. Together, Constantine and Licinius issued the Edict of Milan, which officially sanctioned Christianity as an accepted religion in the Empire. The symbol of Christ painted on Constantine's cohort's labarum now rested on a silver medallion, below the Roman Eagle and atop the labarum's stanchion. Christianity was resurrected from the bowels of the earth to the glory of Rome, 249 years after Nero's Fire.

These dynamic historical winds were lost on Miriam, whose Faith was swept away by doubt and despair. On a Sunday morning in early May 313 AD, a stranger approached Miriam after the Liturgical Services.

"Mater Miriam, it is me, Simon, the merchant from Petra!"

"Who?"

Miriam was clearly confused.

"Simon, the merchant from Petra. Good woman, surely you are Mater Miriam, guardian of the traveler, healer of the sick. You asked me to take Puella to the Holy City. She has taken up your ministry there, healing the sick and comforting the weary traveler." He knelt in front of her, clasping her hands in his.

"Have you seen Philip?" Her voice was monotonous as she stared through him.

"Philip?" Simon had no knowledge of Miriam's past life with Quintus.

Miriam repeated the story she had told hundreds of times throughout the past six months: the cleansing ritual, the rape, her blind son, its demon father, the battered soldier, his beheading, Philip's miraculous cure, and the cruel separation.

Now he understood the sadness that haunted her. The crescent-shaped scar on her face was a continual remembrance of the rape. The scar her heart bore from her separation from Philip was far deeper. Through her kindness and humble Faith in Yesua, she had helped many. He knew of the legendary healing powers possessed by the rags she used to cleanse the sick and weary. On their trip to Jerusalem, Puella had shared Miriam's story of the crucified man, Lupa, and Miriam's journey to the leper colony in Petra.

"Kind woman. You have suffered much, but have given back more. Your Faith will save you. Stay here. I must leave you now, but I will return shortly." He kissed her forehead before leaving to enter the church.

Pope Peter's successor, Achillas, had recently appointed a new presbyter in the Baucalis district, who was renowned as a great spiritual teacher. His following grew quickly. Simon's pilgrimage to Alexandria had been to visit St. Mark's grave. This day, Simon attended the presbyter's first Liturgy. Unaware of the presbyter' reputation, he found his teachings thought-provoking.

"Surely, this holy man would help Miriam, particularly if he knew the story of her suffering and devotion," Simon thought.

Simon found the presbyter alone, deep in prayer and kneeling in the church's sanctuary. Simon respectfully stood behind the man for several minutes, not wishing to disturb his devotional meditation. As if sensing the awareness of another spirit, the presbyter stood, turning to face Simon with open arms, saying, "My friend, how can I help you?"

"Do you know the troubled woman who lives outside the church?" Simon hoped that he would know Miriam's story.

"No. I have not met her. I arrived here just last week. Today was my first service with this congregation. I have much to learn about this flock. Tell me about her."

"I met this holy woman in Petra; there, she ministered to lepers and healed the sick. She raised donations by washing the feet of weary travelers in the city plaza. I was one of her loyal patrons. She publicly displayed a cross-like staff. In these treacherous times, she was undaunted in her outward devotion to Yesua. As she washed my feet, she prayed to Yesua for my safe passage. She was known to all as Mater Miriam, guardian of the traveler, healer of the sick."

"Why did she leave Petra?"

"She is looking for her son. Her story is quite extraordinary. You must hear it from her. I think the many traumas she has suffered, coupled with this quest to find her son, is now driving her to madness. She doesn't remember me. Through her faith in Yesua, this petite and gentle woman has helped so many. Can you please help her?"

Without hesitation, the presbyter said, "Take me to her."

Together, they knelt before Miriam. Before either could speak, Miriam burst into her soliloquy, "Have you seen my son? His name is Philip. He was blind and was miraculously cured by the blood of a martyr. Philip's father was a Roman soldier who beheaded the martyr in our presence and became so enraged by the miracle that he separated us, forever. I was sent into the desert and my son was sent to Alexandria. Surely, someone has met him. Have you seen my son? His name is Philip…."

Before she could repeat the story again, the presbyter gently placed his forefinger on her lips and quieted her with a long shushing sound. Placing his hand under her chin, he brought her face to face and began to study her. His gaze was intense. Finally, he smiled, "Mater Miriam, walk with us into the church."

The presbyter led them into the sanctuary, where they stopped near an urn of water that had been blessed that morning during the Liturgy.

He removed his shoulder stole and soaked it in the water. Miriam and Simon stood together in silence as he knelt in front of her and began to gently wash her feet.

As he toiled before her, with his head bowed in reverent admiration, he spoke.

"The boy's father is Quintus, the butcher of Syria. The merchants that he bribed to bring Philip here were Christians. Instead, they took Philip to Antioch for safe keeping with Lucian, the presbyter. By some twist of fate, Quintus also went to Antioch; there, he had a chance encounter in the market with the merchants, Lucian and Philip. The merchants were captured, but Lucian and Philip escaped on a merchant ship destined for Alexandria."

The presbyter rose to his feet. Miriam's tears rendered her speechless. Simon held her trembling body in a protective embrace. Simon studied the man intently. He was clearly too old to be Philip.

"How…how do you know all of this?" he stammered.

The presbyter replied, "My name is Arius. I am one of Lucian's students. Lucian brought Philip to me for safe keeping. Philip joined several other young boys who were also sent to me for safe keeping. The group traveled to Pemdje, to live in a Christian community."

"Pemdje…Pemdje," Miriam sobbed. Taking a deep breath, she whispered "It ends where it begins. My son is in Pemdje."

Arius paused for a minute before responding, "This is not certain. He was to remain there until Lucian could return from Antioch. Alas, Lucian was captured in Antioch shortly after Quintus, in a horrific public display, had butchered the merchants and a Christian family who had aided Philip's escape. His rage extended to the onlooking crowd. Anyone suspected of being a Christian was also butchered. Quintus delivered Lucian to the Emperor in Nicomedia, where Lucian was imprisoned for many years, until his death by beheading."

Miriam cried out, "Quintus is the demon spirit of the Demiurge himself."

"Perhaps," replied Arius. "News of Lucian's death exalted my resolve to continue his teachings. Unfortunately, Pope Peter opposed these teachings, ordering me to cease or face excommunication. His threat stiffened my fortitude to continue, however. I was excommunicated and exiled; as a result, I have lost all contact with the community in Pemdje. Peter's successor, Achillas, reinstated me. Last month, I was appointed presbyter of the Baucalis district."

Arius soaked his stole in the holy water again, then knelt to continue washing Miriam's feet. As he resumed, he prayed, "Yesua, Mater Miriam's Faith in You has brought her here. May this Faith protect her as she travels to Pemdje in search of her lost son. Restore her Faith in You. Restore her to prayer and the ministry she practiced in Petra. Return Philip to her, so he may love her as You so loved Your mother, Mary."

— CHAPTER 12 —

DESERT HERMITS

I

Over a dozen years had passed since Philip and Barnabas joined the community in Pemdje in 303 AD. Unlike for Quintus and Miriam, little had changed for them within the safety of their environment. By now, both young men were expert scribes. All of the boys with whom they entered the community were older. Most were married with families. Philip and Barnabas remained celibate.

Philip was small in stature, like his mother. His father's features dominated his visage. It was a vexing combination for the quiet young man who rarely revealed his inner thoughts. In stark contrast, Barnabas grew to be over six feet tall. He was lean, handsome and commanding. The community regarded him as a spiritual leader.

A relationship birthed by fate was now bound by affectionate love. Brother to brother, the two were inseparable. Publicly, Barnabas was the protector, Philip the lamb. Privately, Philip was the inquisitor, Barnabas the defender of the Faith. Philip deliberated each word that he scribed from the diverse theological treatise. His days were consumed by his inner dialogue, the evenings his constant questioning, the nights, his haunting dreams. To avoid sleep, Philip often peppered Barnabas with challenging questions; Barnabas in turn attempted to weave Philip's disparate thoughts into a logical fabric.

"Philip. Do you know what tomorrow is?" Tonight, Barnabas manipulated the discussion.

"It is forty days and nights before the day that Yesua was crucified," Philip replied.

"I think we should do something special."

Barnabas was pacing back and forth.

Sitting in front of him, Philip offered, "We do. We fast and pray at this time every year for forty days. You obviously have something different in mind. What are you thinking?"

Barnabas stopped pacing. "I am thinking we should go into the desert like Yesua, to fast and to pray for forty days and nights."

Philip laughed, "Is this another one of your silly re-enactments? Who am I to be, Yesua, or the Devil?"

"Neither. I am serious." Barnabas continued his pacing.

"We are no longer children. We have been in this place for many years. My thoughts are that you and I should travel together in silence, stopping only to pray. We will take our favorite holy books and as much food and water as we can carry."

"Walking into the desert forty nights? The desert is vast. We may never return." Philip was now standing.

"There is another desert that is east of here, which lies between the river and the sea. It is well traveled. We will cross the river and make our way to the desert, then south. The Spirit will lead us."

Vigorously gesturing, Philip queried, "So we will walk east twenty days, and then return here traveling west for twenty days?"

Barnabas responded. "No. We will walk forty days into the desert, praying to Yesua to guide us to our next destination."

"I like it here. Why should we leave?" It was apparent to Philip, however, that Barnabas had given this idea considerable thought.

His perception proved correct. Barnabas pleaded, "You like it here because it is safe, but living here the rest of my life is not my destiny. I have prayed for guidance. The only answer I receive is a growing desire to leave. The Holy Spirit will keep us safe. The holy books tell us that we must give up the temptations of the flesh to enjoy what is truly good. Only through prayer and reason will we find oneness with the Spirit. Earthly affections are hollow. Those who seek the desires of the flesh are dead. We live among the dead. Yesua escaped to the wilderness before He began His ministry. We must do what Yesua did."

After dinner, Barnabas announced their plans to the commune. Before dawn, the duo was headed east to the Nile Valley. When they reached the Nile, they persuaded a Christian fisherman to ferry them across it. Once across, they began a slow, arduous ascent from the Nile valley to a desert plateau. The plateau was sprinkled with rolling sandy highlands, marked by numerous dry stream beds that quickly swelled to receive occasional rains. Rugged volcanic mountain chains spotted the eastern horizon, running north to south. Beyond the mountains lay the Red Sea.

The young men traveled with walking sticks that, if need be, could be used to ward off bandits, hyenas or mountain lions. Their satchel protected a half dozen of their favorite codex manuscripts. Under his robe, in a pouch slung across and against his chest, Philip carried the gospel codex Lucian had given to him.

Although desolate, and at times unfriendly, the desert was passable. It had been so for nomads, miners and merchants for centuries. The region was a rich source of emeralds, turquoise, copper and gold. Consequently, ancient trading routes crisscrossed the region from the

Nile to the Red Sea. Across the southern part of the Eastern Desert, nomads trekked from water source to water source. The Romans reinforced these routes with forts and way stations that all had protected water sources. In 130 AD, the Emperor Hadrian constructed the Via Nova Hadriana, the first confirmed road in the region, which stretched from Middle Egypt to the Red Sea.

Each day they followed a strict routine of prayer at dawn, noon and dusk. The morning prayer included a reading and a lesson that Philip and Barnabas alternated leading. They traveled in silence, reflecting upon the sacred reading and its lessons. The noon prayer was a petition for safe travel. Evening prayers were devotions of gratitude. On the third night, as the duo lay silently staring at the sea of stars against the dark sky, Philip broke the silence.

"I wonder how many others like us are in this desert."

"I know of at least one." Sensitive to Philip's anxiety about sleep, Barnabas decided to break their rule of silence and engage in conversation.

"Anthony?" queried Philip.

"No. The Eastern Desert is home to Paul the Hermit. He is older than Anthony and has been here for decades. In his youth, he was betrayed by a family member to Roman persecutors. To avoid capture, he vanished into the desert. He lives in a cave near a spring. According to legend, a raven brings him a half a loaf of bread every day," Barnabas explained.

"Do you think we might come upon him?"

"Only if Yesua wishes it to be. The desert is vast. I have no idea where the old man might be."

"The heavens are beautiful." As had become customary during evening discussions, Philip veered off to an unrelated topic.

"The Creator's work is unbounded," Barnabas said.

Philip paused for a moment, "What is this place?"

"It is a vast desert."

"No, not this desert. What is this world we live in?"

"It's the earth created for man by God."

"But God created man to be perfect. Why then is the place not perfect?"

"The Judeans said that man lived in a perfect garden, disobeyed God, and was cast out of the garden."

"Into this place?"

"Yes."

"So God created an imperfect world for an imperfect man?"

"Yes."

"Was it created at the same time as the perfect garden?"

Barnabas hesitated before replying, "Well…yes…I think. God created the heavens and earth first. Only then did he create man."

"So how could a perfect God create an imperfect world? Better yet, why would a perfect God create an imperfect world? Did he know that man would sin?"

"God knows all."

"Doesn't seem fair."

"What doesn't seem fair?"

"Well, if he knew man was going to sin, why would a perfect God create a perfect being that he knew would become imperfect?"

"Only God knows. What is your point?"

"Do you believe in the demiurge?" Philip was now off on another tangent.

"No."

"Do you believe that Yesua is an Aeon?"

"No."

"Do you believe that was Yesua is Seth and that he has come to earth many times? Some say Yesua is Elijah."

"No."

"Do you believe that Yesua was created after God?"

"Yes."

"So how is he not an Aeon?"

"Well, I don't believe in the traditions which say the imperfect world was created by the Demiurge or that Yesua was one of many Aeons."

"Do you believe the Father birthed Yesua and the Holy Spirit to save these flawed spirits we call mankind?"

"Yes." Frustrated with Philip's persistent questioning, Barnabas decided that it was his turn to be the questioner. "Enough, Philip! You have not answered my earlier question. What is the point of your questioning?"

"I have tried to understand the books that we scribe. The stories are not consistent. I am not sure what to believe."

"That is why we commit ourselves to prayer and understanding. Our spirits are weakened by the flesh. We are imperfect and can never know all. Those things that cannot be understood require faith to be believed."

They lay in silence, gazing upward. Barnabas sensed that Philip was not primed for sleep. He asked Philip, "What do you believe this place is?"

"It is the place created for fallen spirits," Philip replied. "I believe that all of us were perfectly created by the Birther, because He is perfect and incapable of error. We are in this place because each of us has sinned against Him. A perfect God would not punish me for someone else's sin. As flawed spirits, we refuse to accept responsibility for our action and place blame on others."

Philip paused to gather his thoughts and continued, "I believe our fallen spirit will remain in this place until we reach perfection again. Because the Birther loves all that He has created, He sends Yesua again and again to save us, until finally there is no hope and the only spirits remaining in this place are the perfectly imperfect. Once this is achieved, this place can be destroyed and only perfection will remain."

Silence returned as both contemplated Philip's beliefs. Again, Barnabas asked, "And why do you believe this?"

"It is the only thing that makes sense, the drudgery of this place, Yesua's sacrificial love; my mother's forgiveness of my father; my father's evil spirit. Many who are in this place will be saved, forgiven and escape. Yesua will come again and again, until the only ones left are the unforgiven."

These haunting thoughts left both of them speechless.

The next morning, the two continued their journey. The forty day quest protracted to a year while they meandered across the desert on ancient paths. Just as Barnabas predicted, the desert was vast. Eventually, they journeyed northeast to the mountains bordering the Red Sea. When they reached the foothills, the two took refuge at a small oasis, just below the mountain range.

One morning, Barnabas spotted a raven, clutching a small bundle, flying into a cave on the mountain side. The raven repeated the event at the same time every day. Purely by chance and through the will of Yesua, they had stumbled upon Paul the Hermit. Cautious excitement gripped them. They watched the cave intently for several days, looking for signs of life. Barnabas and Philip debated whether they should make the ascent to inspect the cave. Fearful that the cave might prove to be the lair of something ominous, they kept their vigil under the oasis' lone palm tree.

On the last day of the week, a tall gaunt figure with a long staff appeared at the entrance to the cave. As the raven approached, the figure raised both arms in the air. With one hand, he took the bundle from the raven. When he lowered his staff, the raven perched on its gnarled handle. Silhouetted against the cave opening, the hermit and the raven charmed one another with animated conversation. When the man drew the staff close to his face, the raven nibbled his cheek, playfully kissing it before jumping from the staff to his shoulder.

To their surprise, the hermit did not turn back to the cave, but began a slow descent toward the oasis. As the hermit approached the oasis, both observers instinctively fell to their knees and lowered their heads to the ground.

"Brothers, why are you laying prone before me? Who do you think I am?" The raven cocked his head, as if listening for an answer.

Still prone, Barnabas spoke, "You are the holy man who is called Paul the Hermit!"

"It is so; I am Paul the Hermit. Still, why are you prone before me?"

Refusing to make eye contact, Philip spoke. "Because you are a holy man."

To their astonishment Paul replied, "Young Philip, I am no closer to the Spirit than you. Please rise."

The boys stood. Dumbfounded, they stared at the hermit as he stepped to the spring to fill a water pouch. When the pouch was replenished, he sat facing the boys.

Raising the bread that the raven delivered that morning, he said, "Come break bread with me."

Philip and Barnabas sat on either side of Paul. As the hermit broke the bread, the raven hopped from his shoulder to muster fallen crumbs.

Paul broke the bread into small portions for each of them, saying, "This is the bread of life. Take it and eat it in memory of Yesua who broke bread with his disciples before his merciless death and glorious resurrection."

He passed the water to them saying, "This is the drink of life with which John the Baptizer baptized Yesua. Take it and drink it, so that the Spirit within you may be immersed in the risen Yesua."

The trio ate quietly while contemplating Paul's words. Philip spoke, "How did you know…."

Paul outstretched his forefinger to Philip's lip. "Later. Now is a time for meditation. Be one with the Spirit of Yesua within you."

With eyes closed deep in thought, they sat upright, keenly aware of the sun's warmth as it rose to its peak. After hours of silence, Paul spoke, answering Philip's unfinished question. "I have been expecting you. I received a vision of you and Barnabas entering the desert. The heavens were bright as you lay awaiting sleep. Philip said that he believed this world, or place as you called it, was created by the Birther for the banishment of those who had sinned against God."

Chilled by his comments, Philip was speechless. Barnabas mustered a response. "Was…..is Philip right?"

"Why should it matter?" the old man said. "It is not a thought worthy of contemplation."

Philip mustered the courage to engage in conversation. "Teach us. What is worthy of contemplation?"

"My vision foretold our meeting today. I will say now what I said in my vision. 'Indeed, our spirits are flawed. Yesua is perfection. Being one with Yesua's Spirit is the only way to the Father's house,'" Paul replied. "This is the only truth worth pursuing. All else is of no consequence."

Suddenly, the raven took to flight. With staff in hand, the hermit rose to his feet and turned toward the mountains. As he walked away, Philip shouted, "Wait! Did you see anything else in the vision?"

The old man stopped at a distance, then turned to face them. "There is a woman of deep faith bearing a scar on her face, a scar shaped like a crescent, who is searching for Philip!"

That night, Philip's nightmares returned.

II

It was clear to both Philip and Barnabas that their bond was a blessing that would prevent either one from pursuing a life of solitude such as either Anthony the Great or Paul the Hermit chose to observe. Philip's curiosity about other men searching for the truth in the desert was foretelling. Indeed, he and Barnabas were not alone. The growth of ascetic life was being cultivated by the momentous changes compelling Christianity forwards. The legacy of the few Desert Fathers spawned coteries numbering in the hundreds.

One year extended into three. As they roamed the desert, they met numerous contemporaries who shared a desire to pursue ascetic habits in a communal environment. They also shared a longing for leadership and guidance. The early tradition of the Desert Fathers was to mentor a disciple in the practices of hermetic solitary lifestyles. As yet, the concept of communal monastic life was undefined.

Three years of wandering drew on into five. Or was it more? They had lost all sense of time. Somewhere along the way, their youth sallied. The twosome ultimately made their way to the Via Nova Hadriana, stopping for long periods to live in the hills surrounding various mining villages or forts that marked the road at regular intervals.

The road began at Antinopolis, located on the eastern bank at the Qena Bend of the Nile in Middle Egypt. Sixty miles south, up-river, laid the ancient Egyptian city of Thebes. Fourty miles due south across the desert rested the mummified bodies of ancient pharaohs in the Valley of Kings. The Emperor Hadrian built Antinopolis with the intention of the city becoming the empire's southernmost metropolis rivaling Alexandria. With Antinopolis at its gateway, the Via Nova Hadriana diagonally traversed a region known as the Thebaid. The road terminated two hundred and ten miles southeast at the Red Sea in the ancient city of Berenike, a port along the primary trading routes to India.

The duo's expedition south ended sixty miles from Berenike at a settlement named Apollonos. They were 300 miles from Pemdje. Although strategically situated, Apollonos was smaller than larger settlements, some of which could support up to 2,000 travelers. Philip and Barnabas lived in the surrounding hills for several months. Leaving Appollonus was an impulsive decision, and was prompted by a spirited evening discussion.

"We have been searching for years to no avail. Let us return to Pemdje. I miss the communal spirit there," Philip said.

"The Holy Spirit is telling me to keep searching," said Barnabas, a response that Philip had heard many times.

"Can you ask how long this will take? I am not interested in wandering the desert for forty years like Moses."

"Be serious," Barnabas cautioned.

"I am. Do you remember our encounter with the hermit, Paul? His parting comment was that my mother was searching for me. What is the likelihood of his vision becoming a reality?"

"Philip, we have discussed this many times. The hermit's vision eased your heart about your mother's fate. She was still alive. She still loves you. But as Yesua teaches us, a man must leave his father and mother to follow Him. Each time we discuss this, we chose to pursue this sacred quest. You can be at peace about your mother's fate while you follow Yesua."

"Maybe that was the wrong choice. Maybe the Holy Spirit was leading us to the hermit. Maybe his vision was a message to direct us back to Pemdje. We lived there for over ten years. My mother was born there. If she were alive, wouldn't she return home?"

"Perhaps." Barnabas was softening, "But we met with Paul years ago. Your mother may be gone from there."

"The excitement of our quest has become drudgery." Philip's argument grew animated. "Have you not noticed? The further south we travel, the harder it becomes to find others who are searching, like us? What we have been searching…no… what YOU have been searching for, is not in this direction. We met many others like us further north. For that reason alone, we should turn back toward Pemdje. If we find what you seek, then the will of the Holy Spirit is fulfilled. If not, we will return to Pemdje. Either way, I will be resting in one place…. and, if she is still alive, I might be graced with my mother's presence again."

Barnabas silently contemplated Philips words "…'no…what YOU have been searching for'…" Humiliated by his friend's anguish, he replied, "You are right. This is a wise decision. No more wandering. We shall travel this road back to the river and continue north to Pemdje. We will depart tomorrow."

That night, Philip dreamt vividly. It was a dream such as he had never experienced before. He was alone in an ancient city, wandering through deserted streets. The streets were wet from a storm that had recently passed. He reached the top of a hill that was barren, save for ancient ruins. With the sun rising behind him, he gazed west across a valley to the opposite hill where there he could see the faint outline of a single crucifix at its crest. He wandered down the hill into the city's maze of narrow deserted stone streets.

Ascending the next hill, he was stunned by a familiar smell. It was his father's. He stopped and surveyed his surroundings. All was deathly still. There was no sight of anything living. He turned to face the path ahead. The view up the hill was dark. He felt as if he was looking into a lion's cave. His heart was racing, his breathing shallow. He felt panicky. Is the beast inside? Is this the final abyss? Panic became terror. Is this how my father's victims felt before he murdered them? Is my father at the crest, waiting to murder me?

He sprinted back down the hill. A Roman temple appeared on his right. The smell was overbearing, almost debilitating. He felt as if he was face down in putrid gutter waste, and he searched for something with which to cover his face. In the doorway of an abandoned house, he found a woman's shawl, which he wrapped around his neck, covering his mouth and nose. The putrid stench vanished, only to be replaced by another familiar smell. The aroma was intoxicating. He felt giddy, as if he had just consumed his first cup of wine.

"Mother!"

"They are both here," he thought! "Where is she? Where is she?"

With his mother's shawl wrapped around his face, he continued the ascent. Philip had taken no more than a dozen steps when the stones beneath him became spongy. He could feel mud oozing above his sandals and through his toes. He slowed his pace. The ground turned into blood.

Squish, squish, squish!

Giddy intoxication morphed into grotesque, aching nausea. His head was spinning. The street was spinning. As he reached the crest, his bile rose. He beheld a scene then that shocked him to his senses, as would a breathtaking leap into the bracing cold of an icy river. The stone path beneath his feet was firm and clean. Lying prone before him was a dying woman surrounded entirely by a pack of wolves.

"Mother, mother," he shouted!

He walked through the pack to lie beside her. He pulled her to him. She grabbed his robe in desperation and pulled him to her bosom. Then things morphed once more. Philip's robe parted. His mother leaned down, and her mouth latched quickly to his breast. She suckled, and milk began to flow.

"No, no, no!" Philip screamed. "NOOOOOO......!"

"It's all right. Calm down, my brother. Calm down. Shhhhh. Shhhhhh," Barnabas said. "You are only dreaming, Philip. Whatever it is, it's just a dream. You are safe here, with me. Shhhhh." Barnabas held his friend in a loving embrace, gently stroking his narrow sweat-beaded brow.

III

Taking passage with a caravan, Philip and Barnabas resumed their journey back north toward Antinopolis. Pressed to his chest, Philip carried with him the Gospel codex given to him by Lucian nearly twenty-two years earlier. The codex chafed against his breast; his nipples felt curiously swollen and sore.

They traveled in silence. Barnabas' introspection haunted him. "What have I done? Where has this journey taken us? Has my folly condemned my brother to madness?"

Philip was completely lost to his surroundings. "What happened to me last night? Was that really a dream? Is my Mother alive? Yes, that's it. Miriam lives. She is in danger. I must save her." His mind ignited, his thoughts flashed with glowing lights, which assailed him as if from within a meteor storm. "What is happening? What is this place? Sweet Yesua, show me the way out of here. Father, Birther of the world, please forgive me for whatever I did to offend you. Let me return home to you. Let me return home."

Home, however, was not the destination of their return journey. Unbeknownst to Philip and Barnabas, they were finally bound for the fertile grounds where Christian monastic life first began to take root. The years of wandering, the years of searching, the years of prayer was a test of Faith. Barnabas' folly would indeed be the fulfillment of the Holy Spirit's will.

The year Philip and Barnabas left Pemdje, another young man named Pachomius began his search in the Eastern Sahara Desert. He accepted Yesua's calling in solitude, much like Paul the Hermit. Pachomius' historic journey into ascetic life led to sainthood and he became one of a handful of saints venerated by Oriental Orthodoxy, Eastern Orthodoxy, Catholicism and some Protestant Sects.

There are eight known biographies of Pachomius, each delineating intersecting, alternate and conflicting narratives about his life. According to tradition, he was born to pagan parents in the Thebaid region. His parent's status had afforded him an excellent secular education. From his youth, Pachomius gained a reputation for prudence and sensibility.

At the age of twenty, he was conscripted into the Roman Army. Not infrequently, Roman conscripts were housed in prisons until fully indoctrinated into military life. During Pachomius' indoctrination, the prison was visited by the local Christians who fed the prisoners.

Moved by their compassion and love for their fellow man, Pachomius vowed to become a Christian once his conscription ended.

He was released from service in 313 AD, one year after Constantine's conversion at the Battle of the Milvian Bridge. True to his vow, Pachomius was baptized. With only limited exposure to Christian teachings, he returned to the Thebaid where he lived in solitude near a remote village for three years. Craving deeper spiritual guidance, he sought out a local ascetic named Palemon, who accepted the young man as a disciple.

For many years, the two lived an austere, well-disciplined life, offering manual labor and continuous prayer to God. One day, a celestial voice commanded Pachomius to create a reclusive community at Tabbenisi near the Nile River, north of the Qena bend. Palemon traveled with him to the location; there the two built a cell for Pachomius. Palemon remained with him for a brief period before returning to solitude in the desert. Accounts of Pachomius' divine directive quickly spread throughout the region. Before long, droves of hermits besieged him.

Divine intervention struck again when an angel, clothed in distinctive garb, appeared to Pachomius. The angel bestowed a communal rule for the amassing hermits, balancing communal needs with solitary life. The rule was simple. Hermits would live in individual cells, but would work together for the collective well-being of the community. The distinctive garment worn by the angel would be worn by all. As construction of the first monastery continued, the gathering hermits submitted to the leadership of St. Pachomius. Thus, Christian cenobite life was birthed on the banks of the Nile River at the Qena Bend.

Before his death in 346 AD, the venerated saint established ten monasteries and two nunneries. Seven thousand monks would eventually live by his rule, which then underpinned the foundations of monastic rules as proscribed centuries later by St. Basil and St. Benedict.

The monastery at Tabennisi was well established by the time Philip and Barnabas arrived in Antinopolis.

Following customs dating back to Yesua, Philip and Barnabas found shelter in the home of a Christian merchant named Anub. Anub was well known to the merchant caravans that traveled between Antinopolis and Berenike. He frequently traded with them in exchange for goods from Alexandria and other Mediterranean communities. Although Anub's primary trading route was between Antinopolis and Alexandria, he occasionally ventured as far as Antioch.

Anub considered offering hospitality to holy men an honor. Philip and Barnabas were treated with utmost respect. The pair willingly shared their Christian passage with Anub and his family. Barnabas frequently finished Philip's accounts. Anub listened compassionately to Philip's stories. At times, Anub interrupted, requesting that some detail be repeated.

"The community you seek is being built nearby by a young holy man named Pachomius. Before you choose to join him, you should know that much has changed since you departed Pemdje." Anub was uncertain where to start. "The Romans fought a civil war. A general named Constantine converted to Christianity after a vision before a battle. His army bore into battle combat banners emblazoned with the symbol of a cross. He was victorious in spite of being outnumbered."

"Constantine became Emperor of the West," Anub continued. "Another general, Licinius, was victorious in the East. Together, they proclaimed an end to the great persecution. Peace between the two generals was brief. Another war erupted. Constantine remained loyal to Yesua. His armies carried Yesua's banner into every battle. Yesua never abandoned Constantine, who was victorious to the end."

"The Emperor is Christian?" Barnabas struggled to understand; the claim strained credulity.

"Yes. Yes. Our prayers have been answered beyond expectations. The persecutions are over. The Emperor is Christian. Miraculously, he has proclaimed Christianity as the official religion of the Empire.

"Tell us about the Church in Alexandria. Is Arius the Bishop?" Barnabas inquired.

"No, Barnabas. Alexander is the Bishop. The Emperor does not favor Arius. The Emperor wrote a letter to the Church in Alexandria, a letter proclaiming that Arius' teaching are the work of the devil. He has been excommunicated from the Church and is an outcast. All of his writings are ordered to be destroyed." Anub could sense their anguish.

Always searching for answers, Philip spoke up. "How did this happen? What does a Roman General know of holy men and their teachings?"

Anub explained further. "Arius' teachings were growing in popularity with Yesua's followers. Arius concluded that since the Father begat the Son, there was a time when the Son did not exist. Therefore, the Father is greater than the Son. A great debate erupted among the bishops, fueled by Arius' archrival, a deacon named Athanasius. When Constantine learned of the discord between the bishops, he convened a great council to settle the matter. Three hundred bishops met in a town named Nicaea, which is not far from Nicomedia, the city where Lucian of Antioch was martyred."

Barnabas rose quickly to his feet. "Lucian was martyred? When? How? Why?"

Philip clenched Lucian's codex to his chest. "No. This cannot be!"

"I am afraid so," Anub continued. "As to when, Lucian was beheaded over ten years ago, following many years of imprisonment. As to how and why, he was captured by one of Galerius' murderous henchman in Antioch after returning from a trip to Alexandria to visit his student, Arius. Evidently, Galerius's goon was hunting him for some reason."

Frozen in disbelief, an ashen Philip whispered under his breath, "Father."

Anub finished the story. "Lucian's last words were…"

"I am a Christian!" Philip shouted, preempting, correctly, the end to Anub's tale.

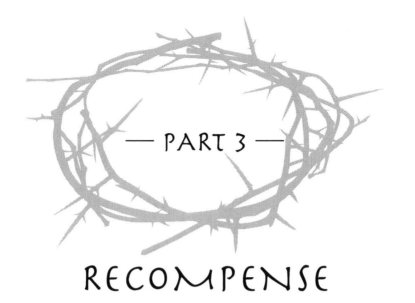

— PART 3 —

RECOMPENSE

We believe in one God, the Father Almighty, maker of all things visible and invisible;

And in one Lord Jesus Christ, the Son of God, the only-begotten of his Father, of the substance of the Father,

God of God, Light of Light, very God of very God,

Begotten, not made, being of one substance with the Father, by whom all things were made, both which be in heaven and in earth.

Who for us men and for our salvation came down from heaven and was incarnate and was made man.

He suffered and the third day he rose again, and ascended into heaven.

And he shall come again to judge both the quick and the dead.

And we believe in the Holy Ghost.

And whosoever shall say;

That there was a time when the Son of God was not,

Or that before he was begotten he was not,

Or that he was made of things that were not,

Or that he is of a different substance or essence from the Father,

Or that he is a creature,

Or subject to change or conversion,

All that so say, the Catholic and Apostolic Church anathematizes them.

In the year 325 AD, from late May to July, three hundred and eighteen Christian Bishops and theologians assembled in the town of Nicaea in what is now modern Turkey. Convened by Constantine, the Council was chaired by Ossius of Cordova. Notable attendees included Eusebius of Caesarea, Eusebius of Nicomedia, Alexander of Alexandria, Arius and Constantine himself.

The purpose for the synod was twofold. Foremost was resolution of the mounting controversy of the Christian Godhead and the nature of Yesua's divinity which reached a climax in the teachings of Arius. Supported by Constantine, the majority of bishops resolved to end the controversy once and for all.

According to traditions, Eusebius of Caesarea drafted a creed that was based on an invocation used in baptismal services in Caesarea. The draft avoided the controversy by ignoring any reference to the nature of Yesua's divinity. Perhaps Eusebius was not convinced; perhaps he avoided the issue in deference to his friend Lucian and Lucian's student Arius. To no avail, a great debate ensued, championed on either side by Arius and Bishop Alexander of Alexandria.

The Arian argument was soundly defeated. The Council published a universal creed of beliefs about the nature of Yesua's divinity that also included a condemnation of false beliefs perpetrated by Arius and his supporters. In a letter to the Church in Alexandria, Constantine supported the Council's decision proclaiming that Arius was under the influence of the devil and the devil alone in promoting such unholy teachings. Constantine proclaimed the end to all ambiguity concerning the nature of the One God.

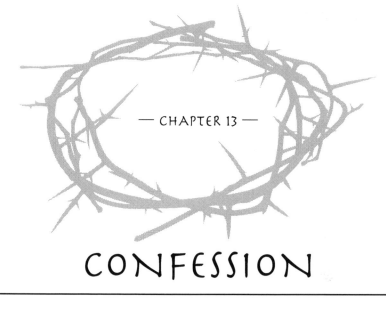

— CHAPTER 13 —

CONFESSION

I

Through over thirty years of service to Rome, Quintus experienced, not to mention initiated, some of the most gruesome scenes imaginable. Not a single one of these, however, had ever fazed him. His feelings fluctuated between indifference, amusement and sadistic pleasure. Emotionally, he had been protected by an impenetrable armor shield, until now. The surreal hauntings of his martyred victims intensified with each recurring nightmare.

"We forgive you….we forgive you!" Their chanting faces were his only clear memory since he had lost his arm at the Milvian Bridge. He could barely recall the events that preceded his coma. His victorious heroics on the bridge were lost in a fog. Like a weary traveler caught in a dark storm on an uncharted slippery mountain path, he was lost, confused and frightened on an endless journey to nowhere. "Is this my reward for unfailing loyalty? Is forgiveness the only reward? What does it mean? Forgiveness? For what? Why do I need to be forgiven?"

"We forgive you….we forgive you!" Their willingness to grant complete forgiveness frightened him the most. This unfamiliar feeling was like a severe burn that renders an incomparable pain as shredded skin exposes raw nerves that reverberate when touched by even a gentle breeze. Quintus was finally broken, both physically and emotionally.

The most feared imperial persecutor was now the crippled bodyguard of a Christian Emperor's mother and she was the gentle breeze that most exposed his fears.

For many years as Helena's protector, Quintus hid this unnerving fear, particularly in her presence. Unlike her son, Constantine, Helena embraced Christianity with such zeal that many believed her faith was forged in her youth. Her piety and benevolence were unbounded. Whereas her son used his growing political power to consolidate his control, she used her influence to build churches and to nurture Christian communities throughout the Empire. Her compassionate nature was a constant reminder to Quintus of the brotherly love which he fruitlessly toiled to extinguish in the hearts of his victims.

At first, Quintus performed his duties as expected. As time passed, Helena quietly observed odd behaviors inconsistent with a battle-hardened legionnaire. When Quintus accompanied her on visits to care for the unfortunate, he would stand at a distance. Sometimes, she caught him staring aimlessly at the afflicted. Unless she requested that he do so, he never approached them. When he did, tremors overtook his remaining hand. Eventually, Quintus spiraled into a vicious cycle. As Helena nurtured these souls, he began to see the faces of his victims in the crowd. His nights grew restless; he feared sleep and the haunting that followed. Insomnia fueled the cycle. Quintus now feared the very presence of those who had once feared him the most.

"What troubles you, sir?" His behavior had grown too obvious to be ignored.

"The memories of war, my lady," was always his only response.

Helena knew this answer to be a lie. She had met men who were haunted by war. Unlike them, however, the sights and sounds of Roman legions and their spoils had no effect on Quintus' behavior. Furthermore, she knew that the afflictions of the unfortunate were no more haunting than the psychological scars of war. No, memories of war were not haunting him. It was something else, something from his past.

Helena knew from conversations with her son that Quintus had a violent past. She preferred not to know the details, because she was devoted to Yesua, her savior, and Quintus was a soul in need of salvation. With her piety came great patience. Penetrating Quintus' hidden secrets would take time. She knew that whatever sins haunted him, Yesua would forgive Quintus.

"I must find a purpose for this man to keep him from descending completely into an abyss," she thought, "a purpose that will lead him to Yesua's redemption. He has lived a life of destruction. I shall make a builder of this broken man." As Helena became the master builder of the empire's churches, Quintus became her master foreman.

There are seven hills in Rome. Overlooking the Forum is the Palatine Hill, the traditional site of Emperors' palaces. For his mother's residence, Constantine chose a location southeast of the Palatine Hill, just inside the city wall. The site included a temple to Venus and Cupid, an amphitheater, a circus and a villa built one hundred years earlier by the Emperor Heliogabalus. Properly renovated, the property was ideally suited for the Augusta Imperatrix, Helena. The renovation was the first project under Quintus' charter.

Roman legions were well versed in construction techniques. Their long campaigns required the building of a variety of projects, including roads, walls and military camps suitable for long sieges. Many of Europe's modern cities trace their origins to Roman military outposts. The French cities along the Rhone river valley owe their existence to Julius Caesar's conquest of Gaul in the first century before Yesua's birth. As a dutiful officer experienced in military construction projects, Quintus was at ease with his role renovating Helena's new residence. Now released from escorting her on her charitable visits, Helena patiently waited to expose this wretched sole to Yesua's saving graces.

II

The peace between Constantine in the West and Licinius in the East was shattered by civil war in 317. A consolidated empire under a single emperor was the prize. A protracted struggle ensued. During his absences from Rome, the duties of governance fell to Helena as Augusta Imperatrix. Helena used her access to the Imperial Treasury to fund the building of churches in Rome and Trier.

Upon a brief return to Rome, Helena briefed Constantine of her activities in his absence as he waged war with Licinius. She updated him about her activities with the poor, as well as the charitable donations from the Imperial Treasury to Christian communities. She commented that the villa renovation was proceeding well, remarking about Quintus' vigilance as foreman.

"His spirit has been renewed somewhat, but a hollowness remains. I will not give up until his soul is saved."

Constantine felt obliged to expose Quintus' past, hoping to temper Helena's enthusiasm. "Your subject was the most vicious Christian persecutor in the Empire. He was trained to destroy body and spirit. Perhaps, most devastating for Quintus was the destruction of his own soul in the process."

Undaunted, she replied, "All souls can be saved. I will not give up."

"Then he has no better champion in his camp." Constantine wished to change the subject. A casual comment by her son presented Helena the opportunity to resurrect a long standing discussion between mother and son.

"Mother, you are becoming quite a builder. What plans have you next?"

Her enthusiasm was aroused. "Building Churches is not enough." Constantine knew where the conversation was leading.

"What more would you have me do? We cannot bring back the dead," he sarcastically replied.

"No we can't, but we can honor them. The misguided acts of your predecessors have destroyed many sacred Christian sites. We must find them all and erect glorious churches to honor Yesua and the fallen martyrs." Helena was already prepared for his next response.

"Mother, you cannot go to the Holy Land."

"Why not?"

"Licinius' troops still occupy that region. Winning this war may take many years to accomplish. Youth is long past. Even if the war were over, you are too fragile to make such an arduous trip."

"Pilgrimage!" she corrected him. "Trip" indeed, she thought, amused.

"As you wish, pilgrimage."

"The distinction makes the topic of my age immaterial." Constantine's dismissive behavior made her feel disrespected, reminding Helena of the belittling divorce by his father and consequent remarriage for political gain.

Constantine grasped the meaning of Helena's piercing gaze as if asking him, "Have I, the one who gave you life, not been loyal to you through all my humiliations?" In spite of the fact that she was now in her early seventies, no one's opinion carried as much weight with him as hers.

"I could never forgive myself if something happened to you. You have been with me even when we have been apart. I love you Mother." He clasped his hands around hers, gazing lovingly into her eyes. "Alas, the answer is still no," he quietly whispered.

After sitting together in silence for several moments, Helena spoke.

"My son, most revered Caesar Augustus, thank you for your generosity building suitable places for worship. Perhaps I can persuade you to undertake such a project in Rome while I wait patiently for my prayers to be answered."

"Resurrect a sacred site, here in Rome? Yesua was never in Rome."

"Peter was. He was crucified in Nero's circus, which survived the great fire. The same circus where Nero fed Christian martyrs to wild beasts after that fire. No site outside of Jerusalem is more sacred. The local bishop told me that Peter is buried at or near the site.

"What do you want me to do, mother?"

"Order the circus razed and Peter's remains uncovered. Then build on the site a large Basilica to honor him."

"Will you lead this effort then?"

"No!"

"Who, then?"

"You will, my son!"

A smile graced his face. "So be it. I know you only too well. Is there anything else?"

"Yes. Have Quintus raze the circus."

The next day, Constantine, Quintus and the imperial architects convened at Nero's Circus on the Vatican hill to survey the site. The local bishop was also in attendance. The bishop was certain of the whereabouts of the Apostle's remains, as the location had been preserved through the oral traditions of the Christian community in Rome. The bishop led the entourage to a location beside an Egyptian obelisk, inside Nero's circus.

"The crucifixion took place here," the bishop said.

"Quintus, this obelisk is to remain as a witness to the crucifixion." Addressing his architects, Constantine ordered, "Incorporate this obelisk into your design."

The architects surveyed the circus, gesturing as they described the potential design. "The obelisk should be placed in the center of a long colonnaded atrium in the forecourt of the entrance," they suggested.

"Agreed. Build a large basilica to honor this martyr," Constantine replied.

"But Caesar, a basilica design is the official audience hall reserved only for the emperor."

"So, what then is the appropriate design?" Turning to the bishop, Constantine asked. "Is your God not the Lord of the Spiritual realm?"

"Indeed," replied the bishop. "Using designs reserved for Roman Temples would be blasphemy."

"Then it must be a design reserved for a Lord." Constantine settled the matter.

The rest of the morning was spent walking the site to outline the details of the complex. The structure would include a wide nave with two aisles on each side. The end of the nave terminated in an apse, the traditional location for the emperor's throne. The discussion of how to differentiate the design from a temporal building was resolved by the addition of a bema or transept before the apse. The resulting "Latin" cross footprint would become the model for future Christian Churches in Western Europe.

"One further request, kind Caesar," the bishop pleaded. He was concerned that St. Peter's grave was not yet incorporated into the plan. "Peter's remains should rest in the Church. Follow me."

The Bishop led them outside, turning north into a cemetery located on a steep incline adjacent to Nero's circus. He stopped at a pagan shrine called a "tropaion," which was highlighted by a concave niche flanked by two columns built over an elevated red brick structure. The eight foot tall, downhill brick foundation wall was severely cracked and supported by a buttress that was not part of the original design.

"Bishop, are you certain? This is a pagan shrine!" Constantine noted that the niche was a traditional pagan detail for the location of an urn containing cremated ashes.

"The pagan tropaion was added to disguise and protect the grave below." The bishop explained the history of the grave, according to traditional accounts that were eventually recorded in writing by a Roman priest named Gaius in 199 AD.

"After Nero's abdication and suicide in 68 AD, Christian followers moved Peter's bones from the catacombs to this site. The bones were buried in a shallow 'poor man's' grave covered with terracotta tiles creating a gabled top."

Gesturing to the surrounding cemetery, he continued, "The remains of other martyrs from Nero's persecution were moved to this slope as well. Through the years, rains eroded the slope, exposing Peter's grave. The red brick retaining walls and closure were added. Fearing desecration by pagans during subsequent persecutions, the tropaion was added to disguise the site." The bishop paused.

Falling to his knees, he gathered a handful of soil, spit into it and blessed himself with the mud. Staring intently at the grave, he said, "Yes, this is his grave. This earth is sacred. The prince of the apostles, Yesua's rock lies here."

Without hesitation, Constantine turned to Quintus, "These bones are not to be disturbed under any circumstance."

Addressing his architects, he commanded, "This grave shall be centered at the intersection of the nave and the transept."

The architects glanced at each other without speaking. Their facial expressions left Constantine with the feeling they were reluctant. "What is it? Speak!" he barked.

"Caesar, centering the basilica here will require that the entire hill be lowered to the level of this grave." In fact, leveling the hill required moving several million cubic feet of dirt to create a site on which to build the basilica.

"My legions have undertaken far greater engineering feats. Are you not up to the challenge?" Constantine was clearly agitated by the response.

Again, they hesitated. Rome's architects were keenly aware of the subtle superstitions that influenced the orientation and siting of sacred structures. Finally, the senior architect spoke. "Caesar, desecrating graves to build a temple is not advised by the oracles."

"Damn the oracles. This is to be an edifice willed by God." Constantine believed that his mother's actions were divinely inspired by the patron deity who would ensure a victorious ascension to Emperor of the entire Roman world.

To appease his superstitious architects, Constantine instructed Quintus, "No graves shall be desecrated. Relocate any remains that you unearth to a proper location for re-burial. Begin leveling the hill tomorrow."

The next day, under Quintus' charge, construction commenced on the largest building to be constructed in the 4th Century. The 350 foot long structure would be capable of accommodating 4,000 worshipers. The re-siting of the basilica changed the orientation with the obelisk, placing it outside the basilica's nave to the south. Its doors opened to the east, providing the remains of the venerated saint a spiritual vista to the Holy Land beyond.

III

Known as the Vatican necropolis, the construction site was an age-old cemetery. In early times, the Romans cremated their dead, preserving them in urns which were safeguarded in sepulchers that often housed multiple generations of ashes. Poorer relatives were buried outside, beside the shrine.

In the second and third centuries AD, the Romans began preserving the bodies in sarcophagi, resulting in the construction of larger sepulchers. Funerary sculptures might be added as memorials for ancestors who held a position of status. Some of the sepulchers were large enough to accommodate family meals, celebrations to honor the dead and to appease their spiritual influence to favor the living.

Early Christian burial traditions preserved the body in hopes of resurrection at the final judgment. Martyrs were initially buried alongside average Christians. Because of their special connection with God, however, these graves were transformed into shrines venerating the sainted dead, particularly those who were victims of the Roman persecutions.

Roman execution techniques regularly resulted in mutilated corpses. Consequently, these shrines frequently contained dismembered bodies, partial skeletons or mere fragments of bone. When nothing was preserved, blood-soaked clothing or belongings were substituted. Hoping to receive special influence beyond death, clusters of ordinary Christian graves girdled shrines of popular martyrs.

The Vatican necropolis which confronted Quintus was an urban microcosm amassed in a web of sacred edifices. Leveling the site was a daunting task under any circumstances. Dismantling the necropolis was an altogether different matter.

Multitudes of citizens, pagan and Christian, arrived soon after excavations began. Citizens of stature were permitted to remove the remains of their ancestors for burial elsewhere. Most respected the Emperor's wishes. However, several groups of devout Christian pilgrims refused to leave venerated shrines of Rome's martyred souls. One such group conducted a continuous vigil over the shrine of a popular, but lesser known martyr.

"It has been decreed by the Emperor himself that a Basilica honoring Peter the Apostle be constructed on this site. These remains must be removed," Quintus ordered.

"Centurion, we are poor and have no means to relocate them. Nor do we own property for such an undertaking." They pleaded instead, "Please ask the Emperor to spare these remains."

"The Emperor is at war in the East. He expects this work do be completed upon his return." A more youthful Quintus would have made an example of the group.

A young priest whom Quintus recognized from Helena's missions then approached him. "Kind sir, please seek audience with the Augusta Imperatrix, Helena. She understands these matters and has favor with her son."

Quintus hesitated. "Very well. I will request audience with her tonight. Meet me here tomorrow. But understand that her orders will prevail."

That evening, Helena greeted Quintus at her villa. "How is my son's new project progressing now, Quintus?"

"Slowly, madam. Very slow." Quintus continued, offering an explanation of the painstaking steps required to prepare the site. Finally, he revealed his conundrum. "All of the graves on the hill above St. Peter's shrine must be moved."

"Why are you troubled by this situation?" She sensed uneasiness.

"Desecration of graves is forbidden. It is a bad omen, and I am already cursed."

"Another tribulation for his guilty heart," she thought. "Do you think the work I plan for you is punishment?" She queried.

Quintus contemplated his response. "Why am I afraid of this woman? Why am I afraid of these nightmares? Why am I afraid at all? What is this feeling that has such a grip on me? Why can't I shake it? Do I tell her the truth? No, that would be a sign of weakness."

Quintus raised his amputated right limb, "No my lady, this is my curse. My destiny is to fight. My destiny has been crushed. I am cursed by your God for the terror I once inflicted on Yesua's followers."

"Is this a confession? Has he breeched the path to salvation? Is he truly sorry, or is this sorrow for the loss of his power?" she wondered.

She looked at him with a gaze at once chilling as well as compassionate. "Quintus, you are not cursed. You are blessed. Yesua loves you. There is nothing that you have done or could possibly do that will change his love. But everything will change for you once you accept His love. Perhaps your change of fortune is a sign leading you to your true destiny."

He had heard these words before, and they invariably enraged him. Yet spoken by Helena, they somehow soothed his ire, but did nothing to assuage his doubt.

She continued. "Quintus, order the pagan citizens to remove their descendants, then move the earth from the crest of the hill and bury the Christian dead below St. Peter's shrine under the heap used to level the site. It would be a tribute for any Christian to be buried beneath the foundations of Peter's Basilica. Move only those remains which are necessary to build a proper foundation without disturbing Peter's body."

This solution eased his concerns. "Yes, my lady. Thank you."

"Quintus, one other request please." Her request was delivered more like an order. "Tell the young priest to ensure that these souls receive a proper Christian burial before they are entombed. To ease your superstitions, perhaps you should join in prayer with him."

Quintus delivered Helena's orders to the young priest the next day at the cemetery. "Assemble your disciples here each morning. I will direct you to the new location to be covered with soil from the crest of the hill. These dead will be entombed with Peter beneath the building. You will be permitted to conduct a Christian ceremony for the dead. The Augusta Imperatrix has ordered me to participate with you in this ritual."

The ordeal of relocating the remains took several months. Quintus excavated a mass grave next to the sloping cemetery within the footprint of the Basilica, while the young priest organized work groups to transfer the corpses and relics.

The day of the mass burial was overcast. Throngs of Christians trekked to the site. The young priest was accompanied by the local bishop. The bishop retold the story of Peter and Paul's martyrdom and consecrated the site as sacred ground.

The young priest read Paul's words from his second letter to Timothy. "May the Lord grant mercy to the house of Onesiphorus, for he often refreshed me, and was not ashamed of my chains, but when he was in Rome, he sought me diligently, and found me. The Lord granted him his mercy on that day. And in how many things he served at Ephesus, you know very well."

The Bishop raised his staff and blessed the grave saying, "Mayst thou live among the saints and may God refresh the souls of these courageous dead."

The congregation replied, "Peace be with them."

Quintus softly repeated their words, "Peace be with them." To himself he said "and may peace be with me, at last."

The skies erupted with a cloudburst, quickly dispersing the crowd. The deluge continued intermittently for weeks, protracting the task of leveling the hill. Eventually, the mass grave was filled and the cemetery disappeared. The rains began anew.

Weeks later, Quintus inspected the site. Unbeknownst to him, the rains had weakened the soil on the hill. As he walked to the center of the mass grave, the foundation retaining wall collapsed, causing an avalanche of mud and bones, trapping Quintus.

With fresh air to breathe it is possible to live for a considerable time. As masters of the macabre, the Romans used live burials as an extraordinarily cruel method of execution. For Vestal Virgins who sullied the oath of celibacy, burial alive was the prescribed punishment. Entombed in a small vault underground with a couch, a lamp, and a table and a scant portion of food, their fate was to die slowly, trapped within total darkness. A claustrophobic torment ensured a death beset with endless panic and horror.

Quintus plunged into the midst of sacred bones, covered over with several feet of dirt. The voids created by the mass of skeletons captured enough air to last for a few hours. As he wandered in and out of consciousness, he recalled stories about being buried alive.

He remembered the account of Diocletian's chamberlain, a secret convert who sheltered other Christians during the persecutions. According to legend, after his secret was exposed, this martyred saint, Castulus was tortured and executed by being buried alive in a sand pit on the Via Labicana.

"I wonder if he could feel the slimy insects eating his flesh," Quintus pondered.

"The German tribes used to bury traitors alive," he reflected. "The cowards were tied to a wicker frame and pushed face down into the mud until they vanished. Infamy must be buried out of sight."

He repeated the thought over and over again as he drifted away. "Infamy must be buried out of sight. Infamy must be buried out of sight."

Quintus' train of thought was interrupted by a bright light and a cool breeze. He was covered in mud from head to toe. He was nude, lying on a table inside a tent made of a white translucent fabric. The blinding light moved closer to him, revealing a young, fair-skinned girl carrying a wash basin. She was dressed in a white flowing gown that fluttered in the breeze as her strawberry blonde hair flitted about. She appeared to float with the wind.

"Why are you here?" he asked.

"To bathe you," she whispered.

He studied her round cherubic face. Freckles peppered the bridge of her nose and cheeks. Her deep blue eyes glistened. When she smiled, her cheeks puffed like peaches of a soft pink hue as the light which outlined her petite frame waxed brighter.

"You must be Celtic, yes?" he inquired.

A wily smile graced her face as she shrugged as if to say, "Perhaps so!"

"What is your name?" Quintus combed for confirmation.

"Aisling." She smiled.

"Sounds Celtic." Returning her smile, he pressed further. "What does it mean?"

"Dream," she replied. Pressing her finger to her lips, she continued. "Shhhh. Let me do my work."

He closed his eyes as she traced cool rags across his body. He could feel her breath on his face and the warmth of her body as if she floated above him. Her aroma was sweet. Her breath was sensually exhilarating.

When she finished, she blew on his eyes as she placed her hand on his right shoulder from which his mangled amputated arm dangled feebly.

"There, you have been cleansed. Now, you are almost ready." Her fingertips traced his bicep.

"Almost ready? For what?" He could feel her fingertips moving down his arm as if his forearm were still intact.

"For Him!" Her smile beamed.

"What is this phantom feeling?" Quintus was vexed, "How is she doing this?" The peculiar sensation intensified. "Is her hand holding my absent hand? Stay focused?"

"You said 'almost.' What else must happen?" he begged.

"You must ask and receive Miriam's forgiveness!" She disengaged, backed out of the tent, turned into the light and vanished.

Just as Quintus caught a fleeting glimpse of two, lily-white body-length wings, the bright light vanished, hurling him back into the dark abyss. He struggled to burrow his way out of the constricting heap of mud and bones.

Quintus was quickly losing his strength, frantically gasping for air. Eventually, the trashing stopped with his realization that escape was futile. He closed his eyes and took a deep breath. Perhaps, it was his last. He waited for the end.

The bright light returned. A dozen hands grappled, pulling him in all directions. Were these his demon escorts to the fires of the underworld? He opened his eyes to be greeted by familiar faces and realized that he had been rescued.

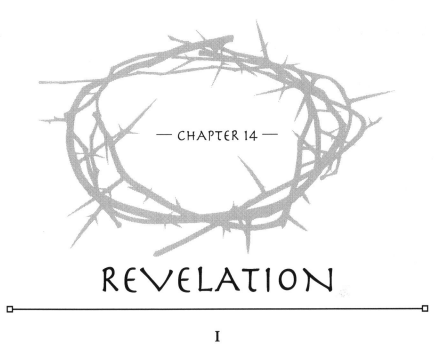

REVELATION

I

"It ends where it begins. My son is in Pemdje. How sweet is the mercy of the Lord," Miriam thought.

In Alexandria, Arius extended his hospitality to Miriam, providing her with food and shelter. Her rehabilitation and return to health took several months. All the while, Arius cautioned her that it had been over a decade since Philip was sent there. Philip was now a young man who might be fulfilling his life's purpose elsewhere.

Simon agreed to accompany Miriam to Pemdje in search of Philip. Miriam eagerly awaited Simon's return from Petra, where he was completing trading transactions from his trip to Alexandria. By the time he returned, Philip and Barnabas were wandering in the Eastern Desert. Locating the community that sheltered Philip and Barnabas was easy. Miriam's heart sank when the heard the news of their departure. Simon remained optimistic.

"The Eastern Desert is well traveled. There will be news of their adventures." He went on to recount the story of Peter the Hermit. "He's quite rarely seen, but his reputation is widely known. Mater Miriam, many of your prayers are answered. Philip may not be here, but he is alive, safe from his father's scourge. For this alone you should be thankful."

The stories of Philip's life in the community were not without angst for Miriam, particularly when she heard of his reclusive behavior. She knew that memories of his father haunted him. Would life as a desert hermit exacerbate his reclusiveness? Would he burrow into a hole from which there was no escape?

"His father's scourge has scarred his memory. I am not sure that the desert can cleanse his spirit," she fretted. "What now? What must I do? Must I search the desert?"

"Do not lose hope. Today is more hopeful than when you left Petra." Simon grasped both of her hands. "Stay here and tell his story to all you meet, as you did in Alexandria. Pray like you have since you were separated. Do not lose hope."

He continued, "I will return to Petra through the Eastern Desert. There is a route which will take me to the sea. I can cross by boat to continue my journey to Petra. I will tell his story to all I meet, letting them know that you are here in Pemdje."

Simon crossed the Nile and headed southeast across the desert toward the Via Nova and the ancient port of Berenike situated on the west coast of the Red Sea. Miriam found refuge with three Christian women who knew the story of her parent's martyrdom.

Miriam revived her Petra routine. She could be found each day in Pemdje's main plaza, bathing the feet of weary travelers. After Miriam prayed for their safe passage, she would query them to see if they knew of Philip and his whereabouts. For those who would patiently listen, she would retell her tragic story, beginning with the beheading of Sergius. As the years passed, Philip's story was known to all in Petra, as well as to thousands of travelers.

As the seas of change about them were sweeping with the rising wave of Christian influence, Miriam and Philip dreamed and prayed for their reunion. Philip never gave up hope that she was still alive. Miriam was resolute in her belief that someone that she or Simon had met would in turn meet Philip. Miriam remembered Simon's story of Peter the Hermit. She prayed to Yesua to send a vision to the hermit should he encounter Philip. She prayed to Yesua for Simon to meet someone who would encounter Philip. Finally, she prayed to Yesua to be reunited with Philip in Pemdje.

Simon's journey to the port of Berenike was largely uneventful. He encountered few religious zealots living in the Eastern Desert. Most shunned contact with him. One prodigious encounter, however, was all that was needed; just one chance meeting with someone who knew or who would eventually meet Philip.

Simon was nearly halfway across the desert when he noticed a figure on a hill about 100 yards from the road. As he approached the figure, it raised its head slightly, but then dropped quickly, as if too weak to move. Near the figure smoked a smoldering warm campfire. The figure was a young man in his mid-twenties. He laid quietly in the fetal position, barely breathing. His walking staff was clutched tightly in his hands.

It appeared as if he had been attacked in his sleep! His face was covered in dried blood. His right ear was missing. His neck and cheek below the ear were sliced open. Though he was bloodied, no major veins or arteries were severed. Both forearms and hands were shredded. Simon gently turned the man over and discovered that his buttocks and left thigh bore several puncture wounds. It was now clear that this young man had indeed been the victim of an animal attack, probably hyenas, or possibly, wolves.

Simon pitched camp, determined to stay as long as it took to nurse the man back to a condition healthy enough to travel. Leaving him to find help would expose the man to further attacks from predators and vultures. Holding his head gingerly, he turned it and trickled water into his mouth. The man lapped the water.

"What is your name?" Simon asked.

"Thomas," he whispered.

Simon was traveling with a donkey and a small cart which he positioned behind the young man to protect him from behind. It was nearly sundown. Simon rekindled the fire and prepared a broth for Thomas. Then Simon cleaned his wounds and wrapped his head in a clean cloth, covering his right ear and cheek.

"How did this happen?" Simon asked.

"Wild dogs," Thomas spoke, struggling to catch his breath. "I was... was adding wood to the fire, when one of them jumped on my back.... knocking me to the ground. He bit my cheek and my ear. The others struck at my arms and legs. I rolled over and one bit me from the rear, attacking my hind-side. It was difficult to see. I could not tell how many there were."

"Speak slowly, Thomas. Slowly. Take your time," Simon urged.

"I tried to stand with my staff, but two dogs knocked me over again. I think, I think that I hit my head.?" he offered, uncertain.

"I think you are correct. You have a large lump here." Simon lightly touched the spot. "How did you finally fend them off?"

"I didn't," Thomas replied. "A larger animal burst through the fire and attacked the dogs. They fought ferociously above me. That's the last thing I remember. I must have passed out. I am not sure how long I've been here."

"The embers in the fire were still warm when I arrived. It must have happened last night." Simon was eyeing their surroundings. "Wild dogs do not give up easily. They may come back tonight. I will stay awake and guard us tonight. Tomorrow, if you are strong enough to travel, we must leave."

That night, Simon fashioned a seat against the wheel of his cart so that he could remain comfortably upright. He stoked the fire frequently. From his supplies, he gathered a whip and a long dagger for protection. Shortly after midnight, he heard the chilling wails of the pack. As the shrieks grew closer, it was clear that the pack was now surrounding their camp. Simon braced for the worst. Given the pitch of the cries, he was prepared for hyenas.

Suddenly, the night grew deathly quiet; the periodic rustling of paws across the sand broke the silence. They were close. Simon gripped his weapons in each hand. He moved from a sitting position into a squat. He stared into the darkness. Something moved beyond the campfire, which illuminated two piercing eyes. The eyes moved back and forth, as if the animal were pacing. Then the eyes disappeared and reappeared, as if it was looking backward then forward. Was this the lead dog? Was the pack close behind?

The eyes grew larger as a figure emerged from the darkness. The silhouette was taller and broader than a dog. The outline of the head and ears revealed a dark wolf. Was Thomas wrong? Had Simon's hearing deceived him? Was this a pack of wolves? Simon was gripped with a strange foreboding fear, as if a supernatural battle were unfolding.

The wolf stopped a few feet from the camp fire. More robust than most wolves in the region, Simon guessed that the wolf was a male. They studied each other; Simon squatting next to Thomas, the wolf standing behind the fire, facing Simon. The rustling of intent began again. Growling, the wolf bared its fangs. The rustling stopped.

Simon stood, anticipating assault. The wolf growled more loudly. Raising his head to the sky, the wolf's howl rivaled that of the most ferocious desert lion. The sound of scampering paws retreated from a certain fight, and then scampered off, whining until out of Simon's hearing. Pirouetting, the wolf continued to howl, then came to rest with his back turned to Simon. The wolf surveyed the darkness. Then, as if he were a sentry, he sat on his haunches with his back to the encampment.

A pack of hyenas is a formidable predator. When defeated, their prey became easy pickings for lions and wolves. Was this the wolf that had chased the wild dogs from Thomas' vulnerable figure the night before? Again he wondered. Is this the dominant male guarding its prey until an entire pack arrives? Uncertain, Simon could not risk disaster. He sat back down against the wagon wheel and watched intently.

Around 2 AM, the growling wolf was on his feet with the hair raised on his neck, back and haunches. He stood at attention for nearly an hour, and then returned to his sentry pose and post. As the night dragged on, Simon started to nod off. Try as he might, he could not avert sleep. He awoke at sunrise to find that the wolf had vanished.

Thomas was more responsive that morning. Though his head was pounding, he was able to sit upright. The two struck up a conversation as they shared bread and water.

"Did the dogs come back last night?" Thomas asked.

"I think so, but I am not certain." Simon went on, explaining the events of the evening. "I could hear the pack close by, but only the wolf came near. Strange."

"How so?" Thomas grimaced as he tried to get more comfortable.

"I thought that the wolf was the pack leader, but as the night grew longer, I came to believe that he had come to protect us. I think he was the beast who saved you from the dogs." Simon was shaking his head in disbelief.

"Have you ever known a wolf to behave like that?" Thomas questioned.

"I know of only one other person who was protected by a wolf, Mater Miriam." Simon recounted her story from the time Miriam met Lupa in Jerusalem.

"How did she get to Jerusalem?" The story was distracting Thomas from his injuries.

Taking this interest as a positive sign of Thomas' recovery, Simon chronicled Philip's miraculous cure at the beheading of St. Sergius years earlier. "The boy was the bastard son of the executioner, who had brutally raped Miriam. She was left with her right cheek permanently marked by a crescent-shaped scar."

"What a dreadful, tragic story! What has happened to the mother and the boy?"

Clearly, Thomas had not heard Philip's story. "Miriam is in Pemdje. She went there recently, searching for Philip, only to find that he and a companion had departed for the Eastern Desert just weeks before. Philip is somewhere in this desert."

Thomas grimaced, trying to reposition himself. The pain was beginning to intensify, distracting him. Simon presumed that Thomas had not chanced upon Philip and Barnabas.

"What are you doing in the desert, Thomas?" Simon inquired.

"I am looking for a hermit who will accept me as his disciple," Thomas replied.

"So are Philip and his companion. Perhaps your paths will cross. If so, let Philip know that his mother awaits him in Pemdje." Simon rose to begin breaking down the camp. "You should rest now. We cannot risk another night here. I will arrange a spot for you on my supply wagon."

Simon let Thomas sleep until late morning, then departed for a mining camp that he had passed the day before the two met. Simon stayed with Thomas for a week before continuing on his passage.

A grateful Thomas wished him well. "What is your destination, kind deliverer?"

"I will cross the sea by boat and travel to my home in Petra, where I will gather more provisions. I must continue to Jerusalem. Living there is a young woman who was raised by Miriam. I am eager to tell her that her dear friend, Mater Miriam, is safe in Pemdje, praying for Philip's return." Simon offered his hand as a parting gesture.

"How can I ever repay you?" Thomas asked.

Thomas could sense a deep compassion in Simon's eyes as he spoke. "Pray that the Miriam and Philip will be reunited."

II

Three haunted souls, actors in the tragic martyrdom of St. Sergius, were adrift in a sea of doubt, wondering if the reunions they desperately needed would be fulfilled. They drifted apart aimlessly for countless years. Each was being driven to the brink of madness. Quintus was trapped in Rome, haunted by his victims. Miriam was paralyzed in Pemdje, fixated on Philip. Philip was lost in the desert, searching for meaning and purpose.

After their meeting with Anub, Philip and Barnabas concluded that the Holy Spirit had answered their prayers. The years of wandering the desert in search of a spiritual community finally met with success. They agreed to stop their journey to Pemdje and travel instead to the monastery at Tabennisi on the banks of the Nile River at the Qena Bend.

The pair was welcomed warmly and accepted into the community. Being experienced scribes made them particularly valuable. The copying of sacred texts was serious work and in many respects, much harder than manual labor in the fields, or laboring to build new monasteries. A scribe's work required fine motor skills and excellent eyesight. More importantly, the role required focus and stamina for what was quite often repetitive, boring work.

Philip and Barnabas were quickly recognized as scribes who possessed superior skills. They were ordered to work in a small chamber with six other monks. There were no rotations, no division of labor. Their days were as long as the light was good enough to work by. Pachomius himself determined what texts to scribe. Their work was so important that he would frequently excuse the monks from prayer services, allowing them to take advantage of the remaining daylight.

As with the rest of the community dedicating their lives to God, all work was performed in silence as a sacred offering. Monks communicated only if necessary to complete a task. Spoken words were reserved for communal prayer. An atmosphere of anonymity cloaked each monk. Barnabas hoped that continuous work and prayer would calm the storm in Philip's psyche.

Recurring nightmares of his demon father worsened with a darkness that prevented Philip's soul from reaching safe harbor. The dreams were played out in different settings, but all had a consistent theme and ending. As each dream unfolds, Philip sees his mother in the distance and races toward her. Before he reaches his mother, she is attacked by a deadly predator. The predator varies in each dream: a snake, a lion, a wolf. By the time he reaches his mother, the marauder has her in its mortal grip. Philip beats the beast off with his staff, battering it to death. Turning the lifeless creature over, Philip is confronted by the monstrous face of his own father, a vision that invariably awakens Philip, leaving Miriam's fate unresolved.

At first, Philip toiled diligently in sacred silence. Then a voice began speaking to him. "You killed me. Murderer! You killed me, but not before I killed her." Try as he might, he could not silence the voice. He tried prayer. He tried reading the sacred scriptures he transcribed. He practiced these distractions in silence, until one day he shattered the calm in the room.

"Devil, get behind me!" he shouted aloud in his first outburst.

Some of the other monks smiled, thinking his utterance the perfect response to the drudgery of their work. A chill gripped Barnabas as if he knew Philip's demons were back. Barnabas moved closer to Philip.

"What troubles you brother?" Barnabas whispered, as he gently placed his arm around Philip's shoulders.

Philip threw Barnabas' arm aside as he shouted again, "Devil, get behind me!"

The other monks stopped their work and stared at Philip.

"Brothers, I am afraid the toils of the day are taking their toll on Brother Philip. He and I will walk in the garden together to refresh his spirit. Please excuse us."

The pair left the building, wandering into a garden that was used frequently for meditations. As they walked, Barnabas recalled the many good times they had shared. "Remember when we first met? I was playing the role of John the Baptist with our friends, baptizing them in the river. Suddenly, you appeared. I called you Yesua."

Philip stared straight ahead, as if in a trance.

"We called each other brothers. We have been friends ever since. I love you, Philip. Be at peace. I would never let anything harm you. Even your demon father, should we meet him." He stopped and turned Philip to face him. "Do you hear me?"

Philip looked into Barnabas' face. By now, he was engulfed by full-blown mania, hallucinating. The face he saw belonged not to Barnabas, but his father, bedizened with Sergius' blood. "Do you hear me?" the beast taunted, hissing as the tongue slithered from its bloodied mouth.

"Be gone with you," Philip shouted, as he pushed Barnabas to the ground. Philip grabbed a tall stake from the plants and battered

Barnabas, shouting, "Evil one! What have you done with her? What have you done, you vile serpent?"

The commotion caught the attention of several monks who were meditating in the garden. Realizing what was happening, they raced to Barnabas' aid. Before they could subdue Philip, he struck Barnabas in the head, knocking him unconscious. Several monks wrestled the writhing Philip to the ground as he screamed like a mad man. Another monk, who ran for help when the commotion began, returned with more monks, including Pachomius.

"Take Brother Barnabas to his chamber. Care for his wounds. Remain with him, praying for his recovery," he ordered. "Take Brother Philip to my chamber and strap him down. We must drive the demons from him!"

Pachomius led the ensuing exorcism. The darkened room was lit only by candlelight. Three other monks prayed with Pachomius. Philip was strapped down for his own protection. As with traditional practices, Yesua was summoned to expel the demon. The quartet prayed to powerful Angels, Gabriel and Michael. They prayed to the Apostles and martyrs. Their efforts were to no avail. Philip's convulsive ranting continued through the night, and on into the morning.

By all rights, his body should have been exhausted of all energy by now. The monks were prepared to pray and fast for however long it took.

That morning, Pachomius opened a vial of sacred oil to anoint Philip. First, he anointed his forehead. When he anointed his lips, Philip bit him and spat in his face. Knowing that the demon was to blame, Pachomius harbored no ill will toward Philip. His heart was filled only with compassion for his brother.

"This one is not yours. He belongs to Yesua. I will not let you prevail," Pachomius told the demon as he smiled at Philip.

The veins in Philip's neck bulged angrily as he screamed. Quintus' bloodied face was all he could see. "Monster. What have you done with my mother? What have you done with her? What? What? Where is she, you wretched beast?"

Pachomius gently placed his hand on Philip's chest, hoping the strength of Yesua's spirit within it would drive the demons from his brother monk.

To his surprise, his hand pressed against a stiff object underneath Philip's robe. He opened Philip's robe and discovered the leather pouch protecting Lucian's precious gift.

Leafing through the book, Pachomius spoke to one of the attending monks. "Go find Brother Barnabas. If he has recovered, bring him here. I wish to speak to him."

Barnabas had regained consciousness soon after he was taken to his cell the night before. The pain from his bruised body paled in comparison to the pain of his heart. His caregivers told him that Pachomius was exercising the demons from Philip. That night, just before sleeping, Barnabas hoped and prayed for Philip. He awoke thinking, "Perhaps the holy man can kill the spirit of Philip's demon father." Although disturbed, he drifted back to sleep and slept until dawn.

The messenger monk found Barnabas bruised and sore, but willing to help his friend. Together, they returned to Pachomius' chamber. The holy man left the exorcism to talk to them.

"Brother Barnabas, how are you feeling?" Pachomius asked, as he clasped Barnabas' hands in his.

"My shoulder and head ache and my arms are bruised, but I am fine otherwise. How is Philip?"

"Our brother is possessed by a demon that harmed Philips' mother."

Do you know this demon? Do you know Philip's mother? Why does he wear this gospel in a pouch around his neck?"

Barnabas recounted their tragedy. "I do not know her, but I do know the story. His father was a vicious Roman persecutor who tortured and murdered Christians. The butcher raped Philip's mother, who was his slave. Philip was born blind. When he was ten years old, his father beheaded a Christian legionnaire in their presence. The blood from the martyr splattered in Philip's eyes. His blindness was miraculously cured. His father was so enraged that he separated them. They were each exiled to remote areas of the empire. Philip saw his mother's face only for a moment. A crescent shaped scar on her cheek is his only memory of her face."

"And the book? What do you know about the book?"

Philip was rescued by Lucian of Antioch, who gave him the book as a gift."

"Lucian of Antioch? The great martyred teacher?"

"Yes."

"Excellent. Then we will call on Lucian to assist us. We should also call on Philip's mother. Do you know her name?"

Before Barnabas could respond, the messenger monk blurted out "Miriam! Brother Philip's mother's name is Miriam!"

Pachomius asked Barnabas, "Is this correct? Is Philip's mother named Miriam?"

"Yes." Barnabas studied the monk with one ear and a badly scarred face. "How do you know this?"

Pointing to his scars, he replied, "A merchant named Simon of Petra saved my life years ago. He befriended Philip's mother. He told me this same story."

"The Holy Spirit is at work here. We will invoke Miriam's aid as well." Pachomius turned to enter the chamber.

"Wait!" Thomas pleaded. "Wait! The merchant asked me to give Philip a message if I were to meet him. Tell him Mater Miriam is alive, living in Pemdje, praying for their reunion."

Barnabas was speechless. A wave of guilt swept over his body. Philip was right. They should have heeded Peter the Hermit's vision and returned to Pemdje. Instead, Philip lay here, in a state of demonic madness.

The rush of emotions was swallowing him.

"Barnabas. Barnabas!" Pachomius woke him from his stupor. "Join us as we pray over Philip."

Entering the room, he walked to a small window, opened it and stood facing Philip. A pleasant breeze extinguished the candles as it refreshed the smell of the cramped chamber. Pachomius was silhouetted against the sunlight. Lucian's heroic imprisonment, torture and murder were well known in the Christian community. Pachomius summoned Lucian's aid by speaking through him to Philip.

Quoting Lucian's last words, Pachomius said, Philip, "This is Lucian. Are you proud to be called a Christian?"

Unable to see the figure clearly, Philip closed his eyes as if blindness had returned. He lay still for a movement. He smelled the fresh breeze. He felt the warm sunlight on his face.

Pachomius spoke again. "Philip, this is Lucian. Are you proud to be called a Christian?"

Philip opened his eyes. "Yes. Yes Lucian, I am proud."

"Philip, this is Lucian. Do you trust me?"

"Yes, Brother Lucian."

"Your father cannot harm you. You are safe with me. Tell his demon to leave."

"My mother! He has done something to my mother!" Philip became agitated again.

"No. He cannot harm your mother. She is also safe. Tell him to go and never return." Pachomius' soothing words calmed the troubled monk. "Tell him, in the name of Yesua, to depart forever."

Philip closed his eyes again. "Be gone murderer. In the name of Yesua, let me be. Stop tormenting me. My mother is safe."

Philip's breathing slowed. The room cooled with the gentle breeze. Peace graced his face. "Mother is safe," he whispered.

All of the attendants watched and waited. Then Pachomius whispered in return. "Philip, this is Miriam, your mother. I am safe. I am here in Pemdje, waiting for you. I am here waiting."

Philip smiled as he listened, as if he could hear Miriam's daily plea, as if he could smell her sweetness. With a look of contentment, his exhausted body succumbed at last to sleep.

III

Philip's slow recovery proved hopeless. His perseveration for reunion with his mother replaced the obsessive fear of his demonic father. Terror was replaced by restless anticipation.

"When can I see her? When can I see her? My mother is in Pemdje. Can you take me there? Can you take me to my mother?" His incantation was nonstop.

Philip relapsed into habitual rocking as he chanted his pleas. Barnabas feared that his friend's madness was permanent. The realization that Philip might never fully recover was not lost on Pachomius. The troubled monk's relentless outbursts were distracting the entire community. A month after the exorcism, Pachomius requested a meeting with Thomas and Barnabas.

"I regret having to say this, but Brother Philip cannot stay in this community." The decision clearly pained Pachomius.

"If not here, where can he live? I cannot leave his side. I must then leave also," Barnabas asserted.

"I thought this would be your response," Pachomius elaborated.

"There are many caves in the cliffs above the river near here. You and Thomas will find a suitable location for Philip. Each of you will be permitted to leave the community one day a week to deliver food to him and oversee his wellbeing."

Barnabas was pondering Pachomius' proposition when Thomas spoke up. "We should take him to Pemdje. He should be with his mother."

"How many years has it been since your encounter with the dogs and the good Samaritan, Simon?" Pachomius asked.

"Ten years, perhaps," Thomas replied.

Pachomius made eye contact with Barnabas, who declared, "Miriam may not even be there. A journey to Pemdje is hazardous. Philip is not well. If we find that Miriam has moved or worse yet, that she has died, Philip may not survive."

Thomas persisted. "It is not a coincidence that we are here today in this place discussing Philip's fate. Miriam's prayers are being answered by her faith in Yesua."

Pachomius had entertained the work of divine intervention, but did not think Philip was capable of making the journey alone. Asking a monk to abandon his life of solitary devotion to accompany Philip appeared to be imprudent. Pachomius rose to his feet. He paced back and forth in front of his window, pondering the conundrum.

Facing the window, he delivered his decision. "Yes, Philip should be with his mother. It is his only hope. However, I fear that Barnabas may not return to the secluded devotion he seeks. For this reason, Thomas will travel with you and Philip. If Miriam is found, leave Philip and return. Barnabas will feel a duty to Brother Thomas to return to the community. If Miriam is not found, return with Philip and carry out my plan."

The next day, the trio departed the monastery en route to the Nile River, where they hope to secure passage by boat down river to Pemdje.

As they boarded the boat, Philip asked his companions, "Are you taking me to my mother?"

"Yes," Barnabas replied. "Yes."

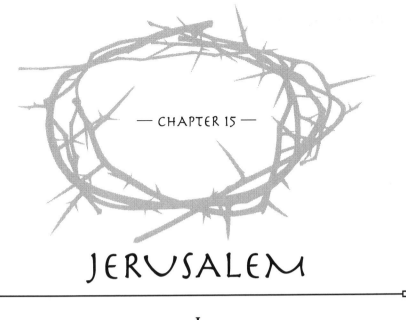

— CHAPTER 15 —

JERUSALEM

I

Under the watchful eyes of Helena, Quintus toiled for eight years on the construction of St. Peter's Basilica. It took nearly three years to complete the site preparations and foundations. As the structure went vertical, his role changed to directing the construction of wooden scaffolding. Once again, his experience in the legions, building siege platforms, proved useful.

Constantine's civil war with Licinius was an intermittent affair lasting seven years. It ended at the Battle of Chrysopolis, fought on 18 September, 324 AD. The final encounter on the shores of the Bosporus across from Byzantium left Constantine as victor, the sole Emperor. With the Empire secure through the unwavering loyalty of his patron deity Yesua, Constantine now focused on strengthening his rule. In May of the following year, eager to resolve the divisions confronting Christianity, he convened the Council of Nicaea. Peace, prosperity and continuity appeared within his grasp.

But Constantine's court succumbed to the intrigue and treachery that haunted imperial politics. Like his father before him, Constantine fathered a child with a woman of little political consequence, named Minervina. Unlike his father, Constantine was a loving, protective father who kept his son, Flavius Julius Crispus, at his side.

Except for the son she bore, Minervina's life remains obscure historically. It is unclear whether Constantine married her. Regardless, she was discarded like Helena. In 307 AD, after succeeding his father as Caesar of Gaul, Constantine married Flavia Maxima Fausta, the daughter of the Augustus Maximian, sealing an alliance for control of the Tetrarchy.

Maximian's son, Maxentius, was jealous of Constantine's success and usurped his father's position, spawning five years of political maneuvering between father, son and son-in-law for control of the Western Empire. Maximian turned on Constantine and plotted to assassinate his son-in-law. The plan was foiled when Constantine captured Maximian, forcing him to commit suicide in 310 AD. Two years later, Maxentius' forces were defeated by Constantine at the battle of the Milvian Bridge, where Quintus ended Maxentius' life.

Constantine's most trusted colleague proved to be his son, Crispus, whom he appointed Commander of Gaul. Like his father before him, Crispus distinguished himself as a warrior in his father's legions, waging successful campaigns in Gaul and defeating Licinius' forces in two critical battles in the east. Because he was much older than his half-brothers, Crispus was the most suitable heir to the imperial throne. Fausta, who bore Constantine six children, feared her husband would favor Crispus over her off-spring. The jealous Fausta convinced the paranoid Constantine that his son was conspiring against him. On his father's orders, Crispus was tried, condemned to death and executed in 326 AD. Soon afterwards, Constantine discovered Fausta's ruse and extracted his revenge by orchestrating her murder. Fausta was suffocated in an over-heated bath.

Crispus was a favorite of his grandmother, Helena, who had influenced Constantine's decision to entrust his son's education to an important Christian teacher named Lactantius. The execution of her beloved grandson shocked Helena. The ensuing confrontation with Constantine was more admonishment than conversation.

"You are not a true believer. How could you be? How could you let this happen? You executed your son and murdered your wife!"

Constantine knew better than to respond.

"Your mistrust and violent temper are not worthy of a true Christian. You must atone for your actions."

A reticent Constantine replied. "I can't bring him back. Fausta had to be punished for her deception. What is done is done. What would you have me do?"

Helena was stern. "You can start by being baptized. You can start by asking Yesua for forgiveness."

Constantine did not respond. He knew that Helena would have no patience for what he believed. However unfortunate these incidents might be, they were fateful circumstances of his position and power. His superstitious loyalty to Yesua was just that. His behavior was reinforced because he was constantly rewarded by this loyalty. Yesua was just an ally, albeit a powerful one, to whom he would remain loyal. But he could not submit himself totally to Yesua. After all, he was the Emperor. There was no higher earthly power.

"Have you nothing else to say?" Helena was clearly frustrated by his apparent apathy.

"It was their destiny." Gesturing to his surroundings he continued, "And this is mine."

"Well, my destiny is the fulfillment of Yesua's will. I am leaving for Jerusalem to find his tomb and cross. I will build churches on those sacred sites and pray that your soul will be saved. Don't try to stop me."

"Very well, Mother," a reticent Constantine replied. "Upon one condition, that you take Quintus with you. He knows the region well. His skills will be helpful in your quest."

The next morning, Helena met with Quintus to deliver the news of his new assignment. Her mention of Jerusalem triggered an avalanche of memories, beginning with the fateful beheading of Sergius and the miraculous cure of his son's blindness. He had banished the slave girl to Jerusalem. Was she there? The Celtic angel's words repeated in his mind over and over, "You must ask and receive Miriam's forgiveness!"

II

A lthough Helena was now 76 years old, she wasted no time in her preparations for the journey. Within a month, her entourage was ship-bound for Caesarea. From there, they traveled east to the ancient city of Jerusalem. Upon arrival, she immediately set out to discover the sacred site of Yesua's crucifixion. She discovered, to her horror, that the Emperor Hadrian had covered over the site so as to build a temple dedicated to Venus. She ordered Quintus to find the temple and report to her when he had an answer.

Quintus made his way through the city to a narrow stone paved street that wound its way up a hill. The street circled the north side of the temple as it passed skeletons of crumbling buildings. A woman's body lay in a doorway. The scene seemed eerily familiar. He hesitated for a moment, but proceeded onward to the temple entrance, where he dismounted in front of its monumental stairs.

Again, he hesitated. "There is something foreboding about this place," he thought. It started to rain as he climbed the stairs. When he reached the portico, there was a thunderous crack followed by an angry gust of wind. A downpour erupted.

The interior of the temple was cold and dark. For all intents and purposes, it appeared abandoned, the need for pagan rituals forsaken. As he walked through the temple, he could sense someone watching him. He stopped, poised like a spider awaiting danger. He stared into the shadows behind the interior columns.

"Is that figure a statue or a human?" he wondered.

"You there, come out," Quintus ordered.

The muted figure outstretched its hands.

"Come out, I said!" Quintus' senses intensified.

The figure stood motionless, its hands outstretched.

Quintus drew his sword. "Identify yourself! Come here, as I commanded!"

"Come to me!" The figure's response was gently spoken.

Quintus' sword suddenly grew heavy, much too heavy to hold. It fell to the floor. The clanging metal reverberated in the hollow temple.

"Who are you?" Quintus said, expecting a response.

Again, silence engulfed the temple. He could not discern the figure's sex. "Is this the Goddess Venus? Is she angered by the void of sacrificial worship?" he asked himself. The tension paralyzed him. His spider-like instincts vanished.

"Come to me!" The voice was hypnotic.

Quintus stepped forward. The floor was wet. He lost his footing. Catching his balance, he stopped and shuffled forward. As he moved closer, a bright light erupted from behind the figure, momentarily blinding his sight.

He stopped again, trying to focus. Instinctively, he raised his right hand to shield his eyes. He was able to discern a man's figure standing in a pool of blood. The man had been brutally tortured. Fresh blood poured from his wounds.

"Come to me!" The outstretched hands were bleeding profusely.

As Quintus lowered his arm, he realized that he had been shielding his eyes with his missing hand. He reached across his body, and tried to clutch it. When he looked down only to find his usual scarred stump, the bright light extinguished.

Quintus lost his footing. He tumbled backwards and onto the stone floor, striking his head. The blow rendered him unconscious. When he awoke, the man was gone. He lay motionless for a moment, trying to gather his thoughts. The floor was dry. Cautiously, he rose to his feet and walked to the temple's portico. The storm had passed. The bright sun rested in a mid-afternoon position. Quintus had entered the temple early in the morning. He had been unconscious for hours. As he mounted his horse, he noticed that his feet and calves were covered in blood. He tried to rub it off, but to no avail. The beheaded mother at her son's crucifixion and Miriam's subsequent rape flashed before him as he slowly made his way across the city to Helena's quarters.

"I must regain my composure. I need to clean off this blood," he thought. "I cannot present myself to Helena in this condition."

Quintus left the temple precinct. The city was alive with activity. He passed through a tight street which opened onto a plaza that had a public fountain. Quintus rode slowly toward it. Sitting beside the fountain was a young woman who was washing the feet of strangers, behind her perched a cruciform staff. His mind raced with memories of his cleansing ritual with Miriam. He waited patiently for others to leave, and then approached the woman.

She hesitated when presented with his blood soaked feet and legs. Looking up, she made eye contact. She sensed his angst. His clothing revealed a Roman officer of great stature. The scars and dismembered arm belied a fearless warrior. His eyes reflected those of one who has suddenly come to grips with his own mortality, only moments before death.

She plucked a rag from a pile of them beside her, and soaked it. Prepared, she prayed, and reached for his leg; her gentle touch seemed to ease the tension in his muscular calves. The stubborn blood stain washed away with ease.

"What happened sir?" she said, her eyes fixed on his feet.

With a slow monotonous voice, Quintus broke the long silence. "I am cursed by the blood of my victims."

She continued to work as they made eye contact again. "Yesua will forgive you."

Quintus studied the woman. She was much too young to be his slave girl. Her face and skin were pristine. She bore no scar.

"What is your name?" he asked.

"My name is Puella," she smiled.

Puella was not the name the Celtic angel had spoken. In fact, until the angel's appearance, he could not remember Miriam's name at all. He had only heard it once before, when she was handed over to the soldiers after the miracle in Rasafa.

Quintus thanked Puella and gave her a denarius for her toils. As he mounted his steed, she called out to him, "Yesua will forgive you. Go to Him when he calls."

Quintus did not respond. He galloped away as fast as his horse would take him to report back to Helena. As he recounted his survey of the temple to Helena, he revealed only that he felt a strange presence as if a powerful spirit inhabited the temple. Helena could feel his disquietude. She knew that whatever he had encountered was indeed powerful. Quintus rarely shared his feelings. When he did, he never voiced each detail, fearful of exposing his vulnerability.

"You have confirmed what we have been told. This must be the place. Raze the temple. Make haste. Use whatever resources you need. Time is fleeting for me. I must find His cross." Helena could not contain her excitement.

The city was still a functioning military fortress. Helena saw to it that all available legionaries in the garrison were at Quintus' disposal. Engineering feats of the Roman legions were notable for both their complexity, as well as the speed with which they were accomplished. The razing of the temple was no exception. Under Quintus' supervision, work proceeded around the clock for nearly a month. He rarely left the site. When he did, it was for the brief respite of a bath and a peaceful meal. On his way to his quarters, Quintus always stopped at the plaza fountain to receive Puella's soothing foot baths.

News of Helena's exploits circulated quickly through the community. Puella was keenly aware of Quintus' charter and eagerly awaited his visits to learn if Yesua's burial chamber had been discovered. Their sessions ended with Puella praying for Quintus' safety and good fortune. Quintus liked this innocent maiden. For the first time in his life, he was developing a genuine concern for another human being. It was an odd feeling.

News of Helena's exploits also reached Constantine, who wrote to Macarius, the Bishop of Jerusalem, ordering him to assist in the search for the true cross. Once the temple was razed, frenzied excavations followed, until a cave entombment was unearthed; it resembled the description of Yesua's sepulcher.

While the excavations searching for the true cross continued, Helena meticulously interrogated the local residents, hoping to unearth clues revealing the identity of the tomb and the whereabouts of the cross.

She uncovered many legends about the site called Golgotha, "the place of the skull," including the belief that Adam was also buried at the site.

"Surely this is the tomb," Quintus told Helena after its discovery. "I am certain of it."

"How can you be so sure?" She was still unaware of Quintus' apparition in the temple.

"He is there. He is watching us," was his only reply.

"Other sacred burial sites are there, including Adam's. Unless we find His cross nearby, we can't be certain," Helena insisted.

The excavations yielded no results. Repeated questioning within the Christian community also proved fruitless. Helena was made aware a rumor that the Jewish community knew the location, but feared their faith would be destroyed by Constantine if Helena found the cross. She convened a meeting with the Jewish leaders, demanding that they surrender and reveal the location of the cross. The assembly refused, feigning ignorance.

"I will destroy the entire city if necessary to find it. There will be no pity on you." Helena's tirade exposed the genus of her son's temper. "You will stay here until I have an answer, or else."

Threats by the mother of a Roman Emperor to destroy the city were not to be taken lightly. Several leaders huddled in conversation until a spokesman approached Helena.

"There is a man named Judas, who inherited a collection of Christian documents." The spokesman's nervousness supported the validity of his statement. "He is very knowledgeable about these matters and seems to know something."

Turning to Quintus, Helena ordered, "Find him and bring him here."

"I will take you too him," the spokesman said to Quintus, who returned within an hour. The man named Judas stood at his side.

"How ironic, a man named Judas will reveal the location of His cross." Helena's demeanor was stern. "Tell me now all that you know."

"Nothing! I know nothing about what you are asking."

Helena stared at the man intently for a moment before she spoke. "Your neighbors don't believe you. I don't believe you."

Hoping to make an example of him, she turned to Quintus. "Can you find out what this man knows?"

"Yes," he said. His penetrating gaze chilled the gathering.

"I know nothing. Nothing," Judas persisted.

Helena motioned Quintus to her side. She whispered in his ear. "Do it without bloodshed."

Quintus nodded and departed with Judas under guard.

As she left the meeting, Helena addressed the leader. "Pray that this man's secret reveals the location of the cross. If not, I will begin the systematic destruction of the city." Before departing, she turned to them and said, "Again!"

Quintus transported his prisoner to the excavation site, where several deep yet fruitless pits had been dug.

"Bind his hands and feet," Quintus ordered the guards.

As they executed his orders, Quintus tied a rope around Judas' waist. "We can stop any time you wish to share your secret."

"I have no secret. Do as you wish," Judas refuted, adamantly.

On Quintus' command, the guards lowered him into the pit. The next morning, they pulled him out, gave him water to drink and questioned him again. Again, he refused to answer them. Again, they lowered him into the pit.

The next morning, he was raised out, given water to drink and asked the question. A small basket of bread was laid at his feet. He would be given the bread to eat if he unveiled the location of the buried crosses. Still, he refused.

The process was repeated for four more days. Each day, the bread basket blossomed with the addition of fruit, dates, and finally dried fish. Still, he refused.

On the morning of the seventh day, he was denied water before being lowered again into the pit. Perhaps, it was his increasing hunger. Perhaps, it was his thirst. Perhaps, it was the seven days of cramped gloomy confinement. Perhaps, it was a combination of all three.

At sunrise on the eighth day, Judas' screams greeted his captors. "Take me out of this hell hole. I will tell you what I know. Take me out of here!"

III

As the excavations progressed, Quintus repeatedly visited Puella on his return trips to Helena's quarters. In spite of the fact that the urgent news he carried this day would please Helena, he stopped at the plaza's fountain to check on Puella. His uncharacteristic fondness for her was a strange but pleasant feeling. Over the past weeks, the young woman developed a troublesome cough, which concerned Quintus.

Puella could not be found in her usual spot. He frantically questioned strangers in the crowd. His concerns were confirmed when he was told that she was gravely ill.

"Where is she?" he asked a stranger.

"A merchant is caring for her at his camp outside the west gate," he was told. "She burns with a fever that is consuming her. She may not see tomorrow, if she is still alive."

Hopefully, she was in good care. Puella would have to wait. The secret revealed by the Jew, Judas, was too important. Helena must be told the news immediately.

Helena's attendants buzzed with excitement upon Quintus' return. It was too early in the morning for him or arrive. He must be bringing news. Quintus was shown to an anteroom, where he paced nervously, awaiting Helena's entrance. The apparition in the temple still haunted him.

Helena entered the room, breathless, "Well?"

"The Jew claims that three crosses and a titulus bearing Yesua's name are hidden in an abandoned cistern buried east of the site," Quintus exclaimed. "The men are excavating the area now. If the cistern is uncovered, I have ordered them to not open it until you arrive."

As she exited, Helena said, "Find Bishop Macarius and meet me at the site."

Quintus and Macarius arrived at the site in late morning, followed by Helena at noon. The excavation work had reached a frenzy. Groups of two and three men wandered off, unsupervised, to dig on their own. The base of the hill buzzed with workers like a hive with the queen bee set to mate. The growing tide of anticipation rose with several false alarms. Near mid-afternoon, two men who were digging near the site's perimeter unearthed a stone structure.

Quintus quickly took control. A ring of guards was stationed around the discovery while he hand-picked men to open the cistern. Helena and Macarius were led to the edge of the structure. At Quintus' command, a trio of legionnaires cautiously pried open the lid. The buzzing that permeated the hill all day was replaced by silence, broken only by the sound of metal methodically chipping away at stone. The stone lid scraped the side of the cistern as the men slowly pushed the lid aside. Quintus grabbed a rope and ordered a sentry to fashion a harness around his torso. Except for Quintus, everyone appeared frozen in anticipation.

"Bring me a torch!" Addressing the men who removed the lid he continued, "On my command, lower me into the cistern."

The cistern was about ten feet in diameter and thirty feet deep. A musky smell rose from below. The rope slackened as Quintus reached the cistern floor. He wedged the torch into a space between two stones. Turning slowly, Quintus came face to face with three rough shaven wood crosses stacked upright against the back wall.

As he edged forward, he stepped on something. Quintus fell to his knees to examine the object. It was a wood plaque with the inscription that read IESVS NAZARANUS REX IVDAEORVN. When he reached down to pick it up, two hands pushed his head down. A barefoot figure stood before him. He could see only two bloodied feet, both pierced with wounds.

"Come to me, Quintus," the voice whispered. "Come to me."

The hands were gentle, but firm. Quintus pressed the plaque to his chest and wept uncontrollably, like a baby thirsting for life-giving milk.

"Quintus?"

"Quintus?"

"Quintus? What is happening?" Helena's voice bellowed.

The hands lifted as the man vanished. Quintus regained his composure, stood and shouted. "Just as the Hebrew described, there are three crosses and a titula with the inscription 'Yesua of Nazareth, King of Judea'" Helena fell to her knees, weeping.

Two men were dropped into the cistern to assist with the removal of the treasures below. The crosses where lifted out, one at a time. Behind the last cross, Quintus found three iron nails. These, coupled with the titulus, proved that one of the three crosses was the mount that Yesua rode to his death. The crosses where relatively well preserved, but moisture from the cistern and three centuries of deterioration left no clear evidence of tell-tale nail holes. In fact, a case could be made that each one of the crosses was Yesua's.

After an hour of fruitless speculation, Helena turned to Bishop Macarius for advice.

"How can this be? How can we determine which is His cross?" asked the distraught Helena. "It will take a miracle."

"Precisely," the bishop replied. "The true tree will be life-giving. We must find a gravely afflicted faithful soul who deserves to live. His cross will provide the cure."

Quintus spoke up. "Bishop, do you know the woman who cleans the feet of travelers at the fountain in the plaza near here?"

"Yes. The woman named Puella?"

"Puella is near death. She is being cared for at a camp very near here, outside the west gate. I will bring her here."

"Hurry, Quintus," Helena pleaded. "There is little sunlight left. I am not leaving here until the true cross is identified."

The camp was easy to find. Puella was in a tent being cared for by the merchant, a man named Simon of Petra. Simon was startled by the appearance of Quintus and the two legionnaires who accompanied him.

"Who are you? What do you want?" Simon was on his knees next to Puella, holding her hand. She was unconscious. Her chest wrenched with each breath.

"I am here for her," declared Quintus, pointing to the dying woman.

"Leave here, now. Her next breath may be her last. She will soon be gone." Simon wiped Puella's forehead with a cool rag.

"Give her to me and she may live." Quintus went on to explain the purpose of his visit. "We have found Yesua's cross. Let her die on it, or better, be healed! Help me to take her to the cross."

The sight of Quintus leading the donkey drawn cart created a stir at the cistern. In his absence, Helena had organized the crosses, laying them in a side by side formation. Simon and Quintus wasted no time lifting Puella from the cart and placing her on the first cross. As they stepped back, Helena stepped forward and gently outstretched Puella's arms on the cross beam. Bishop Macarius began praying, summoning Yesua's saving grace. Puella stopped breathing.

"She's gone," Simon uttered. "Let me take her now."

"No. No." Helena motioned excitingly, "Move her to the next cross."

They lifted Puella to the next cross. The prayers were repeated, but to no avail. Five minutes had passed since her last breath.

"Quickly. To the next cross," Helena urged. "Quickly."

The sun reached the horizon as Puella was positioned on the last timber that remained. Surely, this was the cross. When the incantations finished, the living waited in silence. Another five minutes passed, then ten. The sun's rays glistened on the billowy clouds as the shining orb disappeared on the horizon, the streaming beams of light appearing like a pathway for angels to shepherd Puella to the heavens above. Twilight engulfed the peaceful scene below.

As the gathering wandered away, Simon turned to Quintus, who was next to Helena. "You were right to bring her here. How glorious to send her off, such a beautiful child of God. Thank you my friend. May I take her body now?"

Quintus looked at Helena. Tears dripped from her cheeks as she nodded, yes.

Simon and Quintus knelt on either side of the cross, pulling the corpse to a sitting position. The head fell forward, draping her hair over her legs. A deep, guttural exhalation of air escaped from her lungs as her head suddenly snapped backward, seized by a fit of coughing. Blood coated Quintus' face. Puella had risen miraculously from Yesua's own sacrificial cross.

She gasped desperately for air as she regained consciousness. Her sight was blurred from her groggy sojourn. She could barely make out Helena's figure in front of her.

With her hands outstretched, she called to Helena, "Mater Miriam. Mater Miriam!"

Helena dropped to her side. Embracing her, she said, "All is well, child. All is well. You have been saved. You are well. Yesua loves you."

"Mater Miriam," Puella cried. "Mater! I love you Mater! I love you!"

Carefully, Quintus and Simon carried Puella back to the bed fashioned for her on the cart for the short trip back to Simon's camp. Puella's longing for Miriam dazed Quintus, who wondered about the identity of the woman who bore the same name of his own banished slave girl.

As they approached the camp, Quintus asked Simon, "Who is Mater Miriam?"

"She is a holy woman who adopted Puella when she was young. A remarkable, woman indeed. She was the slave girl of a brutal Roman thug who persecuted Christians in Syria. Her owner raped her when she was young. She bore him a blind son who was miraculously cured of his blindness when the blood from a martyred saint splashed onto his face."

"How was the saint martyred?" Quintus knew the answer.

"He was beheaded in front of Miriam and her son. The head came to rest in the boy's feet," Simon replied.

"What was the martyr's name?" Quintus was reliving the scene in his mind.

"A famous Roman officer named Sergius."

Quintus had trepidation about asking the next question. "Have you met this Miriam?"

"Oh yes. I know her well. I was with her earlier this year. She lives in Pemdje near the river Nile." Simon smiled, fondly thinking of her. "She will be pleased indeed to know of Puella's resurrection upon the miraculous cross of Yesua."

Quintus probed further. "I plan to travel to this region. I would like to meet her. How would I find her?"

Sensing compassion in Quintus, he answered, "You will find her at the fountain in the city's plaza. She washes the feet of travelers. Puella learned her own skills from Miriam. You will know her by the distinctive crescent shaped scar on her face. The butcher gave it to her when he pressed her face into the stone floor while he raped her."

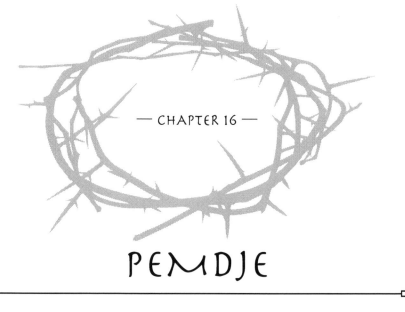

CHAPTER 16

PEMDJE

I

Philip, Barnabas and Thomas traveled on a small boat back to Antinopolis where they again encountered the Christian merchant Anub, who graciously agreed to transport the monks to Pemdje on his sailing vessel.

As they embarked, he instructed them, "I will continue on to the markets in Alexandria. On my return, I will stop again in Pemdje. You are planning to return to the monastery, yes?"

Thomas spoke. "Hopefully, we will find Philip's mother. If we do, only Barnabas and I will need passage. If she cannot be found, we will be taking Philip back with us."

A serious Anub responded. "Philip is fortunate to have you as friends. You are wise to come to me for help. The river can be dangerous. There are treacherous rapids, and large rocks that will easily destroy a vessel. There are river monsters, as well."

For centuries, the inhabitants of the Nile valley were heedful of creatures lurking beneath the river. The ancient Egyptians both feared and worshiped the crocodile. A crocodile god, named Sobek, was depicted in their artwork as a human figure with a crocodile head adorned with a feathered crown and carrying a scepter.

Barnabas affirmed Anub's concern. "We saw crocodiles in Pemdje that devoured small animals and children."

"The crocodiles are even larger on the Nile, growing to be 20 feet long," Anub cautioned. "They are strong swimmers that can catch a boat or a raft. They live in large groups and will strike without warning. They are very dangerous indeed. But the most dangerous peril is the hippopotamus. He is vicious and aggressive. On my last journey, I saw one attack a boat and turn it upside down."

A curious Thomas asked, "Did the occupants survive?"

"It was a most disturbing scene. The boat was close to shore when the hippopotamus casually disappeared beneath the water. Suddenly, the boat with three occupants was thrust from the water. The hippo clutched one man in its hulking mouth and disappeared again below the water."

The tone of Anub's voice was maudlin. "The others swam frantically to shore, only to be greeted by crocodiles that dragged them back to deeper waters. The rapacious reptiles emerged minutes later on the shore with limp bodies that were soon shredded in a feeding frenzy by the pack. The upper torso of the first man bobbed to the surface, only to be devoured by the waiting crocodiles. The river was red with blood."

The story abruptly ended the conversation. Barnabas studied his companions. Thomas gently cupped his mangled ear in his palm as he pulled his hood over his head. He stared aimlessly at the shore. Barnabas wondered. Did the story remind Thomas of his vicious encounter with the wild dogs? Did Thomas regret leaving the safety of the monastery? Is he afraid of what dangers might lay ahead?

Philip retreated to the bow of the ship where he sat with his eyes closed. He started rocking as he pulled his knees to his chest.

"What have I done?" Barnabas asked himself. "I am like that hippopotamus, who without warning, swept Philip away to the desert. The vision that Peter the hermit described was real. Miriam was alive in Pemdje, searching for Philip. My selfish desires were like crocodiles tearing my brother apart. Can he ever be whole again?"

The trip down the Nile did little to allay their trepidation. Each sighting of crocodiles or hippopotamuses sent the monks on an introspective journey to the depths of their worst fears: fears not of the treacherous river, but of the unknown awaiting them in Pemdje.

Try as he might to envision a sweet reunion with his mother, Philip was unable to remember the sound of her voice or her gentle touch. Would he recognize her? Would she smell the same? Would she know him? Would she even be there? Had his father taken her to some foreboding end?

The haunting dreams returned. Philip reimagined Anub's story with himself and Miriam as the victims. The lumbering hippopotamus wore his father's angry distorted face. The crocodiles cackled with his father's sinister laugh. His mind flew from one thought to another. He grew more introspective as they closed in on their destination. Sleep eluded him. His reclusive behavior did not go unnoticed.

"Barnabas, has Philip always been like this?" Thomas asked quietly.

"Occasionally, he goes to a bad place, but never before like this," Barnabas responded.

"What brings him back?" Thomas continued.

"The sacred books. He is very inquisitive. He studies each word, each phrase as he scribes. Our discussions about the books can be very stimulating. He will often arrive at provocative conclusions, even to the point of the most controversial."

Barnabas furrowed his brow, "so controversial that I am careful not to engage him in the presence of others."

"Such as?" Thomas inquired.

Barnabas hesitated briefly, but responded. "He once told me that this place, the earth, is the place of spiritual purification. Each of us was created at some other time in perfect union with God. Each of us has sinned against the Him. We have been banished here to relive our lives until we are either completely purified or eternally damned. Only when our spirit is pure is it possible for us to journey back to the Father, who has sent Yesua many times to lead the way."

Thomas contemplated Philip's postulation for a while. Then he returned to the topic of his mental health. "Do you think he can recover from his current state?"

"I fear his only hope is through a reunion with his mother." Barnabas stared at his friend who was alone at the front of the boat, methodically rocking back and forth.

Anub, who was manning the tiller, had been listening to the conversation. He spoke up. "What happens if she is not there? Perhaps she is no longer alive."

"She must be there. God would not have brought us together otherwise," Thomas replied.

"She has to be there!" Barnabas thought. "Any alternative is unthinkable."

II

"I have been praying for this Quintus," Helena exclaimed. "Ever since the day I met you in the surgeon's tent, I have been praying to hear these words from you. You believe in Yesua! How wonderful is

God's mercy! The miracle of the cross has saved you."

Quintus was having difficulty looking at Helena. "Where do I begin?" He thought, struggling with what he should share with his strong-willed patron.

"Actually, I knew it before the miracle at the cross. He was there!" he mumbled.

"Of course, he was there. Yesua is with us always," Helena replied calmly.

"No. He was there in the temple the day I first inspected it. He was there in the cistern with me. He humbled me before him. I saw his wounds. I felt his hands touch me. His blood gushed from his body. 'Come to me.' He said."

Helena was astounded by this mysterious man who barely spoke more than a sentence when prompted. Now he was pouring out his heart to her.

"Ever since the day we met my lady, I have been haunted by visions of my victims. In my nightmares they stand together, headless and dismembered, chanting 'We forgive you. We forgive you.' I see their faces in the crowds of the poor that you help. When I was trapped in the landslide on the Vatican Hill, an angel appeared to me telling me to go to Him," Quintus rambled.

Now she understood the secret harbored all of these years. He was slowly reconciling himself with his past atrocities. "Please sit down. Calm yourself. You need not confess your sins to me. I will speak to Bishop Macarius. He will be your confessor. Don't be afraid. Yesua will forgive you. Go to Him. Ask for forgiveness."

"Thank you for being so gracious." Quintus hesitated, "There is someone else's forgiveness that I must receive first."

Helena was curious. "Tell me more."

Quintus took a deep breath, "The woman, Puella, who was cured yesterday," he paused.

"Go on, continue." What could this be about, she wondered?

"Do you remember when she called you Mater Miriam?"

"Yes? Obviously she confused me for someone else." She gestured for Quintus to continue.

"Mater Miriam adopted Puella when she was ten years old and became her spiritual guide. She taught Puella how to pray. This woman also bathed the feet of the tired and weary."

Helena was still confused. "How do you know this?"

"The merchant told me," Quintus said. "From his description, I believe I know this woman."

"Why are you telling me this?" Helena replied, her brow furrowed.

Fearing the loss of Helena's respect, Quintus was reluctant to share more.

"Quintus? Tell me. What are you afraid of?" Helena now grasped how difficult this confession was for him.

"I fear that I will lose your respect. I fear that you will think that your prayers were wasted on a wretch like me."

"I know about your past. I know your reputation. Are you truly a believer now? Has your belief in Yesua changed you heart?"

"Yes," he muttered.

"Then my faith in you will not be changed by anything you tell me. Please, continue."

He blurted out, "I must find this woman."

Helena stared into his eyes. This was the Quintus whose shell was so difficult to crack. Obviously, this was a difficult conversation for him. Should she continue? Was there a need to know or was her blessing to find Mater Miriam enough?

Her silence moved Quintus to open up again. "Miriam was my slave girl when I was chief executioner in Syria during the persecutions. I forced her to bathe me after torturing and murdering Christians. The only words she ever spoke to me were, 'Yesua will forgive you.'" He stopped.

"How did you respond?" Helena prompted.

He stared blankly as he continued. "I raped her, violently. I pushed her head to the floor, leaving a permanent crescent scar on her face. She bore my bastard son, who was blind. When the boy was ten, I forced them both to witness the execution of a Christian officer named Sergius. After I beheaded him, his head rolled into the boy's lap. Blood splattered on his face."

Quintus paused, choked by emotion. Then he muttered, "my son's blindness was miraculously cured."

Helena took a few moments to contemplate what she had been told. She gently whispered, "I am surprised that this miracle was not enough to convince you of the power of Yesua's love."

"I thought it was sorcery of some kind." Quintus took a deep breath.

"What is your son's name?" Helena asked.

"I can't remember. I only heard it once." Quintus was in a trance.

"What happened to your son?" Helena smiled.

"I was so enraged that I separated mother and child. I banished Miriam to Jerusalem. The boy was sent to the Roman garrison in Alexandria, but he escaped. I don't know his name or where he might be, if he is even alive." His hand trembled.

For so long Quintus was a callous instrument of suffering and death. For years, he reconciled the hauntings of his victims as his duty to the loyalty he swore as an officer in the Roman imperial army. Now, he was overwhelmed by the realization that forgiveness would truly be granted by simply asking. His feelings for Puella re-kindled his thoughts about the boy.

It wasn't until Puella was resurrected from death that he understood the magnitude of the cruel separation of Miriam from their son. Because of it, he denied his son the joy of his mother's love. Because of it, Miriam was doomed to a loveless life of doubt. Perhaps, it would have been better if the boy were dead. At least she could have reconciled herself to his fate.

Quintus spoke again. "There is something else. The angel who appeared to me when I was buried told me that I must first ask and receive Miriam's forgiveness. I must find her before I can go to Yesua."

Helena spoke. "Is she still here, in Jerusalem?"

"No," he replied. "She is in Pemdje. The merchant visits her often. He told me she is there, awaiting news of her son."

Helena walked closer to Quintus. Placing her hands on his shoulders, she said, "Go now. Find her. Bring her here. Reunite her with Puella. Then, we shall find your son. Together. Go now."

III

Life in Egypt was dependent upon the Nile's annual floods, which were fed by remote jungle rains. It rarely rained in Pemdje. For two weeks, strong winds from the Western Desert pummeled the small city. Wind-blasted sand made ordinary tasks unbearable. A layer of dirt and sand covered everything. Miriam made two fruitless attempts to continue her work at the central plaza. On her second attempt, she huddled all day beneath a shroud with a veil covering her face. Few braved the elements. None were in need of a foot bath.

"My bones ache," she thought. "Almost as much as my heart. He is not coming. He is dead and so am I. My spirit is dead. This foreboding wind speaks to me. Is it time for me to leave? I could walk into the desert as far as these bones could take me. I could walk into the river until I am consumed by its waters. I am so weary, so tired."

She gathered her rags and bucket. Leaving the plaza, she made her way to the room above the warehouse that she shared with three other Christian women. She arrived in time for evening prayers.

The women had been her companions since she arrived in Pemdje over a decade earlier.

The quartet shared whatever possessions they could glean from the results of their menial work. Her sisters knew her well and were constantly amazed at her unwavering faith that she and Philip would be reunited. As part of their prayer routine, they concluded with a prayer for Philip's safe return.

This night, Miriam stopped the concluding prayer. "Not tonight. These ill winds are evil. They bring a foreboding message. Not tonight."

"All the more reason for prayer, sister. Don't despair," they told her.

"No. Not tonight. Not ever. These winds bring only dust. A sign that my son is dust, as well. Philip is not coming. Not ever."

She left the table and retreated to a corner, where she laid on her straw bedding. She woke before sunrise. Taking care not to wake her sisters, Miriam left the room, leaving all of her earthly possessions behind. She walked slowly through deserted streets toward the Western desert, trudging headlong into the howling wind.

The same winds rendered the river unnavigable for Anub's modest ship. Philip and his companions were moored on the river's west bank for more than a week.

"Anub, how much further to our destination?" Barnabas anxiously inquired.

"Two maybe three days," Anub replied.

"How long by land?"

"At least twice as long. But traveling by foot in these winds could blind you. What are you thinking?" Anub was concerned.

"For some reason, I sense an urgent need to find Miriam," Barnabas said.

Barnabas' instinct was correct. Miriam had chosen her fate. As he, Thomas and Philip departed on foot for Pemdje, she was walking into the desert to die. The unrelenting winds slowed her pace. She was determined to walk as far as her body would take her, hoping that no one could find her. Praying that no one would save her.

"I am ready, sweet Yesua. Walk with me to the Father's home. I am ready. Take me." Her request became her cadence. "I am ready. Take me," she said with each stride.

She walked into the night. She carried no water, no food. Exhausted, she lay down. She scooped a handful of earth and smelled the world she was prepared to leave.

"If this is the place, so be it. Take me Yesua, please," she prayed. She woke in a dim, dusty haze, which surrounded her. As she surveyed her whereabouts, she wondered if she had passed into the afterworld.

"Where am I?" she thought. "Give me a sign."

In the murk, she could make out a figure slowly approaching her. It was difficult to make out whether it was man or beast.

"Is it a dog? No. No, it's a wolf!" Miriam tensed. "Am I still alive? Yesua, you once sent a wolf to save me. Have you sent another to kill me?"

Miriam lay back down, anticipating the end. Nothing happened. She sat up and looked in the direction of the wolf. The wolf was laying down, looking at Miriam. When Miriam sat up, the wolf followed suit. Miriam rose to her feet. The wolf stood.

A wave of excitement swept over Miriam as she wondered, "has Yesua sent me Lupa to lead me home to be with Him? Is Philip there, with my parents?"

She called out "Lupa?" At the sound of her voice, the wolf's ears perked. "Lupa, take me home. Take me there."

The wolf sprinted toward Miriam, bolting past her. It stopped and turned to face her, as if beckoning Miriam to follow. Miriam obeyed the command. The wolf walked into the gritty cloud, stopping periodically to make sure her lead was being followed.

The sun illuminated the dust-filled haze to an amber glow, painting a surreal atmosphere. The wolf trotted ahead until sunset, then disappeared. Miriam had been walking for two days without food or water. Her lips were blistered. Her mouth was dry. She was dehydrated and weak. She lay down and immediately fell into a deep sleep.

During the night, the winds changed. Gone were the stinging gusts that tormented the area for weeks. Miriam pushed her body up, looking at the crisp horizon. No wolf. Only desert greeted her. She sat up and turned in search of the wolf.

"Where am I?" Miriam was bewildered. "What does this mean? Why am I here?"

The mysterious wolf was nowhere to be seen. Miriam was staring at the outline of a city. The wolf had led her back to the outskirts of

Pemdje. Summoning her last reserve of energy, Miriam stumbled back to the building that she had left two days before. She collapsed at the doorstep.

"What happened?" Miriam had difficulty focusing when she woke.

"Praise God. You are back. You are back with us." Tears of joy graced her adopted sisters' smiling faces. The room was filled with spontaneous chatter.

"You disappeared so suddenly."

"We found you at our door step."

"You were missing for days."

"You've been delusional."

"We have been nursing you back to heath for three days."

Miriam covered her ears. "Please, please not all at once," she continued. "I walked into the desert to end my life. The desert was veiled in a bright haze. A wolf led me through the wind only to end up back here. Why? What does this mean?"

The women looked at each other. One spoke up. "Philip must be alive. You must continue to pray and wait for him. He will return to Pemdje."

Miriam closed her eyes. She slept most of that day. From the moment they found her, the women never left her side during her recovery. She was lost. Now she was back. They were determined not to lose her again.

As she recovered, Miriam convinced herself that the encounter with the wolf was indeed an omen that Philip would return to her. When she regained her strength, she gathered her blessed cloths and bucket, preparing to continue her healing footbaths in the plaza.

The day was overcast. The dark horizon predicted rain. It rarely rained in Pemdje. The relentless wind ended as abruptly as it started. A thin layer of dust covered everything. Miriam's normally pristine white tunic had yellowed.

Several of her regular patrons greeted her that morning, joyful to hear her soothing prayers as she bathed their feet. The sky grew more ominous by early afternoon. A stranger approached her and offered his right foot. She didn't glance up to study him, but went straight to her task.

"Kind woman, will you help me cleanse my troubled spirit?" The man's soft voice was oddly familiar. A drop of water splattered the dust at his feet.

"A tear?" she wondered.

As she moved her gentle touch to reach his calf, she asked, "What troubles your spirit sir?" His calf bore a wide, ugly scar.

"I need forgiveness," the man begged.

Slowly raising her eyes, she studied the man. Another wide deep scar marred his neck. His right arm had been amputated. She froze as she glanced into his eyes. She could not breathe. Large rain drops spattered around her. Her bucket tumbled as she scrambled back.

"I am here to ask you to forgive me. I was wrong to separate you from our son," Quintus said.

Her fear turned to rage. "Our son? Our son? How dare you, you animal. Now he is OUR son. The only thing you can claim as yours was your vile slime, which you savagely spewed into my womb."

The skies opened on them as she scurried away like a retreating spider. Puddles of mud bubbled in the plaza as the downpour grew in intensity. The plaza emptied, leaving Quintus, Miriam and his horse alone in a sea of mud. Before she could get to her feet, Quintus grabbed her arm, pulling her to him.

"He shall rape me again," she feared.

She spit in his face as she struggled to escape. "Never. Never again," she screamed. "Don't touch me."

"Please listen to me. I have changed. Yesua has changed me. I was dreadfully wrong. Please forgive me," Quintus pleaded.

Quintus panicked. He could only think of Helena's parting words, asking him to return to Jerusalem with Miriam. He mustered all his strength to sling Miriam with one arm over his shoulder. His forearm straddled her ankles as he grabbed the horn of his horse's saddle.

His futile attempt to mount the horse spooked the animal. Rearing back, his steed lost its footing on the slick stone surface, throwing Quintus and Miriam to the mud covered pavement. Miriam slammed head first onto the plaza. Quintus fell onto his one good hand and his knees, struggling for balance. The horse stumbled atop Quintus' legs, sprang to its feet, and galloped away.

Miriam lay face down in a muddy stream of water that quickly change color to deep red. Both of Quintus' ankles were shattered. He dragged himself to her listless body and pushed himself up, kneeling next to her.

He threw his head back as he cried out, "You fool! What have you done? You fool! You wretched, hateful fool! You have cursed the world with misery and death. You don't deserve forgiveness. You don't deserve to be saved."

Instinctively, he slid his sword from its sheath, the same sharp sword that had spilled the sacred blood of martyrs. He positioned the tip below his sternum and determinedly fell forward.

Quintus Flavius Scipio, Supernumerarius in the Roman Legion of the Caesar Galerius Maximianus lay dead in the muddy plaza of Pemdje. His blood soaked sword protruded from his back. His corpse shrouded the motionless slave woman, the mother of his only son.

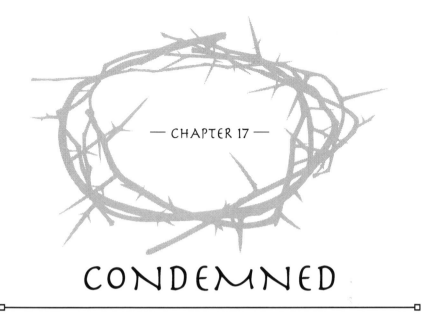

CONDEMNED

The venerable monk was on his death bed. He joined the monastery soon after it was constructed over sixty years earlier. In a community dedicated to silence, continuous hard work and prayer, one's past vanished into blessed anonymity. His age, his life, his heritage, in fact, everything about him was a mystery to his younger brethren.

Most of the monks at the monastery were born after the Council of Nicaea. None of them recalled the Age of Martyrs, which had preceded the Council of 325 A.D. A few of the older monks were babies during those horrific times. The dying monk, however, was old enough to have experienced, first-hand, the pain, the suffering and the controversies that had now miraculously changed Christianity forever.

Though his body was failing, the old man's mind remained sharp. As the young monk attending to him worked in silence, he could not help wondering about the old monk's secrets, which would soon be lost for all eternity.

His attendant was about to spoon feed him broth when the old man caught his eye. "Brother, what I need now is food for my spirit. Would you hear my confession?"

The young man set aside the cup of broth and sat back down next to the death bed. Confession was one of the few opportunities for true dialogue in the community. When requested, it was never denied.

"Tell me brother, what troubles your soul?" The young man gently stroked his thumb on the patriarch's lips, tracing the sign of a cross.

"In Yesua's name, I beg God's forgiveness." Clearly the old man was troubled.

"Tell me the sins you wish to confess. Begin whenever you are ready." The young monk turned away, bowed his head and closed his eyes. "I am listening."

"I am afraid that there is not enough time left to tell everything," the revered holy man mused.

"Take your time. Share what you wish. I am with you until the end," his confessor consoled him. "If you are truly sorry, your sins will be forgiven, whether you finish your confession or not."

"I hope so," the old monk continued. "I must tell a story to provide context. It begins when I was a boy during the last Roman persecutions, a time we call the Age of Martyrs."

Over fifty years had passed since the tragic reunion between Miriam and Quintus. The actors who orchestrated the ascension of Christianity were gone. Helena died in Rome at the age of eighty, less than two years after the discovery of the true cross. Constantine's baptism on his death bed, ten years later, did little to dissuade his enigmatic legacy as the first Christian Emperor. The always political general appeared to be hedging his bet with eternity.

Two years before his death, Constantine ordered Bishop Alexander of Constantinople to restore the heretic Arius back to communion with the faithful. The Nicene Council's resolution of Yesua's divine nature was short lived. Arianism continued to divide the faithful, while the status of both Arius and his arch rival, Anathasius, seesawed between excommunication and reinstatement.

The aged monk was one of many bit players swept up in the ascension of Christianity. As he lay dying, his days were consumed more and more by sleep. His final confession to the young attending monk was now in its fourth day. The patriarch slept into the afternoon. His confessor waited by his side, praying for the opportunity to learn about the fate of the three monks traveling to Pemdje.

The young monk had listened patiently for three days, asking questions periodically to keep both the older monk and his story alive. At times, he felt guilty when he probed. Selfishly, he relished the revelations of the history that had been kept from him for so long. Alas, as his confessor, he would be bound forever to a vow of secrecy.

Although yesterday's session exhausted both repentant and confessor, it seemed a pity for the story to end now. Besides, he had yet to understand what sins, if any, were being confessed by this merciful human being.

"If the devil possessed half of your perseverance, he would surely have been victorious long ago," the old man greeted him with a smile.

"Brother Barnabas, you are still with us. Let me prepare some broth for you." The young monk, named James, rose to his feet.

"No, please sit," Barnabas urged. "There is little time left. How long have I been asleep?"

"Nearly a full day. It is early afternoon," James explained.

"Where did I end my confession?" Barnabas was clearly confused.

"Hardly a confession," he thought, "He shared no sin in need of absolution."

"You ended yesterday with Quintus' death at his own hands in the mud soaked plaza in Pemdje."

"Then I have not finished. Brother James, may I continue?" There was a sense of urgency in Barnabas' voice.

"Certainly. Do you remember what happened next?" James sensed that Barnabas needed prompting to begin again. "When did you, Thomas and Philip arrive in Pemdje?"

"We arrived two days after Quintus took his life."

"Did Philip see his dead mother's body?"

Barnabas sighed, "Neither. By the time we arrived, Philip was blind once more. The first day on foot, we were surprised by a violent wind storm. We strapped our tunics together and walked single file in search of shelter. Philip was in the middle. He babbled constantly, calling out his mother's name. We covered our heads and faces as we staggered forward. I urged Philip to be quiet. I urged him to cover his face. At one point, he threw off his hood. He was screaming. 'Mother, I'm coming. Mother I'm coming.'" Barnabas was now hyperventilating.

"Shhh. Shhh. Slow down, Brother Barnabas. Take a deep breath."

James turned to face the old man. He grabbed Barnabas' hands and began to pray aloud, which calmed the dying monk.

James whispered, "Maybe we should continue your confession at another time."

Tears trickled down Barnabas' cheeks. Ignoring James' request, he continued. "His eyes were caked with sand. We huddled together as we tried to clean his face. Philip would not stop rubbing his eyes. He broke away from us, sprinting into the storm. We could hear him screaming for Miriam, but we could not see him. We covered our heads as we shuffled after him. It took us so long to find him. He was sitting, rocking back and forth and rubbing his eyes. His face was covered with blood."

Barnabas choked back his tears. "It was too late. It was too late. His sight would never return."

Both men were speechless. James worried that Barnabas might not survive his confession. He could not let his broken spirit stray into eternity. James knew that he must ease this kind soul forward gracefully.

He prompted the old man again. "When I asked you if Philip was able to see his mother's dead body, you said 'neither.' What did you mean by 'neither?'"

"Philip could not see and Miriam was not dead!" Barnabas stared at the ceiling. "She broke her nose in the fall. She was unconscious when we found her in the care of her Christian sisters. Her face was hideously disfigured."

James groaned.

Barnabas continued. "We tried to explain to Philip what had happened. His only comprehension was that we had found his mother. We guided him to her side. He knelt beside her, bent over and pressed his head against her chest. He told her, 'I am here to protect you mother. I am here. I love you mother. I am here to protect you.' Then he repeated over and over, 'I will never leave you. I will never leave you. I will never leave you.'" Barnabas' composure returned.

James listened patiently.

"Philip's incantation continued unabated for hours. Finally, the cadence slowed with a whisper as he fell asleep. Thomas and I carried Philip to an adjoining room. We placed our exhausted brother on a blanket. Thomas sat by his side as I returned to Miriam's bedside. The women were washing Miriam's wounds. When they finished, I sat beside her and placed her right hand in mine. I prayed over her for several minutes. I bowed my head as I prayed for my brother Philip who had slipped into irreversible madness."

James' eyes were fixed on Barnabas, who paused momentarily. The two stared intently at each other as Barnabas continued.

"Miriam's hand moved in mine. I looked up to find her staring at me. Tears filled her eyes. 'Philip?' she asked softly. 'Have you come back to me?' As I leaned forward, she put her hand on my neck and pressed my cheek to hers. Without hesitation I said, 'Yes mother, I have come back. It is me Philip. I am here. I will never leave you. I will never leave you. I will never....' Her hand went limp. Her breathing ceased. She was gone."

James rose to his feet weeping and stepped to the window. Barnabas covered his face with both hands. A bird flew into the room through the open window. It flitted around the room, swooped and dipped near to Barnabas. Then it departed as quickly as it had entered. James watched the bird as it drifted out of sight. This clearly was an omen that death was at hand. James returned to his bedside confessional station.

James tried to soothe his spirit. "Brother Barnabas, as unnerving as it may seem, pretending to be Philip was an act of mercy, not a sin. Your soul is not stained by this pretense."

"I know. I knew it then. Do you not know how my soul has been stained?" Barnabas asked.

"Tell me." James anticipated Barnabas' response.

"Philip. Philip was sent to me as a brother. From the moment we met, I was destined to care for him. I failed him." Barnabas' was gripped by remorse.

"This judgment is too harsh. How did you fail him?" James tried to ease his guilt.

Barnabas revealed the burden he carried. "My selfish desires denied his reunion with his mother. Peter the Hermit shared with us his vision of Miriam. She was in Pemdje. She was there waiting for him while we wandered the desert. Philip wanted to return. I rejected his wishes for years, until it was too late. It was not God's will for me to control his destiny. I failed Philip and disobeyed God. These are the sins that stain my soul."

James was determined to calm Barnabas' trepidations. He proceeded to the final absolution.

"Do you want Yesua to forgive you for this sin?" the confessor asked.

"Yes," the repentant replied.

"Do you reject this sin and all transgressions against God and your neighbor?" the confessor asked.

"Yes," the repentant replied.

"Are you resolved to sin no more?" the confessor asked.

"Yes," answered the repentant Brother Barnabas.

"Then by the power of the Holy Spirit and love of Christ, you are absolved of your sins," the confessor proclaimed.

Barnabas smiled. "Thank you."

"Ask and you shall receive. Thank you for sharing this spiritual encounter." James paused briefly. "Do you mind? May I ask? What happened to Philip after you left Pemdje?"

"It took so long for Miriam and Philip to be re-united. I could not bear to separate them. Several weeks after Miriam's death, Simon of Petra arrived in Pemdje. He, too, was dismayed by the tragic demise of Quintus and Miriam."

Barnabas continued. "We discussed at length what should be done with Philip. He was blind and mad. He could not stay in Pemdje. He would be too disruptive to return to the monastery. Thomas recalled that Philip could live in the cliffs near our community at Tabennisa. Thomas and I could return to our duties there. We knew Pachomius would allow us to visit Philip periodically."

"And Miriam? What became of her body?" James queried.

"Simon suggested that she be buried near Philip in the cliffs. I agreed. We filled her corpse with herbs and wrapped her body in linens. Simon joined us on the return trip south on Anub's vessel. At the cliffs, we found a cave suitable for habitation. We buried Miriam near the entrance." Barnabas asked James for a drink of water.

His thirst quenched, Barnabas resumed. "For five years, Thomas and I alternated visits to our friend and brother, bringing with us food and water. As we approached, he could be heard talking to Miriam, as if they were together in the cave. Sometimes, I would respond to Philip as if I were Miriam."

He smiled. "Every so often, we were greeted by Simon, who came to visit Miriam's grave."

Sadness gripped Barnabas again. "Philip died alone in a world of darkness. Thomas found him. Together we dressed him in a clean tunic. We buried him near Miriam with the gospel of Philip that Lucian gifted to him. We placed the codex on his chest, folding his hands upon it."

Barnabas sighed. "My pleas to Philip for forgiveness were never granted."

"I am certain when you meet him again all will be forgiven," James encouraged.

"I am not certain we will meet again," Barnabas retorted.

"What do you say that?" James challenged his doubt.

Barnabas shared Philip's secret belief. "Philip had an odd belief that one could only escape this world if the spirit achieved perfection. He believed that our spirit returned again and again until either it became completely pure or completely corrupt. Only the perfect spirit can be one with God, who is perfection itself."

James' head began to ache. "Brother, I have grown suddenly weary and so must have you. Rest now. I will return to feed you when you awake."

Barnabas raised his hand. "Brother James. There is one more request."

Barnabas pointed toward a large clay pot in the corner of the room, a pot of Coptic red slip with four handles near the opening.

"I have another confession," declared, lowering his hand.

"Yes?" James was curious.

Barnabas continued. "Bishop Athanasius of Alexandria has decreed that all writings, other than those deemed true, shall be destroyed."

"Yes. He was determined to destroy any evidence of heretical teachings. Why?" James had no sense where the conversation was now heading.

"Sealed inside the pot are thirteen codices declared heretical by Athanasius. They were Philip's favorite writings. After my spirit has left this withering flesh, would you be kind enough to bury them at the cliffs near Philip's grave."

"I would be honored to do so." James bowed in reverence.

Barnabas described the location of Miriam and Philip's graves. James knelt beside the fading patriarch, leaned forward and gently embraced him for the last time. The next morning, James found Barnabas' body motionless in the deathbed. His spirit was gone.

To fulfill the monk's last request, James departed with the clay pot the next day. He had no difficulty locating the remains. Fearing that the graves might invite robbers who would discover the codices, he decided to bury the vessel elsewhere at the entrance of a nearby cave. He walked back to the graves, pausing to pray for the mother and son. He finished with a prayer for Barnabas.

On his return to the monastery, he was confronted by a figure walking toward him. As the figure drew closer, he could see there were two, a young woman with a toddler strapped to her back. The woman's hood shielded her from the elements. Her faced was concealed by a veil.

"Kind sir, would you be gracious enough to share a drink of water?"

"Yes, indeed." James was curious. This was an odd location for such an encounter. "May I ask? What is your destination?"

"We are traveling to our father's house," she said.

"How long will the journey take?" he asked.

"I don't know. The journey is long. We have attempted many times, but have never reached our destination." Her gaze was distant.

"A curious reply. What is the meaning?" James thought. He asked the woman, "Why not?"

She gestured to the child behind her, "I won't leave him behind."

The confusing explanation cut short his questioning. He handed her his sheepskin hipflask. She lowered her veil to drink. He noticed that her cheek was graced with a crescent shaped scar. She lifted the flask over her shoulder. The child searched for the flask's spout like a blind pup searching for its mother's breast.

A chill swept over the monk.

"Thank you, brother. Peace be with you!" the woman said as she returned the flask.

"And with you, sister," James instinctively replied.

The woman arranged her veil. Mother and child resumed their journey.

As James watched them disappear around the base of the cliffs, a horseman appeared in the distance on the plateau above them. His horse reared back as he thrust his sword above him. A cross-like sunbeam reflected on its surface. The horseman disappeared over the horizon.

James was frozen, stunned by the surreal scene. He was shaken from his stupor by an animal racing past him.

Chasing after the woman and child, a wolf sprinted toward the horizon.

ABOUT THE AUTHOR

Following a successful business career, Dallas architect and educator C. Douglas Gordon has returned to his passion for the history of religions. He is currently writing historical fiction set in the treacherous and exciting days of early Christianity. A product of five years of research and writing, Blood in the Desert is the first novel in his You Left in Me the Faith series.

Ready for another journey into the exciting and treacherous world of early Christendom?

This time, travel to the last years of Christ's ministry on earth and join young Marit as she witnesses the dramatic events of the transition from Man to Messiah.

Turn the page and read the beginning chapter from C. Douglas Gordon's next novel in the "You Left in Me the Faith" series.

THE TWELVE COINS

— CHAPTER ONE —

Sacred Encounter

The prostitute mother could barely care for herself, much less a daughter who was born with clubbed feet. Nevertheless, she attended to the child as best she could because its disabilities provided an opportunity for added generosity from sympathetic patrons. As her mother plied her trade in the back street shadows, the girl sat on the main thoroughfare maintaining watch, begging from passersby. Her profession was a fatal violation of the theocratic laws of this puppet kingdom. Adultery was a sin against God to be punished by stoning till death.

When the girl was ten, her mother's furtive trade was exposed by a zealot posing as a customer. A handful of vigilantes dragged her past the child, into the street. Bystanders spat in the woman's face and tore her garments as she struggled past her child. The mother glanced at her daughter one last time as if to say, "I am sorry for what you are about to see." The girl sat paralyzed, watching as the crowd, barely thirty feet away, stoned her mother to death in the street.

The whole affair was like a sudden thunderstorm. The sound of the crowd rumbled in the distance as they disappeared into the city. Her mother's disfigured corpse lay motionless as if struck by a bolt of lightning, her blood puddled like water on the cobbled street. A veil of silence shrouded the scene with a calm as deafening as the violent tumult which came and went so quickly.

No one remained to help the girl. It was her duty and hers alone to bury her mother. Slowly she rose to her stubbled feet and waddled to the motionless corpse. It took her the rest of the day to drag the body out of the city to the burial ground on the steep slope below the imposing city wall. Twilight closed in as she chiseled a shallow grave in the porous crust of the limestone hill. Her last task was to cover the corpse with the very instruments of her mother's death. Exhausted, the girl laid down beside the stone rubble mound and fell asleep.

The night should have been fraught with nightmares. Instead she dreamed of her happiest moments with her mother. In her society, this child was lucky to be alive, much less cared for. Not only was she born with club feet, the girl was cursed with thick stumpy legs and a large head with thick unkempt auburn hair. Those teeth that were not missing were either misshapen or misplaced. She walked with the help of two canes fashioned from gnarled olive tree branches. In spite of her maladies, she was generally a happy child who smiled freely and laughed heartily.

She was particularly proud of her name, Marit, given to her by her mother which means "Lady" in Aramaic. A broad captivating smile graced her face whenever she heard her name spoken. Marit's cheerful cherubic face left a stranger with the impression that this child must be a wingless angel whose descent to earth left her battered but not broken. It would be a long time until she smiled again. Sunrise brought clarity to the day, but not to yesterday's events.

For most of the morning, Marit lay quietly on her side next to the grave with her head resting on her outstretched arm. The cool spring air was fresh. Warbling melodies of singing birds filled the air. A playful cluster of crested swallows fluttered by chasing the rising sun. Following their flight, her eyes rested on the tree lined crest of the steep embankment on the opposing side of the limestone valley below. She studied the view, following a precipitous path down to a grove of trees at the base of the imposing but modest mountain named for its abundance of olive trees. The grove was a popular destination for prayer and solitude. Next to the grove was another cemetery nearly identical to the one in which she buried her mother. Her mind drifted, wondering why her mother was murdered and what was to become of her.

The sudden awareness of her surroundings startled her, revealing the reality of her current situation. Today was the beginning of a sacred festival in the city. Soon, droves of pilgrims would be crossing the valley traveling up the road leading to the east gate of the city wall which led to the sacred Temple on the hill behind her. She was exposed, in the open, visible from all directions. A wave of panic swelled within from fear that she might be recognized by a passerby. Her mother's executioners intended for the body to rot in the street and be eaten by dogs, rats and creatures of the night. If Marit was seen here, her mother's grave could be easily uncovered. The vigilantes would exhume the corpse and hurl it into Gehenna, the fiery trash pit in the valley south of the city. It was time for her to leave the burial grounds.

Marit rose to her knees, grabbed her canes, and propped herself up on her club feet. It was a routine she had performed thousands of times. She headed to the road that crossed the valley, stopping occasionally to glance back at her mother's grave. When she reached the side of the road she found a comfortable spot in the shade of an olive tree. She sat, the ground beside her now draped with the veil which she routinely used to collect alms and patiently waited for sympathetic pilgrims entering the city.

Today began the most sacred festival of the year. The city would quickly swell with eager pilgrims. For the people of Judea, this was the city of God, the God of Abraham, Moses and David. This was first century Jerusalem whose normal population of 25,000 could easily swell to 300,000 during pilgrimages to King Solomon's Temple. The religious fervor of these festivals always seemed to breed a corresponding nationalistic fervor with hopes of a great leader, a "messiah" who could free the people from the bondage of the Roman occupiers that controlled their lives. As the city's population swelled, so did the number of soldiers who always accompanied the provincial governor, the visible reminder of Rome's authority.

The governor's palace was 70 miles away on the shores of the eastern Mediterranean Sea in a city built by Herod the Great to honor the first Roman Emperor, Augustus Caesar. Herod had been an ally of Marc Anthony who was defeated by Julius Caesar's nephew Octavian. The Hebrew king traveled to Rome to pay tribute to the victorious young general and profess an oath of loyalty. A wise choice, no doubt, because Octavian proclaimed himself Augustus Caesar, the first Emperor and supreme ruler of the Roman world. As a sign of his fidelity, Herod built a new port city which he named Caesarea in honor of the newly proclaimed Emperor.

The current governor was Pontius Pilatus of the Pontii family, whose authority was of the lowest rank of governors in the Roman bureaucratic hierarchy, the Equestrian order. He was Prefect of the Roman Judea province which was an amalgamation of Samaria, Judea and Idumea. He functioned primarily as a military leader with the additional responsibility for tax collection. His judicial role was limited. He commanded only 3,000 legionaries, barely half a legion, a sparse number for the Judea province, with its diverse geography and challenging terrain. Most of his soldiers were local conscripts or volunteers. A larger army of several legions was garrisoned to the north, 135 miles away in Syria, under the control of the legate of Syria who could reinforce Pilatus as necessary. But moving these forces could take weeks rendering them useless in precipitous uprisings.

The Romans discovered that it was better to interfere as little as possible with the Hebrew laws and customs because of the extreme sensitivity of their status as a Roman province. Consequently, civil administration remained with the local Sanhedrin. The Roman prefect's limited authority included the appointment of its leader. The current High Priest of Herod's Temple, Caiaphas, had been appointed by Pilatus' predecessor, the Prefect Valerius Gratus.

Pilatus experienced the Judeans' explosive temperament first-hand shortly after his appointment six years earlier by Tiberius, Rome's second Emperor. Hebrew custom prohibited the display of false images and effigies within Yahweh's sacred city. Previous Roman prelates had honored this custom by having their legionaries remove any such symbols from their armaments and standards prior to entering the city. During one festival, Pilatus permitted his troops to enter the city in full regalia, complete with effigies of the emperor. Unruly groups gathered to protest this heinous insult.

For five days, tensions grew as the crowds swelled to riotous numbers of close to 5,000. Pilatus ordered a cohort of legionnaires to surround the protesters. Under the threat of death, he demanded the crowd to disperse. The crowd refused, preferring death to the impudent desecration of their sacred laws. Perhaps it was the size and vehemence of the crowd. Perhaps it was a lack of confidence in the local Roman conscripts' willingness to carry out the execution. Nevertheless, Pilatus acquiesced. He withdrew the troops and ordered the removal of the offensive effigies.

By nature, Pilatus was self-willed, inflexible, ill-tempered, and vindictive. He delighted in habitually insulting this stubborn, self-important rabble. On another occasion, to fund the building of an aqueduct, Pilatus appropriated funds from the Temple treasury. Predictably, a disgruntled crowd assembled. Marit and her mother were in the crowd. So too were soldiers loyal to Pilatus who were disguised as protesters. Before the crowd could sprout to uncontrollable numbers, Pilatus released his assassins who butchered all who could not escape. Marit, who posed no threat was spared. However, her mother who was known to legionnaires was dragged into an alley and brutally raped.

As the sun crested the eastern hill, Marit sat quietly by the road reliving the hatred and brutality she had witnessed in her brief existence. She wondered what this day would bring.

A flight of crested swallows burst from the tops of the olive trees in the garden at the base of the mountain across the valley. Marit watched intently as a solitary figure exited the garden, walking in her direction. The slender figure in a hooded white robe moved gracefully across the valley and up the hill. As the figure drew closer, she recognized a man who seemed oddly familiar, a teacher who she had seen in the Temple precinct during other festivals. The man stopped when he reached her.

He smiled tenderly and spoke, "I saw you bury your mother last night."

Cupping her face in her hands Marit wept. The man gently placed his hand on her head and lowered his face to hers.

"Blessed are you child. Because of your mercy, your mother is at my Father's house." He whispered.

Reaching down he gathered a handful of pebbles and placed them on her veil saying, "Come. Follow me. There is someone else who needs you."

Marit sat dumbfounded as she watched him continue up the hill. "My mother is at his Father's house? My Mother? Is this the prophet who is performing miracles in Galilee? Is my mother alive?"

Marit carefully folded the stones in her veil and slid it under her sash. Struggling to her feet she watched the man pass through the east gate to the city.

"Wait. Wait for me!" she shouted. Her maladies prevented her from catching him. "How can I follow him if he won't wait for me?" She fretted.

The man continued his walk. With all her might, Marit tottered up the road after him, losing ground with every lunge. As she passed through the gate, she caught a glimpse of him turning left toward the temple precinct. When she reached that location, she was confronted with a lengthy sheer stairway up to the Temple. The man was already at the top of the stairs.

"Wait! Wait! Please wait for me! I am following you!" She shouted again.

He disappeared. Catching her breath, she stopped at the base of the broad stairway, tightened her sash and launched her arduous ascent. Before she could begin, she was overrun by a handful of men forcefully wrenching along a frightened woman. They were the same vigilantes who executed her mother the night before. Their captive was another prostitute who Marit's mother had befriended. Launching again, Marit scaled the stairway to the Temple. A sudden rage engulfed her, easing her struggle.

When she reached the Temple grounds, she spotted a gathering at the end of the forecourt. The woman stood frozen in front of the gentle teacher. He was squatting down, tracing a stick along the ground as if ignoring the scene before him. The vigilantes were standing behind the woman facing the teacher. As the seemingly disinterested teacher continued to trace the stick, the vigilantes began to leave. First one at a time, then in pairs until none remained. The teacher looked up seeing only the woman. He rose to address her, then quietly disappeared into the crowd. The whole affair was over by the time Marit reached the woman.

The woman stood motionless, staring into a glimpse of eternity. Finally, she turned to leave and found herself face to face with Marit, now breathless and exhausted. As if the memory of this horrific incident had been erased entirely, the woman beamed at the sight of the poor distorted angel at her feet.

The stunned woman spoke, "Oh Marit, sweet Marit. I have been looking for you all night. Since I learned of your mother's death, I have been praying that the evil ones had not harmed you. How are you, sweet child?"

She fell to her knees embracing Marit tenderly. "How are you? Where have you been? How did you follow me here? "

Marit rambled breathlessly, "I followed the teacher here. I buried my mother last night. When I awoke, I made my way to the road and sat beneath an olive tree. The teacher was walking up the road. He…He… oh." She took a deep breath and continued, "He told me to follow him. He said, 'Come. Follow me. There is someone else who needs you."

The reality of the encounter stuck the woman. She whispered, "He sent you to me."

Each stared deeply into the other's soul. Marit broke the silence. "What happened to you just now? Why did those butchers leave? What did the teacher say to you?"

Still trying to comprehend all that had occurred, the woman spoke, "The men found me where your mother was stoned to death. I was there searching for you. One of them said, "The false prophet is in the Temple. Let us present this harlot to him and challenge him on the law." As I stood before the teacher, they challenged him whether stoning was prescribed by the law for my sin. He squatted and picked up stick and started tracing in the dirt. He straightened up and he said to them, "Let the one among you who is without sin be the first to throw a stone at her." Then he bent down and continued tracing. One by one they vanished. When he looked up he asked me "Woman, where are they? Has no one condemned you? "I replied "No one sir." Then he said to me "Neither do I condemn you. Go. From now on do not sin anymore."

Marit thought for about her encounter with the teacher. "Sister, the teacher did something very strange when he met me." Marit pulled the veil from under her sash and gently placed it on the ground. Carefully she unfolded the cloth exposing to her astonishment twelve gold coins.

Marit and the woman embraced again, shrouded in a life-giving cocoon, protecting them while a miraculous transformation piloted them to rebirth into a new life.